APR 1 5

PIRATE'S ALLEY

THE SENTINELS OF NEW ORLEANS

Royal Street
River Road
Elysian Fields
Pirate's Alley

Suzanne Johnson

Pirate's Alley

A TOM DOHERTY ASSOCIATES BOOK

NEW YORK

PIRATE'S ALLEY

Copyright © 2015 by Suzanne Johnson

A Tor Book
Published by Tom Doherty Associates, LLC
175 Fifth Avenue
New York, NY 10010

www.tor-forge.com

Tor® is a registered trademark of Tom Doherty Associates, LLC.

The Library of Congress Cataloging-in-Publication Data
is available upon request.

ISBN 978-0-7653-7697-8 (hardcover)
ISBN 978-1-4668-5284-6 (e-book)

Tor books may be purchased for educational, business, or promotional use. For information on bulk purchases, please contact the Macmillan Corporate and Premium Sales Department at 1-800-221-7945, extension 5442, or write to specialmarkets@macmillan.com.

First Edition: April 2015

Printed in the United States of America

0 9 8 7 6 5 4 3 2 1

PIRATE'S ALLEY

CHAPTER 1

I'd spent the last five minutes contorted into the wizard version of a pretzel. Damn it, what was the point of being a hotshot sentinel with mad elven fire skills if you couldn't put those skills to good use?

I'd been trying to simultaneously turn the starter valve and the gas release to ignite a gas log fireplace. To do it properly, I'd need the wingspan of a bald eagle and a healthy body. Thanks to a compact frame from my Alabama ancestors and a gunshot wound and bruised ribs caused by the crazed elven version of Lizzie Borden, I had neither.

Besides, who'd know if I cheated and used a little magic?

I turned the gas valve, and the nausea-inducing odor of rotten eggs filled the living room of Eugenie Dupre's house.

"Oh God, I'm gonna be sick." My best friend raced down the hallway with a thunder of boot heels and her hand clapped over her mouth. Her face turned a sickly shade of pale green that clashed with her auburn hair.

Ignoring the mental nag that reminded me how often I'd

criticized my father Gerry for saying the same thing about his casual use of magic, I flicked a spark of energy against the gas, watching with inordinate pride as a neat row of flames danced into motion around the ceramic fake log. Anytime my magic involved fire and didn't destroy something or cause an explosion, I considered it a victory.

My victories have been rare.

I slipped my right arm back into its sling, closed the protective mesh fire screen, and waited for the last of the gas fumes to dissipate, soaking the warmth into my skin. New Orleans was rarely pleasant in winter, never mind that winter only lasted about eight weeks. During those weeks, the air hung heavy and damp, constantly buffeted by a cold and bitter wind.

Every once in a while, though, we'd have a true winter. I'd even seen snow once or twice in my lifetime, including Christmas Day 2004, before Hurricane Katrina struck the following August. A white Christmas in New Orleans should have been a hint that the apocalypse, or the New Orleans magical version of it, was fast approaching. The hurricane had not only led to the failure of the levees and almost destroyed my hometown, but its barometric pressure had turned the border between the human world and the preternatural Beyond into a sieve. The city had been flooded with pretes.

Preternatural creatures were like poor relations after a big lottery win. Once you let them inside, they have no inclination to leave. First, they wore down the wizards and persuaded our Elders to form an Interspecies Council to set magical policy. Now, they had the gall to actually demand representation on the council. Negotiations were chilly.

Almost as chilly as the weather. November's balmy and thunderous weather had given way to plummeting temperatures as we headed into mid-December. If we were lucky, today's high might climb to a toasty thirty-three, with snow flurries. Other parts of the world might scoff, but damn it, I was freezing. I'd never tolerated cold well but this year had been worse, and my injured shoulder ached more with every falling degree.

Eugenie clattered back into the high-ceilinged living room and collapsed on the worn orange sofa, a garage-sale find we'd lugged home in my old Pathfinder a few years ago. That would be the Pathfinder turned into a twisted metal carcass by an errant shot of my elven staff, aka Charlie. I missed the SUV. Actually, I missed driving. Since I'd also inadvertently caused the destruction of a rental car, every agency in town had me on some kind of secret "do not rent to this woman" hazard list. Arnie the United Cab driver and I had become way too chummy.

"Feeling better?" I asked. Eugenie's face had lost most of its green undertones. "The gas smells awful, but most of the *eau de sulfur* has burned off. You're looking better."

"I'm okay." She clutched a throw pillow to her midsection and curled up on the sofa. "It wasn't the gas. I probably have a virus or something."

"How about some tea? If I'm going to crash here, you might as well let me take care of you." I climbed to my feet with the speed of a slug. Since my house across the street had burned down last month, I'd been living in the semi-finished first floor of Gerry's old Katrina-flooded house in Lakeview. My significant something-or-other Alex had made it habitable, but hadn't gotten around to installing heat.

He also hadn't gotten around to inviting me to stay at his place during the cold wave, although I knew he wanted to keep up appearances that we weren't in cahoots before we had to testify at tomorrow night's Interspecies Council hearing.

"DJ, nothing personal, but you aren't the caregiver type. I'll settle for some juice from the fridge. You might burn down the kitchen if you tried to make tea." Eugenie's smile was faint but heartfelt. She really didn't look well, so I let the wisecrack pass.

"Gotcha." I shuffled into the kitchen, pulled open the door of the old white Frigidaire, and stared at the top shelf. Last time I'd been here, it had contained bottle after bottle of Abita beer and soda. Now, a menagerie of juice filled its shelves—grape, apple, orange, pomegranate. Lots and lots of cranberry. Not a soda in sight, which amounted to gastronomic blasphemy.

Before Eugenie had talked me into staying with her, I'd planned to spend the cold wave in the warm, posh Eudora Welty Suite at the Hotel Monteleone. The lavish suite, which rented for more money per night than I earned in two weeks, currently lay unoccupied. Its normal resident, the undead pirate Jean Lafitte, was holed up in his outpost of Old Orleans, a border town between modern New Orleans and the preternatural world Beyond.

Ostensibly, he was recuperating from his latest death, one of the subjects the council would be discussing.

In reality, I suspected he was mixing his recovery with a heavy dose of plotting. I expected him to arrive at the Interspecies Council meeting heavily armed and with vengeance on his mind. Jean Lafitte might be handsome and flirtatious, but he was also lethal. He wouldn't roll over and take an act of betrayal, and he had definitely been betrayed.

I picked a bottle of grape juice and one of apple, and let the fridge door slam shut. Setting the bottles on the counter, I opened the cabinet where Eugenie kept the cups and glasses—or at least she used to. Now, the shelves bulged with protein bars, oats, and honey. A freaking bottle of agave nectar taunted me from the bottom shelf.

The glasses had migrated one cabinet over, and I retrieved a couple for our juice and took them into the living room. "What's with all the healthy crap in the kitchen? Looks like I need to make a run to the grocery store for real food."

Because I wasn't consuming cactus juice, no matter what fancy name one called it.

"Yeah, I threw all my junk food out." Eugenie had managed to sit up. Forever the hairstylist, she was trying to fluff the bedhead rumples out of her hair. She'd canceled her appointments for the day and closed her salon, Shear Luck, in honor of her illness. "I'm trying to eat healthier."

"Bad idea." Speaking selfishly, of course. If Eugenie hopped on the Alex Warin healthy living bandwagon, I'd be riding alone on the fried food train to clogged arteries. Chocoholics needed friends with whom to binge. "Junk food nurtures the spirit. I think there's scientific research to prove it."

Eugenie didn't answer, just poured apple juice into a glass and sipped it. She didn't look at me. In fact, she'd been withdrawn since I'd arrived a couple of hours ago, overnight bag in hand.

Maybe she regretted the invitation to let a beer-swilling, fried-food-eating houseguest move in, even temporarily. I was okay with that; the Monteleone had an awesome room service menu.

"Look, we're best friends, right?" I waited until she finally looked up at me. "If you need to do something or I'm getting in the way, tell me. No hard feelings. I can go to Jean's suite like I'd planned, or stay at Alex's." Whether he invited me or not.

To my horror, a stray tear trickled down Eugenie's cheek. "Please don't go. I . . ." She shook her head and resumed her intense gaze at the dark green and rust–colored area rug.

I set my glass of juice on the scuffed coffee table and went to sit on the sofa next to her. We'd been through a lot in the last couple of months, my friend and I. That we were still friends at all—maybe on the way to becoming better friends than before—was a testament more to her than to me. I could admit my own failures. Eugenie Dupre was big-hearted and brave and fiercely loyal, all things I aspired to but didn't always achieve.

I ignored the pinch of the wrap around my ribs when I settled back on the sofa, and reached out to grasp her hand. "Talk to me."

More tears, and she wouldn't look me in the eye. "It's nothing. Ignore me. Hormones."

I squeezed her hand. Not buying that one. "This is me, Euge. Don't give me the 'hormones' crap. What's up?"

She didn't answer for a long time, but clutched my hand like a lifeline. "Well, it's about Rand, sort of."

I should've known. That freaking elf Quince Randolph had caused nothing but misery since he'd opened his Plantasy Island nursery across the street, wooed Eugenie as a way to get to me, and turned on her like a snake as soon as he'd found a way to slither into my life for political gain.

She ended up with a broken heart, and I ended up with a lifelong bond to an elven asshat. Frankly, I thought she got the better end of the deal.

I also thought she'd gotten over him. "What has he done now? Because I'd welcome the opportunity to call him over here and kick his elven assets halfway to Lake Pontchartrain." I didn't know if it would help Eugenie, but it would make me feel better.

She sniffled. "Rand wouldn't come over here even for you, not today. He told me one time he couldn't stand getting out in cold weather. Besides, it's nothing he's done. Well, nothing he's done recently. I haven't even seen him in a couple of weeks. Not since . . . you know."

Yeah, I knew. The night Quince Randolph had told her we were married, a highly exaggerated description of our even-less-than-platonic bonding. Asshat. It was the only word that did him justice.

I tried to set my personal animosity aside and focus instead on what Rand might have done in the past that was only now making Eugenie miserable. There were so many possibilities. "I don't unders—"

"Can elves and humans, you know . . ." She swallowed hard, and her hazel eyes spilled another round of tears down her cheeks as she looked me in the eye for the first time. I held on, waiting for the rest of it. Even with the little bag of herbs around my neck blocking most of my empathic ability, her fear came through loud and clear. She was petrified.

"Can humans have elf babies?"

I'd lived in old houses most of the past decade, and they're rarely quiet. They creak and settle. Antique wood flooring crackles. Plaster chips off between strips of lathing and drifts down the insides of the walls.

You could've heard a feather floating through Eugenie's living room. She looked at me in fearful anticipation of my answer, but my vocal cords had turned to ice. Because, of course, the answer was yes. Their prolific mating with humans was one reason the elves had dwindled as a species.

"Oh God, they can. Of course they can. I can see it on your face." She dropped my hand and clutched her pillow, then tossed it on the floor and stood. "I'm gonna be sick again."

I watched in horror as she ran through the door into the hallway and out of sight. Holy crap. Eugenie didn't have a virus. She had morning sickness—well, in this case, afternoon sickness.

I ignored the retching sounds drifting down the hallway from the downstairs bath and reined in the runaway thoughts and spiral of what-ifs trying to unspool in my brain. The last response Eugenie needed from me was horror or hysteria. A plain-vanilla human, she'd only learned about the preternatural world three weeks ago—including the fact that the lying, manipulative bastard she'd been sleeping with was an elf with political ambitions. She needed me to guide her through this minefield.

Only one problem: I was clueless.

Hadn't they used protection of some kind? Had Eugenie thought a baby would help her hang on to Rand when she saw him slipping away, toward me? Before she knew what he really was? What would a half-elven baby be able to do?

I got up and paced the room, ashamed that my first thoughts had been to cast blame. If I'd learned anything from the New Orleans I'd inhabited since Hurricane Katrina smashed normal life into something unrecognizable, it was to not even go down the what-if road. Blame was a useless emotion, and assigning motive was worse than useless.

To move on, I'd learned, one simply had to take things as they existed in the present and keep blundering forward.

By the time Eugenie returned, looking paler than ever, I'd composed my face into a mask of calm. Beneath, I was shrieking like a model for Edvard Munch, but I looked serene and compassionate, if not exactly competent.

I'd taken Eugenie's glass of juice back into the kitchen and added a little seltzer and powdered ginger to it, and handed it to her when she sat down.

"I doctored it to help with the nausea." She raised an eyebrow, and I smiled. "Don't worry. Nothing magical. Just stuff from your kitchen."

I waited until she drank a few sips before asking, in my gentlest tone, "Are you sure?"

She bit her lower lip and nodded. "I haven't taken a test, but believe me, I know."

There was hope, then. "But it really might be a virus or—"

"You don't know this, but I've been pregnant before, back when I lived in Marrero."

I fell silent, waiting to hear the rest. The time was shadowy between her childhood in the western New Orleans suburbs and her arrival in Uptown, tattooed and henna-rinsed. From late-night girl talks, I knew there had been a man; wasn't there always? There'd been a bad breakup in the old neighborhood of Marrero, across the Mississippi River from the bustle of New Orleans. This was the first I'd heard about a pregnancy.

"I lost the baby near the end of the second trimester." She smiled and swirled the golden juice around in her glass, looking into the past. "It was a little boy. I'd already picked out his name: Charles, after my daddy."

A stab of pity knifed through me at her expression, still filled with love for a child she'd never gotten to hold. "You had a miscarriage?"

She nodded, but when she looked back up at me her hazel eyes had lost their wistful softness. "Not the way you think, though. My ex caused it, by knocking me down a flight of stairs 'cause I was standing between him and the TV set and the Saints were playing the Cowboys."

She shook her head and stared out the window at nothing. "The pathetic thing is that for the longest time I blamed myself. How stupid was I?"

I tried to reconcile the image of my brave friend, the one who'd never backed away from anything, with a woman who'd stay in an abusive relationship. But such a judgment wasn't fair, either. Eugenie was so big-hearted that she believed the absolute best of everybody. I'd been the beneficiary of that too many times to count, and I was willing to bet her ex had, too. God knows, Quince Randolph had.

I wanted to hear what happened to her jerk of an ex, but

first we needed to deal with this still-hypothetical pregnancy. "You're saying you feel the same way now as when you were pregnant before?"

Eugenie sighed and leaned back on the sofa, her shoulders relaxing now that the burden had been shared. "Yeah. Same type of queasiness. Not like a virus. It's just different."

I did some mental calculations. She and Rand had only been together since late October, so she couldn't be more than six weeks along, maximum.

"I recognize that look, DJ." She reached over to the end table, picked up her cell phone, and stabbed at the screen. "I was studying the calendar and I figure I'm about a month along, maybe a little more, if . . ."

The *if* trailed into a long silence.

"If what?" If elves had the same gestational period as humans? If she should even consider having this child, given the circumstances and the fact that the father was a sneaky, manipulative elf?

"If it would show up on a home pregnancy test." Her eyes brightened. "I mean, maybe I'm just panicking. We were always safe; I insisted on it. Would Rand's baby show up on one of those tests you buy at the drugstore?"

I had no idea. "Let's find out. I'll run over to Walgreens and get one, and pick up some ginger ale for you while I'm there. It doesn't have caffeine, and it'll help the nausea." Plus, I felt a growing need for chocolate and the store was stocked with Christmas candy.

I wrapped a scarf around my neck and bundled myself into a hideous orange and purple plaid wool coat I'd picked up at a charity thrift store yesterday, at Arnie the cabbie's insistence. He often shopped there, and a girl needed a coat in this weather, he'd said.

I'd been even more fashion-challenged than usual since my entire wardrobe had gone up in flames just before Thanksgiving, and when I needed basics like underwear and shoes, it seemed frivolous to spend real money on a heavy coat that might get trotted out of the closet once a year.

Not that I had a closet. And no one except a pumpkin and some breeds of cat looked good in orange—and never when it was tarted out with purple, unless one were headed for a Clemson football game.

"Need anything else?" I paused at the front door and looked back at Eugenie. "Pizza? Soda?"

A good, stiff shot of bourbon?

She shook her head, sadness and fear etched into her face in equal measure. I'd be freaking out in her position, and I had a lot of resources she didn't: other wizards, a passing knowledge of the prete world, Alex.

All Eugenie had was me. Maybe I hadn't always been the best friend to her, but I swore to myself: This time, I wouldn't fail her.

CHAPTER 2

One of the few good things about being blackballed by the car-rental places: I didn't have to worry about fighting for a decent parking spot at the shopping center and schlepping my way across a quarter mile of frozen concrete tundra.

A blast of frigid air sent shock waves of cold through me when I opened the cab door and eyed the fifteen or so feet I'd need to run in order to get inside the store. The big entrance sign on Tchoupitoulas Street might say RIVERSIDE MARKET, but the drugstore's location wasn't nearly that chic. The long strip mall backed up to one of the Mississippi River wharves, and I knew it well. My official office was near the other end, a sparsely furnished rectangle called Crescent City Risk Management.

It wasn't a deception, exactly, since I did manage risk. Just not the type of risk for which one bought an insurance policy.

"Man, that be some cold. I'll be waitin' on you, Miss DJ. I'll even turn off the meter seein' as how you're a regular. Ain't you glad you got dat coat?" Arnie gave me a gap-toothed grin. He was old-school New Orleans, of the generation that still called shopping for food "making groceries" and referred to the near-west suburb as "Metry."

"Thanks, Arnie. I don't know what I'd do without you." Sure I did. I'd be riding the bus or forced to ask Alex if I could borrow the pristine Mercedes convertible he'd stored at his parents' house in Mississippi last month. Things located near me, he pointed out, had a bad habit of turning into fireballs.

He hadn't even offered me the use of his uncle Eddie's beater of a pickup that got passed around the family in times of need. He could drive me wherever I needed to go, he'd said. My interpretation: He could control where I went if I had to depend on him for transportation. Thus my newfound relationship with Arnie.

Hurrying into the store, I relaxed at the cocoon of warmth that surrounded me, not to mention the piped-in Christmas Muzak and the reassurance of knowing an unlimited supply of junk food lay at my disposal.

I picked up a blue plastic shopping basket and made my way through aisles crowded with wrapping paper and Santa hats, tree lights and tinsel, weaving toward the back corner of the store where the actual pharmacy had been tucked. My footfalls fell in rhythm with Johnny Mathis crooning about roasting chestnuts on an open fire, which sounded dangerous.

Halfway down the "As Seen on TV" aisle, I lurched to a stop and backed up. For Alex's Christmas present, I'd bought him a membership renewal at the city's most high-tech gym, but the Perfect Bacon Bowl ("Everything Tastes Better in a Bowl of Bacon!") looked like the ideal thing in which to hide the membership card. He'd be totally grossed out, toss it aside, and I could use it without admitting I'd bought it for myself. Alex considered bacon an express pass to heart disease. I considered it one of nature's perfect foods.

Grinning, I grabbed the Perfect Bacon Bowl and wedged it in my basket. My amusement faded as the store's holiday excess gave way to the health-care aisles, and the enormity of Eugenie's situation finally hit me in all of its awfulness.

If she was pregnant, Rand would want the child, and Rand had a way of getting what he wanted even if it meant playing dirty. Oh, he thought he played fair, but the elves had an arrogantly warped worldview in which "fair" equaled "whatever the elf wants."

Or would he prefer that she get rid of the child so his precious pure elven DNA wouldn't be mixed with that of a human? I pondered that down half an aisle, but rejected it. Rand would want an heir. God knows he would never get one from his so-called mate, namely me, and if he had half a brain, he'd realize that.

Where would one find home pregnancy tests? I scanned row after row of vitamins, eye drops, elevated toilet seats, antacids, and finally found them—colorful stacks of boxes in frightening babylike colors of pink and blue and what had apparently replaced green as the new neutral pastel, lavender.

I stared at the half-dozen different brands, overwhelmed not only by the choice of tests but the ramifications of a baby fathered by Quince Randolph. What would a half-elven child be able to do? Look how many elven skills I won in the genetic lottery and I was far, far more removed from elfhood than this kid would be. Could the baby do bizarre mental games in utero? Were elves automatically devious and underhanded, or was that a learned behavior?

What *was* the gestation period for a half-elven child? Nine months like a human or an elephantine two years?

If Eugenie were pregnant, considering she'd lost a child before and the Catholic upbringing she staunchly upheld in the face of the weirdness around her, would she consider ending this pregnancy? Would it be fair to even ask her to consider it?

Okay, I was getting ahead of myself. There would be time later to panic and wrestle with moral dilemmas.

First step: Try the pregnancy test. The boxes all claimed to be ninety-nine percent accurate. Those results applied to humans, I assumed. Not surprisingly, the accuracy rating for half-human pregnancies had been omitted from the package labels. I picked one using the highly scientific method of prettiest logo.

I lingered in the candy aisle on the way to the register, thinking about Rand and piling in enough peanut butter cups and candy bars to replace my blood supply with cocoa and sugar. To balance it out, I grabbed a twelve-pack of diet soda along with Eugenie's ginger ale.

While I stood in the checkout line, I had time to consider Quince Randolph, aka Rand. That would be Rand, my non-husband, newly minted member of the Elven Synod and clan leader of the Tân, the fire elves. Blond, blue-eyed, with broad shoulders and good cheekbones, Rand was the prettiest elf in this world or any other, with an ego matched only by his ambition. And tied to me by a blood bond for the rest of our miserable lives.

A tingle of fear zipped up my spine and across my scalp. I had to be careful. Since the bonding, Rand could no longer read my thoughts or influence my moods, but he would know if I got freaked out or frightened. He could also communicate with me mentally, although I'd gotten adept at ignoring him. I didn't want him picking up any stray fear or tension and feeling the need to sniff around to see what had me upset.

I began slamming up mental barriers as fast as I could visualize them in my head. Ramparts, moats, and thick stone towers, all ringed around my thoughts. I set my brain inside the virtual stronghold of Mount Doom, surrounded by mental orcs dripping green saliva off their fangs and poison off their bow-strung arrows. If Quince Randolph turned his sneaky mental radar in my direction and picked up even a hint of freak-out, we'd have a problem before I could get back to Eugenie's with the pregnancy test to find out the status of the potential elf spawn.

Mental note to self: Do not refer to the child as *elf spawn* in front of Eugenie.

Rand also could both read Eugenie's thoughts and influence them if he was touching her or got close enough. Thank God he'd been cocooned in his house since the cold weather struck, or so Eugenie claimed. Even his mental pings to me—sort of a text message without the text or the device on which to read it—had become less frequent since the temperature dropped.

But the cold wouldn't last forever. Eugenie might have to move. The wizards maintained a facility for criminal and men-tally challenged magic-makers in a remote corner of Greenland. Rand would never brave the frigid weather in Ittoqqortoormiit.

Breathe. Nothing's certain yet.

I'd finished paying and was lugging my bags out the door when my pocket vibrated with Pink's "So What." The song re-flected my pissed-off mood most days now. I'd ditched my mel-low Zachary Richard ringtone the day after both Alex and I had been shot, thanks to a power-mad elf and a necromantic wiz-ard who'd sold his skills for a big payday. The day after the undead pirate, scoundrel, thief, and blackguard Jean Lafitte had proven himself both loyal and incredibly brave.

The day after I learned wizards could be every bit as treach-erous as elves, vampires, and other species my kind thought of as monsters.

My cell phone screen popped up Alex Warin's name and photo. I set the bags down on the sidewalk. "Hey." I wedged the phone between my ear and shoulder and waved furiously across the parking lot, where Arnie appeared to be napping in his cab. "Are you home?" He'd been on some secret mission for the Elders.

"Yeah, want to go to Celebration in the Oaks tonight? Maybe grab dinner at one of the restaurants doing Reveillon?" Alex sounded pumped, his deep baritone more buoyant than its usual tones of sexy silk or grumpy caveman, depending on his mood. Whatever he'd been doing for the Elders, it had been successful. I'd find out over dinner.

"Definitely. Why don't I come to your place about seven?" I needed to spend some quality time with Eugenie and a petri dish, or whatever one used to take a pregnancy test.

Arnie had apparently awakened, because the black-and-white United Cab lurched to a stop in front of me a few seconds later. "Hang on," I told Alex, and piled my bags in the back seat of the cab. I nodded in response to Arnie's stage-whispered question of whether I wanted to head back to Eugenie's house on Magazine Street. "Okay, I'm back," I told Alex. "Seven sound okay?"

His voice dove closer to caveman territory. "What the hell are you doing?"

Since my relationship with Alex had gone from professional to personal, I'd been trying to be mature and tamp down the instinct to dish the crap back to him when he got territorial and bossy, which was way too often. So I refrained from making a snippy comment about my vehicular drought and his lack of help.

"I just picked up some soda and am taking a cab back to Eugenie's." I paused. "Because, you know, she has heat."

Okay, so I hadn't perfected the whole mature thing yet.

"Ah . . . yeah, sorry. I'll get you some heat this weekend." Caveman slid into sexy. "I can keep you warm till then."

I smiled. "You certainly can . . . after dinner and the Oaks."

His low, sexy chuckle made my toes curl involuntarily. "Okay, see you soon."

"That's a man-smile, that's what it is." Arnie watched me in the rearview mirror, and I bit down on my lip to wipe the man-smile off my face. I did not want to be the kind of woman who had a special man-smile. "So, Miss DJ, you think we gonna get snow tonight? I sure don't like to be drivin' in da snow."

I was the last person to ask for weather advice. When Hurricane Katrina made landfall, I was still insisting it would take a last-second turn and hit Florida. "I hope not. I'm ready for spring."

"Yeah, you right."

A few minutes later, Arnie prepared to turn onto Nashville Avenue from Magazine, and I saw three things in quick succession, none of which made me happy.

First, on the right-hand corner, a few stray antique bricks littered a patch of bare dirt, all that was left of the foundation of the 1870s Victorian camelback house where I'd made my home until last month. The last two weeks had been filled with a flurry of phone calls and insurance forms as I made arrangements to have the few unburned parts of it demolished and removed. The last little bits of my home had been hauled away to a landfill two days ago, leaving only a few bricks to remind me of all I had lost.

My sorrow morphed into a scowl when I glanced at the opposite corner, where Quince Randolph had emerged from the doorway of his Plantasy Island nursery and was walking toward Eugenie's house with a purposeful stride. He was bundled in a thick white sweater, a white leather coat, and blue jeans. As usual, he looked like a beautiful, exotic Russian snow prince, all tall and lean, with his long, wavy blond hair and graceful motion. And, today, boots, scarf, gloves, and a fedora-style hat of a shade of deep teal blue that probably matched his eyes to perfection.

He could not get inside Eugenie's house, even if I had to tackle and hog-tie him with his own pretty scarf.

Giving Arnie a generous tip not only to help him out but to ensure he remained my best cab-driving buddy, I lugged my bags out, trying to protect my right arm. I nodded at Rand with a big, fake smile and turned to the third source of my displeasure— Alex Warin, sitting on Eugenie's front steps. What part of *I'll come to your place about seven* hadn't been clear?

Not that I would mind seeing him under normal circumstances, but Eugenie's bombshell had blown us way past normal. I didn't want to tell him yet, either. Not until Eugenie took this pregnancy test and we knew for sure.

Unlike me and, apparently, Rand, the cold weather agreed with Alex. Like most shifters, he was hot-natured, so he not only wore no coat but had the sleeves of his black sweater pushed up. The cold wind blushed his cheeks and nose a ruddy shade of pink that looked good on him.

"How come you're sitting on the porch?" I asked, keeping Rand's rapid approach in my peripheral vision. "But since you're here, help me run interference. Eugenie's not feeling well and Rand can't come in. Shoot him if you have to."

"If I could shoot him without starting a preternatural war, I'd be all over that." Alex stood up and tugged the heavy soda cartons out of my hands, leaving me with my bag full of chocolate and a discreet little box neither he nor Rand needed to see. I wedged the whole thing into the top of the cross-body messenger bag I'd started wearing to accommodate my shoulder wound.

Rand strode up at a fast clip. "I've been trying to talk to you, Dru." He ignored Alex, who set down the soda and crossed his arms, barricading the front door. Bless his enforcer heart. He did intimidation really well, only I wasn't sure Rand could be intimidated.

"I've been busy," I told him. Yeah, busy ignoring his mental pings. The more I responded to his nonverbal comments or questions, the more it would encourage him to use that infuriating skill. I'd gotten good at blocking him out. "What's so urgent?"

He pulled his coat around him more tightly and danced from foot to foot like a show pony. "We need to talk about the council meeting tomorrow. Can we go inside? I can't stand this weather."

"No, Eugenie's not feeling well and you'd upset her." True enough. "I'll call you later tonight."

"Can't we just go in for a minute?" Rand's teeth chattered. What a wimp. It was cold, but it wasn't that cold.

Rand sidled around me and walked toward Eugenie's front door, stopping a foot from Alex, who didn't budge, even when Rand's teal fedora butted his forehead.

"She said she'd call you, Randolph. Go home."

Rand didn't answer, nor did he back off. Within seconds, sweat popped out on Alex's face and the muscles in his jaw tensed. Rand was doing some kind of mental crap on him.

Stop that, you jerk! I yelled at Rand in my head. I yelled really, really loud.

Rand winced and clapped his hands to his temples, and Alex relaxed. Then he pulled a knife out of his jeans pocket and flicked it open an inch from Rand's chin. It was a wicked little combat blade with a jagged edge.

Good grief; we didn't need a preternatural incident on Eugenie's porch. I stepped between them, facing the elf. "Please go home, Rand. I'll call you tonight. I promise."

He dropped his gazed from Alex to me. "You are my mate, not his. Don't forget that, Dru."

Turning quickly, he trotted down the front steps and stalked back toward Plantasy Island.

"Yeah, like I could forget," I muttered.

"Is it legal for him to do shit like that? I have a splitting head-ache. And why didn't you remind him that mate thing is just a formality?" Alex had turned into a petulant five-year-old, so I knew he was fine.

"Believe me, he could do a lot worse, and he knows we're not true mates without me telling him." I hadn't been aware until now that freaky elven mental magic would work on shapeshifters. "What did he do to you?"

"Set my brain on fire, I think. Felt like it anyway."

That was pretty mild, as elven mind games went. If Rand had wanted to really hurt him, Alex wouldn't be standing up-right and whining. Unfortunately, I knew that from firsthand experience. "Why were you sitting outside, anyway?"

"Thought I'd wait for you and enjoy the fresh air," he said, following me through the entry hall into Eugenie's kitchen, wav-ing at her along the way. She was still sitting on the sofa, staring at the fire, and I wasn't sure she'd heard us. Which was good; it meant she probably didn't realize how close Rand had gotten.

"This is perfect running weather," Alex said. "Want to go before dinner?"

No, I had a little science experiment to take care of. "Thanks, but I promised Eugenie I'd help her with some, uh, cleaning."

Alex had beautiful eyes, a dark chocolate brown with long lashes that every woman I knew would kill to have, including me. When he squinted in suspicion, like he was doing now, it ruined the whole sexy vibe.

"You're an organization freak, but you only clean as a last resort when you want to avoid doing something else. You're a procrasti-cleaner. What are you really up to?" He snaked out a hand and pulled on the Walgreens package, whose top protruded from its hiding place in my bag. I snatched at it, but he jerked it

out, upended it on the kitchen counter, and grinned at the mountain of chocolate candy that tumbled out—until a peanut butter
cup rolled to the floor and exposed the lavender box.

If I hadn't been so worried about Eugenie, I'd have laughed
at Alex's expression. Despite my daily grounding ritual and the
small "mojo bag" of protective herbs and stones around my neck,
my empathic abilities echoed his fear.

He picked up the box with two fingers, carefully, as if it might
contain radioactive materials. For all I knew, it might. Who knew
what was in those tests?

"We need to talk about this, DJ." His voice came out in a
froglike croak.

I bit my lip to keep from laughing. "It's not—"

"We're still trying to figure things out between us." He paced
around the counter and put his hands on my shoulders. "I'm not
ready to be a father. You're sure as hell not ready to be . . ."

Too late, he realized he'd stuck a big old size thirteen boot
in his mouth. It would serve him right if I'd let him go on thinking the pregnancy scare was mine, just to see how big a hole he'd
dig himself into. Except I'd promised myself I wasn't going to
keep secrets from Alex. At least not major ones. I was going to be
mature enough to give this relationship a fighting chance, even if
it killed me—or him.

Plus, I couldn't deny that he was right. I wasn't ready to be
a mother. I was well aware that my grumpy, unaffectionate cat,
Sebastian, had become fat, happy, and docile since my house
burned down and he'd moved in with Alex, a canine shapeshifter.
He preferred a dog to me, proving I wasn't even a decent cat
mother.

"It's not mine, Alex." I kept my voice low. "The test is for
Eugenie."

I tried not to be offended at the relief that washed across both his face and his aura. His wonky shapeshifter energy, which had been crawling across my skin like invisible ants, settled down to its usual buzz.

Then it began rising again. "You mean . . ." He looked toward the living room, then out the window, where the front of Plantasy Island sat in plain view. Rand stood framed in the doorway, looking our way. "Holy shit."

I followed the direction of his gaze with my own and nodded. "Exactly."

CHAPTER 3

I paced back and forth behind the sofa; Alex stood in the entry hall, looking out the window at Plantasy Island as if he could will Quince Randolph to permanently disappear. We'd been waiting longer than the five minutes Eugenie needed to get the results of the test, but she hadn't made a sound and the bathroom door remained firmly shut.

It wasn't a good sign.

Alex and I had agreed not to discuss anything this close to Rand, in case he turned his sneaky elven antennae in my direction and found me distressed enough for him to get suspicious and investigate. He needed to be nowhere within ten feet of Eugenie, and especially not within touching distance. Touching her would ramp up his power and he'd know in an instant. Since the child she carried had his DNA, he might be able to communicate with it if he got close enough—or even if he didn't. Who the hell knew?

"It's sleeting." Alex came back into the living room. "Ground's still too warm to stick, but we might have an icy drive to the council meeting tomorrow night if it doesn't get above freezing tomorrow."

"Great. It'll make the evening even more special." At least the baby crisis had temporarily taken my mind off the coming Interspecies Council meeting, which promised to be a debacle. The prospect of testifying had kept me awake most of the last two weeks, ever since they'd decided to meet before the holidays instead of waiting until January. Not that pretes in general hung mistletoe and stockings, but because the current political atmosphere was so contentious.

This would be the group's first official gathering as a governing body, and it scared the hell out of me. What could be worse than a roomful of pompous, self-important preternatural bureaucrats, each trying to prove himself more badass than the prete in the next chair?

Judgments would be passed. Examples would be made. I didn't want to be one of them.

The sound of an opening door wafted down the hallway, and the squeaky hinges were followed by a slow cadence of boot heels on hardwood. These were not the footfalls of a happy woman.

Eugenie's eyes had puffed almost closed and her nose had reddened to the color of a Santa suit. Her expression lay somewhere between stunned and catatonic. "Congratulate me, guys. I'm having a baby elf." She sat heavily on the sofa next to me. "What in the hell am I gonna do?"

I took Eugenie's hand, and Alex sat on the coffee table facing us, his knees touching mine. He cleared his throat, and I had a sinking feeling that he was about to say something awful. Not intentionally awful, but cluelessly awful.

"Is there any chance it isn't his? I mean, have you . . . did you . . . ?"

Eugenie narrowed her eyes and I leaned back to watch the fireworks.

"Well, let's see, the only person I've even fooled around with since Rand was . . . hmm . . . I believe that was with *you*, Alexander Warin. Could it be yours?"

What? I gave Alex my own version of a narrow-eyed look and he had the worst possible reaction under the circumstances: He blushed and stammered. The dog.

"It was, uh, when we thought you really had bonded with Randolph and we were both pissed off at you and, uh, nothing happened." His words tumbled out in a rush. "Really. Eugenie, tell her. Nothing happened."

Eugenie looked at me and shrugged. "Nothing happened. We had one half-hearted kiss, which I started, and then I went home. Point being"—she turned back to Alex—"no, this can't be anyone else's baby."

He closed his eyes. "Sorry, it's just that it would be easier if it weren't his."

Which gave me an idea. "As long as we keep Rand from getting anywhere near you, Eugenie, he never has to even know about it. If . . ." I'd been about to say "If you decide to have it," but I'd been having that conversation with myself all the way to the drugstore and back. I would not advise Eugenie on whether or not to continue this pregnancy. Even if she asked my opinion, I wasn't sure what I'd tell her because I didn't know what I'd do in her situation. It had to be her decision.

". . . If we can just keep him away," I finished.

I slumped down in my seat. Nothing was easy here, because the decision not to tell Rand felt wrong, too. Quince Randolph was a cretin, but for all the underhanded things he'd done to me—including kidnapping and political manipulation—he also had saved my life more than once. In a way, by offering me a

way to avoid turning loup-garou after I was infected, he'd saved
Jake Warin's life, too.

He had a right to know he had a child on the way, and we
needed credible information on human-elven pregnancies. I
couldn't exactly Google "elf spawn." Well, I could, and I had—
while we waited for Eugenie to take the pregnancy test. More
than a million results popped up, which was downright scary. A
quick scroll turned up a lot of World of Warcraft sites, which I
figured would be less than helpful.

Rand might be our only reliable source of information. And
once he knew Eugenie was pregnant, he'd be insufferable.

The longer we could keep this baby a secret, the better for
everyone, especially Eugenie. She needed time to adjust to the
idea, and I needed to find a reliable, discreet source of information on human-elven reproduction.

"Have you considered an abortion?" Alex looked perfectly
and sincerely clueless. He had the tact of a baboon, and his words
hung heavy through a long, tense silence.

"Go the hell home. I hate men. I don't ever want to see another man in this house, human or otherwise." Eugenie pushed
herself off the sofa and slapped Alex upside the head on her way
past. "DJ, get that dog out of here. I'll talk to you tomorrow."

I kicked Alex's ankle. "Nice job, Fido."

"What?" The sad thing was, Alex looked truly perplexed.
"It was a reasonable question, all things considered."

"Let's go to dinner." I couldn't get mad at him about the
question since I'd pondered the same thing, plus he didn't know
about the baby Eugenie had lost. He was also a guy and had no
common sense when it came to two things women did not want
to hear about from men—reproduction and hip circumference.

I grabbed my messenger bag on the way out, but took Eugenie's house key and left my overnighter. As much as I liked the

idea of snuggling up next to my big, warm shifter tonight while the sleet pelted away outside, Eugenie needed me more, even if it was to fetch juice and figure out what one did with agave nectar.

A half hour later, Alex and I piled into his black Range Rover and headed across town to Café Degas, the spot he'd chosen for dinner. Left to my own devices, I'd always go to Commander's Palace, but Alex reasoned that Degas was en route to City Park, where we planned to catch the annual holiday light show before heading back to his place. Then I'd have to fulfill my promise and call Rand. Joy.

Reveillon was a two-week period of prime eating in a city that relished good food—local restaurants offered special fixed-price, four-course holiday meals in December. Tourism always fell off before the holidays, so Reveillon had become a clever gimmick to entice locals onto the restaurant circuit.

We made our way through the airy interior of the café, which tonight promised an array of fried oysters, crawfish ravioli, rack of lamb, and chocolate. I could almost forget the upcoming meeting and the baby crisis.

Almost.

"Does Eugenie's reaction mean she's really going to keep this baby?" Alex had at least noticed Eugenie didn't take the abortion question well.

I filled him in on the child she'd lost, but only after he'd promised not to bring it up in front of her.

"What if it were you?" Alex dug into his fried oyster and rémoulade salad, but was so intent on my answer he probably didn't even taste it.

"I honestly don't know." I poked at my own salad, picking out the oysters to eat and avoiding the greens. "I mean, normally, no, I wouldn't consider ending a pregnancy. If it were your baby, for example, of course not. You'd just have to get over it, whether you thought we were ready to be parents or not."

I shook my head. "But if it were Quince Randolph's? I honestly don't know what I'd do in that situation. Eugenie doesn't truly understand what kind of power the elves have, or how politically strong Rand has grown now that he's become chief of the fire clan and has a seat on the Interspecies Council. Don't forget how new all of this is to her."

Rand had ascended to clan chief when his mother, Vervain, the previous ruler, died at the hands of the undead serial killer who'd been trying to get at me. Chalk up one more death on the Typhoid DJ scorecard. It was a miracle anyone would come within a mile of me.

Alex waited as the waiter replaced our salad dishes with dinner plates artfully arranged with crawfish ravioli. Then he leaned across the table. "Don't let Eugenie wait too long to figure out what she wants, DJ. Zrakovi will want a say in how we proceed."

I chewed my ravioli and rested my fork across the edge of the plate with deceptive calm. Then I leaned across the table myself. "You are *not* to tell Zrakovi. You are not to tell anyone. This is not your news to share without Eugenie's permission. However she *proceeds* has to be her choice, not the Elders'." Or ours, for that matter.

Alex put his own fork down. "Eugenie isn't in a position to decide who does and doesn't know—not about this. There'll need to be damage control." He gave me a hard look. "You said it yourself—she doesn't understand the ramifications."

"Alex, seriously. Don't tell Zrakovi. Not yet. Give it a few days at least."

Willem Zrakovi was a member of the Congress of Elders,

the wizards' ruling body. He represented North American interests and I'd always found him fair and less stuffy than others I'd met among the wizarding elite. But he would stir the cauldron in whatever fashion best suited the Elders, not Eugenie.

Alex pushed his plate toward the middle of the table. I wasn't feeling too hungry anymore either.

I took a deep breath. "Well?" He'd never answered, and I wanted his promise.

"I'll keep quiet for now, but I reserve the right to change my mind after the Interspecies Council meeting. It depends on how things go tomorrow night. If the wizards take a hit and negotiations with the elves look shaky, I might have to tell him. We can't let him be blindsided or have the elves find out some other way and accuse us of hiding it."

"But—"

"DJ, don't be naïve." He waited for our plates to be whisked away and replaced with another course. The leg of lamb made me think of baby sheep, which made me think of baby elves. I definitely had lost my appetite. "If things get more precarious between the wizards and elves and they find out we hid something like this from them, it could be disastrous. Zrakovi needs to know."

I stabbed the damned lamb with the tines of my fork. "It can be disastrous next week, then. Give Eugenie a few days to think things through."

We left it at that, with him unwilling to promise anything outright and me unwilling to push him to the point of an argument. Maturity, that's my middle name.

"So, what were you doing for the Elders today?" He'd seemed pumped when I talked to him before the baby bombshell hit, so maybe we could recover from an argument that didn't have a resolution.

He smiled, and his whole demeanor relaxed. "Jonas Adamson had escaped back to the Beyond, so I was able to go into Old Orleans and capture him."

Ah, he'd gotten to be an enforcer again, the work he really loved, not the investigative assignments he got stuck doing most days now that the borders had dropped for good.

"Did you get to shoot him?"

He grinned. "Of course."

"Good. He deserved it." I knew that sounded harsh, but the unregistered necromancer and fellow Green Congress wizard had done a lot of damage last month.

"I agree, and I finally got to try out that new ammo the Elders approved for enforcer use." Alex chewed enthusiastically. "It doesn't just enter the body like a normal bullet; it does that, plus releases a magical paralysis potion so they can't keep running until they find a transport."

"I've always liked a good paralysis potion." I also liked seeing Alex this excited. When I'd met him, he'd been one of the Elders' most lethal killers. As the prete landscape changed after Katrina, however, his job had changed as well.

We used to be border guards. I was the sentinel, the peacekeeper, and he was the muscle called in when talk failed. Now, we worked in a gray zone where it was never clear who could go where or do what. Alex didn't like gray zones.

No gray zone for Jonas Adamson, though. He was one doomed wizard. He'd sold his necromancy skills to the leader of the water elves, had forced the undead Axeman of New Orleans to try and kill me, and tried to have Jean Lafitte do the same. Axeman had killed Rand's mother and several humans. All for political power and a little bit of money.

Except it hadn't worked. Tomorrow night, Jonas would get his judgment, along with the elves, wizards, and vampires who'd been part of the scheme.

"Who all is going to testify?" I sank a spoon into the chocolate pot de crème. I might not be able to eat lamb, but it takes earth-shattering stress to kill my taste for dessert. "And do we know who ended up as council members once things finally got settled?"

Alex shook his head, shoved his dessert across the table to me, and slid my untouched glass of port across the table toward himself. Good trade.

"Not sure about the council. I heard there will be three or four senior Elders, three reps from the fae, two each from the elves and vampires, and the smaller groups will have one representative. Politically, the fae are the biggest question marks. No one has a clue what side they'd come down on if the groups really start choosing sides."

I pondered what I knew about the fae. They lived in a monarchy, but all I knew of their magic was that much of what the human world attributed to science was their handiwork. Time and tides, gravity and seasons. Next to the wizards, they were the largest group. They also had a reputation for being eccentric and unpredictable.

"As for who will be testifying . . ." Alex finished his port, set his glass aside, and took a sip of mine. "Pretty much everybody you'd expect, including the Axeman himself. Rene Delachaise didn't get called; guess he was too far removed from the action. Neither did Jake. The big question mark is Jean Lafitte, and whether he'll be recovered enough to attend. Have you heard from your buddy the pirate?"

Alex said Jean's name without his usual sarcasm. *Le Capitaine* had earned some respect from the man he called *le petit chien*, not only because he'd saved me, but because he'd saved Alex's cousin Jake, a rogue werewolf loup-garou with control issues. He'd been living in the Beyond and working for Jean for almost a month now.

He might have gained a little respect for Jean, but Alex would never like the man. I, however, liked him a lot. Probably too much for my own good.

"I haven't heard from Jean since the week after he was killed." Make that the week after I killed him, and part of my soul died alongside him. I'd never before used my magic to hurt anyone I cared for, and I would never forgive the people who'd forced me to do it. "He was recovering pretty fast." And was mad as hell, I didn't add. "I'm pretty sure he'll be there tomorrow; he'll want to have his say."

Alex was quiet for a few moments, and I thought we'd moved past the subject of Jean Lafitte. Until he said, "Well, unfortunately, you'll have plenty of opportunity to hear his side of it."

I frowned at him and pushed his half-eaten pot de crème aside. Even I had reached my chocolate limit. "Why is that?"

"I talked to Zrakovi this afternoon after I turned Jonas in," Alex said, giving me an undecipherable look. "He's putting me back on sentinel duty for the next few weeks while you handle a special assignment."

Special assignment had an ominous ring to it. I reached for my water glass, knocking my spoon off the table. It hit the floor with a clatter, even in the noisy restaurant. A waiter was there to whisk it away so quickly I wondered if he were a vampire. Probably not, but one could never be sure these days.

"What kind of special assignment? And why am I hearing it from you instead of Zrakovi?" Elder Z was my boss, not Alex, however Mr. Bossy liked to think otherwise.

Alex pulled out his wallet and laid a credit card on the table. He was picking up the tab without a negotiation, and I let him. I had a feeling I wasn't going to like what he was about to say.

"Zrakovi's going to talk to you tomorrow after the hearing, but I'm all about the not-keeping-secrets-from-each-other thing."

Uh-huh. More like, he thought this was such a juicy piece of news he wanted the pleasure of telling me himself, although he didn't look exactly happy about it.

"Okay, spill it. What's my special assignment?"

"You're going to be babysitting Jean Lafitte and making sure he doesn't try to take revenge on anyone for what happened last month."

Alex gave me a grim smile and held his glass of port up in salute as the pot de crème congealed into a lump in my stomach. "Good luck with that, *Jolie*."

CHAPTER 4

I sat in Arnie's cab off the corner of Tulane Avenue and Broad Street and tried to figure a way to avoid going into the massive Orleans Parish Criminal District Court Building. Fifty years ago, the behemoth of stone and marble had been a marvel of lavish classical architecture. Today, it was a marvel that anyone survived a visit to it.

The weather sucked, the neighborhood reeked of danger, and the fourth floor was probably already full of pretes behaving badly.

Even before the post-Katrina flooding submerged the first two floors of the courthouse in grimy water, wiping out case files and evidence, the building had suffered from dwindling city budgets, ongoing political corruption, and a rapidly deteriorating, gang-riddled environment.

Criminals were everywhere, so of course it made the perfect spot for the first meeting of the Interspecies Council, held after hours to accommodate the vampires. According to Alex (my hotline to the Elders), a horde of Blue Congress wizards, skilled in creation, re-creation, and illusion, had reconfigured the seldom-used fourth floor. The windowless area had been transformed into a meeting space now reachable only via a single transport drawn in chalk on the building's front steps.

A shabbily dressed man lounged near the spot where the transport was supposed to be, but I saw bright, sharp eyes beneath the brim of the worn hat tilted over his forehead. Enforcer.

"Miss DJ." Arnie glanced in his rearview mirror, eyes widened. "You sure you want to be gettin' out here? It's almost eight o'clock. Courthouse been closed awhile, and there's no reason for a woman to be hangin' around Tulane and Broad after dark. Nosiree."

Unspoken was the "and I'm not coming back for you when you get your ass in trouble" message.

"It'll be fine. That's my friend up there on the steps." The probable werewolf posing as a vagrant. Alex had been required to make an early appearance to help set up security; thus, my trip with Arnie.

"Ohh-kay, Miss DJ. You be careful, hear?"

Yeah, as careful as I could be heading into a roomful of vipers. As sentinel of this region, I'd be part of every council meeting in a non-voting capacity. New Orleans had become the grand social experiment of the prete world. If things worked out here with our open borders to the Beyond, the reasoning went, other cities might drop their borders as well.

Before the walls fell following the hurricane, I'd been a sort of border guard. Now, my job was part babysitter, part negotiator, part peacekeeper. Prete-related crimes got shunted to Alex and his Division of Domestic Terror investigators, so he'd be at all the meetings as well.

A loud pop from a few blocks east sent my skin crawling as

I exited the cab, and probably accounted for Arnie peeling rubber. He raced through a yellow light on Broad and hightailed it back toward the gentrified, safer confines of Uptown.

It probably wasn't a gunshot, or so I told myself. Early Christmas fireworks, maybe, or a backfiring car. Right.

The faux homeless guy sat up straighter and actually growled when I approached, so I got straight to the point. "Transport?"

He pushed back the brim of his hat, and I felt his buzzy shifter energy from three feet away. "ID?"

Definitely an enforcer. They all had that charming gift of gab, including Alex when he went all Neanderthal on me.

"You'd be doing me a favor if you refused to let me in." I dug my Green Congress badge from my bag and gave it to him, noting the increased buzz when I touched his hand. Slightly different from what I got off shifters like Alex or my merman friend Rene Delachaise, so I was betting werewolf.

He glanced at the ID and handed it back. "No such luck, sentinel. You're on the VIP list."

Yeah, Very Insignificant Peon, at least compared to most of those who'd be here.

Just past him, I spotted the interlocking circle and triangle of a wizard-powered transport etched across several concrete steps in chalk. "Why couldn't we just transport directly into the courthouse?" I stepped into the transport but waited for Wolfie's answer before leaving.

"Beats me. My guess is that the wizards wanted to inconvenience everybody as much as possible, maybe hoping half the council members won't bother to show up." He paused. "No offense."

"None taken." He was probably right. The Elders refused to meet in Old Orleans because most of our magic doesn't work in the Beyond, plus this had the added bonus of forcing the elves to travel in frigid weather, which they would hate. In my late-night research on the Elders' secure website, searching in vain for useful information on elven reproduction, I had learned that elves were weakened by cold temperatures. Which explained not only Rand's reluctance to venture outside these days, but maybe my own. I wasn't anywhere near half elf, but the cold seemed to bother me more than anyone else I knew and had gotten worse, maybe due to our bonding.

The transport was open and already powered up, so I only had to say the magic words "Interspecies Council" to use it. I knelt and touched a finger to the chalk line, though, to see what kind of wizard had powered it. Definitely Red Congress; the transport was strong. Physical magic was the strength of Red Congress wizards; my specialty was ritual magic, slow but reliable, and not the least bit sexy.

Unlike any other Green Congress wizard, however, I had a righteous staff of elven origin tucked in my messenger bag. I'd picked this particular bag because Charlie (or, as the elves would insist, Mahout) would fit in it with only an inch or two of wood poking out.

After a few unpleasant seconds where it felt as if my head were being sucked through a vacuum cleaner hose, I opened my eyes to the magic-enhanced fourth floor of the Criminal District Court Building. The locals just call it "Tulane and Broad." I'd been here once before, to beg my way out of jury duty, and knew each level of the real building consisted of one long marble hallway with courtrooms and offices on both sides.

The magical version still had the highly polished gray marble floors, but the transport sat at the edge of a lobby area not much larger than the living room of Gerry's house. A few benches dotted the edges on three sides; on the fourth wall spread a massive set of double doors in rich mahogany. Beyond, I assumed, was the Interspecies Council's inner sanctum.

"ID?" A beefy guy wearing a lot of black leather, including a shoulder holster, stood outside the transport. This one's energy buzzed more shifter than were, and I wondered what he turned into. True shifters like Alex and Rene could change at will, unlike were-animals, who remained tied to the phases of the moon.

I pulled out my badge again. When he handed it back to me, I stuck it in my pocket where it would be easier to get at next time. I'd borrowed a trio of red and white sweaters from Eugenie to wear in layers, refusing to make my first appearance before the world's most powerful pretes dressed in a thrift store coat of eye-gouging plaid. Wearing jeans—the only pants I owned now—and with my right arm in a tasteful black sling, I hoped I looked sufficiently conservative but not to the point of sucking up.

Unlike Alex, who I spotted as soon as I slipped through the double doors. He wore a suck-up black tailored suit that highlighted his broad shoulders and narrow waist, and a cream-colored shirt that looked suspiciously like silk, open at the collar. Deep in conversation with an older man who sported a wild Einstein-ish shock of white hair, Alex looked healthy, wealthy, and sexy enough to make me forgive almost any boorish behavior.

I caught his eye and waved, and got a hot little smile in return, complete with that sexy crease on the left side of his mouth that was almost, but not quite, a dimple. Maybe our relationship was going to make it after all. I'd had my doubts in the last month, but we'd both been working at it, trying to keep the external stuff from blowing us apart.

I reined in my appreciation and looked around the room, trying to figure out where to sit.

According to Alex, the room had been patterned after the Supreme Court chambers. A long table stretched across a carpeted platform in front, with chairs that faced the room. Before each chair was a placard inscribed with the council member's name. I made note of where *Capt. Jn. Lafitte* would be seated and scanned the rest of the room. A small wooden table sat in front of the dais, with two chairs facing the council, probably for who-ever was giving testimony. And rows of seats behind.

I was prime peanut-gallery fodder, so I plopped myself at the end of the row of seats nearest the front and counted the chairs behind the long table. Fifteen, each with a microphone stand before it.

Despite my terror at having to testify and dread of seeing Adrian Hoffman and the Axeman again, my adrenaline pumped enough to make the room seem brighter and louder. I'd done a good grounding before leaving Eugenie's to keep my empathy in check. I didn't know which species I could read and which ones I couldn't, so better to be safe.

"Hey, sunshine. Care if I sit with you?"

I looked up and smiled. It was the first time I'd seen Jake Warin in weeks, not since I'd fled to Old Barataria to escape the elves and the Axeman.

I scooted over and Jake took the aisle seat.

"What are you doing here?" I whispered. "You don't have to testify." Being here could be dangerous for him; he'd acci-dentally infected me with the loup-garou virus last month, which in some ways had set the whole ugly elven conspiracy in motion. The Elders still didn't know about his involvement, and I hoped it didn't come out today.

"I'm security for the boss." Jake's dimples made an appear-ance, and his amber eyes twinkled like they had before all this loup-garou mess started. Maybe he was finding his way back to being Jake, and that made me happy. "You know, your pirate BFF."

I looked around but didn't see Jean. "How's he doing?"

Jake shook his head. "His body's healing, but you knew that. His head? Well, let's just say he is one pissed-off Frenchman."

Great, and I had to babysit him. "Throwing tantrums? Making it hard on his people?"

"Oh no." Jake looked around to see if anyone was nearby, then lowered his voice. "If Jean's noisy and carryin' on, he's mostly putting on a show. It's like theater for him, you know? He likes an audience. When he's really pissed off, he gets quiet. And he's been like a damned church mouse ever since Thanksgiving."

Better and better. "I hear my next assignment will be keeping Jean under control," I said. "Any idea how I can accomplish such a thing?"

Jake laughed. "Good luck, sunshine."

Yeah, seems like I'd heard those words before.

Alex joined us, and for the next half hour, we watched as members of the Interspecies Council arrived with varying amounts of fanfare. The people with charges against them were being held in a room behind the dais, which left me free of worrying about seeing Adrian Hoffman again and able to gawk at the pretes.

The Einstein talking to Alex turned out to be Toussaint Delachaise, my merman friend Rene's father and council representative for the water species. A sour-faced gremlin represented the group I liked to call "gods and monsters," sort of a catchall prete class, none of whose components were big enough to have their own representatives. The head of the enforcers, a werewolf who'd been Alex's boss before he'd begun answering to Zrakovi, filled the were-shifter council seat.

"Where's Lafitte?" Alex whispered, then slid his gaze past me. "What the holy hell is that?"

I didn't feel self-conscious turning to openly gawk at the

newcomers, because a silence had fallen over the room. Everyone else gawked, too. A tall, razor-thin woman with a cascade of silvery-blue hair glided down the room's center aisle. She wore a heavy blue floor-length coat trimmed in white fur with a long fur tail that slid along the floor behind her like a snake. Trailing her were two men also dressed in long, fur-trimmed coats.

"Faeries," I whispered to Alex. "Has to be. They have three council seats."

He nodded. "The queen is really . . . old."

I studied the woman, who'd walked onto the dais and taken the seat pulled out for her by one of her male companions, the one with short black hair as opposed to the one with short blond hair. Both men looked to be in their early thirties; the woman was a pickled ninety if she was a day. Although she could be a thousand.

Note to self: Look up the life span of faeries. I hoped the faery search would be more fruitful than the hours I'd wasted trying to learn about elf reproduction while Eugenie cried in her bedroom.

Finally, the other council members filed in from the room behind the dais. First came a man too pale and perfect to be anything but vampire. "That's Garrett Melnick, the head of the Regents," Alex whispered. "Etienne was going to be their other council member."

Melnick looked like actor James Franco if he joined Mötley Crüe. Boyish posing as hair-band grunge, all in black leather.

The elven contingent of Mace Banyan and Quince Randolph needed no introductions, although they both looked gratifyingly cold. Rand's gaze locked on to me as soon as he walked in the room, and he smiled. I gave him a finger-wave, the most I was willing to concede, although damned if he wasn't pretty in his powder-blue snow-prince sweater. He must have a closet filled with every shade of blue.

We'd had a short conversation last night after Alex and I returned from dinner, deciding the weather was too awful to visit City Park. He'd not been able to tell me much of what to expect today, except to keep my eyes open and be ready to think on my feet. That didn't bode well.

"That's the Elder from Asia, from Tokyo, I think. His name's Sato," Alex said, nodding toward the dark-haired man who entered with Willem Zrakovi. Both wore ankle-length black robes.

"Since when do wizards wear robes?" I whispered. "That's falling into every human stereotype ever created." Jeezum. Next thing you knew, they'd be waving around magic wands.

Speaking of which, I moved my bag containing the elven staff between my feet so I could get at it if I felt the need to wave something around myself.

"The First Elder thought they'd look more intimidating in robes than in business suits," Alex whispered back. "They look like they're on their way to a costume party at Hogwarts."

Finally, a handsome black man of indeterminate age walked out of the back, accompanied by a handsome Frenchman whose age I knew all too well.

Jean Lafitte looked great for a 230-year-old pirate who'd recently died for at least the fourth time that I knew of. He was six-foot-two of alpha pirate, his dark hair pulled back in a short ponytail, his dark blue eyes sharp and serious. He had full lips, a strong chin, and a jagged scar along his jawline in case one forgot how lethal he could be.

The indigo double-breasted waistcoat emphasized his slim waist, and light-colored breeches were tucked into black leather boots that almost reached his knees. Add the ruffled white shirt and he was ready to attend any nineteenth-century ballroom in style.

He gave Jake a light, somber nod and let his gaze linger on

me a second before taking a seat next to Toussaint Delachaise. His companion took the center chair and pulled the microphone toward him.

"If everyone could take a seat, please."

This was my first look at Adrian Hoffman's father, Geoffrey, the First Elder and also the representative for the UK and European Union wizarding communities. I saw the resemblance to his son. He wasn't as flashy as Adrian, but had the same bone structure, the same good looks, the same haughty bearing. I guess one didn't become grand poobah of all wizards without cause for arrogance. He'd probably been horrified that his baby boy had fallen for a vampire, conspired with elves, and gotten himself turned.

I'd spent a lot of my sleepless nights thinking about the First Elder, putting together my theory as to what he knew, and when he might have known it. I was ninety-nine percent certain he was up to his robe-wearing ass in the whole elf-vampire-wizard political mess. I couldn't prove it, however, so I had no intention of sharing it here unless I got backed into a corner.

After the introductions, including an awkward moment when Hoffman forgot the Faery Queen's name and called her Ravine instead of Sabine, the room fell quiet. I waited with my eyes glued to the closed door behind the dais. Of all those charged with crimes, who'd come out first? Would it be Adrian himself, who'd conspired against a fellow wizard and set me up to be killed? Lily, the elf who'd started the whole conspiracy? Etienne, her vampire conspirator? Jonas, the necromantic wizard who'd turned against his own people for money? Or the Axeman of New Orleans, the big, lumbering undead serial killer who'd become the conspirators' weapon?

"The first thing I'd like to do this evening," drawled Hoffman, looking down at a stack of papers he'd placed before him, "is call for the testimony of the person who was at the heart of all the problems experienced in the preternatural world three weeks ago. The person, indeed, at whose feet the bulk of the blame could rightly be placed."

Good. Lily would go first. She deserved every punishment they could throw at her.

Hoffman looked up, and I froze when his cold brown eyes came to rest on me.

"I request that Drusilla Jane Jaco, the sentinel of the New Orleans region, take the stand."

Oh, shit.

CHAPTER 5

The world around me had turned alien and surreal. I took a deep breath to steady my nerves. The First Elder's son was in trouble, and he needed a scapegoat. As sentinel, I might as well have cloven hoofs and little nubby goat horns sprouting from my head.

I just thought it would take him longer to go after me.

My knees shook when I stood up. *Be ready to think on your feet,* Rand had said, and I wished I'd pressed him more on what he meant.

Walking to the front with my chin held high, I kept my eyes on First Elder Hoffman. I hadn't done anything wrong, other than be born with enough elven magic for both wizards and elves to find it threatening. Hoffman would do everything possible to put Adrian in a good light, which meant putting me in a bad one.

He wasn't getting away with it. If he thought I'd stand by meekly and take one for the team to avoid ugly political fallout, he had the wrong wizard. I'd almost died, Alex had been shot, and I'd been forced to kill Jean.

Jake had shoved the messenger bag containing the elven staff in my hands as I climbed over him to the aisle. I didn't find it reassuring that he thought I needed to be armed. The tense posture and sudden alertness of both Rand and Jean as I took my seat behind the witness table offered an important reminder, however. I had allies on the council. Strong allies. They just didn't happen to be sitting in the First Elder's chair.

The next surprise came after I'd vowed to tell the whole truth and nothing but the truth upon pain of having my powers stripped, or some equally horrible fate. The door behind the dais opened and another security guy escorted the prisoners out of their holding room.

If I hadn't been trying to keep a wary eye on the First Elder, I'd have smirked at the vision of Jonas, Adrian, Etienne Boulard, and the Axeman attached to each other with glittering, magic-enhanced ankle shackles. Except there should have been a fifth person in that group. Lily was the guiltiest culprit. She'd hired Jonas to use his necromancy in resurrecting the Axeman to kill me, which had led to the death of Rand's mother. She'd blackmailed Adrian into betraying a fellow wizard, forced Jean to shoot me, and conspired to overthrow Mace Banyan as head of the Synod.

I glared at Rand, making use of our ability to telepathically communicate by bellowing, *Where the hell is Lily?*

He winced and hunched his shoulders. *Stop yelling!* Leaning to one side, he whispered something to Mace, and the Elven Synod leader's dark gaze slid to me before he spoke. "Mr. Hoffman, before we continue, I'd like to address the absence of one of the defendants tonight, Lily Aleese."

Hoffman's face compressed into a sour look very much like his son's habitual sulk, which told me Lily's absence hadn't been scripted. "Ms. Aleese is key to these proceedings, Mr. Banyan."

Mace assumed a sorrowful expression that looked about as genuine as a cheap cubic zirconia in a diamond mine. In his gray suit and gray band-collared shirt, with his perfectly matched heather-gray overcoat thrown across the table, he looked urbane and oh so sincere. I knew better; he'd had the same expression when he apologized for kidnapping me and then plundering through my mind with the finesse of Ferdinand the Elven Bull.

Freaking elf.

"Unfortunately, the severity of the charges against Lily precluded our waiting for the council to assemble." He reached across the table and dug in a pocket of his overcoat, pulling out an envelope. "Lily Aleese was executed, as per elven custom, forty-eight hours ago in Elfheim, following a Synod trial. I have time-stamped photos of her body, with and without her head, should you wish to take and examine them."

Photos could be doctored. It took a lot of effort for me to remain seated and silent, and I shot a questioning look at Rand. He hated Lily as badly as I did. If he said Lily was dead, I'd believe him.

He gave me a tight smile and nodded. Inside my head, I heard him as clearly as if he'd spoken aloud: *Mace insisted we do it by the old rules, but she's definitely dead. I killed her myself. And she suffered.*

Somehow that didn't make me as happy as I would've expected. The elves were brutal. I'd seen what they did to Rand after he'd helped me escape Elfheim. He'd been beaten, and badly. The only reason he didn't get another punishment for bonding with me was that our alliance, and his mother's death, had made him too powerful. I had no doubts he could dish out suffering as well as the next elf.

While Hoffman examined the photographs, I looked over at Jean to see how he was taking the news about Lily, but his attention rested with one person only: Etienne Boulard. They'd been friends in their human lives, before Jean had become so famous he earned a magical form of immortality, and Etienne, a French Louisiana plantation owner, had become a Regent of the Realm of Vampyre. Etienne had betrayed Jean, and they both knew it.

Much like the question of whether or not I'd continue an elven pregnancy should I find myself in that predicament, I had no answers to the question of whether I'd stop Jean if and when he tried to exact revenge on Etienne. That had a much greater likelihood of happening than me getting pregnant with elf spawn. Jean didn't forgive a betrayal, plus he had a couple of major advantages. He couldn't be turned vampire and he couldn't be killed, at least not permanently.

I didn't like Etienne's odds.

From the vamp-in-dawn's-early-light look on his face, Etienne didn't like his odds either. He fidgeted in his seat and looked everywhere except at Jean. His gaze came to rest on me briefly, and I saw a flash of the insolent, confident vampire he'd been a month ago. Only a flash before he looked down at the floor.

"Very well." Hoffman passed the envelope back to Mace. "In future, however, I hope the elves will abide by the procedures we've established for the council."

"In future"—Mace looked at Rand—"we'll have no more such treachery within our ranks."

Rand was starting to look a lot like the Mona Lisa. I never trusted her little smile, and if Mace had any sense he wouldn't trust Rand's. I had no idea what my significant elf was up to, but I had no doubt that Rand had a scheme. He always did.

Then again, Mace deserved whatever he got.

"Ms. Jaco." Hoffman slipped on a pair of reading glasses,

probably to give him a more scholarly appearance to go along with his silly black robe. Nearsighted wizards used magic to correct their vision. "Is it true that you conspired to interfere with the affairs of the Elven Synod during the last two weeks of November?"

"Uh . . . no?" I hoped that little question mark at the end wasn't evident to anyone but me. I expected Hoffman to accuse me of setting up Adrian, not interfering with Synod business. Where was he going with this?

He peered at me through his little glasses, which gave him a piggish appearance.

"Does that mean you deny entering into a blood bond with Quince Randolph, who at that time was the incumbent clan leader of the fire elves? And that the nature of this bond was purely for Mr. Randolph's political gain?"

Rand's jaw clenched, but he didn't say anything. This was Mace Banyan's work; he hadn't wanted Rand on the Synod, much less sitting on the Interspecies Council. Rand had gotten the council seat because our bond gave him an in with the wizards.

I gave Mace my most evil stink-eye. "I wouldn't say it was purely political, no."

Hoffman took off the glasses and settled them atop his shiny bald head. Now he looked like a pig with glasses on his head. "You're telling me that you and Mr. Randolph are living as husband and wife, as such bond-mates are called in our culture?"

He smiled. Evil bastard.

Damn it. Everyone knew Rand and I weren't living together, but if I admitted that I only bonded with him to avoid turning loup-garou, Jake would be in big trouble. That wasn't going to happen.

"Mr. Randolph and I are working on our relationship after entering the bond based on our intense physic"—I choked and

grabbed the bottle of water on the table, wishing it were rum—
"physical attraction."

Behind me, Alex coughed, or maybe it was Jake. I didn't dare
look. I kept my eyes on Hoffman.

"I see." He paused and rolled his eyes heavenward. Pig pig
pig.

"Is it true you refused to cooperate with the Synod when
they attempted to determine your powers after you were claimed
by the ancient elven staff known as Mahout?"

"Hey, they kidnapped me." This was starting to piss me off.
I was not the one sitting over there bound in magical ankle bling
after being caught with the proverbial smoking gun.

"And is it not true, Ms. Jaco, that it was you who killed Captain Jean Lafitte last month?" He looked down the table at Jean.
"*Kill* being a relative term, of course."

That one was true, and I met Jean's gaze with what I hoped
was an apologetic look. He was beyond apology. His dark blue
eyes were hard as the marble on the courthouse floor, and his
movements as he got to his feet were slow and deliberate. The
pirate was still healing.

"This is a farce, Monsieur Hoffman. You attempt only to
excuse the actions of your son, and every man and woman in
this assemblage is aware of it. I suggest we allow Mademoiselle
Jaco to tell her story as it happened, and then deal with those
who are truly guilty. I can assure you that she, like myself, was
a victim. Do not use Jean Lafitte for your perverse behavior. I
will not tolerate it."

Yeah. What he said.

Hoffman and Jean stared at each other for what seemed like
a week and a half before the First Elder backed down. "Very well,
out of respect for you, Captain Lafitte. Ms. Jaco, would you give
us the account of your *victimization*?"

If ever a word had dripped with sarcasm, it was that one, but I resisted the urge to dish it right back. I'd call him names in private later, and I'd hunt like hell for proof that he needed to be in that lineup of bling-wearing suspects. Tonight, I had the clear moral high ground and I planned to keep it as long as possible without slinging mud.

So I began to talk. About taking elf lessons with Adrian. Taking him with me to the vampire club L'Amour Sauvage, where he met Terri and where we'd seen Lily talking to Etienne. The meeting with wizard Jonas Adamson, the only registered necromancer in the area.

"Did you suspect that Mr. Adamson was in league with Lily Aleese?" Hoffman asked. He'd remained bland-faced throughout my story until Jonas was mentioned.

"I wish I had suspected him, but no. I didn't see anything to link him to Lily or to L'Amour Sauvage." I looked over at Jonas, who had kept his eyes on the floor since entering the courtroom. His toast was so burned, I almost felt sorry for him.

I went through the rest of the story as I had rehearsed it, taking Alex's advice to stick to the facts and not make any statements of opinion or emotion—until I got to the part where Jean received a direct order from the necromancer to kill me, and instead urged me to kill him first. And then I couldn't help it. I cried. I would never, ever forget that act of sacrifice.

"Please, Ms. Jaco, spare us the female histrionics." Hoffman's voice was dismissive. "After all, it's not as if Captain Lafitte really died."

Female histrionics? I'd seen Jean's face when my magic hit him. I'd watched him die. Maybe it wasn't a permanent death, but he suffered as much as if it had been.

I'd give the First Elder one thing; he knew just the words to cut off this female's histrionics. I'd been prepared to move cautiously, build a case against the First Elder, line up the proof that he was involved.

Forget it. Gloves? Off.

"Might I ask you a question now, Mr. Hoffman?" My heart still pounded but it was no longer from fear.

I heard Alex, or maybe it was Jake, hiss behind me. In my peripheral vision, I saw Willem Zrakovi lean forward. Even Sabine, queen of all faeries, who'd been studying her nails for most of the meeting, leaned forward with interest, and the faery guys whispered to each other behind her.

How far was I willing to take this?

Hoffman's eyes danced merrily beneath the faux glasses propped on his head. "By all means. Ask your little question."

Amused, was he? I kept my tone conversational. "Is it true that the whole time Adrian was being blackmailed by Lily Aleese to keep you from finding out about his vampire girlfriend, you already knew about it? Is it true that you were already in league with the vampires yourself, conspiring against the elves while the vampires pretended to be their ally?"

The heavy silence that followed was so deep my rabbit-racing heart was probably audible in Old Orleans.

Is this true? Rand shot me a mental zing. *Do you have proof?*

I'm sure of it. Somebody needs to question Jonas. The more time I'd had to think about the First Elder's involvement, the more certain I'd become. Adrian wasn't good at keeping his mouth shut, for one thing, and he and Terri hadn't been secretive about their affair. Plus, Etienne Boulard was a Regent; he would never have turned any wizard into a vampire without approval from higher up. Which meant either from his Vice-Regent or the First Elder.

Hoffman had sold out his own son. And with Lily dead, Jonas might be the only one who knew the truth.

"That is ludicrous." Hoffman wasn't twinkle-eyed anymore. "I should have you brought up on charges of treason. Return to your seat immediately. This council doesn't want to hear your desperate lies."

Get Jonas on the stand, I told Rand as I grabbed my bag and returned to my seat. Jake scooted down next to Alex, putting me on the aisle. Good. The way things were going, I might need to make a run for it.

"I believe we've heard enough," Hoffman said, straightening his stack of papers and setting his glasses on top of them. "I vote the council makes a recommendation on the proper punishment for—"

"Excuse me, Elder Hoffman. If I might make a request?"

Hoffman looked as if he'd swallowed a lemon. He turned his head slowly to the left. "Mr. Randolph?"

"I'm sure my mate was mistaken about her allegations. She's just overwrought."

I gritted my teeth and refrained from shouting at him, at least until I figured out his angle. Then I'd show him what overwrought looked like.

"No need to defend her—"

"But," Rand interrupted, "I would be interested in hearing at least one other account before we decide the prisoners' fates. These are serious charges, particularly against Jonas Adamson. I'd like the chance to question him using elven methodology, if I might."

Jonas raised his head for the first time, staring at Rand in horror. Mace leaned back in his chair and looked thoughtfully from Hoffman to Rand to Jonas. If I was right, and the First Elder was conspiring against the elves and the vampires were playing both sides, Mace would want to know.

So, apparently, would Elder Zrakovi, who spoke for the first time. "Geoffrey, I think Mr. Randolph's suggestion is a good one. It's the most expedient way for us to conclude this matter and move on. Perhaps we should let the council vote on it."

Sabine reached a wrinkled hand to her microphone stand and slid it toward her. When she spoke, her voice was husky and made my skin crawl. English was not her first language. I definitely needed to do some faery research. "The entire delegation from Faery agrees with the elf. Let the necromancer speak."

"I see no reason for it." Vampire Vice-Regent Garrett Melnick's blue eyes turned frosty, and he flashed fang. "We have the sentinel's testimony against her fellow wizard. What more do we need?"

"I agree." Hoffman gave Zrakovi a thunderous look.

"You're right. He knew."

Silence fell as everyone looked for the source of the voice, breathless and a bit squeaky. Jonas Adamson stood, his fists clenched at his sides.

"You will sit down!" The First Elder looked like a water balloon on the verge of a big, wet explosion, but on either side of him, Mace Banyan and Jean Lafitte jumped to their feet. Hoffman settled back and took a deep breath. I held mine.

"Fine, Mr. Adamson." Hoffman put his glasses back on. "Have your say."

Was it my imagination, or did Big Daddy Hoffman look nervous?

I leaned forward to get a better look at Adrian. He'd been stone-faced through the entire proceedings, but now he stared at his father with wide eyes. Initially, I'd thought Adrian and his father might be coconspirators, but that look told me he was a victim, too.

One of the wizard guards released the magical shackles, and Jonas made his shaky way toward the witness table. I dropped all my mental barricades to gauge his mood. He was scared and depressed. No kidding.

Rand edged around the table and walked from the dais to stand in front of Jonas. He looked over Jonas's shoulder at me. *Ideas?*

If Jonas felt doomed, the thing that would get him to open up without force was the possibility of survival. *Reassure him. Make him calm. Make him think that if he talks, we can save him. Don't dig the memories out of him unless you have to.* I hated what Jonas had done. I had no respect for him as a wizard, and little sympathy for the chaos he'd created. But I didn't wish that kind of suffering on anyone. Having elves dig in your mind and memories was painful, something I knew from hard experience.

Rand pulled a chair next to Jonas and sat down, reaching out his right hand and placing it on Jonas's arm. Within seconds, the wizard's posture relaxed, his shoulders dipped, his rapid breathing slowed. Even from one row back, I sensed the tension diminishing around his aura. Rand's happy vibes were working.

"Jonas, was Drusilla Jaco's account of the last two weeks of November accurate?"

Jonas nodded his head. "Yes."

I wished I could see his expression, but I'd have to be satisfied with gauging Rand's reactions.

Rand kept his voice low and calm. "Are there other things you can tell us that Ms. Jaco left out or was unaware of?"

I held my breath, grasping the strap of my messenger bag in both hands. I think half the people in the room held their breath. I prayed Jonas would talk and not make Rand pull the information from him by force.

"DJ only knew part of it, and Lily only knew part of it." Jonas's voice was surprisingly forceful. "The First Elder was in on it from the start, working with the vampires to join forces against the elves. If Lily got rid of DJ, he guaranteed the wizards would break the elven truce by blaming them for DJ's death. If she survived, the First Elder agreed to have Adrian turned vampire so the wizards would feel obligated to side with the vampires against the elves anyway."

Holy crap. I'd been right.

There was a split second of silence before the wooden railing in front exploded into a torrent of splinters and wood dust, and the whole room fell into chaos. Security rushed the dais, tripping over the council members who were trying to dodge flying bits of wood and waves of magic. Next to me, Jake cursed, shoved me to the floor, and threw himself on top. I landed on my right shoulder and my head hit something hard.

"DJ, you okay?" Alex leaned down to where my head was wedged under a chair, then didn't give me time to answer. "Yeah, you're okay. Jake, perimeter left. I'll take right."

"Gotcha."

Just like that, they were gone. I stayed low and hazarded a quick look over the top of the chair in front of me, trying to figure out what had happened. Jean had leapt over the council table, blade drawn, prowling toward the prisoners. Their magical shackles appeared to have been broken, and the Axeman lumbered toward the back room, preventing Etienne from getting around him.

Jean wasn't officially my assignment yet, so if he chose the present time to take revenge on Etienne, it was none of my business.

I finally saw the source of the flying splinters. Hoffman, half hidden behind his seat on the dais, flung Red Congress magic like errant bolts of lightning, exploding furniture, lighting, and whatever else he happened to hit—all to keep Zrakovi and Elder Sato away from him. He flung a curse I thought was aimed at

me, but it hit Jonas Adamson square in the chest. His body stiffened and toppled like a felled tree. At least, unlike Lily, he went
quickly.

The room plunged into darkness when one of Hoffman's
bursts of magic knocked out the last of the fluorescent lights.
Everything quieted for a few seconds before a brilliant yellow
glow lit the room from the direction of the dais.

The blond representative from Faery stood atop the council
table, cupping his hands in front of him. Above them floated a
ball of swirling light so bright it hurt to look at it directly.

The room had been stunned to silence, everyone mesmerized by the floating orb. Everyone except Etienne and Melnick,
whom I saw disappearing through the door behind the dais. They
were making a run for it. The Axeman had already disappeared,
and I didn't see Adrian. Behind the vampires slinked Geoffrey
Hoffman, a gleam from the faery light bouncing off the back of
his bald skull. I'd lost track of Jean.

Damn it, either that back room was getting awfully crowded
or they'd set up an escape transport in case everything went south.

I fumbled with my bag and pulled out Charlie. "Time to
go to work, my friend," I muttered, scuttling like a cockroach
between the row of chairs to the far wall, then hugging the edge
until I reached the door.

Things slowly came back to life. Zrakovi wrenched his
gaze from the faery light and scanned the room, stopping when
he reached me. I pointed at the door and held up the staff, but
didn't wait for his go-ahead. In my experience, when it came to
the Elders, better to act and ask for forgiveness later than to ask
for permission beforehand and wait for them to weigh all the
political pros and cons.

I slipped through the door and spotted the interlocking
circle and triangle of a magical transport just as Jean Lafitte lunged

into it, joining Melnick, Etienne, and First Elder Hoffman. The Axeman had already disappeared.

He was the least of my concerns. The vampires and Hoffman weren't getting away that easily, and I didn't like Jean's chances against all three of them.

As Melnick uttered the words "Realm of Vampyre" and they began to dematerialize, I threw myself into the transport with them. Time for a field trip.

CHAPTER 6

Usually, the experience of transporting is unpleasant but benign. One gets squeezed through some kind of magical vise and then pops up in a new place or time.

Then again, one usually isn't in the middle of a fight while transporting, so I couldn't say for sure whether Garrett Melnick sank his fangs into the skin above my collarbone before we left the magical fourth floor of the Orleans Parish Criminal District Court Building or as we landed on a grassy field, presumably in the Realm of Vampyre. Or somewhere in the ether, in between space and time.

All I knew for sure was that it felt as if lit gasoline raced through every vein and my blood burned like hellfire itself. I hit the ground on my back and he followed me down, pulling at my neck with his fangs. Then he raised his head and spat out a mouthful of blood on the ground beside me. His brown eyes glowed a little in the dim lights that surrounded whatever type of clearing we'd landed in. It had the look of a bizarre amphitheater.

He spat again, and used his right hand to scrub the blood off his lips. "You taste utterly vile."

I gave myself a half second to be offended, and another half second to be grateful. Then, because I still had a firm grip on Charlie, I zapped him with a nice shot of elven fire, right in the ass.

He rolled off me, hissing, fangs bared, and my skin stung with the power flowing off him. I'd thought Etienne gave off a lot of power, but he was an infant compared to Melnick. The guy might look like a fun-loving, playful man who should be wielding a mean electric guitar and screeching indecipherable lyrics, but he wasn't the Vice-Regent of Vampyre by accident.

Still, my first vamp feed had been disappointing. "And you hurt like hell. I thought vampire bites were supposed to feel good."

Pointing the staff at Melnick, I climbed to my feet in time to sidestep a pair of flying pirate boots. Jean sailed past me and landed heavily, still holding his cutlass with its wicked curved blade. Etienne had tossed him like a football spiraling downfield on a Hail Mary pass.

"You'll pay for crossing me, Drusilla Jaco." Melnick's words dripped with melodrama, but his delivery sent another wash of power across me. I did not want to see him and his pointy fangs again. Ever.

He faded into the shadows of the arena—more arena than amphitheater, I'd decided, with stone columns rising on multiple levels along three sides. The fourth edge seemed to drop off into a black abyss.

With Melnick gone, our odds had improved. It was now Jean and myself against Hoffman and Etienne, and Hoffman had been sitting on the ground looking stunned since we landed. All I had to do was buy a little time. Zrakovi should be materializing in the transport at any second with reinforcements.

With much grunting and swearing and trash-talking in French, Etienne and Jean engaged in a bit of knife play a few feet to my left, doing a lot of thrusts and parries with wicked-looking blades. Jean seemed to be holding his own, so I pointed the staff at Hoffman. Did I dare make a sentinel's arrest of the First Freaking Elder?

"Don't move a muscle." Did my voice sound squeaky? I lowered it an octave. "I'm officially detaining you, under my authority as sentinel of the New Orleans region."

I'd never gotten to use those words before, although I'd practiced them in front of the mirror. Not in my wildest nightmares had I imagined I'd ever use them on the First Elder.

He crossed his arms over his chest and raised one dark eyebrow. "Who the hell do you think you are, you meddling little half-breed?"

I was not a half-breed. I was at least eighty percent wizard. Fortunately, my other twenty percent could wield an elven fire staff in the Beyond and have it work.

"I'm the person who's taking you back to New Orleans. The Interspecies Council can decide what to do with you."

I wished Zrakovi would get his robe-wearing ass here. My arm was getting tired, and I could swear my bullet wound had reopened. Either that or I'd learned to sweat from one shoulder.

"You troublemaking bitch. I'm supposed to be afraid of you?" Hoffman climbed to his feet and raised himself to his full height, which was considerably more than mine. I backed away, but my hand on the staff was steady. I had the better firepower here, or at least I hoped I did.

Without warning, Hoffman flung a finger toward me and, on instinct, I threw myself to the ground and rolled to the side, bracing myself for a magical hit. My heart rate returned to a steady gallop when only a few sparks flew from his fingertips.

Thank God. I knew physical magic didn't work well in Old Orleans or Elfheim; apparently it didn't work in Vampyre either. Hoffman must not have gotten the memo. He cursed and flung his hand at me again.

I got back to my feet, propped one fist on my hip, and grinned at his expression of outrage.

My enjoyment ended when a train, or at least it felt like a train, hit me from behind. My body flew in one direction, the staff in another. I landed with a jolt, my chin cushioned by a puddle of mud. I guess it rained in Vampyre.

What had hit me? Damn it; I had to find the staff. I crawled in the direction it had flown, and finally spotted it. Then I looked over my shoulder to see what had derailed me—or who. It sure wasn't Hoffman; the First Elder had disappeared.

It had been Jean. A few feet behind me, finally bested by Etienne's vampire strength, he lay on his back, panting. Etienne knelt over him with one hand on Jean's throat, holding him in place. The other held a knife above Jean's chest.

Jean struggled, but Etienne only pressed harder on his windpipe. "You might not die forever, Jean, but this will hurt like hell while you're healing."

Damn it, Jean was about to get himself killed again.

I clutched Charlie more tightly and rolled to my knees, pointing the staff at Etienne and willing it to fire. A heavy rope of red flame shot from its tip and ignited the grass to Etienne's right.

He jerked his head up but didn't release his hold on Jean's throat. Jean's breath had turned to a definite wheeze and he'd quit struggling. I had to save him this time. I shifted the aim of the staff to the left. That had been a warning shot. Even I couldn't miss from here.

"Move. Away."

"To hell with you. Everybody knows your aim is worse than that of a blind man." Etienne gave me defiant flash of fangs and plunged the knife into Jean just as I released my pulse of elven magical energy.

From this range, I could hit anything. The flames of fire wrapped themselves around Etienne, burning into his clothing and reaching skin within a fraction of a second. His screams echoed around the arena . . . and he disappeared. How the hell could he disappear?

A flash to my right sent me into a crouch, ready to fire the staff again. Etienne had reappeared at least a hundred yards away, near one of the stone columns. His shirt hung in scorched tatters, and bloody red stripes stretched around his neck. Probably below the tatters on his chest as well. Good. I'd scorched the fanged son of a bitch.

I pointed the staff at him and fired, but again he disappeared, causing my shot to blow out a chunk of the stone column behind where he'd been standing. Creepy vampire. How did he do that?

I scanned the arena, waiting for him to materialize in another spot, but all was silent except for Jean's labored wheezing and the drip of water from somewhere nearby. Etienne seemed to have joined Melnick and the First Elder, skulking away to regroup.

Turning my attention back to where Jean lay unconscious, I crawled to him and took in the blood quickly soaking his right side just above the waist. Damn it, where was Zrakovi?

I didn't dare put down the staff with Etienne popping in and out like a half-burned, bloodsucking whack-a-mole. Sitting on the ground next to Jean, I kept Charlie at the ready with my right hand while reaching over to pull aside Jean's shirtfront with my left. He was wheezing less, but the stab wound was deep, the outer edges jagged. Etienne had used a serrated blade and twisted it on the way out.

Jean's blood coated my fingers when I pulled the ragged fabric away from the injury. The historical undead were immortal unless they were forgotten and no longer had the magic of human memory to sustain them in the modern world, but otherwise they appeared purely human. They breathed and bled like humans. They didn't have superstrength. They didn't have extraordinary speed or magical talents.

In other words, they weren't that hard to kill. True, they didn't stay dead, but they felt the pain of death. Until he healed, which he would do fairly quickly because he was probably fueled by more memory magic than any other famous New Orleanian, Jean would be in pain.

I didn't want that. I *so* didn't want that.

"Jean, damn it. I should've taken out that vampire from the start and forgotten about Hoffman."

My useless sling still hung around my neck, so I pulled it off, folded it, and pressed it on the wound. Above me, a full moon hung low in the black sky, and the soft lights hanging at intervals around the arena cast heavy shadows in which a million vampires could be lurking. Could they feed from Jean? Would the blood scent lure them here? Obviously, I tasted like crap.

And what the hell did vampires watch at an arena anyway? Somehow, I doubted it was football or soccer. I shivered, and it had nothing to do with the temperature. In fact, Vampyre was toasty warm.

Where the *hell* was Zrakovi?

I'd waited long enough. I was getting the crawling creeps, and everyone who needed killing or arresting had fled the scene. My magic might not power up that transport, but Charlie's would. I just had to drag a hefty unconscious pirate a couple dozen yards and never mind my bloody shoulder and bruised ribs. No problem.

I studied the pirate in question. He'd ditched his fancy waistcoat, his hair had come loose from its ponytail, and his light-colored pants were a mess of grass stains and dirt and blood. Then again, he had more money than God; unlike me, he could replace his wardrobe.

It would be easier to drag him by his boots, but somehow I doubted he'd appreciate his head bouncing along the ground. He had almost a foot of height and probably sixty or seventy pounds of weight on me, but I had determination on my side and a strong streak of stubborn.

Kneeling behind his head, I hooked my hands under his arms and heaved. His head lolled against my chest; pity he wasn't conscious to enjoy it. I got to my feet after a couple of tries and pulled him a dozen steps toward the transport before needing to rest. My shoulder throbbed, and my breath wheezed like I had a vampire pressing on my esophagus.

Okay, time to do it again. I leaned over and screamed as something grabbed my wrists and flipped me a complete one-eighty.

I landed hard on my back and my failing breath was knocked out of me by an elephant landing on my chest.

"Drusilla? Forgive me, *Jolie*. I thought you were that blackguard Etienne."

Drawing in a deep, gasping lungful of air, I flipped my lids open to find a familiar pair of dark blue eyes an inch or two above mine, narrowed in concern. An elephant hadn't landed on top of me, but a pirate had. And he seemed disinclined to move.

"I'm not Etienne." I was fast developing a reputation for my witty repartee under pressure.

"Non." His gaze dropped to my lips and I thought for a second he was going to kiss me. How would I respond if he did? Add that to the list of questions for which I had no answers.

"We're still in Vampyre, but Etienne and the others are gone. Do you think you can walk to the transport?" I took a deep breath as he rolled off me with a groan and sat up.

"Oui. The wound is painful but not deadly. Your fire stopped Etienne before he could finish his dark work." Jean got to his feet more easily than I did; in fact, he had to help me. "You are covered in blood, *Jolie,* and I do not believe it is all mine."

Neither did I. My whole freaking shoulder burned as if it had another bullet in it.

We limped toward the transport. Neither of us would be in any road races soon, although I fully planned to get the ingredients for a healing potion for myself and maybe one for Jean as well. My supplies had been so low, and my access to a magic-friendly workspace so limited, I'd been trying to heal the hard way—like a human. Forget that; the prete world was too unstable for me to be out of commission. I needed my staff-shooting arm fully functional.

Jean glanced around the arena. "Where went Etienne? And the Vice-Regent and your First Elder?"

I shook my head and stepped in the transport. "No clue. And I don't think Hoffman's going to be First Elder after tonight."

Jean stepped into the interlocking circle and triangle and reached out to pull a leaf from my hair. "Why did Monsieur Zrakovi and your elf and your dog not follow to assist you?"

Well, wasn't that a million-dollar question? "I don't know, but I sure intend to find out."

I didn't have to wait long. In fact, we had only to transport back to the Orleans Parish Criminal District Court Building and walk into the council meeting room to see the problem.

The place was on fire.

CHAPTER 7

Jean and I paused in the doorway that led back into the meeting room, momentarily speechless.

"*Merde,*" Jean finally said.

"Exactly," I added.

Flames engulfed the long table where the council members had been sitting. On either end, Zrakovi and Elder Sato had taken off their robes and were using them to beat at the flames, to little avail.

"Where have you been?" Alex yelled as he rushed past me and grabbed the arm of Toussaint Delachaise. "I'm having to take people out in the transport a couple at a time. Can you make the transport bigger?"

"Not without shutting that one down and creating another one," I shouted to his retreating back. Mr. Delachaise's Einstein hair was in more disarray than ever.

I turned to get a better overview of the scene. Jake and several of the werewolf security people were trying to stop the fire from spreading to the carpet by stomping on sparks. Apparently the Blue Congress wizards in charge of decoration hadn't used flame-retardant fibers.

Floating several feet above the chaos was Sabine the Faery Queen, who laughed while the dark-haired faery yelled at his blond counterpart, who apparently had lost control of his fireball. Now he stood with a stubborn expression on his face and his arms crossed over his chest, glaring at his colleague. Some enterprising wizard had at least equipped the room with emergency lighting, although the flames cast eerie shadows on the walls. The fire was spreading slowly and so far had been confined to the table, so either the table was fire-resistant or the flame was some kind of magical faery business. My bet was on the latter.

I moved closer to the faeries. I wasn't sure where Jean had gone, but we probably didn't have long before the building's smoke sensors would alert the NOFD, if they hadn't already.

The faeries were fighting among themselves.

"Put the damnable fire out!" Dark-haired faery's chiseled features flushed an unbecoming pink. He shouted with a slight accent I couldn't place. "Make it rain, you overgrown clump of crabgrass!"

"Make it rain yourself." Blond faery waved his arm in the direction of the fire, and a sudden wind gusted through the room, blowing the sparks beyond the werewolf stompers and igniting the carpet beside the council table. "Sabine is enjoying the show, and she needs to see proof of my powers."

Oh good grief. Dueling faeries, plus a roomful of prete politicians who couldn't figure out how to put out a fire. Could this night get any more ridiculous?

I hobbled to my messenger bag, still on the floor beside my chair, and pulled out a container of unrefined sea salt. Ignoring the flapping and shouting around me, I laid down a containment circle to rim the burning table and the section of carpet that was on fire, shooed Elder Sato outside the circle, and touched Charlie to the salt. I watched with satisfaction as my magical barricade sprang into place.

Just in time, too. The carpet fire quickly reached the containment circle and climbed an inch or two up the side of my invisible cylinder, but went no farther. Too bad I didn't have the proper gear to form a bubble. I could have cut off oxygen and killed the fire.

I also didn't have the ingredients for a replenishing charm, or I could have multiplied the water left in the bottle on the witness table.

With the fire momentarily contained, I looked for Zrakovi. The flames wouldn't spread outward, but they would continue to burn until the floor beneath the circle caved in or something shorted out.

I found him with a once again earthbound Sabine, arguing. "You must tell him to put out that fire, Your Majesty. In a moment, the human firefighters will be summoned."

"Florian needs to reach that decision on his own," she said, and her husky voice brought dry grasses and cicadas to mind. She was one creeptastic queen. "This is a test of his judgment."

"But Your Majesty . . ."

I'd heard enough. If Florian was the blond firebug, he had no judgment worth testing. While Zrakovi played diplomat and followed political protocol, the courthouse would burn down around his ears. Not to mention a hundred human firemen were going to rush in and find a serious freak show that would make one think Mardi Gras had arrived a couple of months early.

I pushed past the dark-haired faery and pointed the elven staff at his companion. "This is *my* fire-maker, Florian, and unless you put some rain on that mess you made, I will give you a personal introduction to it. You won't like it."

"What?" Florian unfolded his arms and looked at me uncertainly, then at Charlie. "Wizards don't have fire-making ability."

"Yeah, well, I'm a half-breed." I zapped him on the arm, and he jumped back a foot. Behind me, the dark faery started laughing. "Put it out. Now." I sent a few tendrils of fire shooting out from the end of the staff to reinforce my point.

He rolled his eyes. "Fine, although that fire is pathetic." With a flourish of arms and a few guttural words, Florian did whatever faeries did, and the heavens opened from the courthouse ceiling. The last time it had rained this hard, we were having a hurricane. Outside. I doubt it had ever rained this hard inside a closed building.

Funny how being soaked made people more compliant. Alex and Jake were able to quickly get every soggy person into the transport, and only then did I realize I hadn't seen Rand or Mace. I snagged Jake as he ushered in a team of newly arrived wizards I assumed was a Blue Congress cleanup squad. "Where'd the elves go?"

He rubbed the water out of his eyes. The rain had slacked to a light sprinkle inside, but the room was a mess, the magically powered emergency lights were flickering and sizzling, and I could swear I already heard sirens. "They took off as soon as the vampires and Hoffman escaped, yapping about a conspiracy." He looked around. "We've gotta get out of here. Wonder what the firefighters will make of this shit?"

❧

Six hours later, about 9:00 a.m., I could answer that question. Jake had gone to Old Barataria with Jean so the pirate could lick his new wounds, and after a treacherous ride with Alex through streets of icy sludge, I'd ended up at his house, waiting for Zrakovi. I hadn't wanted to wake Eugenie by schlepping in looking like a drowned wizard. Plus, although it was selfish of me, I couldn't deal with baby drama again. Not yet. Rand would be too busy hatching conspiracy theories with the Synod to be turning his elven antennae in my or Eugenie's direction.

After showering, I found a pair of my jeans and a black sweater in Alex's closet, and stole a pair of his socks. I'd left my water-logged boots inside the back door, drying on an unfolded section of the *Times-Picayune*. Sadly, they were my only existing pair of footwear since my house burned. Maybe I'd hit the thrift store and find some orange shoes to match my ugly coat.

I forced Sebastian into sharing a few minutes of quality wizard-feline time. I missed the grouchy old thing, but I couldn't say it was mutual. He loved Alex; he tolerated me.

After he'd finally escaped, I created an open transport on the living room floor for Zrakovi, and Alex and I snuggled on the sofa. We drank black coffee that warmed me up for the first time since the courthouse deluge, and watched the breaking news story on TV about a mysterious fire that had broken out on the top floor of the parish criminal court building. The fire of unknown origin had just as mysteriously been doused by a flood of unknown origin. Soot-faced firefighters theorized that a plumbing pipe had burst because of the freezing weather and had probably saved the historic building from burning to the ground.

Sounded reasonable to me. At least the Blue Congress wizards appeared to have gotten the walls back in the right place before the firefighters had to explain a building renovation of unknown origin.

Alex leaned over and treated me to a Rhett Butler kiss, slow and deep but not too sweet. He once told Scarlett something to the effect of how badly she needed kissing, and by someone who knew what he was doing. Alex knew what he was doing. By the time he finished proving it, I was breathless. I rested my head on his shoulder, basking in his warmth and filling my lungs with his scent. "What was that for?"

"That was to show you how glad I am that we got out of that mess in one piece and that we're here together." He extracted his arm from around my shoulders and sat back. "Now let's talk about your crazy stunt."

Damn it, Rhett did that, too. He'd kiss Scarlett silly, then lecture her. "If I'd waited until Zrakovi convinced the Queen of the Faeries to intercede, we'd all have been standing there on the morning news, surrounded by firemen." And probably a few police officers and, possibly, mental health workers. "She was floating around like a balloon from crazy town and laughing at the whole debacle."

I'd been the only person in the room acting sensibly, in fact. "And besides that—"

"Hush." He pressed a finger over my lips. "I wasn't talking about that. You probably saved all of us by containing the fire and forcing Florian to act. That was smart. What wasn't so smart was racing off with Jean Lafitte to catch Hoffman and the vampires. You could've been killed—or bitten."

Yeah, I'd show him *bitten*. I clamped my teeth down on his fingers before he could jerk them away.

"Ow. Stop that. Did you break skin?" He examined them for blood. "Do you know how many germs are in the human mouth?"

Yeah, well, he'd gotten them all over his tongue and hadn't minded.

I was sore and exhausted. I'd used up half a roll of paper towels getting my shoulder cleaned up and stopped bleeding. I'd need more stitches if I couldn't get my hands on the materials for a healing potion. To do that, I'd need to go to my heatless house. And to do *that*, I'd need a vehicle.

"We're not having this discussion." Scarlett might have let Rhett get away with it, but I wasn't taking lectures from Alex just because I'd done something he hadn't approved of. On the whole, during an extremely bizarre evening, I thought I'd handled myself well. "I did what I thought was right. I did what my job calls me to do. And because there was no one else there and I had a split second to act, I went alone."

Alex was quiet a whisper too long. "You weren't alone. You were with Lafitte."

The silence stretched between us and tightened around my throat. Damn it. "Is that what this is about? Jean? I thought we'd moved past that."

He sighed and got up to look out the front window. "I thought we had, too. And yet, there you went with him on another half-assed adventure, acting without thinking. Jumping from one chaotic scene to another. I repeat, you could've gotten killed or bitten. He can't die. You can."

I tugged aside the crew neck of my sweater, and could tell by his widened eyes when he spotted the two puncture wounds. "Melnick," I said. "He spat my blood out and said it tasted vile."

Alex opened his mouth, then closed it, then opened it again. "Where was your *partner?*" He said it much as one might say *pus-filled boil.*

"Trying to kill Etienne Boulard," I said, not willing to sugarcoat it. "Unfortunately, he didn't succeed. I burned Etienne's ass with the staff, though." And Melnick and, now that I thought about it, Hoffman. Charlie had been a busy staff. "And before you ask, yes, they all got away, even Hoffman."

I wanted to share the hilarity of watching the pompous First

Elder's expression of horror when he realized his magic wasn't going to work against me, but knew Alex wouldn't think it was funny. I wanted to tell him how badly I needed to save Jean after what had happened last month, but realized he wouldn't understand. Not only wouldn't understand, but would be angered by it. In Alex's black-and-white world, Hoffman was now a criminal who needed to be apprehended. Jean Lafitte was a menace he'd prefer to never lay eyes on again. I was the woman who didn't have the sense to stay out of trouble.

That realization hurt most of all.

Tears built behind my eyes, and I fiddled with a loose thread on the arm of the sofa. Damn it, I wasn't going to cry like a girl just because I was tired and he'd hurt my little feelings. Until he said, so softly I thought I might be imagining it, "I'm sorry."

I looked up at him, one telltale tear escaping. He returned to the sofa and pulled me into a hug. It sent a blast of pain through my shoulder, but I didn't care. Damn it, I wanted to make things work with Alex, but why did it have to be so hard?

"Let's forget it." He stroked my back, making me want to purr like Sebastian with every stroke of his fingers. "I keep underestimating how well you can handle yourself. And Lafitte pushes my buttons."

"He shouldn't." *Or should he?* I pushed the annoying mental question aside.

A sizzle of power flicked across my shoulder blades, making me shudder.

Alex pulled back. "What is it?"

"Daddy's coming home." I pointed at the transport, where Willem Zrakovi materialized a few seconds later, carrying the smoke-infused tatters of his black robe.

He broke the plane of the transport and stepped out, walking straight to the recliner in the corner and collapsing with a noise that sounded like half sigh, half wounded water buffalo. "I need to talk to you two briefly before heading to Edinburgh. We're having an emergency meeting of the full Congress of Elders in"—he looked at his wristwatch—"two hours. We have to form a strategy and establish stability before reconvening the Interspecies Council day after tomorrow to finish this sordid business."

"What about the First Elder's seat?" I briefly gave Zrakovi an account of following Hoffman and the others into Vampyre.

"The Congress's first order of business will be to formally remove Geoffrey and name an interim replacement as First Elder. If that person is not from the UK or Europe, we'll need a new Elder for that position since Geoffrey served as both."

Alex stood up and paced, which he tended to do when he was thinking hard about how to phrase something. "You're the senior Elder, sir. It would make sense for you to step in as First Elder."

That could be a good thing, and Zrakovi had a hard time feigning disinterest. The idea had occurred to him already; I could feel the surge in his emotions. My empathic grounding had worn off sometime during the courthouse monsoon.

"Well, we shall see." He leaned forward, a short, balding, soot-covered man in a ripped black business suit, in whose hands rested the fates of wizardkind and, to a great extent, the other pretes and the human world beyond. "I have assignments for both of you in the meantime. Alex, form a team to monitor the two main transports into New Orleans from the Beyond—the one at St. Louis Cathedral and the one at City Park. I also want someone watching L'Amour Sauvage around the clock. If Garrett Melnick or Etienne Boulard show up, they're to be detained."

Alex propped an elbow on the fireplace mantel. "And if they resist?"

"Don't kill them. We need more proof than the word of Jonas Adamson—the *late* Jonas Adamson—that Garrett Melnick was involved and playing the elves and wizards against each other. It would be easy for him to pin everything on Etienne. Our best hope is getting Etienne to turn on his Vice-Regent, but that won't be easy."

"Jonas spoke the truth. I could tell, and Rand could tell," I said, trying to settle my shoulder into a comfortable position. It throbbed like it had its own heartbeat.

"I have no doubt of it," Zrakovi said. "Which brings us to you, DJ. I have something for you."

He reached in a pocket and pulled out his wallet, then extracted two plastic cards and held them out to me.

I took them and frowned. The first one was a corporate American Express gold card, with *Drusilla J. Jaco, Crescent City Risk Management* as the cardholder. The second card was sable and gold with a magnetic strip on one side and a fleur-de-lis on the other, with no writing.

I held it up. "This looks like a hotel key card."

Zrakovi nodded. "I've taken out a room for you at the Hotel Monteleone, directly across the hall from Jean Lafitte—that took some serious negotiating with hotel management, I assure you."

He paused, waiting for me to respond. Given the conversation Alex and I just had, my wisest response would probably be *forget it*. But I was a woman with two plots of land, a third of a house, no vehicle, and no heat. "When should I be there and what, exactly, do you want me to do?"

"Keep close tabs on Captain Lafitte. In fact, you should go to Old Barataria now and find out when he plans to return to the city. I don't want him to go anywhere without you either accompanying him or following him."

Alex's face was as revealing as a clay mask, but his anger levels had ratcheted way up.

"Uh, that could be difficult," I said, dragging my gaze away from Alex. "And is it really necessary?"

It seemed awful to even think it, but would the world be such a bad place if Etienne Boulard no longer occupied a spot in it? Once Jean took care of his former friend, he'd probably be willing to play political footsie again with the elves since Lily and her head had parted ways.

"It is absolutely necessary." Zrakovi stood up, looking at his watch again. "We can't afford for him to go off on some vengeance-seeking mission and stir things up with the vampires and elves. And we need Etienne Boulard alive."

He paced the length of the room once before stopping in front of me. "Relations between all the species are more sensitive than ever after what just happened, especially given Geoffrey's involvement. The wizards' position is very precarious." He frowned at me. "I wish you'd told me your suspicions about the First Elder before bringing them out in such a public way."

I nodded, swallowing down the scathing comments I wanted to make. Namely, that had I told him, he wouldn't have believed me. Not without proof. "I apologize for that. He took me by surprise, trying to pin everything on me."

Zrakovi nodded. "Perfectly understandable. Anyway, Captain Lafitte will want revenge, and probably deserves it. But he can't worsen our standing with the other species. I have given my guarantee that he will be held in check." He paused and speared me with fierce brown eyes. "So hold him in check."

"Check. I guess." I looked at Alex, but he was staring at the floor like Sebastian trained on a bug.

Zrakovi held out the stinky robe. "Can you throw this damned thing away? One of Geoffrey's stupid ideas. It's high time some things changed back at headquarters."

I took the robe. It sounded like Zrakovi already had First Elder kinds of plans.

He walked toward the transport, but Alex stepped in front of him. "Sir, could you stay a few more minutes? There's a situation you need to be aware of." He glanced at me. "It's of a delicate nature."

Alex was nervous. Alex never got nervous. Damn it. He was going to tell Zrakovi about Eugenie.

"Of course," Zrakovi said, glancing at his watch for the third time. "I can give you ten minutes. What's the problem?"

Alex looked at me. "DJ, don't you need to be heading to Old Barataria, to check on Lafitte?"

Oh hell no. "I can wait a few more minutes, thanks."

"No," Zrakovi said, clueless to the relationship dynamics swirling around him. "I really would feel more at ease knowing you were on your way."

"I don't have a car," I said, glaring at Alex. "I'll have to call a cab. By the time Alex has discussed his *delicate situation,* it should be here."

By God if he told Zrakovi about Eugenie's pregnancy, I would sauté his boy parts and feed them to the cat.

He stuck a hand in his pocket, retrieved his keys, and tossed his key ring to me. "Take the Range Rover and leave it near the cathedral. I'll get a ride from Jake and pick it up later. I have another set of keys."

Alex had never, ever, ever offered to let me drive his vehicle, even before I'd proven a talent for burning them. But he and Zrakovi stood and stared at me, waiting for me to leave. Zrakovi tapped his foot, and I could tell he itched to take another look at his watch.

"Fine. See you later."

I walked out, got in Alex's SUV, drove across the street, and parked next to Eugenie's back door. She didn't know it yet, but we were going to visit a pirate.

CHAPTER 8

I wedged Alex's behemoth vehicle into a semi-legal space two blocks from St. Louis Cathedral, then texted him to let him know where it was. The only message I added was "heater works well." I didn't mention that Eugenie was with me, or that I'd already driven out to my half-finished house in Lakeview to change into clean clothes, attempt some quick—and useless—research on elven reproduction, and cook up a quick healing potion for myself and a second one for Jean Lafitte.

Alex didn't deserve bonus information.

"You've been stewing all the way across town and back," Eugenie said, pulling her coat around her more tightly. The high temperature today was supposed to be twenty-five but at least it was sunny and the sky was a rich shade of blue. I'd reluctantly donned my orange and purple nightmare of a coat. "You might as well tell me what's bothering you so I can reassure you and tell you it doesn't matter. Then I can enjoy visiting Jean Lafitte. I'm so excited I can't stand it! So tell me now."

I blew out a frustrated breath and swiveled in the seat to face her. "I might be wrong. I hope I'm wrong, but I'm pretty sure Alex is telling Willem Zrakovi about the baby. That's why I wanted to get you out of the house—in case Zrakovi decided to pay you a surprise visit."

Eugenie blinked, her eyes clear and guileless. She was such a good person; I hated to even think of her getting drawn into the messy world of prete politics. "Zrakovi's the wizard boss, right? I mean, that's okay, isn't it? He seemed like a good guy the one time I met him, although I didn't know he was a wizard." She paused. "Anyway, I don't know why he'd care, but you always say you like him. So it's okay for him to know, right?"

I willed my tight shoulders to relax. I shouldn't assume the worst of Zrakovi. He'd always been fair. But he also had his potential First Elderhood on the line, so caution was in order. "I'm sure it'll be fine. I just wanted you to come with me today in case he got the bright idea to pop over and take you by surprise." I tried not to think about Alex's assessment that Zrakovi would assume he had a say in whatever Eugenie decided to do. Might as well not worry about that unless it happened.

"Zrakovi will be interested in how you decide to handle things with Rand because the elves and wizards aren't always on the best of terms," I explained. Talk about putting lipstick on a pig.

Eugenie shrugged and opened her car door. "Well, I'm feeling good for a change and I'm tired of being sick and scared. What Quince Randolph doesn't know won't hurt him, at least not today. I want to visit the pirate's lair and I'm not going to let that stupid elf or your paranoid wizards ruin it."

Maybe she understood more than I gave her credit for.

I got out, pressed the button to activate Alex's alarm, and stuck the keys in my bag. If he came and got the SUV before we returned, we'd have to take a cab back to Eugenie's. I could break in the Elders' credit card. This whole visit to the Beyond was Zrakovi's idea anyway.

"Tell me what to expect. Does Jean Lafitte live in a house in the swamps kind of like a fishing camp?" Eugenie stuck her hands in her coat pockets and hunched her shoulders. I had found a pair of buttery soft black leather gloves in Alex's backseat and had stolen them, even though they made my ugly coat look even shabbier.

"Jean's not a fishing camp kind of guy," I said. Most of the fishing camps around South Louisiana were simple wooden houses built on piers over the wetlands or bayous. Not the Frenchman's style. "Jean's pirate lair is a two-story house overlooking a narrow stretch of beach on the Gulf side of Grand Terre Island," I said. "In our time, nobody lives there and most of the island has gone underwater."

"I've been to Grand Isle a few times." Eugenie sidestepped a local shop owner sweeping the sidewalk in front of his door. "Jake's living with Jean now, right?"

"Actually, there are a bunch of people who live on Grand Terre. You know, people Jean remembers from his human life." Specifically, a bunch of undead pirates, fueled by Jean's memories. Their village of thatched-roof cottages lay adjacent to his mansion, as big an inequality in the afterlife as in the actual life. But only one guy in Jean's real life had ever challenged his authority, and the guy didn't live very long.

"Oh-em-gee." Eugenie practically danced across Decatur Street. "A bunch of pirates. Do they sit around and drink rum all day? Are they all French? Are there women there? What do they wear? Are all the pirates as hot as Jean?"

Oh boy.

"Jean prefers brandy to rum." It struck me that I probably knew a whole lot more about Jean's likes and dislikes than was good for me. "The pirates are all nationalities, I think, but they mostly seem to speak French and not English. There are women there, but I don't know how many. Jean dresses a whole lot better than the average privateer—for God's sake, don't call them pirates in front of him. And no, most of them are not the least bit hot."

In fact, half of those I'd seen urgently needed a trip to the dentist.

"We aren't going to be there long," I warned her, in case she had delusions of hanging around to meet the undead pirate of her dreams. Been there, done that. Well, okay, I hadn't *done* that. "I just need to see how Jean's doing and when he's planning to come back to New Orleans." And then get back to Alex's and see if I needed to do damage control, depending on what Zrakovi's reaction to the news had been.

"How bad was Jean hurt? Did that vampire bite him?"

I hoped curiosity didn't kill the human. "No, he has a stab wound, but I don't think it's too serious. He's probably immune to vampire bites."

She shook her head. "I can't believe you got bit and you didn't even get an orgasm out of it. I guess *True Blood* isn't true after all."

Thank God for small favors. The road to O-Town was somewhere I never wanted to travel with Garrett Melnick or any other vampire.

We walked the length of Jackson Square, stopping to look at the work of a couple of artists who'd set up their sidewalk shops for the day.

"Look." Eugenie stopped in front of an acrylic painting of a mustached man with curly dark hair, hooded eyes, and a big hooked nose. He looked like he'd steal the hubcaps off your grandmother's Cadillac.

"It's Jean Lafitte, our most famous pirate," the artist said. "He was quite a character."

She had no idea. She also had badly missed the mark on his looks. His hair wasn't that curly, he'd been clean-shaven the whole time I'd known him, his nose was straight and in perfect proportion to the rest of his features, and he didn't have hooded black eyes. Still, he might find it entertaining. "How much?" I asked.

"Fifty for the print, but I can sell you the original for only fifteen-hundred."

I handed her my Elder Express card. "The print's fine, thanks." The Elders could pay for it. I hadn't been given a per diem and, besides, pirate bribery was likely to be required on an ongoing basis if I had any hope of keeping Jean *in check*.

Tucking the rolled print under my arm, I led Eugenie down Pirate's Alley, the narrow passage with the cathedral on one side and shops on the other. Local lore claimed it got its name from the pirates who once hung out here, but seeing as how the alley runs between a church and the old "Calaboose" prison, where Jean's brother Pierre had done hard time, it seemed an unlikely spot for pirate frivolity.

"Turn here." I led Eugenie in the gate to St. Anthony's Garden, which lay across the alley from Faulkner House Books. I'd had a contentious run-in with a crabby undead William Faulkner and some of his author cronies shortly after Hurricane Katrina, but he rarely came across from the Beyond. Unlike Jean Lafitte, most of the historical undead were content to let the modern world chug along without their ongoing presence.

"How does this work, exactly? I'm getting nervous." Eugenie seemed to finally have grasped what we were about to do. It's not every day a person leaves one world behind to visit another.

"It's sort of like squeezing through a really tight space, but it only lasts a few seconds." I pointed to where the transport of colored stones and glass lay, masquerading as a rock garden. "I checked, and there's nothing that should hurt the baby or you." At least it wouldn't hurt a human baby, and I assumed half-elven spawn were of much hardier stock.

Since being officially named to the Interspecies Council, Jean had paid for a private transport to be set up between the French Quarter and his house in the Baratarian outpost of Old Orleans, the anything-goes border town between modern New Orleans and the Beyond proper. On my first visit to Barataria's Grand Terre, the island south of New Orleans where Jean had lived in his human life and in whose magical version he now resided, I'd had to transport to a remote sand dune and walk a mile of dark, pirate-strewn beach to find him. In the modern world, Grand Terre was a federally protected wildlife area.

I stepped into the transport and pulled Eugenie in behind me. "Nice rocks," I said for the benefit of a couple of tourists wandering past. They didn't need to see two women disappear into thin air. Once they'd turned the corner, I knelt and touched a finger to the edge of the transport, willing a flash of my native physical magic to power it.

"Holy shit!" Eugenie squeaked, and threw her arms around my shoulders, as if the transport weren't squeezing me enough. At least the healing charm had gotten the pain from my gunshot wound within range of bearable. I'd need another application tonight.

"Close your eyes," I told her. "It helps."

The air around us settled, and I opened my eyes to the wide verandah of Chez Lafitte, lit with flambeaux that flickered against the red brick of the house walls.

"Um," Eugenie whispered, "is it supposed to be dark?" We'd left New Orleans at a sunny ten a.m.

Oops. Forgot to mention that. "Yeah, it's always night here, always a full moon." Actually, there was a grayish hour before dawn and at dusk where one could see, but I didn't plan to stay that long and Eugenie was on need-to-know status.

"Take a wrong turn, sunshine? And you brought along a friend."

Jake Warin had walked out of the double doors that led into the center of the house and grinned as Eugenie rushed over and wrapped her arms around him. I smiled; he looked genuinely pleased to see her. In fact, he looked more at ease than I'd seen him in a long time. I'd been too stressed out at the council meeting to notice the absence of the worry lines that had set up around his eyes. He looked like himself again, his pre–loup-garou self. Who'd have thought working as Jean Lafitte's factotum and living in the Beyond would agree with him so well?

I gave him a quick hug after Eugenie finally let him go. "How's your boss doing?"

"He's in a temper." Jake glanced behind him. "Let me tell him you're here. Might cheer the old bastard up."

I choked on a laugh. Somehow, I doubt Jake called Jean "the old bastard" to his face.

Eugenie and I sat on the steps and looked into the darkness. "You can't tell right now, but we're only about thirty or forty yards from the beach," I said. "This wooden banquette stretches almost to the water." I'd seen the beach in both its dawn and dusk version of daylight.

"I could just lie out here in that hammock and listen to the sound of the waves." Eugenie closed her eyes. "It's peaceful. N'Orleans is a noisy city. You don't realize it so much till you get out of town."

"Yeah, you got dat right." She looked at me, and we burst out laughing at my impression of her Yat accent. She was spot-on, though; the water was soothing. After the glacial temperatures of this morning, the Gulf breeze whispered warm caresses across my skin, and the banana leaves flapping against the columns of the house made me want to curl up and nap.

I was so freaking tired. Not just from the all-nighter and a run-in with my first set of fangs, but from the stress of the last two months. Since the borders to the Beyond had officially dropped in early October, life had ricocheted from one disaster to the next. I didn't see an end to it, or at least not a good one. And my personal life kept getting tangled up with my job. On the plus side, at least I had a personal life. On the minus side, the whole job-relationship balance wasn't working very well.

"You guys can come in." Jake reappeared in the doors leading into Jean's receiving parlor. Beyond that, I knew, we'd find a large sitting room filled with heavy, masculine furniture and lots of polished wood. Bedroom suites were in the back, with what passed for an early nineteenth-century version of plumbing. I had no idea what was up the wide central staircase, except Jake had told me there were windows on all sides with loaded cannons in them. Pirates and Boy Scouts—always prepared.

Jake walked with us through the receiving room. "He's in here, doing okay but still getting around slower than usual. I've gotta say good-bye here, though. Alex sent a courier to say he's calling in security reinforcements to watch the transports, so I'm heading back to New Orleans."

In the world of the Division of Domestic Terror, or DDT, the Elders' preternatural security team, Alex was boss and his cousin Jake a newbie. After a rocky start, both of them now seemed okay with it. Jean had told me once, when Jake first began working for him, that as a soldier Jake was wired to follow orders. And God knows Alex was bossy and liked to give orders. Although, to be fair, he was working on it.

"Yeah, Alex was talking to Zrakovi when we left New Orleans and Zrakovi mentioned the security issue." They were talking about more than that. I understood why Alex felt the need to keep Zrakovi informed about Eugenie's situation, but for me, Eugenie's welfare outranked politics.

"This is beautiful." Eugenie ran her fingers along a massive mahogany sideboard, on the top of which rested a red velvet sash with fine embroidery on it and, on top of the sash, a silver dagger. That little vignette was Jean Lafitte in a nutshell. Refined gentleman and renegade. Velvet and violence.

"Bonjour, Jolie."

I turned to the sitting room door, and he stood framed in the doorway, back in his casual loose cotton tunic, black pants, and black boots. Our glances caught and held, and we didn't have to say it: He was glad to see me, and I was glad to see him. I had needed visual reassurance that he was okay, even though in theory I knew he couldn't be killed. The events of last month had changed the tenor of our relationship. I just couldn't quite put a finger on how it had changed, or what it meant.

After what was probably a couple of seconds too long, he turned his attention to Eugenie. "Welcome to my home, Mademoiselle Eugenie. This is an unexpected and delightful surprise."

She started to shake hands with him, then half-curtsied, then threw her hands in the air. "I don't know how I'm supposed to greet a famous pir . . . uh, privateer."

He laughed and took her hand, raising it to his lips for a kiss. "This is the proper way for ladies and gentlemen of my time."

Yeah, Jean was just an old-fashioned guy.

"To what do I owe this pleasure?" Jean led us into the sitting room, which was much as I remembered it from last month. Lots of dark wood, plush fabrics, and wealth. The "gentleman pirate" had been an extremely rich man in his human days, so I guess it was only right that his immortal version continue to enjoy the spoils of his piratical plundering.

"I needed to talk to you about political stuff, and Eugenie needed an adventure." An escape, more like, but I hadn't decided whether or not to confide in Jean about that. Eugenie's situation was absolutely none of his business, but I'd found him to be a source of surprisingly sound advice. He read people very, very well, which made his betrayal by Etienne Boulard sting him all the more. On the other hand, he was often narcissistic, scheming, and way too smart for his own good.

From a delicate writing desk, I picked up what looked like a scrimshaw sailing ship and held it up to the lamplight, trying to tell if it was carved of real ivory. A deafening *clang* startled me into dropping it, and I made a nifty midair catch. Heart pounding, I turned to see if hordes of undead British troops were storming the beach, but I found only Jean ringing a large handbell loud enough to wake the undead.

What would arrive at that summons? A flock of maidens bearing refreshments? A pirate legion, come to do the master's bidding?

I had only a few seconds to wait before a young woman appeared from the porch. She had a tousled mane of black hair, a perfect tan, and eyes the color of jade. She was stunning, and I forcibly stomped down the spark of jealousy that sprang to life, beating it to ashes. Jean's personal life was no concern of mine.

"Drusilla, Eugenie, this is Collette." Jean presented her without further explanation, which I found extremely annoying.

Collette wore khaki shorts and a Pat O'Brien's T-shirt. She was not of Jean's generation. "So, what do you do here for Jean?" I asked purely as a matter of sentinel business, of course.

"He's been nice enough to let me live here part of the time,"

Collette said, smiling and holding out a hand for me to shake. Darn it, she was so gorgeous I wanted to hate her but she was perfectly lovely. She also wasn't human, alive or undead. The energy signature of her handshake was very familiar. "You're loup-garou?"

She nodded. "It's hard to fit in with my old life in New Orleans since I was turned, so I had been living in Old Orleans until I met my boyfriend there a few weeks ago—my fiancé, actually. I moved out here to be with him." She paused, and what looked like a flash of uncertainty crossed her face. "You both know him. I haven't gotten to meet his cousin yet."

Eugenie and I looked at each other and then back at Collette. "You're engaged to Jake?"

"Your rogue wolf has found a mate, *Jolie*," Jean said, his (quite good) teeth flashing white in his tanned face as he grinned. "Are you jealous?"

CHAPTER 9

If Jean expected me to froth with jealousy over Jake's fiancée, he had it wrong. I'd always care about Jake, but whatever we almost had or might have had in terms of romance lay firmly behind us due to both temperament and circumstance. My only worry as far as his engagement was concerned had to do with how fast it had happened.

Then again, Jake had been hanging out in Old Orleans for months now, unbeknownst to Alex or me. He could've known Collette for a while.

I watched through the window as she and Eugenie walked off the verandah and onto the shadowy path toward the pirate village. Jean had summoned her not for an introduction but to keep Eugenie entertained while we talked business, sneaky pirate.

"Do you like her?" I asked Jean. "It happened awfully fast, but Jake seems happy." Happier than I'd seen him in, well, ever.

"*Oui,* she understands Jacob's struggles. He has come far in accepting his new life since meeting her, and as I understand it, such attractions happen quickly with the loup-garou." Jean settled into his favorite chair with a sigh, and I turned to study my host.

Not just my host, or my job assignment. My friend. How strange that seemed, given that we'd started out trying to kill each other. Although, in retrospect, neither of us had tried very hard.

"You look tired."

Jean smiled, a hint of the old playful twinkle returning to his cobalt eyes. "Such flattering words, Drusilla. I will become overfull of myself."

Like he needed help with his ego. I laughed and took a seat on the end of the settee nearest him. "I hate that you got hurt again."

He shrugged, then winced. "One grows weary of pain, but it is a temporary thing. However, as pleased as I am to see you once again in my home, to what do I owe the real nature of this visit?" He paused. "Have Etienne or his treacherous Vice-Regent been found? Does your First Elder remain free?"

I nodded. "So far they're all unaccounted for, but the Elders are meeting as we speak. They'll remove Hoffman as First Elder and appoint someone else to take his place, at least on a short-term basis. Maybe Zrakovi."

"*Très bien*. Willem is a fair man, although he is also a man of ambition." Jean reached toward the side table to pour himself a brandy, but I could tell each movement brought a jolt of pain. His movements were too careful, too slow.

That I could help. "I almost forgot. I brought something to make you heal faster."

While he poured some brandy into a glass, I dug in my messenger bag for the jar of sweet olive and clove ointment that had been infused with magic. Wizards' physical magic didn't work in the Beyond, but potions and charms—nice, geeky Green Congress stuff—seemed to work fine. "Spread this on the wound, and it should cut the healing time by about two-thirds."

Jean sipped his brandy, studied me a moment, then set the glass aside. "Perhaps you might assist me, *Jolie*."

He stood up and slowly unbuttoned his tunic, and I wasn't sure where to settle my gaze. He wanted me to look at him, and I wasn't falling for it. Even though my eyes itched to check him out.

I studiously examined my cuticles, which really needed a good manicure. Maybe I'd treat Eugenie to a nice, relaxing mani/pedi on the Elder Express card when we got back to New Orleans.

Jean's soft laugh drew my gaze upward and there he was, shirtless and sexy, the white bandage wrapped around his belly and a ragged scar on his left biceps only accentuating the tanned skin and firm muscle. He was 230 years old, damn it, and I was in a committed relationship. Never mind that most of Alex's and my commitment seemed devoted to arguing right now.

"Would you tend to my needs, *Jolie*?"

I gasped. That was outrageous, even for Jean. I cleared my throat and hazarded a fierce look at his face. He was grinning, which sent laughter bubbling through my sore ribcage and I snorted like a pig, which made me laugh harder.

Finally, with some effort, I got myself under control.

"You have a charming laugh, Drusilla. I hear it too seldom." Jean picked up the jar of ointment, unscrewed the lid after some finagling, and sniffed it.

Come to think of it, I'd laughed twice since arriving in Old

Barataria. I don't remember the last time I laughed in New Orleans; the years since Katrina had been a somber shade of black. Maybe I should visit the Beyond more often.

Or not.

"Turn around," I told him. "I'll tend your wound since it's hard for you to see. But the rest of your needs are on their own."

He handed me the jar and feigned a hurt expression. "One cannot blame a man for his desires, *non*?"

"Whatever." I waited while he pulled the bandage away from the stab wound and turned to the side so I could get to it better. The skin around it flamed red and angry, but he didn't flinch as I spread the mixture over the worst of it. The rich, tangy scent of cloves and sweet olive filled the room and blended with the rich scent of tobacco and exotic spices that seemed to accompany the master of the house.

I replaced the lid and set the jar on the side table. "Put some more on it in a few hours. By morning, it should be mostly healed, although you'll probably be sore for another day or two."

"*Merci*. I had planned to return to the city this very evening, and your gift will ease my passage."

Well, we'd see how the rest of my news eased his passage. "I'm also here on an official visit, to ask your plans toward Etienne Boulard, and toward the others involved in Lily Aleese's take-over attempt last month." Never mind that the person who actually killed him was me.

Jean remained silent for a few moments, and I let him consider his answer while I cleaned my hands at a corner basin. When I turned around, he'd retrieved his glass of brandy and was staring at the rich brown liquid.

He looked up when I returned to my seat. "Are you certain you wish me to answer honestly, Drusilla?"

Which pretty much answered my question. He was going after Etienne, and I couldn't really blame him. The vampire had taken his trust and trampled it like yesterday's garbage.

"I do want you to answer honestly," I said. "In return, I'll be honest with you. Zrakovi asked me to shadow you and keep you from stirring up a political hornets' nest."

His dark brows dipped and contracted. "Might I assume that colorful turn of phrase means you're to follow me and attempt to prevent me from seeking the vengeance I deserve?"

"Follow you, or accompany you, yes." I hadn't decided about the prevention part yet. Because to be completely honest with myself, I had to admit that if he was determined to go after Etienne, I couldn't do much to stop him short of physical restraint. The first time I met Jean, before Katrina had toppled the borders between our worlds, I'd pretended to seduce him in order to trap him and send him back to the Beyond.

We'd come a long way since those days. I wasn't the same naïve girl and he was a far more complex man than I'd imagined. Plus, we *were* friends. It would take a lot to make me use my magic against him, especially after what happened last month.

"Very well, I shall both enjoy your company and honor you with the truth." Jean sipped his brandy. "I will have my revenge on my old friend Etienne, *oui*. Such a betrayal cannot go unanswered. But I did not rule my empire by being a stupid man, *Jolie*. I can afford to be patient, and for your benefit will attempt to bring about Etienne's misery without casting shadow on myself or jeopardizing the wizards and their politics."

That tactic was as much for his benefit as mine, but it served us both well. He was just going to torment Etienne, not kill him. "Sounds fair."

"I must add one more thing, however."

Intuition told me that one *thing* would be unpleasant. "What?"

"The preternatural world, as your wizards call it, is marching toward war, Drusilla. I do not see enough people of unselfish nature and good will to prevent it. At some time, and perhaps soon, you will be forced to decide on which side you will stand."

I took a deep breath and let it out, the pain from my bruised ribs, an injury beyond the help of my healing potion, helping to ground me from the worry that sprang up at the talk of war. I'd been privately concerned about the same thing. Power was an intoxicating prize, and no one—including my own people—wanted to share.

But figuring out the power balance had been the whole point of the council formation. "Surely those of you on the Interspecies Council will do whatever's needed to prevent a war."

"My apologies, but I do not believe this is so." Jean got up and moved to sit next to me on the settee. He was walking with less stiffness than before, so my potion had already done some good. "Drusilla, you must listen well. The council members might surprise me, and I pray this will be the case. But I believe the wizards will find themselves opposed more strongly than they expect."

I twisted to face him. "Now that Melnick's been exposed, the vampires—"

"The vampires will side with whoever they believe will win the war." He propped his arm on the back of the settee. "They wave to and fro like a flag on a storm-tossed vessel. Garrett Melnick is not a reliable ally."

Not that Jean was exactly unbiased. Then again, that freaking vampire had bitten me. "I know the elves hate us, but . . ." I trailed off at Jean's look of impatience. What was I missing?

"The elves and the wizards are more closely aligned than you might believe, as long as Monsieur Banyan and your Quince Randolph remain in power. Their alliance with your wizards must hold if the wizards hope to prevail."

"He isn't *my* Quince Randolph. But if the elves and wizards are aligned, and the vampires go with whoever's in power, that just leaves the small groups and . . ."

Jean raised an eyebrow.

Oh shit. That left the second-largest group, the fae. They'd stayed out of preternatural affairs for so long I tended to forget about them. Which probably wasn't wise.

"You think the people of Faery will oppose us? I'd heard they stayed too busy fighting among themselves to fight anyone else." They were a huge question mark. Would faeries plus vampires outnumber wizards plus elves? It would be close in terms of numbers. In terms of power, I had no clue.

How ironic if a war broke out and the tipping point lay with the alliances of small groups like the water species and the historical undead. With people like Jean Lafitte. My friend the pirate could end up being the key to who held power in the entire preternatural world. I wasn't sure whether that was a good thing or bad, but I sure bet he was aware of the potential.

Jean watched me as I processed it all. "I do not know where the support of Faery will fall," he said. "There is a struggle between two princes, brothers, as to who will ascend to the throne once their aunt, the Queen Sabine, is gone. She is childless and quite ancient."

I narrowed my eyes. Jean stayed awfully well informed about prete politics, and often told me things the Elders hadn't yet learned. I suspected this might be one of those things. "How do you know all this?"

He shrugged. "A wise man watches as if he were *un aigle* and listens as if he were *un faucon*."

Eagles and falcons. Both predators. Appropriate.

My French predator leaned toward me slightly and twined a strand of my hair through the fingers of the hand he'd stretched along the sofa back. I steeled myself for the wandering fingers or the smarmy comment, waiting to see which would arrive first.

"You should wear your hair up as the women of my time often did, *Jolie*. I enjoy seeing the graceful neck of a woman." He smoothed the strand of hair away from my neck, then frowned and grasped the crew neck of my sweater, jerking it aside and almost pulling me facedown on the sofa. "*Mon Dieu,* explain this. *Tout de suite*."

I slapped his hand away and straightened up. "Stop it." How did I seem to always attract bossy men? "It happened last night in the transport. Garrett Melnick decided to have a taste. You were preoccupied."

He frowned. "My apologies. Your protection should have been my first concern."

Oh please. Who did he think he was, Alex? "I can take care of myself, thank you. Besides, he said I tasted vile."

Jean laughed, which made me laugh. Again.

I tried an experiment. "You also missed seeing First Elder Hoffman trying to fry me before remembering his magic wouldn't work in the Beyond. He was not a happy wizard when he flung a spell at me and nothing happened."

Jean's smile widened into a grin. "I should have enjoyed seeing his face. He is a specious toad."

See? I knew it was funny.

The laughter faded as my thoughts returned to the fae and the worsening relations among all the pretes. I needed to do some faery research along with my elven-reproduction research. I didn't know a damned thing about the fae except what I'd learned from Gerry's sketchy history lessons. At least I still had my collection of black grimoires—the only thing among my personal possessions that had made it through the house fire unscathed. Apparently, the books of black spells and illegal magic were protected with so many dark charms that even a couple of grenades detonated by an undead serial killer couldn't destroy them.

Male and female voices sounded from outside, accompanied by footfalls on the verandah. "Sounds like Eugenie's back." I got to my feet. "Let me know when you get to New Orleans. I'll be living in the Monteleone, in the room across the hall from yours. You know, so I can keep an eye on you."

He smiled again. "You could keep both of your eyes on me"—great, he'd learned a new modern phrase—"if you resided in my rooms alongside me. Madame Eudora Welty would not object, nor would I."

Uh-huh. Madame Eudora Welty would probably mind a great deal that an extremely expensive and lavish hotel suite had been named after her, only to have it occupied long-term by an undead French pirate.

"Thanks, but you probably snore in French."

The front door opened, sparing me what was probably going to be an outrageous comeback, judging by Jean's animated expression.

Eugenie and Collette came inside, chatting like they'd known each other forever. Two men walked in behind them. One I knew very well. The merman Rene Delachaise and I had once done a highly illegal and ill-advised power exchange to solve a murder case. The case had been awful and the power exchange had been freaky, but we had ended up friends. Whenever I came up with a harebrained idea and needed backup, Rene was my man. He was fearless and didn't bother himself too much with the ramifications of whatever scheme we might be undertaking.

The other guy looked familiar, but I couldn't place him. About six feet, well built, dark hair flopping over green eyes, LSU T-shirt and jeans. Maybe I'd seen him with Rene.

"Well, if it ain't my favorite wizard." Rene pulled me into a hug, and I absorbed the happy vibes of his shapeshifter energy. Like most of the water folk, the merpeople hated wizards for past misdeeds, so I was proud of the friendship Rene and I had forged despite all our species baggage.

"And I am Christof," his companion said, smiling.

"DJ." I smiled back but inside I was racking my brain, trying to place him. I also didn't detect any aura on him, and a quick scan of his visible body parts didn't reveal any peridot jewelry— often used by pretes to hide their species. There was quite a black market for wizard-bespelled peridot on eBay, as I'd learned from Quince Randolph, a frequent buyer. Oh well, I'd call Rene later and ask him to dish on Christof.

After some quick farewells, Eugenie and I made our way back across the verandah toward the transport. I had a few hours to check in to the Monteleone and take a nap before Jean returned to the city, or I could do the responsible thing and track down Alex.

"Why don't you come to the hotel with me and hang out?" I asked her as we stepped into the transport, and I used the staff to power us back to New Orleans. "I'll treat you to a mani/pedi on my Elder Express credit card."

"Maybe a rain check? I have something else I need to do." She didn't elaborate, but closed her eyes until we materialized behind St. Louis Cathedral, made sure the coast was clear of tourists, and left the transport. "I hate that squished feeling, and I'd forgotten how cold it was here."

We quickly bundled ourselves back into our coats and set out to see if Alex's SUV was still parked nearby. We'd been gone almost four hours, so I didn't have much hope.

"So what do you have planned?" Whatever it was, I hoped it didn't involve going anywhere near Rand.

"I need to think about things for a while. I want to go home and put my feet up, enjoy the fire, and just think," she said. "It was good for me to get away from all the worries for a few hours. I don't feel so much like I'm drowning. But Rene agreed with you about the wizards."

"Which part?"

"He said the wizards will—how did he put it? They'll stick their big noses in my business and try to control everything, including my pregnancy. So I need to decide what I want and how I'm going to handle things before I get the choice taken away from me. Was he exaggerating?"

She looked at me with such a serious intensity that I knew she deserved the truth, without sugarcoating. "No, he wasn't exaggerating. It's why I wanted to get you out of there today before Zrakovi could barge in and start barking orders or asking questions you weren't ready to answer."

She nodded and we walked along silently for a few moments. "Thanks for being honest. Don't try to protect me from the truth. You're the only one I can really trust to be on my side. Promise me."

That stung a little, but if I'd been straight with Eugenie from the beginning that Rand wasn't who or what she thought, she might not be in this situation. I wasn't letting her down again.

"I promise. I'll be straight with you, and I'll always have your back, no matter what."

She stopped in the middle of the sidewalk and pulled me into a hug. I closed my eyes and hugged her hard, thinking how close we'd come to losing a friendship that meant a lot to both of us. I didn't know where all this would end up, but she'd be okay. I would make sure of it.

"What do you think will happen next?" She glanced in the shop windows as we resumed our walk through the Quarter.

I thought about all the possible scenarios. "Damned if I know." That was the God's honest truth. "It depends on what happened with Zrakovi, so I've got to talk to Alex and see how he reacted."

We turned the corner and, as expected, Alex's SUV was nowhere to be found. "Let's walk back toward the Monteleone and find a cab."

The sidewalk was still slushy in the shadows where the sun hadn't reached, and if it got as cold as predicted tonight, we'd have treacherous layers of ice to walk on.

"What did you think of Collette?" Quince Randolph notwithstanding, Eugenie had pretty good instincts about people, and she'd spent a couple of hours in Collette's company. "Did you like her?"

Eugenie laughed. "Yeah, I did. She's crazy about Jake, too. She said something that made me stop and think about my situation a little differently."

Pregnancy advice from a loup-garou? "And that was?"

"She told me about being turned into a super-wolf and how her life had changed. She used to be a model and had all these plans to go to California and try to make it big-time. Now she has some of the same problems as Jake. You know, keeping everything under control." Eugenie pointed at a cabbie parked in front of another hotel, and we sped up to make sure we got it before a sneaky tourist slipped in ahead of us.

Score one for the locals. "So, what did she say that made you think?" We settled back in the cab and gave the driver Eugenie's address. If Alex wasn't home, I'd get my stuff and have the cabbie drive me right back to the Quarter.

"She said meeting Jake had made her happier about her life, but sad that she couldn't have kids. That she might even be willing to have a wolf kid if it were possible but it isn't. Meeting someone made her feel that loss more." Eugenie looked out the window, although somehow I didn't think she was looking at the rundown buildings of Central City whizzing past. "I don't care who this baby's daddy is, DJ. I don't care that it will probably be able to do stuff that scares me or I don't understand. It's still part of me. It's still a gift." She looked at me, and the tension wafted off her. "Is that, I don't know, irresponsible? Crazy?"

"No." I wasn't surprised, and I might have reached the same conclusion if I'd been in her shoes, even knowing more about the ramifications than she did. "It won't be easy, Eugenie. As much as you don't like it, and neither do I, Rand's going to have to be involved. He's the only one who can tell us if there are special things you need to be doing."

Or maybe not. I realized with a jolt that there might be one other person who could fill us in on elven pregnancies, and it was a wizard. Only problem was, I didn't know where Adrian Hoffman had escaped to when the whole courthouse melee went down. Maybe he was still in custody and I could talk to him; Alex would know. Adrian knew a lot about elves. He might have learned it from books and secondhand sources, but he knew it.

I shifted my gaze to the rearview mirror and caught the cab driver watching us. He thought he was hearing juicy gossip, and would probably go home and laugh with his wife or girlfriend or buddies about the Uptown women trying to figure out what to do after getting knocked up. If he only knew the daddy was an elven chief.

"I know you're right about Rand being involved, but he's so unpredictable," Eugenie said in the understatement of the century. "How do you think he'll react?"

"Maybe he'll be reasonable." I didn't believe it for a nanosecond. At best, my non-husband would react like an entitled jerk. "I think I should be there when you tell him. Maybe Alex needs to be there, too." Maybe with a gun.

The cab pulled to a stop in front of Eugenie's house, and I was relieved to see no signs of Rand either banging down her door or visible inside Plantasy Island across the street. Unfortunately, Alex's SUV wasn't in his driveway, either.

"Can you wait here while I run in and get a bag?" I asked the cabbie.

"Sure, sure. But run meter." English was not his first language; I think that was a requirement for cab drivers around the country. Old-timers like Arnie were a vanishing species.

It wasn't until I'd retrieved my overnight bag, checked again to see that Alex wasn't home, and settled back in the taxi for the return trip to the Quarter that I had a moment to reflect again on the trip to Barataria. It had been good to see Jake and meet Collette. Eugenie wasn't the only one who'd found it relaxing to get away for a few hours. Another dose of healing potion on my shoulder, a hot shower, and a nap would do wonders.

I wondered what crazy business deal Rene and Jean were up to, which reminded me of Rene's friend Christof. Where had I seen that guy? His face had looked familiar, but not the hair. Not the clothes or the . . .

Crap on a freaking stick.

Now I remembered where I'd seen him. His hair had been

brushed back and styled. He'd been wearing all white, with a fur-trimmed coat. He'd been at the Orleans Parish Criminal District Court Building, yelling at the blond firebug.

Christof was one of the princes of Faery.

Which led to the burning question: Why the hell was a faery prince visiting Jean Lafitte?

CHAPTER 10

By the time I checked into my room at the Monteleone, knocked on the door to the Eudora Welty Suite to confirm that Jean hadn't returned from the Beyond, and took a quick shower, I'd decided Christof must have been slumming, getting a few hours away from Faery. God knows I'd want to escape that wackadoodle Florian and their floating queen.

Christof might know Jean from Interspecies Council business, or at least know of him. Rene's father, Toussaint, also was a council member, so he could've met the merman before. Maybe he liked the music and beer at Tipitina's and Rene took him to Barataria to warm up.

Because any other reason for his appearance at Jean's house—a conspiracy between the pirate and the fae and maybe the water species, for example—gave me a big, nasty headache.

I eyed the king-size bed, which was fluffy-pillowed and ready for napping, but decided I shouldn't put off the things I needed to do.

The first one was a long shot, so I tried it first, pulling a vial of iron filings from my portable magic kit and forming a small summoning circle on the floor of the bathroom—the only windowless space to which I had ready access. I couldn't summon Adrian Hoffman unless he was in the Beyond, but by all logic he should be there, unless he wanted to be arrested again or unless he'd been arrested again. I hoped he was in Vampyre, giving dear old dad a hard time.

I couldn't summon him to my room. Vampires didn't die at dawn like in the movies, but they didn't trot around in sunlight, either. If I were going to summon him to this side of the border, I'd have to give him a light-tight space.

To be safe, I rolled up a towel and wedged it at the bottom of the bathroom door. If I fried Adrian, I couldn't ask him questions about elves.

Then I realized I didn't have four items closely related to Adrian in order to power the circle. I had a business card, which I placed at due north, and a pen belonging to him that I'd accidentally stuck in my pack after our last elf lesson. I set that down at due South.

I sat on the edge of the tub, thinking of what else I might use. Adrian was a Blue Congress wizard, not Green Congress like me, but otherwise our badges should be similar, so I set my badge at due east. Lacking anything else, I scribbled his name on a sheet of hotel stationery, folded it, and laid it atop the circle at the western side of the arc.

Using a penknife from my pack, I pricked my left index finger and dropped blood on the circle as I touched Charlie to it, shooting out a bit of energy and speaking Adrian's name.

I'd really expected this experiment to fail, because if I'd been hiding from the Elders and wanted to avoid being summoned, I'd set up wards to protect myself from the summoning magic. But he materialized within seconds, looking panicked as he felt the containment circle and glanced wildly around to see if there was a deadly light source nearby. He stared at the closed bathroom door a moment, then turned to me.

"What the hell do you think you're doing, you stupid woman?"

Adrian and I had had a slew of contentious conversations for three years before finally meeting in person, and we hadn't liked each other any better at close range. I'd thought being a fugitive vampire might make him less haughty, but not so.

It occurred to me that if I were a good sentinel, I'd call Alex and have Adrian arrested. But I was wearing my friend-of-Eugenie hat, and getting him arrested meant it would be a while before I could pump him for information, if ever.

I reached out my foot and broke the circle. "I want to talk about elves."

He was silent so long that I was sure he was trying to figure out a way to escape, but he finally sat on the toilet lid. "I have nothing to say about that. I can't believe you summoned me to a hotel bathroom to talk politics."

Oh, good grief. "Let me rephrase my question. I don't want to talk about politics or conspiracy plots or even how you almost got me killed last month. I want to talk about elf reproduction; specifically, pregnancy. You know. Length of gestation. What the baby can do in utero. What skills a baby elf has at birth and what he'd develop later. That kind of thing."

His eyes widened, and he gave me a head-to-toe appraisal. "Oh my God. You've let Quince Randolph knock you up. I didn't think even you were that stupid."

Now I remembered why I disliked Adrian so much. "I'm not . . ."

Wait. I needed to think about this. What would be more dangerous: Adrian running back to Vampyre with the news that

I had an elf in the oven, or that it was Eugenie? I was better able to defend myself. She probably didn't taste nearly as vile as I.

"I'm not ready for this pregnancy to be common knowledge," I told Adrian. "But I do need information and I didn't know where else to go."

He sniffed. "Why on earth should I help you?"

God save me from self-serving, smartass wizards-turned-vampire. "Oh, because you owe me, for one thing. Plus, you're outside the Beyond and trapped in my bathroom until nightfall. One phone call, and the Elders would have you back in their little underground vampire jail cell before you knew what hit you."

He bared his fangs at me, a disconcerting sight. I was used to Adrian the wizard, not Adrian the vampire. "Fine." He glared at my midsection. "How far along are you?"

I closed my eyes and cursed the day I'd met Quince Randolph—or the day Eugenie had met him. It galled me for Adrian to think I'd had sex with the elf, or that he might tell anyone else, but this was for Eugenie. "About a month."

"You probably don't have many symptoms yet, then. Let me think . . . it's been a while since I studied this. Does Randolph know? I really had thought you were lying when you said you had a real marriage."

Ugh. "It surprised all of us." So far I hadn't lied, technically.

"He could tell you more than I can, but since you're asking me I assume he doesn't know yet and you don't want to ask him."

I perched on the edge of the tub again. "Good assumption."

Adrian sighed. "I don't know a lot—you're eventually going to have to see an elven midwife. Gestation is seven months, so you should be showing within another two or three weeks."

Great. An elven baby bump.

"Average birth weight is relatively large and you're, well, not. So you might need . . . surgery."

"The elven version of a C-section?" Better and better.

"Right."

"What can the kid do before it's born?" I prayed his answer was not much.

"Quite a lot, actually. It's fascinating."

Oh, I just bet it was. "Fascinating like a work of art, or fascinating like a freak-show zombie?"

He laughed. 'Cause I'm just that funny.

"The baby will be able to communicate with both of you, but especially with the father since Randolph is a pure-blooded elf. Your magic is a wild card. If you were human, you'd probably sense the baby's feelings but not as strongly. But the kid's half wizard, don't forget. Your pregnancy might be more like that of a wizard."

Which was exactly like a human pregnancy, since magical skills weren't evident until a year or two after birth.

For the next half hour, I talked with Adrian about everything I could think to ask, and by the time I formed a transport and let him go on his way, I was exhausted. Eugenie could expect to be in labor at least seventy-two hours, and the labor would be both mental and physical. I didn't envy my friend any of this.

The baby might or might not be able to influence her moods or actions closer to term. I prayed that wouldn't happen. Things would be difficult enough with his or her manipulative ass of a father trying to control everyone in sight.

I filed Adrian's musings about the elven-wizard genetic mix in my brain's *hope-I-never-need-to-know* category.

Some of the information was positive. Other than weird smoked-meat cravings, which Adrian thought was specific to the fire elves, there were no bizarre physical symptoms to expect. And the elves revered their young. Their species had dwindled in number through the eons, and the Tân were the smallest of the four clans. This child would be celebrated.

I just had to make sure Eugenie didn't get trampled in the process.

Speaking of trampled, I needed to talk to Alex. I wanted to find out what Zrakovi had said about the pregnancy, but even more, I didn't like the way we'd left things this morning. The longer we let things ride, the more apt they were to blow into major problems. We had enough real issues without developing new ones.

He answered on the fourth ring, just as I was sure the phone was going to voice mail. From the noise in the background, I deduced that he was either at a restaurant or bar—lots of overlapping voices and clanking dishes or silverware.

"You're back from Lafitte's?" Never one to waste time on niceties like saying hello, my Alex.

"I'm at the hotel. Are you at a place where you can talk? I want to hear how things went with Zrakovi."

He paused, and I heard a voice in the background yelling, "Two gumbos up!" Restaurant then. "You mean you're speaking to me?"

No, he was imagining this phone call. "Sounds like it. How'd the conversation go?"

"Let me finish up here first. The enforcer team's at the Napoleon House, dividing up assignments. I'll come by your room. I have other news you need to hear."

Joy. News I *needed* to hear rarely turned out to be news I *wanted* to hear. He wouldn't say more, though, so I left him to his business and lay down with the room service menu. It was never too early to plan tonight's dinner and tomorrow's breakfast.

I dozed off somewhere between French toast and bagels with lox and cream cheese.

"Tell Eugenie to answer her goddamned phone."

I had to be having a nightmare, because Rand was yelling at me. I tried to ignore him.

"We need to discuss my baby and it's too damned cold to walk over there. But if she doesn't answer her phone, I *will* be on her doorstep and she *will* let me in."

Definitely a nightmare.

With a disgusted groan, I opened my eyes. I still wore the Hotel Monteleone robe with nothing on underneath, and my hair was damp and curling uncontrollably. Rand wore at least two sweaters and cords, and had a blanket draped over his head. We sat on white-painted wooden benches inside an ornate gazebo.

I recognized it; the structure sat in the corner of the greenhouse area of Plantasy Island. The last time we'd sat in it, it had been no dream. Rand had kidnapped me, taken me to Elfheim, and I'd been mind-raped by Mace Banyan and his merry band of elves.

I knew this was a dream; dreamwalking was an elven skill, and I'd been dragged into enough unpleasant dreamwalks by my late father to recognize the difference.

Rand had hijacked my nap. I tightened the white bathrobe around me so he also didn't get a free dreamwalking peep show.

"Go away, I'm sleeping." I couldn't throw him out of my dream, but I didn't have to talk to him. Except . . . wait. What he'd said finally sank in.

"What baby?" I could play dumb. How the hell did he know about the baby?

"Zrakovi told me. You're my mate; you should have been the one to tell me." His voice took on a wounded edge. "After all, we'll be the ones to raise the child. You'll be a beautiful mother."

"Mother?" I sputtered. The cold air clearly had frozen his brain. "Eugenie is the child's mother. I'll help the two of you work out something that's good for both of you and for the baby." Just add prete-human parental custody counselor to my list of sentinel duties, alongside undead pirate-sitting.

"Unacceptable." His voice dropped lower. "The child is elf."

God, I hated that imperious *elf* thing Rand trotted out when he encountered a roadblock and didn't get his way. It wasn't even grammatically correct.

"Look, give Eugenie a little time to come to terms with this, and then she'll talk to you. She knows you have to be a part of this child's life."

"A part. A *part*." His voice turned to ice. "We'll talk, Dru."

I started awake with my face pressed against a photo of a large plate of shrimp rémoulade, which I took as a sign that I should order it. I'd brought all my candy from Eugenie's, so I had dessert covered. I wasn't going back to sleep anytime soon.

While I waited for the order, I called Eugenie, who sounded edgy. "He keeps calling me, DJ. I'm not taking his calls. He can't possibly know, can he?"

Damn it. "He knows. You need to go on the offensive."

"What? How could he know?" It clicked home. "The wizard Elder told him, didn't he? Alex Warin has a big mouth. Don't sleep with him again until he apologizes. Loose lips get no sex."

I thought that sounded like a reasonable tactic to take with the loose-lipped enforcer. Damn him and his overdeveloped sense of duty. "Here's my suggestion. Call Rand and tell him you're glad he knows. Then—"

"But I'm *not* glad he knows." Eugenie was heating up fast; the last thing we needed was for her to piss Rand off even more.

"I want Rand to leave me the hell alone until . . . until . . . until the kid hits adulthood."

I closed my eyes and prayed for patience. Negotiating was not my strong suit; I wanted to beat people over the head, bend them to my will, and move on. Funny how that never worked. "I know you aren't glad, but tell him you are. Lie through your teeth. You've gotta play this smart, Eugie, so he'll be reasonable and cooperative. You know how pigheaded he can be."

She gave a piglike snort into the phone. "You're not telling me anything new."

"So play him like a fiddle." We could outsmart him. Maybe. "Call him, and be all charming and sweet. Tell him you're tired today but ask if he could drop by tomorrow afternoon. Even better, since it's so cold out, tell him you'll come to see him. I'll go with you."

That would give us a little time to prepare, not to mention a chance for me to share the info I'd gotten from Adrian. The extra time also would give me a chance to talk to Alex, find out what direction Zrakovi's thoughts were taking, and plan a strategy. Because me taking Eugenie's baby and raising it with Rand like some preternatural version of *The Brady Bunch* wasn't going to happen.

When Eugenie sighed so loud the noise distorted through the phone, I knew she was going to agree. "Fine. About two tomorrow?"

"Yes, and call to let me know what he says." I had been pacing around the room as I talked, but stopped short when I glanced through the five or six inches of daylight showing through the curtains. "Holy cow, is it snowing in Uptown?"

"I dunno. I was trying to sleep when Rand started calling every thirty seconds." I heard her walking to the window. "Man, it's like freaking Alaska out there. How much are we supposed to get?"

"Hopefully, enough to keep Rand inside until tomorrow." The weather could play in our favor.

Room service arrived shortly after we ended the call, and I ate shrimp rémoulade and drank a diet soda in the desk chair, which I'd pulled up to the window so I could watch it snow. The last two days of cold weather had chilled the ground enough for it to stick, or at least I thought so, judging by the rooftops visible from my eighth-floor vantage point. The heavy flakes fell so fast and thick I couldn't see the ground. Later, I'd worry about how much we were supposed to get, and what streets were closed, and how I'd get to Eugenie's, and what form Jean Lafitte's vengeance would take.

The streets would be like a bumper-car rally. Since New Orleans flooded on a regular basis from ordinary thunderstorms, we thought we could drive through anything. I hoped Alex would walk from the Napoleon House instead of moving the SUV. I'd hate for him to have a wreck before I got to bitch at him for being an Elder-loving suck-up.

Eugenie called to report that Rand had been frosty but agreed to the afternoon meeting. "He didn't like it." She paused. "And he said something else. That the two of you are going to raise my baby. Tell me he's lying."

My skin heated from the pent-up anger. "He is a lying horse's ass, not to mention delusional, and you know that. Seriously, Eugenie. I wouldn't raise a houseplant with Quince Randolph."

She sniffled. Oh good grief, she was crying. I gritted my teeth and counted to five. "Look, Eugie. Rand's freaked out and he's mad that he had to find out about the baby from one of the wizards. By the time he processes it and tomorrow rolls around, he will have calmed down." *And so will you, I hope.*

"Okay. You're right. He just gets on my last nerve."

"It's his greatest talent." That earned a chuckle at least, and

Eugenie hung up with a promise to call me if Rand made contact again. Unfortunately, it was harder for me. I might never be able to sleep again.

One thing was for sure. I had to come up with a Rand-friendly compromise by two o'clock tomorrow afternoon, but first I needed to talk to one loose-lipped, might-never-have-sex-again enforcer.

CHAPTER 11

After an hour during which the snowscape had rendered me semi-comatose, I forced myself to get up and roll the food cart outside the door for housekeeping to retrieve. I felt my bigmouthed shapeshifter long before I saw him rounding the corner. His shifter aura, fueled by adrenaline, radiated more strongly than I'd ever sensed it. Then again, he usually kept his brain buttoned up when he was around me lest my empathy pick up on something he didn't want me to know.

Plus, I'd never encountered him after he'd been with a whole bunch of testosterone-laden enforcers, most of whom were either werewolves or alpha shifters. Even the women, or so Alex had said.

Enforcers, he told me, were drafted based on badassitude, not gender.

His badass self turned the corner from the elevator, and I stifled a smile. Black boots, black combat pants, black sweater with the sleeves pushed up, and no coat. His dark hair was its usual tousle of almost-too-long dark waves, and his cheeks had a rosy glow from the brisk wind. He was gorgeous.

I had to remind myself how annoyed I was with him, especially when he treated me to the sexy grin that caused a sexy crease on the left side of his sexy mouth. Damn his eyes, which also were sexy.

"Hey, beautiful," he said, wrapping me in a bear hug and lifting me off my feet. He put all that pent-up energy into one hell of a kiss. Man, I hated to ruin this by bringing up problems, but all I had to do to get in the proper mood was envision Rand's petulant face as he talked about being elf.

I wrenched my mouth from his with some effort. "Put me down."

"Uh-uh. Don't wanna talk." He kissed me again, full of promise of what we might do if I'd just let it go and enjoy the ride. He nibbled his way down my neck, edging close to my souvenir from Garrett Melnick.

I threaded my finger through his thick hair, still damp from melted snow, singled out a few strands, and jerked them out.

"Ouch." He let me go and rubbed his head. "You play dirty."

I turned and went back into the room, holding the door open for him. "You can't kiss this conversation away."

"It almost worked. Maybe more tongue next time?" He gave me a grin that made him look about sixteen. Well, a really hot sixteen. It was hard for me to stay mad at him, and he took shameless advantage of it.

"Look, let's talk about Zrakovi and Eugenie and then we can kiss the rest of the night." If the talk went well, anyway. I figured if Jean Lafitte had half a brain, he'd stay in nice, warm Barataria until morning. I should have a few pirateless hours to spare.

"Fine." Alex stretched out on the bed, and I pointedly pulled the straight-backed chair away from the window, planted it several feet from him, and sat in it with my arms crossed. If I got anywhere near that bed we wouldn't be talking. He knew that, too, which was why he stretched like a cat, causing all the muscles under that sweater to flex.

Cheater.

He huffed out a sigh. "Yeah, okay. I told Zrakovi about Eugenie, as I'm sure you know. I understand why you wanted me to wait, but I didn't want him blindsided if Rand found out another way and stirred up a conspiracy theory."

All of those things were true, even the part about Zrakovi needing to know. He just hadn't needed to know this morning. That brigantine had set sail, though, so I let it go.

"What did he say? And what did you expect him to do once you'd told him?"

Alex sat up and swung his legs off the bed, probably either deciding I wasn't going to join him or figuring he needed his feet on the floor in case the situation called for a quick escape. "His exact words were, 'Oh my.' Which, with him, is like dropping an f-bomb." Alex scraped his hands through his hair. I think he was going for sexy bedhead but kind of crossed into crazed territory. Or maybe I was just annoyed.

"I figure he'll go back to Edinburgh and think about it for a day or two," Alex said. "As far as I know, that's what he's done."

I crossed my legs and examined my un-pampered cuticles. I thought the Monteleone had a day spa I needed to visit, at Zrakovi's expense, and I planned to tip big. "Well, you are dead wrong. He made a detour before he went back to Edinburgh, or either came back once the Elders finished their meeting."

He leaned forward and propped his elbows on his knees. "What do you mean?"

"Zrakovi went straight to Quince Randolph." I told him

about the dream visit from my non-husband, and my follow-up call to Eugenie.

"Maybe it wasn't Zrakovi," Alex said. "Maybe Randolph pulled the information from you since you share your secret elven mating bond." He managed to put an extra dose of snark into those last four words. He'd better watch his step; I was the queen of snark and he couldn't out-snipe me even on his best day. I could skewer him and smoke him on a spit.

"Alex." I took my most patient tone. "Rand told me he learned about it from Zrakovi." I paused. "That was right before he chastised me for not telling him myself since he and I were going to be raising this child as our own."

Heh. That got his attention, and his brows lowered in an appropriately outraged expression. "Is he fucking nuts?"

We both pondered that a few seconds, but the answer was an obvious yes. "Look," I finally said. "He's going to be an ass, and that's no surprise." What I wanted from Alex was an apology, damn it. "Just admit that you misjudged how Zrakovi would react, apologize for putting Eugenie in an awkward position where Rand heard about the pregnancy from someone besides her, and we can move on to damage control."

I thought I was being mature about the whole thing. An apology wasn't too much to ask for, although he really should apologize to Eugenie.

His chocolate-brown eyes hardened. "I'm sorry that Eugenie got put in a tough situation by Rand, but I won't apologize for doing the right thing. That awkward conversation with Randolph would've happened eventually anyway because he's an entitled jerk. How Willem reacted was out of my control."

Willem? Well, wasn't that chummy.

I examined the subtle pattern in the carpet and took a deep breath. To let this disagreement escalate into a full-blown fight would be taking the easy path. We'd both say things we couldn't take back, things we'd have to work to overcome, maybe even things we *couldn't* overcome. "Weigh your battles and then use everything you've got to win the ones worth fighting," Gerry used to tell me when I'd be impatient or fly off the handle at something insignificant.

This wasn't a battle I wanted to fight. We didn't disagree in principle, only in the timing and execution.

"Okay." I got up and pulled my interrogation chair back to the desk, stopping to look at the dense curtain of snowflakes illuminated by the light from my window. Darkness had fallen, but I could barely see the streetlights below.

Suspicion infused Alex's voice. "Okay? That's it?"

I looked back at him and smiled. "That's it. We disagree. It's done. We'll deal with whatever comes next."

He stood up, brows lowered over squinty eyes. "Did Lafitte ply you with brandy, or have the body snatchers been here?"

I laughed. "No brandy and no body snatchers." I pondered whether or not to tell him about Christof being at Jean's house and about my summoning the fugitive Adrian, but decided against it. I didn't know what the Christof thing meant, I'd promised Adrian that I wouldn't turn him in, and despite my new and improved maturity, Alex had lost a bit of ground with me in the trust department.

It wasn't fair for me to tell him something with potential impact on prete politics and ask him to keep it to himself. In matters of keeping my secrets versus supporting the Elders, especially Zrakovi, I'd always lose. It's what made Alex good at his job, and that sense of responsibility was one of the things I loved about him most of the time. The rest of the time, I'd just have to live with it. Or keep my own secrets, as long as they didn't hurt anyone.

When he saw that I really didn't plan to start a fight, his tension level went down, which in turn helped me relax. I hadn't refreshed my mojo bag in a while, which meant a trip to the unheated house in Lakeview, assuming I could get there in the snow. I needed to set up a transport from the Monteleone to my house.

"Where is your oversize French babysitting charge?" Alex pulled a bottle of water out of the minibar. "I half expected him to be here in your room."

Alex sat on the cream-colored upholstered chair wedged into the corner, which left me the bed or the interrogation chair. I sat on the bed; too bad the Elders hadn't gotten me a suite like Jean's, complete with wet bar, entertainment area, and two windows big enough to drive a bus through.

"He's still in Old Barataria, where it's warm. If he's smart, he'll stay there until the snow melts. Forget Jean. You said you had something else to tell me."

Alex became engrossed in the upholstered arm of the chair, a tactic that looked a lot like my cuticle examination. Whatever he had to say, he wasn't sure how I'd react. "I talked to Willem after the Elders' meeting, and he's been named interim First Elder. He sounded pretty jazzed about it."

"I guess so. Not a big surprise, though." Despite his recent lapse of discretion, Zrakovi was a distinct improvement over his predecessor, and I hoped he got the job permanently. "That was your news?"

"No." Alex thrummed the fingers of his right hand on his knee. It was his one nervous tell; my anxiety level ratcheted higher again. "They're issuing a warrant for Elder Hoffman's arrest, by the way, along with Adrian, Etienne, and Melnick—there'll be a new Elder to represent the UK and European Union."

Which impacted me how? Not at all. "So?"

Alex squared his shoulders as if he were heading into a battle and expected to encounter heavy fire. "So, did you know Gerry had a brother?"

I stared at him, parsing out his sentence to make sure I'd heard correctly.

"Are you serious?" I should know that. True, I hadn't discovered that Gerry was my biological father until just before he died, and the way I found out—in a journal entry and a couple of dreamwalks—still stung. There had been no time to find out vital details like siblings, and DJ the idiot child hadn't thought to ask. Apparently, no one had thought to tell me. "Well, that's a surprise."

"I knew you'd never mentioned a family except on your mom's side." Alex leaned back in the chair, more relaxed now that the conversation had been started. What, he'd expected me to get hysterical over newfound relatives?

My mind stuttered and jumped from thought to thought. My mom had died when I was six, and Gerry had been the wizard who'd taken me a year later when my exasperated family wanted to get rid of me. Gerry had taught me how to be a wizard, how to question authority, and, like himself, how to be a bit entrepreneurial in my problem-solving skills. Or so people kept telling me.

Gerry had talked about growing up in Aylesbury, just northwest of London, and about the death of his parents in an accident when he was thirty. About school adventures. About wizardry and history and what stuffed shirts the Elders tended to be. He was teacher, mentor, boss, friend. *Father,* to me, was still Peter Jaco, the human man my mom had married, whose surname I still used, the one so freaked out by my magic he sent me to live with a stranger.

But what Gerry hadn't told me could fill books. He never

mentioned that he'd met my mom, much less gotten her pregnant. He made it sound like New Orleans was the place he'd chosen to be sentinel, but I later learned that he'd been exiled here by the Elders for being a rabble-rouser. He had never mentioned a brother.

"What do you know about this brother?" I paused. "Is he the only one?" I might have a huge family of strangers in England.

Alex raked a hand across his evening stubble. Like me, he'd been up more than thirty-six hours and looked tired now that his enforcer adrenaline rush had drained. "I asked that. He's Gerry's only sibling and is six years younger. His name is Lennox, and he's probably going to be the new Elder, representing the UK and Europe."

Lennox St. Simon. How terribly British. "Why am I just now hearing about him? He and Gerry obviously weren't close."

Other than myself and Tish Newman, Gerry's longtime significant other, he hadn't been close to anyone, which was kind of sad. Tish had been dead only a few months, and the weight of losing her slammed into me all at once. With the prete craziness, I hadn't dealt with her murder or Gerry's either, not really, and their loss tended to wallop me upside the head when I wasn't expecting it. Like now.

As I'd done every time before, I swallowed down the lump of pain that had risen in my throat. One of these days, it wouldn't work and I'd fall apart. But not tonight. This time, once again, I held it together. "Is he Red Congress like Gerry?"

"Yep, and pretty powerful, I hear." Alex moved back to the bed, kicked off his boots, and stretched out again. This time, I crawled up beside him and snuggled in tight. He was warm and solid, and I savored a flash of contentment before letting my mind veer back to this newfound relative.

"Did Zrakovi say what he's like? Does he look like Gerry?"

"Don't know what he looks like, but Willem described him as the anti-Gerry in terms of attitude. Very buttoned-up and proper." Alex traced lazy circles up and down my arm with his fingers. "He's against making concessions to the pretes, and thinks New Orleans is the place to make it clear they don't belong in our world."

Great. We'd no doubt get along famously since everyone told me I was just like my father, and I thought the pretes had as much right to a say in magical affairs as the wizards. Well, almost as much. "Does he know about me?"

"Only recently, since the borders dropped in October, and he's been asking a lot of questions. Willem says he's curious about you, but thinks it's awkward. If he becomes an Elder, though, he'll be here in New Orleans for the council meetings. You're bound to meet him soon; it's why Willem wanted you to know. They're trying to pull another council session together for day after tomorrow."

I snorted. "Somewhere besides the courthouse, I assume." According to the news, the trials scheduled for the next six weeks were being rescheduled or moved to other venues, and the building had been closed to repair the water damage. We'd have to find another public building to destroy.

"Dunno." Alex yawned. "Oh, and Lennox is divorced, but you do have a cousin."

I sat up. "What? Where? He has a kid?"

Alex smiled. "You're gonna love this. Her name's Audrey and she's twenty-three, with physical magic as her dominant skill set."

Strange way of putting it unless . . . "She isn't Red Congress?"

His smile widened. "She's flunked the congressional exam twice, and is apparently driving her dad crazy. She has a reputation for being undisciplined." The sexy crease beside Alex's mouth appeared. "Willem told him it seems to run in the St. Simon family, and I don't think he was talking about Gerry."

I slowly formed a solid fist, made sure Alex saw it, and then punched him in the stomach. "Stop laughing." Which made him laugh harder. "I am not undisciplined. I'm creative. I'm sure poor Audrey is as well." I liked her already.

Settling back into the warmth of Alex's arms, I pondered this newfound family. Uncle Lennox sounded like he'd have a serious stick up his backside, but I liked the idea of a cousin, and she was only five years younger than me.

"Do you think he'll bring her to New Orleans with him?"

When Alex didn't answer, I noted his steady breathing and raised my head enough to confirm he'd fallen asleep, so I snuggled in again. I didn't dare go to sleep because I didn't want a visit from Rand, but I could close my eyes and listen to Alex's heart beating beneath my cheek and . . .

I'm gonna get in trouble; I'm gonna start a fight.

Alex and I both sat up, blinking. "What the hell is that?" His voice creaked with sleep.

I leaned over him, wincing at the pain in my ribs. "It's my phone."

"What happened to your Zachary Richard ringtone?"

I finally raked my fingers across the phone and got hold of it before Pink started another fight. "It's part of my new attitude." I looked at the caller ID. "Uh-oh."

Punching the screen to put the call on speaker, I said, "Eugenie, what's wrong?" The clock on the nightstand read one a.m.

"Rand's on the porch, banging on my door." She must have held the phone out because a loud pounding sounded through the speaker, along with a strident male voice. It sounded like Rand was shouting in his guttural elf language. Good Lord. So much for waiting until the two p.m. meeting, although I'm sure it was two o'clock somewhere in the world.

Alex had already rolled out of bed and begun pulling on his boots.

"Say whatever you need to say to keep Rand calm," I told Eugenie. "Alex and I are on the way."

I dug under the bed for my own boots and tugged on the ugly coat. "You got a gun on you?"

Alex raised an eyebrow. "Yeah, why?"

"Make sure it's loaded for elf."

CHAPTER 12

The two-block walk to Alex's SUV was treacherous. The Quarter lay deserted, odd even for one a.m. on a weeknight, and we didn't talk as we trudged through at least a foot of snow that had a layer of ice underneath it. The temperature had dropped, and part of what hit my face stung like pellets of sleet.

Mostly, we kept our eyes on the ground, sticking close to buildings so we wouldn't accidentally tumble off a curb and break an ankle. The sea of white across Royal Street lay flat from building to building, with no street or sidewalk edges discernible except for snow-covered lumps I could only assume were cars.

My head had begun to pound after the first five minutes, and a couple of waves of dizziness had me wondering if the stress was finally getting to me. Mostly, though, my limbs ached and I had an overwhelming urge to lie down. I blamed it on the physical exertion of trying to walk in this mess, because the other option was an impending case of the flu, and I didn't have time to be sick.

After almost ten minutes, with the big lump Alex identified

as his Range Rover finally in view, I stopped trying to keep up
with him. He'd gained a block on me and had begun freeing
the SUV's doors from their prisons of snow and ice by the time
I caught up.

"You okay?" He jerked on the passenger-side door and helped
me climb in. "You look kind of green."

"I'm freezing. Nothing a little heat won't cure." *Because,* I
told my body, *you are not getting the flu. You have pirates to chase,
elven non-husbands to pacify, political shenanigans to avoid.*

Once inside, Alex ran the defroster and we waited while the
layer of ice on the windshield melted enough for the wipers to
operate. Within a few minutes of the heater turned on high, I'd
finally begun to thaw, my energy flooding back with a gratify-
ing rush.

I'd never again make fun of this behemoth of an SUV, even
if I did need a ladder and an altitude-sickness potion to climb in
it. It was big and heavy, had heated leather seats, and its vents
shot out enough warm air to melt the snow that had frozen into
crystals on our eyelashes and hair.

"I can't believe Rand went out in this mess." I reached over
and brushed ice off Alex's shoulder. Even Mr. Hot-Blooded
Shifter had pulled a leather jacket out of the backseat and put it
on. I wiped the cold water off on the leg of his jeans, earning a
playful swat.

"I would say Randolph is a horse's ass, but that would be
unfair to the horse." Alex pulled carefully out of his parking space
and inched through the Quarter. "I'm gonna stick to the main
roads just in case there are other idiots out here who've plowed
a trail. I can't see the edges of the street."

We maneuvered the pinball arcade of Canal Street, filled with
abandoned cars and people who'd parked on the neutral grounds
like they did when they expected a flood, and headed to Uptown

along St. Charles Avenue. Alex navigated the curving road by aiming the SUV at the midpoint between the ancient snow-laden live oaks lining both sides of the street and using the overhead streetcar electrical lines running through the middle of the neutral ground to stay on course.

Finally, we cut over toward Magazine Street, dodging stalled vehicles. Alex lurched to a stop by letting the truck slide its right front tire against the curb in front of Eugenie's house—at least we assumed it was a curb.

The house was a big, solid early-century Victorian painted light blue, with cream-colored hurricane shutters, a broad front porch ringed by a gingerbread rail, and a side entrance for her Shear Luck salon. The porch light was on, and through the thick fall of snow and ice I saw a dark lump near the door, but no sign of Rand. Maybe he'd left a package and gone home like a good elf.

The snow here was deeper, up to my knees, so I waited for Alex and his long legs to blaze a trail to the house and I followed in his wake.

"What the hell?" Alex's voice took on its gruff enforcer tone.

I couldn't see around him until he got up the stairs, and I realized the big dark lump on the porch was covered in fur. "Is it a dog? Must be a stray, poor thing."

He bumped the lump with the toe of his boot, and it rolled over. "No, it's an elf in a fur coat."

Rand's eyes were open just enough to be covered in ice crystals and look creepy as hell. He would be a perfect elven mortuary display. "Is he dead?"

I hope my words didn't sound like wishful thinking, because while I wanted Rand to leave me alone, I didn't want him dead. His bonding scheme had almost gotten me killed, but it also had kept me from turning loup-garou. We could probably be of help to each other if he'd get over the notion that we were married. The very mistaken notion, at least in any real sense of the word.

There was also the possibility that if Rand died, it might kill me as well because of the bond, so I had a practical reason for wanting him alive.

"He's not dead," Alex said after spending a few seconds with two fingers placed over Rand's carotid artery, assuming that's what elves had. "I think he's just unconscious. Call Eugenie and tell her to open the door; if we knock, she's gonna think it's him and not answer."

I placed the call, and in a few seconds the dead bolt clicked, the scrape of a chain latch sounded, and Eugenie pulled open the heavy cypress door, wielding a butcher knife. She looked from Alex to me and, finally, down at Rand.

"Is he dead?"

Okay, Eugenie definitely sounded hopeful.

"No, he's sleeping off his stored fat, like a bear in hibernation," I said, looking down. He didn't have an ounce of fat on him.

"Let me drag him in," Alex said, grabbing Rand's ankles and pulling him toward the doorway. His head bounced on the rough wood.

"Good grief, Alex. You're a shifter. Pick him up." It wasn't the same as little ole weakling me dragging two hundred pounds of Jean Lafitte across a field in Vampyre, which had given new meaning to dead weight.

"Goddamned elf." Alex scooped up his unconscious nemesis and hauled him through the doorway. The way he let Rand's head crack against the doorframe had to be intentional.

"Where do you want him? Never mind, I see a spot." Alex carried Rand to a rug in front of the fireplace and unloaded him in a heap, and none too gently. Eugenie kicked Rand's calf as she walked past to turn up the gas flames. I almost felt sorry for him. Almost.

Alex and I sat on the sofa and Eugenie in the adjacent armchair, and we watched Rand intently as if he were a circus act. I had no idea what to do with an unconscious elf, and was fresh out of smelling salts. As his body warmed, he gradually lost the stiff, embalmed look and instead turned into a pretty sleeping elf prince. He was cute enough to set on the mantel for decoration as an Elf on a Shelf. Well, if the Elf on a Shelf spontaneously spouted outrageous pronouncements without warning and had the potential to set off a preternatural war.

I stretched out a leg and nudged his shoulder with the toe of my boot. "Rand. Wake up, honey bun."

Alex poked me in my sore ribcage.

Rand turned his head in my direction, but didn't open his eyes for another minute or so. When he did, they were the clear, cerulean blue of a tropical sea, but not quite focused. "Hi, Dru. You look beautiful."

Alex made a low growling sound and poked me in the ribs again.

It was enough to make Rand wake up and realize he wasn't in friendly territory. He sat up and looked at me, then Alex, and, finally, Eugenie. He started that scary glowing thing. Whenever he was angry, his inner fire started up. Too bad his lack of consciousness hadn't knocked that out of him.

"You would have let me die out there," he said to Eugenie.

She raised an eyebrow as if to confirm it.

Oh, good grief. "Let's start over. Rand, are you okay? What happened out there? Do you want something hot to drink?"

And could you quit glowing?

He wrenched his glare from Eugenie and looked at me. The

anger drained quickly. "Elves don't tolerate cold weather well. Our systems shut down to protect our vital functions."

I stared at him. "You mean you really do hibernate?" My earlier comment had been a joke, or so I'd thought. "Like a bear?"

"Elves are not like bears. Bears are like elves. It's a very advanced survival system." He looked offended at being compared to Yogi and Boo-Boo.

"Right." I wondered if I had enough elven DNA to blame for my flagging energy on the walk through the snowy French Quarter, and set that aside to ponder later. "Would it help to have something warm to drink?"

Rand smiled. "Tea would be nice, Dru. Thank you."

"I'll get it." Alex sprang off the sofa so fast it was almost preternatural. Unlike vampires, however, shifters couldn't do that speed-of-light thing. Now that Rand was awake, Alex was just trying to escape a scene that was likely to be messy and emotional. Alex hated messy and emotional.

He wouldn't be gone long, though. As much as he hated emotional stuff, he'd want to monitor anything with political overtones.

Rand looked down for a moment, seeming to gather his thoughts. Then he climbed to his feet and approached Eugenie slowly, as one might walk toward a skittish puppy. I moved to the edge of my seat and put my left hand in the vicinity of Charlie, just in case I needed reinforcement.

But he knelt in front of her and reached his hand toward her abdomen, still moving cautiously. "May I?"

Eugenie looked at me and I nodded. Rand touching Eugenie was probably the next best thing to a prenatal exam, given the fact she couldn't see a human doctor and wizard doctors wouldn't know crap about elven reproduction. Thanks to Adrian,

I now knew a lot more than before; I just hadn't had a chance to tell Eugenie.

"Okay." Her voice shook. "Don't do anything to me."

"I won't. Promise." Rand reached out gently and slid his long fingers beneath her sweater, resting his hand on her belly. He closed his eyes and sat perfectly still for what seemed like a week and a half.

"It's a boy. I have a son." He opened his eyes and looked up at Eugenie, and then at me, his face lit with genuine joy. I realized I'd never seen him truly happy. Scheming, angry, playful, and petulant, but not happy.

"Only . . ." He cocked his head at Eugenie. "You had another baby boy, one who died. It still hurts you."

Eugenie's eyes widened and she again looked at me. I seemed to have become the referee and interpreter here, whether I wanted the job or not. Again, I nodded. She knew in theory about Rand's mental magic, sensing moods and reading thoughts, but she hadn't experienced it. Before we were bonded, he'd used it on me a few times, but it no longer worked. He was being very gentle.

He also could manipulate people's feelings, which was not acceptable in my book and I was on the lookout for it. So far, he hadn't tried it.

"Yes, it was a long time ago." Eugenie blinked away tears. "It wasn't my fault."

"No, I can tell that. You loved him." Rand withdrew his hand and settled on the floor. "My son will have a life worthy of a prince. He will be the heir to the Tân chieftain title and powers as my eldest son—unless, of course, Dru and I have one within the next year or two who might rival him for power as a legitimate heir."

He looked at me, took my gaping mouth as an assent, and

nodded. Alex, who'd returned with a cup of steaming something-or-other, poked me again on his way to hand the cup to Rand.

Alex needed to find a new way to express himself; I'd have bruises.

"And of course you'll have the very best medical care in Elfheim," Rand continued. "Our clan midwife is excellent, I'm told."

"Uhhh . . ." Eugenie gave me a panicked look.

"Rand, would it be possible for your midwife or doctor to see Eugenie either here or at your house across the street? It would be a lot less stressful for her and the baby than traveling to Elfheim."

I was going to change my name to DJ Kissinger.

Rand frowned a moment as he considered it, then nodded. "I don't see why not. The midwife probably won't agree to come until the weather warms up, but that's okay because I can tell the baby is healthy. He's strong."

Good news, then. "What else does Eugenie need to know, in the meantime?" I'd see if Adrian's book-learning matched reality.

"Yeah." Eugenie cleared her throat. "Are there things I need to be eating or doing?'

Rand considered this. "Just the usual things, I think, but I'll find out. Plenty of rest, fresh air, no caffeine, lots of smoked meat."

Alex coughed and cleared his throat, probably swallowing some inappropriate comment. I moved farther away from him on the sofa lest he decide to poke me again.

I pretended this was a surprise. "Smoked meat?"

"Sure. Protein, cooked on an open fire or smoked. We are the fire clan. She'll crave it."

Eugenie put a hand over her mouth. "Oh my God. I ate a

whole package of smoked salmon this morning. I thought I was going nuts. I couldn't get enough of it."

Great. I saw lots of steakhouse dinners over the next . . . "Do elven pregnancies last nine months?"

"Oh, right. Forgot about that." Rand pulled out his phone. "Our gestational period is seven months. I can tell you're four weeks along, plus averaging out human and elven times . . ." He punched the screen a few times. "My son should be here in the middle of July, give or take a couple of weeks."

"No," Eugenie said, frowning. "Not *your* son. You've said that three times now. *Our* son. Yours, but also mine. Ours."

He studied her with his eyes narrowed, and I sighed. I knew that look of challenge, where his eyes focused like a laser and his mouth curved up just at the edges. He was going to say something horrendous. Something that would undo all the goodwill he'd built up in the last half hour.

In my head, I yelled, *Rand, whatever you're about to say, don't!*

He flinched, but didn't look away from Eugenie. "Well, of course you can see him," said Mr. Reasonable. "I'd like for Dru and myself to raise him in Elfheim, but I know she'll want to stay here in New Orleans at least part of the time until I can convince her to quit her job and raise our own family. We can have a tutor that travels with us and can—"

Oh holy mother of God. This elf was worse than delusional; he was insane.

Alex growled, sounding an awful lot like his canine entity, a pony-size dog I called Gandalf. Eugenie jumped to her feet and kicked Rand in the kneecap, eliciting a hiss. "You and DJ are not raising my baby. Not there. Not here. Not at all."

She turned to make a dramatic exit, but Rand snaked out a hand and caught her ankle in his grip. She twisted around, probably to wallop him, but stopped when she saw his face.

Rand's eyes had narrowed, his frown etching deep grooves between his eyebrows. Not to mention he was glowing again. "I'll have you restrained." His voice was low, and vicious. I'd never heard this tone from him before.

"Don't test me, Eugenie. I won't allow you to harm this child." He let go of her ankle and got to his feet, looming over her. Eugenie's eyes had widened in fear and she scrambled away from him, pressing her back against the living room wall.

He turned from Eugenie to me. "Dru, she's thinking she'll kill my child before she lets me raise him, but I warn you all now. My son is elf. He will not be reared by a common human. I won't allow her to destroy him, no matter what it takes."

Holy shit, what was Eugenie doing? She couldn't even *think* crap like that around Rand. I needed to give her some tips on how to shield her thoughts, although her nature was not to be secretive or reserved. I wasn't sure she'd be able to do it.

"She doesn't mean it." I kept my voice even and calm. "You felt how much Eugenie loved the baby she lost, so you can tell she loves this child already. She's just scared, Rand. You can be overbearing." And pigheaded, and devious, and did I mention an insensitive boor?

"You're all talking about me like I'm not here, so I'm leaving." Eugenie ran from the room, but at least she had the sense to not go outside. She clattered down the hallway and ended her grand exit with a slammed bedroom door.

Well, that had all been just peachy.

Time for damage control. I sympathized with Alex, who was always lamenting the fact that he had to negotiate with pretes rather than just shoot them and be done with it. I could shoot something right now.

"Rand, please go home," I said. "I guarantee you that Eugenie is not going to do anything to intentionally harm this baby."

Of that much, I was confident. "Give her time to calm down. Remember, this whole world of ours is new to her. She only found out things like wizards and elves existed a couple of weeks ago."

I was so going to take him to task for that *common human* remark, but now wasn't the time to push him.

"I'll go only if you guarantee me access to her whenever I want, and assure me that if any decision is made that impacts my son, you will tell me if he can't."

I nodded before I realized what he'd said. "What do you mean if he can't?" Adrian had said the child would be able to communicate, but how soon?

"If this were a full elven pregnancy, by the fourth month the child would be able to communicate mentally with both parents. Not words, of course, but just general feelings. Happy. Sad. Excited. Stressed. Since he's half human, I don't know. It might happen on schedule, or late, or not at all."

"That is just . . . freaky." Alex uttered his first complete sentence since dumping Rand on the floor.

Rand ignored him. "Dru, can you do a transport back to my house so I don't have to go back out in the snow?"

"Sure. Not a permanent one, though. Eugenie would have to agree to that and now's not the time to ask." I retrieved my messenger bag from beside the sofa and took out my portable magic kit, which badly needed replenishing.

Taking a vial of unrefined sea salt, I spread a slapdash interlocking circle and triangle on Eugenie's living room floor and looked up at Rand. "What's the name of the transport in your greenhouse?"

"Rivendell," he said with a crooked smile, and I burst out laughing. So sue me. Every once in a while, he was funny.

After he stepped in the transport, I pulled Charlie from the messenger bag and touched the tip of the staff to the transport. "Fly to Rivendell, Legolas," I said.

Rand was smiling when he disappeared.

If only I could banish him to Mordor for the next six or seven months.

CHAPTER 13

Waking up with Alex wrapped around me like a big warm blanket should've been the perfect morning-after finale to a night—well, make that an early morning—of great makeup sex. As he'd noted, despite our lack of sleep, we had nervous energy to wear off and we'd almost argued, so makeup sex was appropriate.

We'd finally drifted off sometime after four a.m., boneless and satiated and brimming with endorphins. I no longer felt deprived by my first, and I hoped only, vampire bite.

But I awoke with thoughts first of Rand, which was libido-killing enough, followed by thoughts of Jean Lafitte, from whom I tried to keep my libido at a safe distance. It finally occurred to me that since elves found misery in cold weather, a historically undead pirate bent on revenge might see a snowstorm as an opportunity.

I reached for the nightstand, grabbed my phone, and punched speed-dial number four. I'm not sure if it was practical or pathetic that the Elders had dropped off my phone list and my top four programmed numbers were now Alex (cell), Eugenie (cell), Rene (cell), and Jean Lafitte (hotel suite). Maybe I'd get the pirate a cell phone for his 231st birthday. Or not.

"*Bonjour, Jolie.* Where are you?"

Lying in a nice, warm bed with a man who isn't dead. "At Alex's. How'd you know it was me?"

Said living man grumbled a couple of four-letter expletives in a bad French accent, turned over, and jammed a pillow over his head.

"The telephone"—Jean still stumbled over the newfangled word a bit—"has a square on it where names of people magically appear when they call me. Did the wizards invent this magical square? It is quite clever."

The wizards could take credit for many innovations, overnight delivery service via transport from the wizards' central supply house, for example. Caller ID was not among them, however. Many of the older wizards still thought cell phones were the work of demons. Real demons.

"Nope, that's a human miracle. When did you get back, and what are your plans for the day?"

"I arrived shortly after sunrise so that I might avail myself of the hotel's . . . what odd words do they use . . . ah. Breakfast buffet. One can eat as much as one wishes, for as long as one wishes, all for the same amount of money. It is a quite interesting experiment, although I do not feel it is practical for the building of wealth."

I tried to envision Jean Lafitte lining up at the trough of a hotel all-you-can-eat breakfast buffet, stuffing down muffins and omelets and pancakes. I failed. "They make up for it by charging more for the rooms. And your plans for today?"

He paused, which raised my warning flags up the mast of life's sailing ship. "I thought I might explore the city. One does not often see *Nouvelle Orleans* under snowfall. I imagine it is quite beautiful."

Sightseeing? Something smelled rotten in the state of the historical undead. "I'd enjoy that, too." I'd hate every second of it and might well freeze to death. "Can I go with you?"

Another pause. Damn it. He was up to something.

"But of course, Drusilla. We will have a dinner date at noon and then we shall enjoy a stroll."

Explaining the difference between a lunch date and a dinner date didn't seem worth the effort. I glanced at Alex's bedside clock. Holy crap; it was almost eleven a.m. already. "I'll come to your room as soon as I can get back to the hotel from Uptown."

Next to me, Alex grumbled something into the mattress. I probably didn't want to know.

"I shall await your return." Jean hung up.

"Yeah, bye to you, too," I said to the undead air.

"Pirate's on the move." I poked Alex in the hip, probably harder than necessary, but I owed him. "I've gotta go."

"Au revoir," he said into the pillow.

I waited a moment to see if he was joking, but he went back to sleep, or pretended to. One way to find out. "Okay, I'll just take your keys and leave the Range Rover with the Monteleone valet. I'll text you the ticket number."

He jerked the pillow off his head and threw it on the floor. "Having you sleep here seemed like such a good idea last night. Now, not so much."

Yeah, well, he hadn't complained during the makeup sex. One of us had to work for a living, even if it meant babysitting an undead pirate who was plotting some type of mayhem.

If possible, the drive back to the Quarter was worse than last night's trip. The snow had tapered off, but more fools like us were out trying to drive around. The city had made a valiant attempt at dumping sand on a few of the major streets to provide traction but all it did was make a mess.

By the time we turned onto Royal Street, my nerves were fried and I wasn't even driving. "Why don't you park and come into the hotel for a while? Don't you have transport watch at the Napoleon House in a couple of hours?"

Alex grunted, which is what passed for conversation with him until he'd been up awhile.

"I don't speak caveman. You'll have to translate."

He pulled the SUV to a cautious stop in front of the Monteleone, which meant his answer was no. "I don't want to see Lafitte before I've had coffee. Or after. And don't let him touch you."

I kissed him, lingering over it a moment. We needed more time together than half an argument followed by makeup sex; our fledgling relationship was already treading water. Maybe all the pretes would retreat to their respective corners of the Beyond for Christmas and leave us alone for a day or two. A girl could dream.

"Talk to you tonight?"

"Later, *Jolie*." He must be waking up. He'd managed to smile instead of scowl.

I took off my coat as soon as I got inside the Monteleone lobby so security wouldn't mistake me for a panhandler with bad fashion sense and toss me out on the curb. Then, on the elevator ride to the eighth floor, I felt guilty for that thought, and wondered how the city's shamefully large homeless population was faring during this weather.

Many of New Orleans' homeless were the working poor, whose hard minimum-wage jobs didn't provide enough money to pay the city's inflated rent and utility costs. Between misbehaving pretes and personal crises, I hadn't heard the news in a couple of days.

A dark-suited room-service waiter exited Jean's room as I approached down the eighth-floor hallway. "Is Mr. Lafayette in?" I asked. "I'm staying across the hall and was supposed to meet him for lunch." Maybe Jean had gotten tired of waiting for me and ordered his own meal.

The young man smiled. "The dude ordered two entrees, so unless he's really hungry he ordered for you."

Great. Lunch *a deux* in the pirate's suite. "How thoughtful of him. I'll have to give him a special thank-you."

If he ordered me snails, he could eat them himself.

I knocked on his door before going to my room. I heard a clatter of dishes behind the door, and then it opened to the man himself. "Ah, *Jolie*. You . . . Pardon, but do you realize your attire is the same as when you paid me such a delightful visit yesterday in Old Barataria?"

"Thanks for noticing." When I'd put the clothes back on last night, I hadn't anticipated an all-night elven paternity intervention followed by makeup sex. "I need to take a quick shower and then will come back for lunch. It'll take a half hour." Give or take thirty minutes.

"You are welcome to avail yourself of the shower in Eudora Welty's rooms. I could be most helpful with your *toilette*." He grinned, and I grinned back. One of these days I would agree to one of his smarmy suggestions and freak the hell out of him. But not this one, and not today.

"I'll see you in a few."

"A few what, Drusilla? Truly, your modern folk have the most disagreeable habits of language."

Whatever. I unlocked my door, retreated to the quiet warmth of my room, and gave a longing look at the neatly made bed. I'd rather eat and nap than let Jean drag me all over the frozen city. I was part elf, after all. I now had an excuse for my winter-phobia.

The hot water of the shower finally beat the rest of the chill out of my skin, and I took my time choosing layers of clothing that would add warmth without bulk: a T-shirt that said NEW ORLEANS: IT'S NOT THE HEAT, IT'S THE STUPIDITY, a thin black sweater with a tight weave, a bulkier red sweater, and black cords. Two pairs of socks, one wool. I finished drying my hair, looked at my makeup bag, and left it closed. This wasn't a lunch date. Normal women carried oversize purses filled with cosmetics and personal items. I walked across the hall carrying my ugly coat, the elven staff, my boots, and the messenger bag containing my portable magic kit.

Jean must have heard me because he flung open the door to his suite and greeted me before I had a chance to knock.

He too wore layers. He'd added what looked like a long, fitted suede jacket over his usual white linen tunic. I fingered the lapel; it was thick but soft. "This is spiffy. Did you buy it or tan it?"

"It was given to me in trade by an Acadian who wished to purchase a pirogue. In those days we did not experience such winters, so I had little use for it."

I couldn't help myself. "And what year might that have been?"

He pursed his lips and shrugged. "I do not recall, but believe it was before the war."

That would be the War of 1812. "It's held up very well." Of course, so had he.

"*Merci*. And I must say you look . . ." He appeared to struggle for a word I wouldn't find offensive. Captain Lafitte and I had very different ideas about the proper attire for a woman, modern or otherwise. ". . . warm."

"Exactly. And I'm hungry." I eyed the room-service cart buried under silver-covered dishes. "You didn't order snails, did you?"

"*Mais non.* I inquired, knowing how anxious you were to sample these delicacies, but the weather delayed the ship filled with escargot for the hotel."

I started to explain that a *shipment of escargot* differed from a *ship of escargot,* but why bother. Thank God for blizzards. "That's a real pity."

Much to my surprise, he had ordered burgers dressed with bacon, creole chutney, and cheddar cheese. Extra fries had been piled onto his plate in an artistic pyramid. I'd have to jog through the snow to work this off.

I gave him a mock salute. "Congratulations, Jean. You have discovered hamburgers, a great American tradition." The few times I'd been around him during meals, he'd proven to have an adventurous palate—developed at sea, no doubt, during a time when one ate whatever one could catch, trap, or plunder from an enemy vessel. If he'd ever resorted to trying *long pork,* as roasted human flesh was called due to its supposed porklike flavor, I didn't want to know.

"Our mutual friend Rene introduced me to this *hamburger* delicacy, although he has been unable to explain to me why it is called thus when it contains no ham. No pork at all, in fact."

I stopped with a French fry halfway to my mouth. I thought it had something to do with Hamburg, Germany, but wouldn't bet on it. "Did he explain why French fries are called thus even though they don't come from France?"

He picked up a crisp potato and studied it. "I beg to differ, *Jolie.* Even in my youth, we consumed *frites* at my home near Bordeaux and later in Saint-Domingue. We did not have the sweet red sauce, however." He dumped a quarter of a bottle of ketchup on his plate and dragged a fistful of fries through it.

We spent the next half hour discussing the many variations on the hamburger, leaving Jean anxious to try a Big Mac—I think it was the lure of special sauce that attracted him, plus my opinion, after much sampling, that Mickey Ds had the best fries in the universe.

"*Très bien,* that was most enjoyable." He settled back and gave me a sly look that sent my antennae of suspicion skyward. "Do you still wish to join me in a walk through the city, to avail yourself of its winter beauty? Or perhaps you would prefer to rest while I enjoy my stroll."

"I want to stroll." Actually, I'd rather crawl under the duvet in my own hotel room—alone—until spring. "I'm ready when you are."

I noted he'd never said he *wanted* me to join him on his stroll. With the pirate, the words he didn't utter were often more revealing than the ones he did.

"Shall we then?" He opened the door as I struggled into my coat, but then blocked my way. "Pardon, *Jolie.* Your coat does not do justice to your beauty. Do you have another you might wear?"

What a delicate way of saying the coat was hideous and he was ashamed to be seen with me. "I can't afford a whole new wardrobe as well as a new coat, not being a wealthy historical figure with an unlimited supply of gold at my disposal."

"Ah, well, we must remedy this." He turned and strode down the hall toward the *lifting room,* as he called the elevator, leaving me to chase after him. I wasn't sure what his remedy might be, but maybe he'd get me a raise.

I barely managed to jump into the elevator before the doors

whisked closed and took off for the lobby. So that's how we were going to play it. He was going to do his best to wear me out or ditch me, whichever came first.

Game on, pirate. My stride might be short but my competitive spirit was gargantuan.

As soon as he walked and I trotted through the lobby and out the front door onto Royal Street, I slipped my arm through his. He either had to walk at a pace I could maintain or blatantly brush me aside, which I didn't think he'd do, courtly old-world gentleman pirate that he was.

I nailed it. After a suspicious glance at my arm, his mouth twitched. I'd seen through him; he'd seen through me.

"Ah, *Jolie*. We are perfectly suited to one another, as I must continue to remind you. A woman of your intelligence is wasted on such as *le petit chien*."

I'd let the slam at Alex pass. "Where are we going?"

"Let us stroll to see the cathedral, even though it means I will be forced to also regard the monument to the arrogant Andrew Jackson."

Rumor had it that Jean had won the historical undead representative's seat on the Interspecies Council after a contentious election with the undead former president Jackson. During his human life, Jackson had lived in New Orleans briefly during the time of the Battle of New Orleans in 1814, which gave him enough local memory power to pop over occasionally in his undead form.

Rumor also had it that Jean had won the election by cheating. Since the source of said rumors was Alex, they were likely true.

During weekdays, Royal Street was open to traffic. Which meant that not only were the streets a slick layer of ice since the city had made some attempt to shovel the snow to the sides, but every few yards we came across people staring morosely at their fender benders.

"It does not appear snowfall is useful to automobiles and— *Mon Dieu!*" Jean dodged an icy snowball lobbed by a red-faced, cursing Mini Cooper driver. He'd been aiming at a pickup owner who'd turned the back of his cute little car into mangled yellow aluminum foil. The only thing dumber than driving in this mess was driving a car that weighed less than my cat. Of course, that was a low shot coming from a woman who no longer had access to anything motorized.

I retained a firm grip on Jean's left arm and elbowed him in the ribs. Once he'd escaped the flying ice ball, he had slipped his right hand inside his Daniel Boone coat, where, if experience proved true, he'd stashed a weapon. It was too cold for a preternatural incident.

"Don't you dare shoot anybody. I'd have to clean it up." My teeth had already begun chattering, and it would take forever to modify all those human memories. Plus, I'd have to call Blue Congress wizards to erase the bloodstains from the snow; I had nothing in my portable kit that would work.

"Bah, very well. My intention was to stab the blackguard, not fell him by pistol." Jean resumed his speedy charge toward St. Louis Cathedral, tugging me along, slipping and sliding beside him.

We made it to Jackson Square with no further life-threatening situations, and I couldn't help myself: I pulled my phone from my pocket and began snapping pictures like every other snow-struck New Orleanian who'd wandered into the streets.

Jean scooped up a handful of snow and packed it into a firm snowball. In perfect pitcher's-mound form, he threw a hard line drive at Andrew Jackson's snow-covered, bronze head. Hit him right between the eyes.

"Nice shot. Do you feel better?"

"Bah." Jean turned back and smiled at the sight of St. Louis Cathedral draped in snow and ice, which I had to agree was a pretty spectacular sight. "It would prove more enjoyable had I been able to strike the arrogant toad himself."

No love lost between the pirate and the president, apparently. Alex said Jackson had been banished to Old Tennessee after causing such a public stink over the election-cheating incident that it threatened to expose the historical undead to humans.

"Can we go inside the cathedral for a few minutes?" I was so cold my blood seemed to be coagulating inside me. "I'm freezing."

Jean gave me a sidelong glance. "It is not so very cold, Drusilla. Perhaps it is your elven ancestry."

Huh. So he knew about that little elven quirk. Of course Jean seemed to know all the prete secrets; he could've probably filled me in on elven pregnancies.

I tugged his arm toward the church. "Maybe, but that doesn't make me any warmer. Just for a couple of minutes."

He stalled. "Perhaps we should return to the hotel, *Jolie.* Cold weather has dire effects on elves, and, pardon, but you do not look well. Your health and comfort are my greatest concern, as always."

Something was getting deep around here and it wasn't just the snow. Never bullshit a bullshitter, as my friend Rene would so eloquently put it.

"Look, I know you're trying to ditch me, and it's not going to work."

Jean frowned as he tucked my hand around his crooked arm again and began a very slow stroll back toward the Monteleone. *"Qu'est-ce que c'est* ditch?"

I didn't even dignify that with an answer because he knew

exactly what I meant. Besides, I wasn't sure I could talk anymore; my teeth were chattering too violently. My whole body was chattering violently. I had tolerated the cold up to a point, but now I seem to have turned some type of elven corner.

My pirate tour guide had changed tactics. Instead of his earlier breakneck clip, he now walked so slowly I could've outpaced him on hands and knees—all the better to freeze me out.

As we walked, Jean kept up a running commentary on the ice formations hanging from the shop awnings ("I am reminded of a deep cave I once visited in Cartagena"); merchandise available for sale, particularly sex toys and lingerie ("The fondness of your modern folk for such scandalous items and clothing is most distressing"); and snowstorms he had known ("You do not realize the treachery of hoisting anchor on a vessel whose deck is coated in ice, *Jolie*").

Fortunately, he seemed to require only an audience and not a partner in conversation.

I kept my eyes on the white ground in front of me, willing one foot at a time to move me forward. The world around me blurred, and I saw only the toes of my black boots crunching on white. Again and again.

My thoughts had frozen as well, but Rand's voice came through loud and clear. *Dru—what the hell are you doing? Get inside.*

With effort, I raised my head and looked around. "Freaking elf," I muttered. In my head, I tried to form words. *Babysit pirate.*

Get out of the cold, you stupid wizard. You have my blood in you now; you'll spontaneously hibernate if you get too cold.

Huh? "Bear?" I asked.

Jean frowned down at me. "*Qu'est-ce que c'est* bear? Drusilla, you do not look well, and we do not yet reach the hotel for two additional thoroughfares. We must walk in haste now. *Tout de suite.*"

"Elf," I said, trying to make Jean understand. But he pulled me along too fast, and my elven feet stopped moving.

The world tilted as I watched the snowy sidewalk shooting toward my face at an alarming pace, or was I moving toward the snow? Was Jean shouting at me, or was it Rand?

Sleep. The word filled my head as I rested my cheek on a cold, white, fluffy pillow.

CHAPTER 14

DJ, are you awake?

Freaking elf. "Go home, Rand."

I am home. Where are you?

I frowned and burrowed my face into the soft down pillow. Which was very different than the pillow I remembered falling into.

Holy crap. What had happened?

I sat up and took in several observations at once, none of which made sense and all of which sent my heart rate jack-rabbiting so hard I could feel my blood pressure zooming into the ozone.

First, I was lying beneath a heavy bedspread woven in a rich blue-and-cream print. The bed was an elaborate confection made to look like an antique half tester, and a brass chandelier hung overhead.

I recognized the Monteleone. I recognized Jean Lafitte's bedroom in the posh Eudora Welty Suite in the Monteleone. I didn't have a clue as to how I got here.

Second, I wore only a bra and panties. My clothes were thrown across a chair in the corner. I had no recollection of removing them.

Third, the pillow next to mine still held the clear indentation of a head, and there was water running behind the closed bathroom door.

What in God's name had I done?

Rand! Where are you? So help me, if that elf was behind this, I'd splay him open like a catfish and watch his guts fall on the floor. Then I'd batter and deep-fry him.

God, Dru. Stop shrieking like an elven shrew. I think you got too cold and went into a survival state. Like I did on Eugenie's porch.

Survival state? Then I remembered, and shame joined panic. I had gone into hibernation like a bear, right out on Royal Street in front of God and everyone. *Quince Randolph, you sonofabitch! Why didn't you warn me that would happen?*

Stop yelling. How did I know you'd be stupid enough to go traipsing through the snow to the point of unconsciousness? I can tell you're in the Quarter, but where are you?

Catch you later.

I slammed shut every mental door I could imagine and then troweled imaginary caulk in any imaginary cracks around said doors. I was vaguely aware that, off in the distance of my mental stronghold, Rand was yelling at me.

Had Jean hauled me back to the hotel like a sack of *pommes de terres*? How had he explained a hibernating blonde to the hotel management? At least my dark blue underwear matched. Had he taken advantage of me? No, it wasn't his style. Which meant I'd consented.

Holy crap. Alex was going to kill me if I didn't kill myself first. I wasn't sure hibernation-brain was an adequate defense.

The bathroom doorknob rattled and I dove under the covers, even though I realized it was like closing the barn door after the half-naked cows had escaped.

From my hiding spot, I heard the door open and footsteps cross from tile to carpet before stopping with a rustle of fabric. "Hey, babe. You finally back from the dead? Whatcha doin' under there?"

"Rene?" I poked my head out and frowned at my buddy the merman, fully dressed in jeans and a Saints sweatshirt. His feet were bare, and he walked around the bed and climbed in as if either one of us belonged here, much less at the same time.

"What are you doing here? What am I doing here? Who undressed me? Where's Jean?" And, as an afterthought, "Why are we in bed?"

Now that I realized I hadn't acted like my licentious great-aunt Dru and slept with the pirate, I transferred my anger to the proper place and it wasn't to myself. I'd kill that sneaky Frenchman if he weren't immortal.

Rene was not immortal, however, and he was within reach. "You better start talking, fish boy."

"Aiyeeee." Rene cackled like the Cajun he was, and fluffed the pillow behind his head. "I told Jean you'd be spittin' mad. Nothing happened, babe. Your clothes were wet and I was just trying to keep you warm. I'm a shifter, you know. We run hot."

"Oh, do you now."

That made him laugh harder.

I threw off the covers and stomped over to my clothes. He'd seen whatever I had and I knew he didn't want it, so there was no point in hiding. I picked up three soggy layers of T-shirts and sweaters, and cords so wet they weighed about ten pounds.

My breath hitched. The staff; I'd lost the staff. I whirled to Rene, who sat propped against the lush draped fabric that covered the headboard, watching me with a grin. "Where's my bag?"

"In the living room. Everything's there, babe, even your magic stick. Jean, he took care of you."

Yeah, I just bet he did. It was hard to argue effectively in underwear I'd intended only Alex Warin to see, so I went into the living room, dug my room key out of my messenger bag, and stuck my head out the door, looking up and down the hallway.

"I'll be back. Don't go anywhere," I yelled at Rene, and made a run for it, jamming the key card into my door lock and slipping inside before I was spotted. If hotel cameras caught my mad dash on security footage, well, I'm sure they'd seen stranger things. This was New Orleans, after all.

I dug out clean jeans and a black sweater to match my mood, and realized my only pair of boots were still across the hall and probably soaked. Damn it. I was an adult woman of reasonable intelligence, most of the time. I should have a house with actual furniture. I should have a car. I shouldn't have clothing scattered across friends' houses all over town and be plotting revenge on an undead pirate.

Not to mention his merry cohort the merman. I looked at my snarling tangle of hair, brushed it out as best I could, and charged back across the hall.

Rene took his sweet time opening the door. "You calmed down some, wizard?"

"That depends on what your buddy Jean is up to." I went in and slumped on the sofa. "And I'm hungry. I just came out of hibernation."

Rene laughed as he picked up the room service menu. "What you want?"

"Something with andouille in it." I was craving smoked sausage. Freaking elves and their smoked meats.

He studied the menu. "Red beans for one, coming up."

I found the TV remote and hit the power button, flipping

channels to the local NBC affiliate. Brian Williams was doing a news report on New Orleans' historic winter storm. "What time is it?"

"Little after six," Rene said. He tossed the menu back on the coffee table after he ordered the food and settled onto the sofa opposite the one I occupied. "I got a date at eight, so the pirate better get his ass back."

Good Lord. I'd hibernated for more than four hours—plenty of time for Jean to cause all kinds of trouble. Zrakovi was going to kill me, too. I wondered if the hibernation angle would earn any sympathy, or just ridicule.

"Okay, let's have it." I set the remote aside and gave Rene my most intimidating look. He smiled. I needed to work on being more authoritative, although he probably knew me too well for it to ever work. "What is Jean doing?"

Rene stretched and propped his feet on the coffee table, crossed at the ankles. "I got no idea."

I threw a sofa pillow at him and he batted it back to me like it was a beach ball at a rock concert. "Don't give me that crap, Rene. You and Jean are business partners; you know all his dirty little secrets."

I could've called a halt to their long-running smuggling operation months ago. They took everything from tobacco to antique furniture to spices in and out of Old Orleans at huge profits. But it wasn't hurting anybody, so I looked the other way. That could change.

Rene busied himself putting his socks and shoes back on. He had changed out of the Saints sweatshirt while I was across the hall and had donned a red sweater that was a good color for him with his short black hair, Vandyke beard, and eyes such a dark liquid brown they almost looked black. His date clothes, I guessed.

"Not this time, babe. I told Jean that you and me, we're friends, and I don't lie to my friends without a damn good reason. So whatever he's doing, I told him I don't wanna know about it. That way, when you yellin' at me and asking what he's up to, I can say I don't know.

"So, I don't know."

Damn it. Rene had never lied to me. Ever. He wasn't lying now.

"Tell me how you got mixed up in this."

"Jean, he called me last night and asked if I'd stay with you today if you, how'd he put it . . . 'if Drusilla perhaps is unable to care for herself for a matter of hours.' Told me to wait in the lobby, and if he didn't show up by four, to go on home."

Jean knew, damn it. He knew if he couldn't ditch me, he could drag me around in the cold until I did that whole humiliating hibernation thing. How did he know so much about elves?

I closed my eyes. "Go ahead. Tell me the rest."

"So I'm there in the lobby, tryin' to figure out how big that old grandfather clock is, and here comes Jean about two fifteen, totin' you in like Sleeping Beauty. Except for that ugly plaid coat."

I looked around. I hadn't seen my coat.

"Jean threw that bad boy away," Rene said. "I woulda done it if he hadn't."

Great. Fashion criticism from a man who wore mesh tank tops nine months out of the year. Never mind it was on his commercial fishing boat.

"What did he tell the manager?"

Rene cackled again. "Bellman, security guy, manager all come rushing over, wantin' to call an ambulance, but Jean had his story ready."

Yeah, I just bet he did. "Which was?"

"You got some kinda fainting-goat disease that makes you

fall asleep without warning. Seein' as how he pays cash for this suite a year in advance, they didn't question it."

A knock at the door interrupted my latest wave of humiliation, and I went to sign for room service, putting it on my tab. I hated to charge my meal to the man I was going to . . . well, I didn't know what I was going to do to the pirate yet, but I'd come up with something. Fainting-goat disease, my ass, although I wasn't sure hibernating-elf disease would get any more respect.

I carried the tray to the coffee table and sat in the floor, sucking down red beans thick with spices and big chunks of andouille. "Anything else? What's supposed to happen next?"

Rene reached over and stole a slice of my French bread. "Jean's supposed to be back in time for me to go on my date."

"Who's the lucky girl tonight?" Rene was a bit of an aquatic-shifter playboy. As I'd learned all too well during the time we'd done the power-share and lived in each others' brains a few days, he had a prodigious appetite for both food and sex. Fortunately for both of us, we'd become good friends and had no desire for benefits. As he often pointed out to me, he didn't like wizards. I was an exception.

"Nice little river nymph that lives over in Belle Chasse," he said. "But, you know, not too nice."

Uh-huh. He planned on getting lucky. "The river nymphs haven't started up their 'escort service' "—I made little quote marks with my fingers—"in the Quarter again, have they?"

I'd shut them down a few months ago after they brought satyrs in to "escort" the female clientele. A nymph could mainstream with humans, but satyrs couldn't. They might hide the nubby horns and long tails, but the cloven hooves just couldn't fit in any kind of shoe that looked normal.

"Not that I know of. Mina wasn't involved in that mess anyway."

"Well, I've recovered so you can go ahead and go on your date whether Jean's back or not." I chewed on a chunk of andouille. It was awesome; I wish I'd just ordered a big plate of sausage. "Then you won't have to witness me eviscerating your business partner."

Rene laughed. "That would almost be worth staying for." But he got up and checked for his keys and wallet. "You sure? Jean should be back soon."

I smiled. "Yeah, have fun."

On his way out, he stopped next to the desk, bent down, and pulled my coat from beneath some papers in the trash can. "Think I'll take this with me, babe. Force you to find something else."

Fine. I'd buy an overpriced coat in the Quarter and charge it to the ElderCard. Don't leave home without it.

Once I had the room to myself, I turned up the TV and finished my dinner to the drone of the local news. I'd fallen completely out of touch the last couple of days. A former city official was being sent to jail on corruption charges, where he'd have plenty of friends waiting for him. I figure politicians made up at least twenty percent of the state's inmates. Fortunately, his trial had been in the federal courthouse instead of the closed-down parish district court.

Mostly, though, the local newscasters talked about the weather. A guest meteorologist from Baton Rouge had come in to rant about the "once in a lifetime" weather pattern New Orleans was experiencing. We'd gotten two feet of snow, were enjoying a short respite, but could get another two-to-three feet of white stuff tomorrow. Outside a twenty-mile radius in any direction from the central city, however, normal winter weather in the fifties prevailed. They couldn't explain it.

It wouldn't go above freezing the next forty-eight hours. What the hell could I wear to avoid a repeat of the hibernation fiasco? Of course I had no car; maybe the concierge would send someone to buy some long johns and polar fleece at one of the sporting goods stores, if they weren't sold out. Maybe I'd get some for Rand, too.

No, forget that. It was convenient having him essentially imprisoned in his house, and he didn't deserve special consideration. He could've warned me that our bond left me vulnerable to spontaneous hibernation, plus he was being an ass about Eugenie. Surprise surprise.

Sirens are almost a constant in New Orleans, and I'd learned to ignore them. But when what sounded like a whole fleet of NOFD ladder trucks roared by, sirens blasting, I ran to the window. A half-dozen police cars followed, nudging the few pedestrians out of the way and turning toward Chartres Street.

"We have a breaking story from the French Quarter," the TV reporter said, and I turned to watch video of people pouring out of a building from whose upper windows smoke billowed and flames licked at the night sky. "A multiple-alarm fire has struck a crowded nightclub called . . ."

I didn't need to hear the rest. I recognized the place. It was the vampire bar belonging to Etienne Boulard, former friend and now avowed enemy of the unaccounted-for Jean Lafitte.

L'Amour Sauvage was in flames.

CHAPTER 15

Calling Jean every bad name I could think of, I jammed my feet into the cold, wet boots and looked around helplessly. Rene had taken my coat. Going out in wet shoes was risky enough; coatless, I was asking for another round of hibernation.

On the other hand, it should be toasty warm next to the burning vampire club.

I went into the bedroom and opened the armoire where Jean kept his clothes. I considered the heavy terrycloth hotel robe, but if it was already snowing, the terrycloth would just absorb all the cold water. Damn it. The pirate didn't have anything useful.

More sirens sounded outside. This had to be bad. I grabbed my messenger bag, made sure the staff was wedged firmly inside, and ran down the hallway. The elevator moved at the pace of an elf in Antarctica, but finally it arrived at the lobby. I cut into the gift shop, grabbed a couple of heavy sweatshirts, charged them to the room, and pulled them on as I crossed the shiny marble floor toward the street.

The doorman smiled as if he might be going to make jovial conversation, but thought better of it and rushed to open the door for me without a word. He probably feared I'd keel over in a dead sleep from my mysterious fainting-goat disease and hoped it wasn't contagious.

As soon as I cleared the doorway, the wind hit me full-force. God, it was cold. My feet began to go numb before I'd taken a dozen steps, but I rushed onward, moving as fast as I dared. I cut over one block to Chartres Street and slowed, not only because the whole area ahead of me lay jammed with emergency vehicles and people, but because the fire roared like a living thing, its flames bright enough to make the snow falling between me and the club appear as a dark, moving curtain.

Was Jean insane? The Quarter was older than him—ancient by U.S. standards. Its venerable buildings were always in some state of disrepair, making us the American originator of urban grunge. Dilapidation was admired and coveted in New Orleans, especially in this part of town. The Quarter was also a monstrous firetrap.

On the positive side, by the time I began working my way through people and got within a block of the fire, the warmth hit me and hibernation was no longer an immediate concern. Every few seconds, I scanned the moving throngs around me, trying to catch a glimpse of a familiar, tall Frenchman dressed in a Daniel Boone coat.

I finally spotted a familiar face. Vampire Regent Etienne Boulard stood still as only vampires can, a rock amid the moving sea of firefighters, paramedics, cops, and ash-covered club patrons. He looked mad enough to chew wooden nails, but at least he wasn't dead. I wasn't sure I'd point that out to him as something for which to be thankful, however.

My first instinct was to turn around, return to the hotel, and pretend I'd seen nothing. But damn it, I was the sentinel here. New Orleans was my town, and if anyone was going to set fires in the French Quarter it should be me and my elven staff. I had to investigate. Besides, it might have nothing to do with Jean Lafitte.

I stepped up beside Etienne, hoping he didn't hold a grudge after the little burning incident in Vampyre. He didn't turn in my direction and I didn't think he'd seen me until he hissed, "I hold you entirely responsible for this."

So much for not holding a grudge. "If by *this* you mean the fire at L'Amour Sauvage, think again. I just got here."

When Etienne turned to me, I winced. His blue eyes shone like marbles in a face covered in soot and tight, reddened skin. He'd been close to that fire. "You saved Lafitte, though, and he's behind this."

"Did you see him set the fire?" Besides that, we had a bigger issue. Namely, that Etienne should've been arrested the second he crossed back into New Orleans. I hadn't seen the warrant yet, but I was pretty sure conspiracy and attempted murder were on his preternatural rap sheet. Should I call Alex or try to arrest him myself?

"I didn't have to see him." Etienne's French accent had grown heavier. He usually sounded more Louisianian than the Frenchman he'd been back in his wizard days as a plantation owner. He'd lost his magic after being turned.

"Then you have no proof." I startled as the glass blew out of an upper window and sent a shower of blackened shards to the sidewalk.

"As soon as the club opened this evening, it filled with undead pirates, behaving like ruffians and driving away my regular customers." Etienne seemed to have forgotten his shaky legal status. He was so angry he'd even flashed a bit of fang, which meant I could add *reckless exposure to humans* to his list of crimes.

He turned back to watch the fire, the muscles in his jaw working as he clenched his teeth. How that teeth-clenching thing worked with fangs, I wasn't sure. "Did you see one of the undead pirates set the fire? Otherwise, it could've been anyone."

"God. Are you that stupid or are you being deliberately obtuse to protect your friend Jean?" Etienne motioned to someone in the crowd, and I saw the L'Amour Sauvage assistant manager heading toward us. He was a very polite metrosexual vampire who monitored the entrance of the club, keeping the crowds in check. His usually polished suit and tie were gray with ash, but I could still read his name tag: Marcus.

"Everyone got out," he told Etienne, who nodded.

"Get my attorney on the phone and tell him to get his ass down here. He'll need to deal with the human authorities. I"—he glanced at me—"must return to Vampyre immediately."

Oh no he didn't. I needed handcuffs, or a good obedience spell. All I had was Charlie, so I pulled the staff from my messenger bag and discreetly pressed its tip against Etienne's side.

He stiffened. "You wouldn't dare use that here."

He was probably right. "Don't try me. You're still wanted by the Elders, so you aren't going anywhere except . . ." Holy crap. Now that I had the vampire, what the hell was I going to do with him? Haul him back to the Monteleone to wait for the breakfast buffet? "Except to Edinburgh."

Etienne Boulard was the Elders' problem, and it was the job of the area's enforcer, Alex Warin, to send prisoners to Elder headquarters in Scotland. He'd need orders first, though.

I pulled out my cell phone and managed to unlock my screen.

I'd just hit Zrakovi's number on my speed dial when someone barreled into me from behind, knocking me, my cell phone, and a street busker with an acoustic guitar into a heap on the sludgy street. The crowd edged away so we'd have a clear path to the ground.

"You broke my neck." The musician sat in a puddle, looking like the last reject from *Duck Dynasty*; the icy mud dripping from his face did nothing to improve the squirrel's tail of hair dangling from chin to waist.

"What?" I looked him up and down. "You're sitting up and talking. I don't think you can do that with a broken neck."

"My guitar." He held up a fretboard with dangling strings and nothing attached. Now I knew what had broken my fall.

"Sorry, hold on." I rolled to my knees and scrabbled around on the ground until I found my cell phone inside the remains of the crushed guitar. I looked around to see what had knocked us over, and thought Marcus had an awfully guilty look on his grimy face, especially when he looked away the second we made eye contact.

If Etienne hadn't remained exactly where he'd been before the tumble, I'd have accused Marcus of creating a diversion so his boss could escape.

At least the staff, still duct-taped together after last month's chaos, remained intact since it had landed on my head. The phone didn't have a scratch. Alex, who knew me way too well, had bought me a super-indestructible, waterproof case.

I climbed to my feet, turned my back to the whiny musician, and tried my call again.

You have reached the Elders. We can't take your call right now. If this is an emergency, call your local sentinel.

Seriously? The Elders had voice mail and were sending calls

to me? This would never have happened while Adrian Hoffman had been manning the phones.

I made sure Etienne was still in view and got ready to call Alex. I had a missed call from him that had just ended, so he shouldn't be too hard to reach if . . .

"Excuse me. Sentinel?"

Marcus stood hesitantly next to me. Last time we'd met, I'd been bleeding profusely from my bullet wound and he'd made me sign a release form promising not to hold any vampires responsible if they got carried away and bit me. Apparently, I tasted vile so it was just as well no one had tried.

"What is it?" I tried to peer around his shoulders at Etienne, who remained in place, watching the fire. I couldn't believe the arrogant jerk wasn't concerned about being arrested.

"Can you put out the fire? With your magic?" Marcus cast a worried glance over his shoulder as another window burst from the heat.

Was he nuts? "I'm sorry, Marcus, but this is too big for me to handle, especially with all the humans around. It's best left to the firefighters. How did it start?"

He shook his head, still pretty and pale and androgynous even with ash smudges on both cheeks. "I'm not sure, but I think it started in the back, either in Etienne's office or the men's room or the mechanical room between the two. Our heating unit is old, and it's been running nonstop this week."

A slight flame of hope ignited in me. Maybe Etienne was wrong about this being Jean's handiwork. Maybe it was nothing more sinister than an overworked, malfunctioning central heating unit.

Marcus stood on tiptoe to try and see over the people in front of us. "But we also had a bunch of the historical undead, friends of Jean Lafitte the pirate, filling up the bar tonight. I saw one of them coming from the hallway right before we smelled smoke."

Or maybe I was kidding myself.

"What about Terri?" I wasn't sure Etienne's personal assistant had returned, but then again I'd been surprised to see Etienne. Terri hadn't been proven guilty of anything except having the bad luck of falling for Adrian Hoffman.

"Terri hasn't been back since the troubles, and as far as I know, Adrian's in Vampyre."

The troubles. That was a nice way of putting it. If I ratted Adrian out, he'd be tossed in a wizard prison until the protocol for an interspecies trial could be worked out, as would Daddy Elderbucks. They could keep Etienne company.

"Sorry about the club. Hope you guys can rebuild." I edged around Marcus and headed toward Etienne. I wanted him within discreet reach of Charlie while I called Alex.

Etienne turned when I nudged him in the side with the staff again . . . only it wasn't Etienne. This guy had the same ash-coated blue suit, the same blond hair, even the same freaking fangs, which flashed openly as he grinned at me. "Sorry, honey. Etienne had to run."

Marcus patted me on the shoulder, edging past me and standing next to Etienne's body double. "Kirk looks so much like Etienne, doesn't he?"

Damn it, I had been played like the busker's broken guitar.

My phone buzzed again, and I walked away in disgust. W. ZRAKOVI showed up on caller ID.

"L'Amour Sauvage is going to be a total loss, but at least no one's hurt," I said, not bothering with a greeting. "We might need a Blue Congress team, but it's too early to tell."

"Damn." Zrakovi sounded as annoyed as I felt. I couldn't

believe I'd let myself be distracted while Etienne pranced back to Vampyre unchallenged. "Where is Lafitte?"

Good question. I pivoted around and stepped away from the onlookers so I could see more people. Heat from the fire baked one side of my face, while the other was wet with snow and already half frozen now that I'd moved away from the crowd.

"He's been at the hotel," I hedged.

I hadn't intended to lie for him, but I also couldn't cast blame his way without talking to him. Sending his undead pirates to annoy Etienne wasn't illegal, and there was some chance the fire started innocently. Not much chance, but some.

"The vampires think it could have been a problem with the heating unit," I added. A long silence on the other end of the call. "You know, overworked because of the cold snap."

Finally, Zrakovi asked, "Then why might we need a cleanup team?"

God, I was getting in deep snow here. "There also might have been some undead pirates in the club just before the fire started." I tried to make my voice sound matter-of-fact and unconcerned. "There's no way to know if one of them had anything to do with the fire, of course, but a Blue Congress team should be on-site, just in case they dropped a rare doubloon or something."

"Undead pirates. Oh no, they'd *never* start a fire." Was it my imagination, or was Zrakovi's voice more than a tad sarcastic?

"Well, we don't know yet." I dug my hole deeper.

"And you say Lafitte was with you?"

Sneaky Elder. "No, I said he was at the hotel. But I did hear about the fire on the TV in his suite, in fact."

Where I'd been sitting alone, eating andouille.

Since when did I start lying to the Elders to cover for Jean Lafitte? Now, apparently.

"Yes, well, I'll get a Blue Congress team on its way. And DJ . . ." Zrakovi paused, and I held my breath, praying I wouldn't have to lie to him again. "I know you owe Lafitte your life, and that the two of you have gotten . . . close."

I thought *close* might be stretching it. Especially after the hibernation incident.

"That doesn't mean I can't do my job," I said, wondering if that, too, had become a lie.

"I hope so, because we need you."

He couldn't have made me feel any more guilt-riddled had he trotted out the inevitable comparison to my father.

"I wouldn't want you to make some of the same mistakes that Gerry made."

I sighed. "Definitely not, sir."

"Well, we need to get together after the Interspecies Council meeting to talk about your friend Eugenia and the child."

I didn't correct him on Eugenie's name. The fact that he didn't know it said a lot. "I look forward to it."

Lies, lies, and more lies.

There was no more I could do here. The fire seemed to be under control and hadn't spread to the adjacent buildings. Etienne was gone, at least for the time being. I'd go back to the hotel, order a bottle of wine, and figure out what to do. Only then would I call Alex. Lying to Zrakovi was one thing; lying to Alex—not just neglecting to mention something but outright lying—was another matter.

By the time I found the busker and gave him all the cash I had on me to help pay for a new guitar, the snow fell harder and was piling up fast. My teeth chattered again before I cleared the next block, and the entire lower half of my body was as wet as my boots since I'd done the street dive with the bearded busker.

A block from the hotel, I got the same surreal sensation that had overcome me just before the hibernation, and willed myself to move faster. My feet slipped and slid, but I didn't slow down. If I fell and broke my neck it would solve a lot of problems.

I crossed over to Royal Street and saw the lights of the hotel shining through the heavy snow like a homing beacon. I walked toward them and almost fell when I pushed open the door and entered the lobby. The doorman gave me a fearful look, but I waved at him. No hibernating bears or fainting goats here.

To my left shone the lights of the Carousel Bar, and I could think of nothing that might warm me up faster than an Irish coffee, or maybe just the Irish without the coffee. As always, the bar pulled me in two directions. It was funky and fun and clever. It also was bizarre and disconcerting. The polished wooden bar in the center was round, with brightly colored stools ringing it on the outside, and a circular, mirrored display of liquor bottles on the inside. The whole thing revolved slowly so that you'd make a full rotation every half hour or so.

Business was brisk; the tourists still in the city had wisely decided to stay inside instead of roaming the French Quarter. But I spotted a couple leaving and somehow propelled my frozen, numb feet to hurry and claim a stool.

"What's the warmest thing you have?" I asked the dark-suited bartender.

He laughed. "Martini or cocktail?"

Martinis were too small. "Cocktail. Big one."

"Well, you're lookin' kinda pale. We got one called the Corpse Reviver—gin, Cointreau, absinthe, Lillet Blanc."

Ironic. Too ironic. "Maybe something sweet." Okay, I'm a wimp.

He studied me, as if my bedraggled appearance might give

him the perfect cocktail suggestion. "The French Double-O-Seven: Grey Goose, pomegranate liqueur, and champagne."

"Now you're talking." Because when I saw the Frenchman, I was going all James Bond on his ass.

By the time my drink arrived, the bar had made a quarter turn. I paid the twelve bucks plus tip with my own credit card, since it seemed wrong to make Zrakovi pay for the drink I was consuming to help me forget how much I'd lied to him. Sweet heat filled my mouth and burned its way down my happy throat, settling into my stomach, and I found myself wishing for a bag of smoked beef jerky.

Freakin' elves.

As the bar turned, I studied the changing view of patrons sitting at the tables that were scattered around the edges. There seemed to be an even mix of tourists and business people. Maybe a few locals who'd come to the Quarter to see the snow and decided to warm up at the bar.

I glanced up at the glittering mirrored display of alcohol in the center of the bar and did a double take. Had that been Truman Capote?

I swiveled and scanned the tables looking for him and, instead, found myself capturing the gaze of a long-haired man with a vaguely familiar pair of green eyes. I couldn't see who was with him because of a couple of businessmen who'd sat at a table between my perch and his, and I couldn't quite place him. His eyes looked sort of like those of Christof, the dark-haired faery who'd been at Jean's house in Barataria, but this guy had shoulder-length brown hair with a lot of red highlights.

He smiled at me and leaned over to say something to a companion. Finally, the businessmen moved to seats at the bar and left me with an unimpeded view. The green-eyed man might not have been Christof the faery, but his companions I recognized.

Truman Capote, a card-carrying member of the historical undead, and his equally undead companion.

I'd found Jean Lafitte.

CHAPTER 16

Call me suspicious, but I had no doubt Truman Capote's only purpose in being at the Carousel Bar with Jean Lafitte was to serve as his alibi. Probably the other guy, too.

"Well, if it isn't Cat Woman," Capote drawled.

"You remember me, then." Good. Not having to explain who I was made things simpler.

Capote had been part of the William Faulkner dustup after Katrina. A bunch of historically undead New Orleans authors had come across the border and broken into Faulkner House Books near Jackson Square, where the man himself had lived in his human life for a while. They proceeded to get drunk until I'd done a nifty bit of magic, turned them all into cats, rounded them up, and sent them back to the Beyond in boxes. As I recalled, Capote had turned into an oversize Maine coon.

"I'm not likely to forget such an experience." He took off his dark glasses and signaled the waiter for another drink. The historically undead Capote was middle-aged and cocky, his neck draped in a pastel-striped scarf whose purples and pinks looked unsettling next to his somber black suit and fedora.

I was ignoring Jean Lafitte and his knowing little smile, so I held out a hand to the auburn-haired guy. "DJ Jaco. You look awfully familiar. Have we met?"

"We have." He took my hand and pressed it to his lips in an old-world, courtly way that reminded me of the pirate I was ignoring. "I am Christof, the Faery Prince of Winter and, I hope, next in line to the monarchy. We've met twice, I believe."

"But . . ." The eyes were the same, green and slightly almond-shaped. But he'd had dark hair slicked back at the council meeting and tousled at Jean's—and not nearly this long. His title finally sank in. "You're the Winter Prince? And why do you look different?"

"Perhaps you should give Drusilla a demonstration, Christof." Jean stared at me a moment and suppressed a broad smile. What was that about?

"Of course. Excuse me for a moment." The Prince of Winter got up and made his way out of the bar, disappearing into the lobby. I swear, I needed a vacation. Life had grown too bizarre.

The waiter brought a fizzy drink and set it in front of Capote, who took his little plastic spear, stabbed a cherry, and held it out to me. "Suck it. Let's see those tongue skills," he said.

I choked on my French Double-O-Seven. "I beg your pardon?"

Jean's smile widened into a full-out grin. "One should not wear such clothing if one does not wish to receive such invitations, my pet."

Huh? I looked down at my sweatshirt for the first time. I'd grabbed the first thing I saw in the gift shop and hadn't even pulled the price tags off. A line of gold crawfish claws danced across the front, with lines of enormous purple type above and below that said "SUCK DAT HEAD" and "PINCH DAT TAIL."

Gah. "It's talking about crawfish, not sex. If either of you had been alive in the last twenty years, you'd know that." Damn it. This was almost as humiliating as hibernating in public. I jerked the sweatshirt over my head and tossed it on the floor. The one beneath it was identical, so I pulled it off as well. I was inside now; my black sweater would be fine.

"If someone hadn't thrown my coat away and then set a fire I had to run outside to investigate, I wouldn't have been forced to wear suggestive sweatshirts," I hissed at Jean.

"Ah, yes, this awakens my memory." He leaned over and reached beneath the table, bringing out a large plastic bag. "Your eyes will look like jewels wearing this, *Jolie*."

Bribes would get him nowhere, but I opened the bag anyway. Holy crap. I pulled out a coat of buttery soft lambskin dyed to a rich teal. I surreptitiously held it up so I could see the size was a six and should fit. It was the most gorgeous thing I'd ever seen, and I couldn't possibly take it. If he thought giving me a . . . I glanced at the sales receipt that had fallen out on the table, and almost choked. If he thought giving me a $4,000 coat would get him off the hook for today's behavior he was not only dead but dead wrong.

"This is beautiful, but I can't take it, Jean."

"Bah. I chose it for you, so you must have it." He looked over my shoulder. "And here is Christof."

I turned and stared. The green eyes still twinkled with good humor; the stylish dark trousers and white shirt were the same. But nothing else. His face had lengthened, cheekbones grown more pronounced, and his hair was not only stylishly short but a sun-streaked blond. "You're like a shapeshifter, only you change human appearance?"

Christof sat down and sipped from the glass of wine he'd left behind. "Not a bad analogy, Sentinel Jaco. May I call you DJ?"

That would be a welcome relief, since Jean refused to use my "alphabet letters" and Rand insisted on calling me Dru. "Of course. Is this an ability unique to the Winter Prince or to all of the fae? Can you change gender as well?"

"Every one of us who is of pure faery blood can change our appearance at will," he said. "Of mixed-species fae, it varies. But no, we do not possess the ability to change genders, although that would be . . . illuminating. Perhaps then I would understand women."

Somehow, I doubted it. I really had to find time between fires and babies and political crises to do my faery research. "You and Jean and Mr. Capote are friends?"

"Why, yes, indeed." Christof looked at both of his companions with a bemused expression, and something that had been niggling at the back of my mind finally came to the fore. Gerry had once told me that faeries couldn't lie, but were masters of obfuscation.

I needed to be very specific and very literal. "How long have you been friends?"

Christof cocked his head and fixed his bright gaze on me. It was probably my lack of sweatshirts, but the temperature around us seemed to drop. "How does one measure friendship in such mundane things as hours or days or years?"

Exactly what I thought. "Have you known Mr. Capote more than six hours?"

It wasn't my imagination; the room grew colder. People at

the next table looked around for the waiter and tugged on their coats. "No," Christof said.

"Did you know I was born here at the Monteleone?" Capote asked, pulling his suit coat more snugly around him. "Well, that's what I always claimed back in the day."

I'd be polite, but my radar wasn't getting deflected that easily. "I'd heard that, actually. So it wasn't true?"

"No," Capote said, laughing. "I was born down the street at Charity Hospital, or where Charity was before Hurricane Katrina destroyed it. Fine old hospital." He sipped his cocktail and stared into the ether of time. "My mother lived here while she was pregnant with me, though, and a member of the hotel staff drove her to the hospital when labor started."

"Did she live in the rooms of Eudora Welty?" Jean asked, sending the whole insane conversation into Wonderland territory.

As they discussed the literary history of the Hotel Monteleone, I pondered the drop in temperature and the sudden buddy status of Jean Lafitte and the Faery Prince of Winter. Silent across the table, Christof kept his gaze on me like a jagged iceberg.

I leaned back and focused instead on the large-screen TV playing in one corner, hoping to bore him into warming things up. Its sound was turned down too low to hear, but the picture switched from a report on the Saints' NFL playoff hopes to—what else—the weather.

Snowy vista after snowy vista filled the screen, replaced by a red-nosed, heavily bundled reporter whose breath plumed in white clouds as he talked into his microphone. Heavy snow swirled behind him. A map appeared on the screen, showing the Southeastern U.S., where everything was green and clear except for a big white circle sitting over that part of Louisiana just south of Lake Pontchartrain.

The Faery Prince of Winter arrives in town at the same time we have the unexplainable winter of a lifetime. We have the winter of a lifetime at the same time Jean Lafitte, said prince's new BFF, wants to punish the elves for their part in last month's fiasco.

This weather had crippled them. Rand was the only one still staying in New Orleans and couldn't leave his house without risking hibernation. Mace Banyan had fled back to Elfheim. The elves, Jean wouldn't want to kill—Lily had already been decapitated. But he would enjoy tormenting them.

Crap on a freaking stick.

I shifted my gaze back to Christof, and in his cold stare and another dip in temperature, I saw the truth in my suspicions.

"Christof," Jean said, touching the prince's arm. "Perhaps you should go back to Faery this evening and appease your queen. As you yourself said, she is displeased with your continued absence from her court."

"Very well, my friend." Christof leaned back, and I sighed in relief as the temperature rose again. "You will take care of this problem?"

I didn't look up at him, but I was pretty sure "this problem" meant me.

"*Oui,* give my regards to your queen and your brother."

Christof laughed. "Well, my queen perhaps. Florian and I do not talk more than is necessary, as you know."

He bade good-bye to Truman Capote, who'd fallen silent during the exchange, and turned last to me. "I'm sure we'll meet again soon, DJ."

I kept my eyes on Jean. "Undoubtedly. Safe travels."

He shrugged into a long wool coat and swept from the room. The temperature continued to rise.

Capote began chatting again, telling stories and engaging

Jean in conversation, which was fine with me. I needed to think.

I owed Jean Lafitte my life, as Willem Zrakovi had pointed out. More than that, I considered him a friend. Maybe not the most straightforward friend, but I had no doubts that if push came to shove, he would protect me. I also felt certain he would never betray me, even at cost to himself.

If I turned him in for burning the vampire club and using the Winter Prince to make the elves miserable, he'd lose his spot on the Interspecies Council at the very least. He might face prosecution for consorting with the fae while the Elders were still paying him to provide them with updated navigational maps of the Beyond.

I also was likely not the only one turning a blind eye toward his business dealings with Rene, and those could be shut down, which would hurt both of them. Jean could even be confined to the Beyond, which would hurt him far worse than a temporary physical death. He was adventurous and independent. Chaining him down would kill his spirit even if his body survived forever.

So far, he hadn't actually hurt anyone. He was playing mental games, like a big old French cat toying with a vampire mouse and a few elven cockroaches.

There was another issue that factored into how I dealt with Jean. I considered him a friend, and I owed him. Beyond that? I had avoided thinking too hard about my feelings for him, and had no idea what his were toward me. We'd been flirting for years. He'd made it clear that he found me desirable, and I'd unfortunately not hidden my attraction from him nearly well enough or Alex wouldn't continue to see him as a threat.

I couldn't make a reasonable decision about his dealings with the fae or his potential arson case until I knew where Jean and I stood. For Alex, it would be black and white. Jean broke the law, so Jean should be punished, whatever that meant. I couldn't think that way. I didn't want to think that way. Right or wrong, my heart had a say in whatever decision my mind reached.

Jean had told me a time would come when I'd have to choose sides. I hadn't thought it would be now, or in this way. Then again, maybe it wasn't as complicated as I was trying to make it. There was only one way to find out.

"Jean." I interrupted Capote in the middle of a rousing story about his adventures growing up in the city. "We need to talk."

Something on my face seemed to tell him this was not a light request. "Truman, *mon ami*. Our time here draws to a close."

Capote looked from Jean to me and back. "Good, I was tired of talking. I can expect that portable computer tomorrow?"

Jean gave a single nod. *"Bien sûr."*

"And you'll set up lessons for me on how to use it?"

Jean looked at me, eyebrows raised.

Oh, hell no.

My go-to-the-devil look must have been enough; Jean turned back to Capote. "My friend Rene will arrange these lessons."

Guess laptops were the cost of an alibi in the financial realms of the historical undead, and Rene would be making a visit to an electronics store. The Geek Squad probably didn't make house calls to Old Orleans.

Capote wandered out of the lobby and turned toward the central Quarter. I wasn't concerned about him being recognized, and he was smart enough to keep his identity hidden. He was just one more eccentric guy in a city full of them.

What concerned me was the man who sat next to me at the

table, watching me with cobalt-blue eyes that had seen much and were often far too perceptive.

He held out his hand, and after a pause, I took it. "Shall we, Drusilla?"

God help us, we shall.

CHAPTER 17

Throughout the walk across the hotel lobby and into the elevator, I tried to talk myself out of having this conversation. It wasn't too late. We could go upstairs, Jean would ask if I really wanted the truth about his involvement in the fire, and I would tell him no. Then he could spin a few lies about his lack of involvement, both of us knowing they were lies. I could then pretend to believe him and pass the lies on to Zrakovi.

Here was the problem: I'd also have to pass the lies on to Alex, because if I told Alex the truth, he'd tell Zrakovi. Never mind that it hurt Rene as well as Jean. Never mind that it hurt me. He'd do the right thing as he saw it; he might feel badly about it, especially if it hurt me, but he'd believe he had no choice.

I admired that about Alex, his sense of moral absolutes. I also hated that about Alex, his inability to acknowledge the gray areas and shadowy corners of life.

Maybe one of the reasons I didn't want to have this talk with Jean was that it would make me confront my feelings about Alex.

Did I love him or did I just desperately want to love him? Did he love me? Even if the love was there and was real, was it enough?

One crisis at a time.

Before following Jean into the elevator, I slipped my mojo bag from around my neck and stuck it in my messenger bag. Normally, my empathic abilities were more crippling than illuminating. The more of other people's emotions I could filter out, the better, and my daily meditation and my locket of magicked herbs and chips of gemstones helped strengthen those filters.

Tonight, I wanted a read on Jean's emotions and I was glad that, unlike a lot of pretes whose readings were hard to interpret, I could read the auras of the historical undead just like any other human. I wasn't sure Jean knew I could filter and absorb emotions. I had never told him and, if he knew, he'd never mentioned it. Advantage: DJ.

So as we walked side by side on our silent way down the hall to Jean's suite, I knew he was worried. I didn't know if he was worried about his deal with Christof being exposed, concerned about our pending conversation, or fretting about the value of gold bullion in Europe.

The lack of specifics were empathy's greatest shortcoming. I knew what he was feeling, but not why. It required a lot of interpretation on my part. For better or worse, I was pretty good at it, and my instincts told me he was as worried about upsetting the status quo between us as I was.

"Would you like to have our talk in the rooms of Eudora Welty or in your accommodations?" Jean asked.

"Your suite." There was nowhere in my room to sit other than the bed and an armchair, and he had a nice, neutral living room.

When we reached his suite, the edge of a white sheet of paper stuck out from beneath his door. Looking across the hall, an identical sheet stuck out of mine.

I walked over to procure my folded sheet, then followed Jean into his room. The sound of the door closing behind me had an ominous finality to it, as if momentous things would now take place within these walls. I pulled my cell phone from my pocket, noted a missed call from Alex, and turned off the ringer.

Jean, meanwhile, had unfolded his paper. "The Interspecies Council will meet once again, on the morrow," he said. "Where is this meeting place?"

I opened my sheet. I was not a voting member of the council, but as sentinel I'd always be dragged into their meetings because chances were good that anything they had to discuss would somehow involve me. The announcement, handwritten in a florid script, said the meeting would take place at ten a.m. tomorrow morning on the third floor of Hebert Hall on the Tulane campus, which already had closed for the holidays.

"It's a building at Tulane University," I said. "Across from Audubon Park, where the de Boré plantation sat during your day. There's no reason to hold the meeting at night since the vampires aren't invited."

I knew this because the sheet contained a list of the expected attendees. Both Alex and Jake, as well as a couple of names I didn't know, would be on security duty. Noticeably absent from the list were Garrett Melnick, any other representative of Vampyre, and Geoffrey and Adrian Hoffman. Noticeably present was Lennox St. Simon, my mystery uncle representing the UK and EU, and, at the head of the list, Willem Zrakovi, Acting First Elder.

At the bottom of my sheet, scribbled in blue ink, was a postscript:

DJ—Please be prepared to discuss what you know about Eugenita's intentions toward the elven child of Quince Randolph, as well as Etienne Boulard's whereabouts and Jean Lafitte's involvement in the burning of his club.

—Wm Zrakovi

I had an overwhelming urge to run away from home. Except unless I jumped over to the Beyond, the Elders could track me down using my unique magical signature. And the number of places in the Beyond where I didn't have enemies was dwindling fast.

"Might I interest you in a brandy, *Jolie?*"

It couldn't hurt. "Please."

When Jean handed me the glass of amber liquid that I knew would set my insides on fire but numb the panic building inside me, I handed him my paper. "Read the note at the bottom."

He studied it a moment and tossed it on the coffee table.

I sat in the middle of the sofa facing the large windows, and he sat on the matching sofa opposite me—exactly where Rene and I had sat earlier this evening. It seemed like a week ago.

"We appear to be at a crossroads, you and I." Jean's voice was soft and deep, without a trace of smarminess or sarcasm. His mood was somber but no longer nervous.

I looked at this undead pirate who was causing me so much inner turmoil. Really looked at him. He bore the scars of the difficult life he'd led in his human years. His skin was tanned and smooth on his face but for the jagged scar across his jawline. But there were stress lines at the edges of his mouth. Deep blue eyes conveyed so much, from arrogance to sincerity, but often distrust as well. His dark hair had been pulled back and tied with a leather cord.

He was very handsome, without a trace of prettiness. He had

a mouth that could be cruel. A mind that was nimble and sharp as razor wire. A sense of values that were his own and no one else's.

What did he see when he looked at me? A child, or a woman? A valuable ally? A potential lover? Or a means to an end?

"Let's start with the easy part," I finally said. "Did you order your men to burn Etienne's club?"

He settled back on the sofa with his brandy and regarded me, lips pursed. "Do you wish the truth, Drusilla? Once I have told you, the burden of what to do with that truth falls to you. You may yet postpone your time for taking a stand, and I might yet postpone my time to decide whether or not to place my fate in your hands."

"I know that." Oh, how I knew that. My gut told me now was the time, though, while the crisis was relatively minor, while I still could think and not just react. "I can't make an honest decision about what stand I should take—or if I should take one—unless I know the full truth. And the time for honest decisions is here, I think."

Everything—Eugenie, Alex, Jean, Rand, the council, the political tensions—seemed to be hurtling toward various cliffs, with me standing at a series of crossroads between them and their destinations. I felt it in my gut; if I didn't choose which cliff I was going off, and with whom I'd take the plunge, I'd be torn to shreds as they each tried to take a piece of me.

If I were Alex, my answer would be simple. I'd go in whatever direction the Elders were headed. I'd side with the wizards, right or wrong, because that was what was expected of me. At one time, even as recently as a few months ago, I'd have thought my choice was that simple, too.

But I'd seen too much since Katrina's aftermath had thrown our world into chaos. The wizards' political machinations and paranoia were as much to blame as anything for the current interspecies tensions.

A sudden realization hit me upside the head like a two-by-four, and put into perspective why I was struggling so hard to take a stand: The people I really cared about, the ones I loved each in his or her own way, were unanimous in one aspect. None of them were wizards. That revelation almost took my breath away, but I had to set it aside for now.

"Tell me the truth," I said to Jean, digging in my heels at the crossroads, preparing to make the first of what my heart told me would be a line of hard decisions.

Jean stared at the floor, thinking, his aura bathed in indecision. I was asking him to trust me without any assurance that I wouldn't do something to hurt him. I knew when he'd made up his mind; a hum shimmered across my skin like a stone sending a ripple over a lake, and his mind calmed.

He looked up at me. "Very well, Drusilla. Here is the truth, as you asked. Although you are not fully elven, you hold much of their magic. Thus, I escorted you into the snow, believing you would eventually succumb to what the elves call their survival state." The emotions coming off Jean ramped up, but he remained outwardly calm. As long as that level of calm was there, he was being honest. "I knew you would not be harmed as long as I returned you to the hotel immediately, and I had Rene waiting to watch over you. Your life will never be placed in mortal danger by Jean Lafitte."

"How did you know I'd hibernate?" One could use pretty words like *survival state,* but if it oinks you might as well call it a pig. "Why did you want me to hibernate?"

"Certainty eluded me, of course, but I had observed you on the night of the council meeting," Jean said. "While others were chilled, your countenance was very much like that of your elf—

quite pale. I was concerned for your health, and Christof explained this odd elven trait, as he has dealt with elves for many lifetimes."

Freaking elves.

"As for why, well, it was what my friend Christof called a policy of insurance, lest you attempt to interfere with the plans I had made."

Plans that involved arson, no doubt. "What happened after you left me with Rene?"

"I met Christof as planned, and we proceeded to make ourselves seen at the . . ." Jean paused and frowned. "*Bar du Carrousel.* Throughout the week, I had arranged for some of my men to visit L'Amour Sauvage and disrupt Etienne's business while spending very little gold. He is an arrogant man, with no fear of the authorities, and I knew he would not remain in Vampyre for long if his financial affairs were in distress."

The old hit-'em-in-the-pocketbook tactic. It would be an effective strategy to use on Jean as well, although I thought it best not to point that out. The pirate liked his gold.

"Disrupting Etienne's business is not a crime unless your men attracted the attention of humans," I said. For better or worse, a bunch of disheveled French-speaking guys dressed like pirates would attract no attention at all in New Orleans.

"Arson is a crime, however," I added. "Humans inside the bar could have been killed. The fire could have spread to other buildings in the Quarter. The firefighters could have been killed."

"Yet they were not." Jean's gaze on me was steady, as was his emotional temperature. "My men were instructed to ensure that everyone, human and vampire, including Etienne himself, was shepherded safely from the building."

"Still, the fire could have spread. You jeopardized the lives

of the firefighters and the people who work and live in the
adjacent buildings." He'd committed a crime that had involved
humans, although the nagging little voice in the back of my mind
pointed out that he'd risked our discovery less than the debacle
at the parish courthouse.

Jean narrowed his eyes. "Do you judge me, *Jolie*? Etienne
had called himself my friend for almost two centuries, only to
betray and manipulate me in the way he knew would be most
hurtful."

I nodded slowly. I did understand. Jean had once told me he
didn't like being controlled during his human life, and he wouldn't
tolerate it in his immortal life. Etienne had put him under the
control of a necromancer who'd taken away his free will, and
had played him for a fool.

I didn't condone arson, but I understood the urge for revenge.
And I understood that for a man like Jean, who would be dealing
with other pretes for eternity or damned near close to it, he had
to appear strong, decisive, invulnerable. He'd exercised restraint
by sparing Etienne's life and settling for annoyance.

Yet he'd still broken the law. Arson, definitely. Exposure to
humans, possibly. Treason? Or at least treason as the Elders would
define it.

I took a deep breath. "Exactly what is Christof's dog in this
hunt?"

Jean frowned. "Pardon, *Jolie,* but Christof does not possess
un chien. The fae do not like them."

Good to know; I filed that away for future reference. If I
had a home to take it to, I'd visit the Humane Society today and
adopt a mutt as a bit of faery protection. Although I guess Alex
would work. "I meant, why is Christof involved in this at all?"

Jean laughed, and affection for the faery filtered through his
emotional aura. They really were friends and not simply politi-

cal allies, which relieved me. "He has no interest in the vampires beyond the council business, so he was not *involved*, as you say, but for my companionship."

Yeah, as an alibi. Or maybe he was smuggling items into Faery. "Do you have any type of business arrangements with Christof?"

"Bah, women and their questioning nature." Jean paused, answering my question by avoidance. Another tidbit to file away. "Again I must ask, Drusilla. Do you wish to know the truth in this matter?"

No, I wanted to move somewhere warm, where I'd never see another prete and would never be in danger of hibernating. "Just tell me."

"Sabine, the monarch of Faery, is quite old and is childless."

I knew that. "Right, and Christof and the other guy both want to be the grand poobah of all Faery."

Jean stared at me a moment and I waited for him to figure out *grand poobah*. Finally, he grunted and nodded. "*Mais oui.* He and his brother Florian, the Summer Prince, are the eldest of Sabine's family—nephews, perhaps several times removed. Pardon, I am unsure. They both wish to be this *poobah*."

I twirled my finger in the universal symbol for *get on with it*.

"Florian is a foolish and careless *bouffon,* and would be quite unfit for the monarchy, but he curries favor among the others of Faery."

I was beginning to see the picture. "So Christof wants allies on the council who will support him in taking the monarchy if and when Sabine bites it."

Again the confusion. I hadn't realized how often he had to stop and try to interpret my slang. "When Sabine dies," I clarified.

"Ah. *Oui,* just so. I wished to make life uncomfortable for the elves without incurring their wrath, and Christof suggested a brutal winter. It seemed quite clever and hurts no one. The humans who study such things are quite excited. In return, I have promised him the support of the historical beings when he is in need of it, and have promised to attempt to convince others to support him as well."

Uh-huh. "Others like me?"

He shrugged. "You, and the wizards and even the elves. Christof is much more serious of mind than his brother. The support of the council should be his whether I speak on his behalf or not. The problems created by Florian at the last meeting should prove this."

Yeah, Florian hadn't quite seemed the soul of maturity.

We sat in silence for a while before Jean finally spoke again. "Now that you know the truth, Drusilla, there remains the question: What will you do?"

I took a deep breath. I had no idea. Plus we had one more thing to discuss.

Us.

CHAPTER 18

I tried to figure out how to broach the subject of Jean's and my relationship, and like any master procrastinator, decided there was no need to have this conversation now at all. I could play duck-and-run with Zrakovi a good long time and feign ignorance at the council meeting.

That last thought almost stopped my heart. If I were planning to lie to the Interspecies Council and my new First Elder—even by a lie of omission—I had chosen sides already, hadn't I? And if I lied to the council, that meant I had to lie to Alex. I wasn't sure what it said about me that lying to the Elders didn't bother me. Lying to Alex bothered me a lot.

God, shoot me now.

"Will you tell your Elders that I burned Etienne's business establishment, Drusilla?" Jean asked. "Moreover, will you tell your lover?" He put a little spin of disdain on that last word.

Alex, my heart whispered. Alex was the reason this conversation couldn't be postponed, whether I wanted to have it now or not. If I were going to lie to Alex about something this big,

I needed to have a damn good reason, and I needed that reason to be perfectly clear in my mind. Maybe getting things between Jean and me in the open would bring clarity to my muddied, swamp-bogged thoughts.

I didn't love Jean Lafitte—not in a romantic way, no matter how attractive I found him. A little lust was good for the soul, I always said.

I did, however, admire Jean, and I liked him. I liked him a lot. I enjoyed spending time with him. I saw him as a kindred spirit in some warped kind of way; he played by his own rules and had a peace of mind with it that I envied. I wanted him to be happy. I wanted him to be safe.

Which meant I wanted to protect him, as stupid as that sounded considering I was mortal and he was not.

I wasn't sure how to begin this talk, except with the truth. "Jean, if I am going to lie for you, I need to be convinced that you aren't playing me—using me, I mean. I need to know whether I'm a political asset, or a friend, or maybe both—a friend who could come in handy during a political showdown." That was my best guess.

I paused. "I know I'm young." Hell, even Zrakovi was a pup compared to Jean. "I know I can be too trusting. I know I let myself act on impulse too often, and you've done a lot to help me after we got off to such a rocky start."

Jean smiled at that understatement. "Because you deceived me and attempted to harm me, *Jolie*?"

I smiled back. "You got your hits in." Literally.

I couldn't believe I was opening up to Jean like this, but he had trusted me with the truth so far, and I was asking for more. I had to give a little in return. "I'm grateful for all the times you've helped me and I've come to care for you a lot, but I need to know *why* you help me. All the reasons. Why did you sacrifice your-self to keep me safe last month?"

Jean was giving me what I thought of as his too-shrewd look, so I took another deep breath. "Alex and I have been working hard to build our relationship and make it last. I want it to work. If I am going to lie to him, I need to know what I am to you."

There, I said it. My heart pounded so loudly he could prob-ably hear it, and I opened my senses to his, trying to gauge his reaction. I needed to monitor his stress levels and aura to deter-mine his truthfulness. Without my empathic shielding, I was like a lie detector with legs.

Jean was thinking, but not in a scheming way, which would have come across as tension. He was just . . . thinking.

"These questions I will answer, Drusilla, but there are other matters that I would like you to consider also."

I nodded. "That's fair."

"You say that you and Monsieur Warin are working hard to build a relationship—those were the words you spoke. Do you mean that it requires work in order for the two of you to live in peace? That it is a chore, a difficulty?"

"No, but, well, yeah." I mean, weren't all relationships like that? Not that I had a lot of role models, but wasn't that what adults did? They worked through problems in order to strengthen their bonds. Neither Alex nor I were people who opened our hearts easily, so we'd worked hard to get to this point.

Jean got up and poured himself another brandy. He held the decanter up with his brows raised in question.

"No more, thanks." Not yet anyway.

"One more thing I would say before I reveal my own heart." Jean reclaimed his seat on the opposite sofa. "From the words you say, I believe that it is your Alexander to whom you are concerned about telling lies, rather than your Elders. Perhaps you had not realized this thing."

"I realize it." I just wasn't sure how to feel about it.

"Is your concern about lying to Monsieur Warin because you wish to protect him, or because you do not trust him to keep your innermost feelings safe from those who would harm you and those you care about? And is trust not necessary for the success of your *liaison amoureuse,* your relationship, as you call it?"

I needed that brandy after all, and propelled myself off the sofa and straight toward the decanter. My hands shook so badly some of the amber liquid splashed on the top of the bar. Jean had drilled down to the heart of the matter in mere seconds. The issue wasn't how he felt about me. It was all about Alex.

I loved Alexander Warin. There, I'd put words to it, finally. I loved the idea of Alex, and of being with him. I loved the way he smelled, and the way he growled in the morning before his coffee. I loved the way he touched me and made me feel like the most beautiful woman on earth. I loved the way his long lashes rested on his cheeks when he slept. I even loved that he got possessive and overprotective, although he still sold me short most of the time.

I loved Alex, but I didn't trust him to put me first. Because he might love me in return, but I didn't think he was capable of putting love before duty. He wasn't wired that way. Oh, I'd dragged him off course a few times for minor things, but our lives were changing. The foundations of the wizards' place in the prete world stood on quicksand. The stakes rose daily, and if Alex had to decide between supporting me and doing his duty for the Elders, I would either lose or he'd rip himself apart trying to choose, in which case he'd end up hating me for it.

There was the truth of it, in all its knife-edged glory.

Alex would never hurt me deliberately. He would protect

me from physical harm with his life, and I'd do the same for him. But I had to follow my heart, whether it was beating in time with the Elders or not. Whether it was beating in time with Alex's or not.

"I don't know what to say." I looked up at Jean, and felt his sympathy. I didn't want pity. I wanted clarity, damn it. For once, I wanted to see things in black and white.

"Then I shall tell you the truthful answers to the questions you asked, about my own intentions and motivations. They are not so simple."

Somehow, that came as no surprise.

Jean twirled the brandy glass stem between his fingers as he spoke. "Do I find your value as an ally to be an alluring thing? *Mais oui,* Jean Lafitte is not a stupid man. But is that why I help you? Why perhaps I make sacrifices for you? No, Drusilla. If I only needed an ally in politics, there are many ways in which I could achieve such a thing. Gold will buy many allies."

Well, okay. That was probably true. Since he'd begun his navigation work with Zrakovi, he had a lot of contacts, maybe even wizard allies who were a lot less trouble than I. Although, like me, he might not fully trust them.

"Then why?"

He cocked an eyebrow and his cobalt eyes took on a playful sparkle. "If I were to avow that you are my immortal life's great passion, that I would give up immortality itself to be at your side and in your bed, you would not believe me, *n'est-ce pas?*"

I bit my lip to keep from laughing. Damn straight. In fact, had he proclaimed his undying love and devotion, I'd have slapped him for lying to me after all our soul-baring. Even now, thinking about it, I couldn't keep a straight face. I snorted out a burst of laughter. He was so not the Lord Byron type.

Jean laughed with me. "And there is your answer, *Jolie.* I am not the type of man to fall upon his sword for the love of a woman, nor do I want a woman who wishes for such devotion. Yet my feelings for you are matters both complex and serious."

My laughter died. "And those are?"

His face grew solemn. He put his glass down and paced to the window, standing with his back to me. "The world is a bigger and more wondrous place than ever I dreamt as a mortal man." He pulled back the curtains, and over his broad shoulders I could see the heavy fall of Christof's snow piling on the windowsill. "But to live into eternity is a lonely enterprise, Drusilla. I might find companionship with a human woman, but she could never know who or what I am, and I do not wish to live such a lie. I might find companionship among my kind, yet many of their lives exist only due to my memories, and that is shallow company. They offer no surprise."

He turned and looked at me, and his aura radiated genuine affection tempered with something else I couldn't quite put my finger on. Loneliness, maybe. Longing.

"When I see you, *Jolie,* I see a woman who is far more than she realizes but who will someday grow into her powers. One who is much stronger than those who would trap her inside their cages or try to put her to harness. One with a bold intelligence, with whom I can laugh. One who surprises me."

He paused, and when he spoke again, his voice was so soft I had to strain to hear. "I see a woman who makes me feel alive again, like a man, and not like a wraith who has lived beyond his usefulness in a world that no longer needs him."

I didn't even try to stop the tears his words drew from me. Whatever I'd thought he might say, it wasn't this flaying open of his soul, laid bare for me to stomp on.

Jean walked to sit beside me on the sofa, and leaned in close, so that he had only to whisper for me to hear him. "Of course,

Jolie, you would make me feel even more like a man should you throw aside *le petit chien* and allow the famous privateer Jean Lafitte to woo you like a proper suitor. I should like to understand more about the signs on the shirt you wore earlier. What was it: *Eat the tail and suck the head*?"

I blinked up at Jean through tears that dried quickly when I saw the laugh trying to escape his twitching lips. Thank God. If ever a serious moment needed a bit of smarmy relief, it was this one. I had no doubt the things he'd told me were true; I felt the honesty of them. But he'd saved us from diving so deeply into that pool we'd both drown.

I smiled. "It isn't crawfish season yet; I'll show you then." By spring, hopefully he'd forget.

"And now, Drusilla, I must ask for you to be equally honest with me. What is Jean Lafitte to you, and how will you use the information you have been given?"

Good question, and I didn't know the answer. I'd come here to find out how Jean felt, but instead of the clarity I'd hoped for, all it had done was show me what a muddle my own feelings were.

Love and friendship, duty and loyalty. Sorting them out shouldn't be this hard.

"Pardon, *Jolie.* I did not wish to bring you pain." Jean wrapped an arm around my shoulders and pulled me against him. I inhaled the scents of tangy cinnamon and exotic spices and rich tobacco that was unique to Jean. He was solid and warm, and the auras of our affection for each other mingled. But it wasn't romantic love, not what I felt for Alex. Not for either of us. Lust, I could handle.

After a few seconds, he leaned in and kissed my forehead. "You perhaps should return to your room, *Jolie.* You have much to consider. I only ask you this: If you decide you must tell your

Alexander about my involvement with Christof and the burning of L'Amour Sauvage, will you tell me of this decision before
the council meeting? Surely you will allow me adequate time
in which to prepare my defense."

I finished the last sip of brandy, set the glass on the table,
and turned toward Jean. "I won't betray you." Jean Lafitte had
given me a precious gift tonight: his trust. I had to treat it with
respect, however I decided to handle things.

On my way back across the hall to my door, I pulled my
cell phone from my bag and checked the call log. Two more
missed calls from Alex.

It had been a night for revelations, not that they'd proven
helpful. What Jean's eloquent words had done, however, was un-
derscore how much Alex and I needed to sort things out. We
needed to talk calmly, without a looming crisis. That didn't seem
to be possible, so I'd have to settle for whatever I could squeeze
out between now and tomorrow's council meeting.

I didn't listen to the messages but called him instead. He
picked up on the first ring.

"Where the hell are you? Why the hell haven't you taken
my calls? If that goddamned Lafitte has been—"

"Stop it." My tone could cut ice and, to my surprise, he shut
up. After a couple of seconds of silence, I said, "Can I come over?
We need to talk."

"More than you know." He waited a few beats. "You need
a ride?"

"I can take a cab," I said, hoping he'd offer to come anyway.

"Let me come and get you. It's rough out there and my SUV
handles the roads pretty well."

I smiled. Just the fact that he'd offered was enough. "No,
keep the fire lit and the house warm. I'll be there as soon as I
can."

I called the concierge desk to see if any cabs were running, and the über-efficient Monteleone staff person assured me he would conjure a taxi from snow if he had to. Everybody was into drama tonight.

I brushed my hair and put on a touch of makeup. For Alex, I'd at least make an effort to look like I hadn't been crying. I wouldn't go out coatless, though, and I looked at the white plastic bag containing the coat that had cost more than my monthly salary from the Elders. If I wore it to talk to Alex, what would that say about me? That I was choosing my friendship with Jean over my love for Alex? That I was willing to take a bribe?

I decided it would only say that I was a practical wizard with elven blood, who chose not to risk spontaneous hibernation in a taxi. I pulled the tag off the coat and ran my fingers along its buttery leather, then slipped it on. It was a little wide in the shoulders, but otherwise pretty close to a perfect fit. And Jean was right; teal was a good color for me.

By the time I reached the lobby, a yellow Metry Cab sat in front of the door, ready to dash me through the snow to see the man I loved.

Why did I dread it so much?

CHAPTER 19

The three-mile taxi ride took almost forty-five tense minutes. After twenty minutes, with signs of a familiar mental fugue setting in, I asked the driver to please roll up his window.

"What, you don't like da fresh air?"

"Only when it's above thirty degrees."

He grumbled but rolled it up, and slowly my mind came back online.

I tipped him extra when I got out at Alex's. He might have to come back for me in an hour or two, open windows and all. I hoped not. Just in case things went well, I'd gone ahead and set up the transport in my hotel room, powered it up, and left my extra key card under Jean's door, reminding him to pronounce Hebert Hall, our meeting place, as "aye-bear" like a Frenchman and not "hee-bert," or he might end up somewhere in Mississippi.

I went to Alex's front door, glancing catty-corner across the intersection of Nashville and Magazine at Plantasy Island. There was no sign of Rand. A few times during the evening, I'd sensed him trying to make contact, but I definitely didn't want to deal with the elf tonight. The undead pirate, the merman, Truman Capote, and the freaking Faery Prince of Winter were bad enough.

By the time I got out of the cab, Alex had already opened the door and stood waiting, and my heart melted a little. Damn it, I wanted our relationship to work, and I wanted to be loyal to Jean Lafitte, and I wanted to protect Eugenie, and I wanted to be a good sentinel. How was I supposed to accomplish all of that?

He gave me his crooked smile as he moved aside to let me in. "Nice coat. I'm glad to see you got rid of that ugly plaid thing. That's a sexy color for you." As if to prove it, he kissed me, then kissed me again. I should have told him Jean bought me the coat, because it was entirely possible that Jean would mention it himself to annoy Alex, given the chance. Jean might trust me with the truth, but his ability to resist poking at *le petit chien* was another matter.

Then, after another kiss, soft and sweet, Alex turned faster than a starving gator after a piece of rotten chicken. "Where the hell have you been? Why weren't you answering your cell phone?"

I took off my jacket and hung it over the back of one of his dining room chairs, then walked toward the kitchen. I pulled a soda out of the fridge and took my time returning to the living room. He hadn't moved, his body fixed in a wide stance with his arms folded over his chest and his eyes narrowed in suspicion. Sort of piratelike.

I decided on the truth. What a novel concept. "I spent most of the afternoon in bed, trying to recover from spontaneous hibernation."

That hadn't been the answer he expected, obviously, because his face blanked. "What?"

"I tailed Jean Lafitte through the Quarter today, just like

Zrakovi told me to do." I sipped the soda and wished I'd taken the time to make hot chocolate. "Until we'd traipsed all the way to Jackson Square and halfway back to the Monteleone in the cold, I didn't realize that I also had that freaky elven hibernation thing, probably because of the bonding with Rand." I wouldn't mention fainting-goat disease. "I don't go down as quickly as a pure-blooded elf, but if I get cold enough? *Bam.* Hibernation sucks."

God, had the scene with Rand only been last night? No wonder I was exhausted.

Alex grunted like a caveman. "You hibernated?"

I nodded and grinned. "Right on Royal Street in front of God, man, Jean Lafitte, and the Hotel Monteleone bellman. How humiliating is that?"

Alex didn't come close to smiling. "It's not funny, DJ. Although you seem to be okay, and I'm sure Lafitte was happy to ride in and be the hero."

Not taking the bait. I wasn't going to let this be about Jean, at least not unless I had to. "Actually, Rand was the one who tipped me off as to what was happening—you know, through his mental communication thing. But by the time he got through to me, I was down for the count."

Of course it would've been nice if the elf had warned me that our bonding might leave me open to such a thing.

"Are you sure you're okay?" Alex tipped my chin up to look me in the eye, maybe to see if I had dilated pupils or any other sign of hibernation hangover. "I was worried when I couldn't get you. You should put a tracking device on Lafitte; it would make trailing him easier."

I stepped back and stared at Alex. My mouth probably hung open in sheer awe. "That is freaking *brilliant*. Why didn't I think of that?" I was a Green Congress wizard; making charms was my thing. I should have thought of it. Of course, not having a heated space in which to make potions and charms was cramping my style.

"Because you need me." He kissed me again and treated me to a quick flash of that sexy crease at the side of his mouth before it disappeared. "We do need to talk, though."

"Yeah, we do." So much for romance. I followed him to the dining room table and we took chairs facing each other. Before me lay a massive sea of earth tones. Alex was all about subtle colors, from the dark brown hair to eyes the color of dark chocolate to the warm caramel color he'd painted his walls and the pale cream of the molding and woodwork. The only splash of true color in the tidy, comfortable middle room of his classic New Orleans shotgun house was the signed poster of Sir Ian McKellen as Gandalf I'd given him as a housewarming gift.

"I guess while you were hibernating, Lafitte trotted back out to burn down L'Amour Sauvage," Alex said. "Unless you know of an alibi. I'm sure he has one."

I looked up at Sir Ian, his wizard's staff raised above the bridge at Khazad-dûm, making his stand as the Balrog approached. *You shall not pass.* Of course, then the Balrog dragged him off the cliff. Unlike Gandalf the Grey, I didn't think I'd be resurrected as DJ the White.

I planted my feet on the Magazine Street version of Khazad-dûm and held out my imaginary staff, because Charlie was too short to bang on the ground. Then I reconsidered. I had other options. No point in facing the Balrog yet. "Actually, as soon as I woke up and realized what happened, I went to the fire scene and talked to Etienne."

That sentence had the desired effect. Alex sat up straighter, his enforcer face on alert, Jean Lafitte a distant memory. "Boulard is in New Orleans? Why didn't you call me?"

I'm sure we'd get back to the subject of Jean's guilt but for now, Alex was distracted. Score one for the master procrastinator. "I tried. I called the Elders first, but got voice mail."

I waited for that to sink in, but it didn't get the response I'd hoped for. I thought it outrageous that the Elders' hotline even had voice mail.

"Yeah, and?"

"Just as I was calling you, one of Etienne's vampires knocked me over in a puddle of icy sludge, along with a street musician. By the time we got untangled, Etienne was gone."

I left out all the bits about the broken guitar and Etienne's body double. Gone was gone.

This time, Alex did smile. "You've kinda had a rough day."

"Tell me about it." I said a silent prayer for forgiveness. "When I got back to the hotel, Jean was sitting in the Monteleone bar. It looked like he'd been there awhile, and he was with Truman Capote, who'd definitely been drinking awhile."

Alex blinked. Twice. "Truman Capote."

I nodded. "Did you realize his mother was living at the Monteleone when she went into labor with him?"

The muscles in Alex's jaw twitched. One of these days, he'd crack his molars from clenching them together. "So you're telling me Lafitte's alibi is Truman Capote and that as far as you know, he didn't set the fire?"

You shall not pass.

"I'm telling you that by all appearances, Jean was at the Carousel Bar with Truman Capote when the fire took place. I can't say for sure, of course, because I was hibernating."

Alex wanted to roll his eyes; I could see it on his face. "That's the testimony you'll be giving tomorrow morning at the council meeting?"

God help me. "Yeah. I mean, maybe Jean set the fire or maybe he didn't. But innocent until proven otherwise—isn't that the way it goes?"

Alex leaned back in his chair, and we stared at each other for what seemed like a month. Finally, he shook his head and almost smiled. "Okay then, that's the way we'll play it. Nobody was hurt, and it's good to know Boulard is hanging around. I'll put a couple of guys at the bar to see if he comes back. See if I can get my hands on one of those old trackers I used to carry."

"What about the council meeting?"

Alex shook his head. "I'll have to get a subpoena for Truman Capote. That should liven things up."

I tried to imagine Capote testifying, and couldn't. Jean's alibi was his problem, however. I'd done my part. I felt guilty for lying by omission, but not that guilty.

"There's something else we need to talk about," Alex said, and my senses picked up his elevating tension. "Eugenie."

I snorted. "You mean Eugenia? Or would that be Eugenita? Zrakovi can't even remember her name."

"It's not funny." Alex raked a hand through his hair, a sure sign he was stressed.

This was why he'd been calling me, then. My heart began a steadily growing thud that pounded in my ears. Alex usually had better control over his emotions, but he was stressing like mad. "What's happened?"

"Zrakovi had been trying to get in touch with you and, when he couldn't, he finally put it on me to tell you." Alex looked into the living room, then at the light fixture. He wouldn't meet my gaze.

"You're scaring me. What does he want?"

"He wants her to get rid of the baby. Well, he wants you to do it, actually, with a potion that he's authorizing as First Elder. He'd like it done before the meeting tomorrow, but I told him that wasn't possible. I tried to buy you some time." Alex finally looked at me, and I could tell he was miserable, and maybe a little afraid. "I'm sorry, DJ. I think he's wrong, but he's convinced it's the best solution for everyone."

I tried to wrap my mind around the idea that Zrakovi would even think I'd go along with such a plan. "It's not the best solution for Eugenie. She'll never agree to it." Even if she agreed to it, I didn't. I wouldn't make a killing potion for my best friend's unborn child, even if its father was a scheming elf.

Alex cleared his throat. God, there was more.

"What?" My hand gripped the soda bottle so fiercely that I almost knocked it over.

"Zrakovi said if Eugenie didn't agree to it, you were to do it anyway."

A chill that had nothing to do with the Winter Prince of Faery raced across my scalp. "By 'do it,' you mean kill that baby? Using a potion? Without Eugenie's consent?"

"Pretty much."

I searched Alex's face for any sign that he agreed with Zrakovi, but he looked miserable. "Alex, I can't do it. I won't."

He took a deep breath. "I don't like it either, DJ. Eugenie's in way over her head and it's not her fault. But Zrakovi wants Quince Randolph focused on council matters, and Mace Banyan sees the baby as a threat—a new generation of elves with no loyalty to his clan."

My voice was calm, but the rest of me grew angrier by the second. "Did Rand do something to change Zrakovi's mind? I thought we'd all agreed that an elven midwife would take care of Eugenie at her house, and once the baby came, we'd deal with it."

Alex shook his head. "Randolph's insisting that the council give him formal assurances tomorrow that he will get custody of the child. Mace will be livid, so Zrakovi wants it to be a non-issue by then, or at least soon afterward. Of course, it should go without saying that Randolph can't know anything about this."

I fumbled in my pocket for my cell phone. "I want to talk to Zrakovi."

Alex hesitated a few seconds, but then nodded. "He has a new cell number. I'll text it to you. But DJ, it isn't going to change his mind. I really did try."

I had no doubt that he had tried, nor that Zrakovi wouldn't budge. But I wanted to hear the order directly from the First Elder. This wasn't Alex's fight, and he didn't deserve to be stuck as the messenger. In fact, I thought less of Zrakovi for trying to put Alex in the middle.

"Hello, DJ." He'd answered in very short order. "Is it done?"

I gripped the phone hard enough to crush it. "No, and I'd like to talk to you about it, sir." I'd be respectful as long as I could. "I know Eugenie and Rand better than anyone, and they will be able to work this out. We can do damage control with Mace Banyan. There's no need to take this step."

The sound of pouring liquid and rattling ice cubes filled the silence on Zrakovi's end of the call. "This isn't up for discussion," he said, finally. "The full Council of Elders has agreed that it's the best course to take. We must ensure that the alliance of wizards and elves is not threatened, and the presence of this child threatens it." He paused. "It's after ten p.m. I suggest you proceed."

I needed time to think. "This is a direct order? There's no room for discussion?"

"None." Zrakovi's voice was flat. "And it is a direct order. Take care of the child."

"You mean kill the child." I wanted him to say those words.

He barely missed a beat. "Good night, DJ. I'll expect to hear the sad news at tomorrow's council meeting."

I ended the call, but kept staring at the cell phone's screen as if it might offer up some answers.

Alex didn't ask what Zrakovi had said; there was no need. He looked at his watch. "You might be able to get Eugenie tonight; that would be better than putting it off. You can at least broach the subject with her."

"No." I was getting pretty good at using my sharp, icy voice.

Alex thrummed his fingers on the table. "Look, DJ, I know this isn't something you want to do. It's not fair to Eugenie. But it's—"

"It's wrong." I fought to keep my voice steady. "It's not fair to Eugenie, and it's not fair to Rand. It's sure as hell not fair to that baby. And it's not fair to me, damn it. I'll tell Eugenie that this is what the wizard leaders want, but that's as far as I step into it. If she wants to abort her child, I will help her find someone to do it. But it's her decision. Not mine, not yours, not Zrakovi's, not Mace Banyan's. Not even Rand's."

My voice had grown steadily louder, and from my messenger bag on the table, the end of the elven staff shot out a spew of sparks without my touching it. Charlie agreed with me.

Alex raised his voice to match mine. "DJ, I agree with you, but it's out of our hands. This is bigger than us and what we think is right or wrong. What if the fae get their hands on Eugenie and use that baby as a bargaining tool? Or the vampires, or the other elves?" He dropped his voice. I hadn't done a grounding ritual in a while, and I felt his absolute misery. He was torn in half over this. I tried to feel sorry for him, but pity couldn't escape its blanket of anger.

"Alex, I know it's your job to do what the Elders tell you, and I know you take it seriously. I know this is tearing you up

inside." I had to try getting through to him. Like it or not, Zrakovi would listen to Alex before he'd listen to me. "Zrakovi is
probably right that this baby is going to cause problems, but this
isn't the answer. You know it's wrong. Somebody has to stand
up for Eugenie in all of this, and we're all she has."

He closed his eyes. "We can't win this fight, DJ. If we don't
do it, Zrakovi'll find someone else who will. Someone who
doesn't give a damn about Eugenie at all. And who knows, it
might be better for Eugenie in the long run."

I'm a snarky person, I'll admit it. I could be downright cranky.
But true, bone-deep anger? I didn't feel it often, but I recognized
it. My veins heated like fire, and my voice burned with it. Alex
could tell himself that little lie all night long to make himself feel
better, but that wouldn't make it true. "I seriously doubt Eugenie would feel that way."

Alex rubbed his eyes; the strain showed in every movement.
"I repeat: It's going to happen, whether you or I approve or
not. Zrakovi said it himself when I was trying to change his mind;
you aren't the only Green Congress wizard in town. I thought
you'd rather it be you doing it than a stranger."

"I see." I saw far, far too much. I had prayed for clarity, and
now I had it. The thing that finally turned my world black and
white wasn't what I did or didn't tell Alex, or how I did or didn't
feel about Jean Lafitte. It was Eugenie, and our friendship, and
her baby, and my own sense of right and wrong. It was what I
could live with at the end of the day, and what I couldn't.

I pushed my chair back. "I'm sorry you got pulled in the middle of this, Alex. I know you care about Eugenie." Those things
were true; the next part wasn't. I planted my imaginary staff on
the Khazad-dûm of Magazine Street and took my stand against
the Balrog of political bullying. "I better go and talk to her now.
This news is better coming from me."

The relief rolled off Alex thick enough to choke me, but I didn't tell him his trust was misplaced. If he thought about it hard enough, he should realize I would never agree this easily. He was desperate to avoid a conflict, however, and I couldn't blame him.

I hoped he'd forgive me.

"This will take a while, so plan on seeing me at the meeting tomorrow morning. I'll either transport from Eugenie's or be back at the hotel. Is your transport still powered?"

"Sure, I'm good. Zrakovi was in and out a couple of times today." He stopped me halfway across the living room. "Hey, don't I get a good-bye kiss?"

I let him kiss me. I kissed him back like it might be my last chance, and it hurt like a knife wound to my chest. I didn't want to lie to him, to let him think I was supporting him while I turned around and did just the opposite. But I also couldn't put him in the middle. If I asked him to side with me against the Elders, he'd be a wreck no matter what decision he reached. Better to just let him be pissed off at me but at peace in knowing he'd done what he could.

Alex might reach his own crossroads later, but not tonight. Tonight, it was my turn.

I opened the door, and the snow hitting my face camouflaged the tears that had started up again. "I'll see you tomorrow, Alex."

When the troubles would really begin.

CHAPTER 20

I had very little time to make a decision.

Not about the baby. The clarity I'd been seeking all night had shone clearly on that issue. I wasn't doing what they'd asked me to do. Period. What's more, if I could prevent it, Zrakovi's hired Green Congress wizard wouldn't do it either. Eugenie had to be my first priority. Prete politics would come and go, but friends were more important.

So as I fought the wind and snowdrifts to make my way across the vacant lot where I once lived, and across the street to Eugenie's house, my first thoughts were to make her disappear. She could go to Shreveport and visit her sister—if she could get out of New Orleans. Doubtful. Even if Christof called a halt to his winter storm this instant, the airport was closed. The bridges over Lake Pontchartrain were closed. There was no way out of town that wasn't every bit as dangerous as a Green Congress wizard with a toxic potion.

The other quick solution would be getting Eugenie to the Beyond and setting her up in Old Orleans, or even in Barataria.

I didn't want Jean mixed up in this fight, however. He had his own tricky maneuvering to do, and Old Orleans was a wild, lawless border town between the modern world and the Beyond. An overly curious soul like Eugenie, with no experience in the prete world, could get into a heap of trouble very fast.

I'd been dithering on the first step to Eugenie's porch, but now did an about-face and went back down to the sidewalk. I was going about this all wrong. Getting rid of Eugenie wasn't the answer. I needed to go to Rand.

My limbs had already begun to move sluggishly, and I opened my mind wide to my non-husband and yelled: *Rand! Come downstairs and let me in!*

Somehow, he managed to convey a mental wince. *Stop yelling. We need to work on your manners.*

Yeah, well, when I had a spare moment. By the time I made it halfway across Magazine Street, my legs were barely shuffling. If there had been any traffic, I'd be a pancake.

The world turned upside down as I lost my footing. My sluggish thoughts registered how sad it was going to be when I was found either hibernating or frozen in the middle of Magazine Street come daylight. I seemed to still be moving, however, and it took a few seconds to filter through my iceberg of a brain that Rand had hustled out and thrown me over his shoulder.

⁂

Great, let him take care of things. I needed to sleep.

"Dru, wake up." Something hot gushed down my chin, startling me awake. I was stretched out on the sofa in his upstairs sitting room, and Rand sat beside me, holding a mug. He'd been trying to give me hot liquids, I guess, but missed my mouth. I held out my hand and he placed the cup against my palm, hanging on to it until he was sure I had it in a firm grasp.

I sipped, and recognized the taste. Sort of like warm apple juice, but with some elven mojo stirred in to clear my mind. After Tish Newman had been murdered on my porch and Rand found me, he'd given me this same stuff. I needed all the mental help I could get, so I drank the rest of it.

"How long was I out?" We didn't have time for me to waste hibernating.

"Not long. Less than a half hour, I'd say." Rand took the mug and set it on the end table. "It's just before eleven. What were you doing out there?"

I hadn't planned this far. I didn't want to cast Zrakovi as the evil villain. He was not an inherently bad man, just an arrogant politician who thought the ends justified the means. Plus, if Jean's assessment of the preternatural power breakdown proved true, the elves and wizards needed to be allies.

The stakes were high. Rand had to understand that he couldn't bully his way through this one. He had to play it smart and with finesse.

"Just tell me, Dru. You know I can't read your thoughts anymore."

Which was a good reminder that he *could* read Zrakovi's. He'd even done a little mental manipulation on the Elder in the past. I had to be straight with him. Seems like I was being honest with everyone tonight except the man I most needed to be honest with, but I'd think about that later.

"Okay, but you have to promise something first." I gave him my fiercest look.

He smiled, and I thought he was going to make one of his outrageous, suggestive comments. He seemed to think better of it, and the smile faded. "Promise you what?"

"That you are going to be calm. That even though you aren't going to like what I'm about to tell you, you're going to talk it all through with me and not get on your high and mighty 'I am Elf' horse."

He looked a little offended but, after an inner struggle, managed to stay off the horse. "I'll try."

"Okay, I need your help." God, I needed Your help, too.

"You know I'll help you when I can." Translation: *I'll help you if it furthers my agenda.* Rand, I understood very well.

"There are certain people in our world, both mine and yours, who do not want your baby with Eugenie to ever be born."

He'd already started bristling, and I sat up. "I'm serious, Rand. You stay calm and talk this out with me or I will zap you." Thankfully, those responsible for hibernation rescue had, so far, all thought to rescue my messenger bag and staff, including the elf sitting beside me.

"Who doesn't want my baby to be born?"

I hesitated. Thinking about telling him, and actually telling him, were two different matters. But Rand wanted his son.

He grimaced. "You might as well tell me. I can bore into the minds of everyone in that council meeting tomorrow except yours and Mace Banyan's. And I know Mace doesn't give a damn about the baby because whether or not I have an heir doesn't affect him."

I thought he gave Mace way too much credit but, at least in this case, his Synod leader wasn't the problem.

"It's Zrakovi," I said, God help me. "He wanted me to talk Eugenie into letting me abort the baby using my Green Congress magic, or do it without her permission if she didn't agree."

I felt a wide imaginary T for "traitor" etch its way across my forehead. So I talked faster. "You have to understand where he's coming from, Rand. The whole prete world is in chaos, and he's afraid the baby will divide Elfheim and, ultimately, sever the alliance between the wizards and elves." Even I thought that sounded cold and lame.

Rand's inner glow had begun to spread across his face, and heat from his body radiated across the width of a sofa cushion. I still hadn't quite figured out what that did for him other than make him look like a pretty Russian snow prince with a sunburn. It obviously didn't prevent hibernation.

"Do not say a word." I shook a finger at him. "Not. One. Word. You will listen to me."

His jaw was clenched and his nod no more than a nano-dip of his chin, but it was a nod.

"The elves and wizards need each other," I told him. At least this part of my argument was something I believed. "We need our people to be allies, and you and I can make that happen. We don't know who the fae will side with, and the vampires are totally unreliable. We have to be smart about this."

Rand blinked. "I've heard the people of Faery might oppose us, especially if Sabine dies and Florian takes over. He's the Summer Prince, the eldest of Sabine's nephews, but he's a total fruitcake. It would be a disaster. Christof is a fruitcake, too, but Mace thinks he might be more reasonable."

I didn't know whether or not Christof was a fruitcake, but he was scary as frozen hell.

"But if Zrakovi does anything to my child," Rand said, glowing again, "the elves will not align themselves with the wizards, no matter the consequences."

"Are you sure?" I had to make him look at this without his emotions. "Think about it, Rand. Are you so sure Mace would support you with his air clan? Or Betony and the earth elves? Or Lily's daughter with the water elves? Without the full Synod behind you, you can't speak for the elves."

Rand pondered this while he made more mugs of apple stuff.

"The question is, why does Zrakovi care about my son? This baby has no bearing on council business."

Maybe. Maybe not. "He's thinking of it as an insurance policy," I said, sipping the warm, fizzy juice. "If there's no baby, then Mace doesn't worry about a new generation of non-air elves taking over. If there's no baby, that's one less thing the vampires could use as leverage to sway your support over to them, or force you to betray the Elders. Or the Fae. Zrakovi thinks the baby makes you vulnerable to blackmail."

Rand's glow settled back to normal. He seemed to be calm and thinking. Yay for apple stuff. "Then I shall kill Zrakovi."

I mentally pulled out a few hanks of hair, both mine and his. So much for clear thinking. "No, you will not kill Zrakovi. I don't know who would move into his spot, but it might be someone worse. We just have to outsmart him for tomorrow's meeting. We're intelligent people; we can do that."

The trick would be to thwart Zrakovi's plans without him realizing he'd been manipulated.

"I could touch him somehow, maybe help him off with his coat," Rand said. "If I could touch him, I could suggest a counter-notion."

I nodded. "Like how the baby would actually be valuable in bringing our people together. Your son would strengthen the elven-wizard alliance."

He shot a cagey look my way. "Because you and I would be raising it together in an elven-wizard household?"

"If that helps you get through the day, you can make that mental suggestion to Zrakovi."

He smiled, the arrogant oaf. "You'll come around."

Not before the child reached the age of consent, whatever that was in Elfheim. I wasn't sure where my relationship with Alex was headed, or if we'd even have one after tomorrow, depending on how things went and how suspicious he was feeling. But whether or not I stayed with Alex had no bearing on my relationship with Quince Randolph. We could coexist but we would never, ever, ever cohabit.

"Okay, that's Plan A. Can you influence Zrakovi's thoughts without Mace Banyan realizing it?" Otherwise, there was no point.

Rand chewed on his lower lip as he thought. "Probably not. His magic is strong, so I'd need some distance from him."

I doubted the attic conference room of Hebert Hall was anywhere near the size of the district court building fourth floor. "You might not be able to get that far away from him, so let's come up with some other options."

We sat in silence for a long time, staring at the fire popping and crackling in Rand's fireplace. The last time I'd been up here, on the second floor of the Plantasy Island nursery, I'd been half crazed and trying to escape the undead Axeman of New Orleans. It had been a dark and bloody business during which Rand's mother had been killed.

I stayed so annoyed with him most of the time, I'd been as insensitive and self-absorbed as I accused him of being. "How are you doing?" I asked him. "I'm sure you miss Vervain."

His eyes widened in surprise, then crinkled as he gave me the real smile. The sweet one I'd seen when he first felt of Eugenie's tummy and realized he had a son. "I do miss her." He stared into the fire. "It's one of the reasons I decided to stay here in New Orleans despite the weather, instead of going back to Elfheim. The house is full of memories of my father and of her."

I knew how that felt. It was why, even though Alex and Jake had worked hard to make Gerry's house in Lakeview habitable except for the lack of heat, I had trouble staying there. The bones of the house remained the same. The quality of the air. The ghosts of memory were always around.

"Why don't you build yourself a new house in Elfheim? One that's just yours alone? You can make new memories. I mean, it would be a place for your son to build his memories as he's growing up." I didn't know that the kid would live in Elfheim; maybe he would, or maybe not. That was for Rand and Eugenie to work out, with me as referee if necessary. But he'd certainly need a home there.

The smile again. "That's a great idea. I've been so focused on making sure Eugenie didn't do anything stupid, I haven't made plans."

I shrugged. "There's plenty of time for that."

Rand gave me a sidelong glance. "You're being awfully nice, Dru. Are you up to something?"

I laughed. "Nothing I haven't shared with you. It's just that you're actually listening to me and I'm listening to you. It's called a conversation. We need to try it more often."

He sighed. "Yeah, after we figure out Plans B and C."

CHAPTER 21

I looked at my bloodshot eyes in the mirror of Rand's bathroom. We'd strategized until almost dawn, and had come up with a Plan B so beautiful in its simplicity that it had supplanted Plan A. No point in tipping off Mace Banyan and risk Rand getting caught doing secret mental manipulation on the man who'd probably become the permanent First Elder.

The downside? With this plan, Zrakovi would know he'd been played. The plan was to make Rand the player, not me, and the elf had promised to keep me out of it. If he didn't, I was so angry over Eugenie's intended treatment that I was almost beyond caring.

Almost.

Every one of the seventy-two hours since I'd enjoyed even a semi-restful sleep showed in the dark circles under my eyes. If I were a faery, I'd be able to put on a new face in an instant and wouldn't hesitate. Handy skill, that one. Plus, as Jean would be quick to point out, I'd been wearing the same black sweater as when I went off to investigate the burning of L'Amour Sauvage what seemed like a month ago.

Rand stood in the bathroom door behind me, looking perfectly rested and perfectly perfect, damn him.

I turned to him. "You got anything I could wear that doesn't, well, look like I borrowed it from you?" No way I could rock the whole tall Russian snow prince thing.

"Some of Vervain's clothes are still in the closet of the spare bedroom. She brought them with her when she fled Elfheim." I appreciated him not saying *when she fled Elfheim because we'd bonded and she knew Mace Banyan would punish her for it.*

Rand pulled a ring of keys from his pocket and I followed him into the hallway, where he unlocked the door to the middle bedroom. "I rarely go in here since . . . since it happened."

Oh man, I hated to wear a dead elven clan chief's clothes, especially those belonging to the woman who'd given birth to Rand. "Never mind, this will be fine. Black is versatile." I discreetly pulled the neck of the sweater away from my body and sniffed. Other than a bit of brandy, magical elven apple stuff, and smoke, it smelled fresh from the dryer.

"Don't be silly. I don't mind if you wear her clothes. I'd actually forgotten they were here."

I followed him into the room. The last time I'd been here, only a month ago although it seemed like years, the room had been filled with antique furniture and pretty earth-tone accents—all with a heavy coating of blood. Some mine, some Rand's, some the Axeman's, but a lot of it Vervain's. Now the room lay empty but for a set of gold drapes that hung over the window. A splash of brown stained the bottom of one side. Dried blood.

I swallowed hard to get the images out of my head; I could see why Rand didn't come in here. "Why do you keep it locked?"

He'd opened the closet door and had returned to stand in the hallway just outside the room. "It's stupid, I guess, but it helps me pretend it's not here. Would you lock it back when you leave?" Without waiting for an answer, he hung a right toward what I assumed was his bedroom and disappeared.

Rand better be careful or I might start liking him. I doubted he could go twenty-four hours without pissing me off or making a mess I had to fix, however, so I wouldn't worry about it.

I stared in the closet at the filmy, gauzy, tie-dyed, earth mother smattering of clothes hanging inside. Rand apparently came by his crunchy-granola hippie persona honestly. There wasn't a pair of pants or top to be seen, but only dresses. Hadn't the woman gotten tired of shaving her legs? Didn't she want to have an occasional stubbly-leg and socks day?

One dress after another, I pulled out and rejected. One looked like Jerry Garcia's grandmother should be wearing it to a costume party. Another was so sheer and low cut, I wouldn't be caught hibernating in it—although it might create a diversion at the council meeting. Another would out-bling Her Royal Highness Sabine, which she'd probably resent. The only dog I had available to sic on her, Alex, would likely not be speaking to me after this morning.

I finally settled on an ankle-length dress with a burgundy and gold print skirt below an empire waist of gold brocade. The bodice of black velvet was trimmed at the neck and cuffs with burgundy lace. Vervain had been an inch or two shorter than me, so with my sturdy black slouch boots with the silver buckles and a flash of bare leg showing between the boots and the dress, I looked like I should be taking the stage at an Alien Sex Fiend concert. I needed more black eyeliner to complete my undead goth look. At least I'd managed to shave my legs in recent memory.

Oh well, it was far short of my new standard for humiliation—hibernating on Royal Street in broad daylight—so I'd make the best of it.

I locked the door behind me when I went back into the hallway. I stuck my head in the sitting room, but didn't see Rand, so I knocked at the door to his bedroom. A muffled "c'mon in" sounded from inside.

This room, I'd never visited, and I had to admit I was curious. Rand was in the bathroom, so I took an opportunity to snoop.

The bedroom of the Tân clan chief was surprisingly normal, without a stitch of tie-dye in sight. A four-poster king-size bed with heavy posts of what looked like birch matched a heavy chest of drawers. There were lots and lots of textiles—hanging on the walls, layered on the floors, and covering the furniture, all in pale, pale tones of blue and white with an occasional dash of copper or gold. Russian snow prince colors, same as those Rand wore.

The only things of real interest hung from the ceiling near the head of the bed and adjacent wall.

Over the bed dangled something that looked like an ornate dream catcher, only instead of leather or rope, it was woven of copper wire, and the feathers hanging from it were encrusted with blue gemstones. In the center of the dream catcher circle, an orange stone was suspended. It appeared to have a live flame flickering inside it.

On the wall beside the bed hung a large shield of tooled leather. It looked ancient. The background was the same rich blue as the dream catcher gemstones, but layered on top of it, in worn leather, was a dragon the size of a breadbox, his wings outstretched, an orange leather flame erupting from his open mouth. Tiny white claws of carved bone, or so it appeared, stretched from his fore and hind feet.

"That's my clan's ceremonial shield." Rand's voice came from behind me, and I jumped, startled. When I turned, he took in my outfit and laughed. "I can't wait to see the reaction you'll get from your shifter, but I like it. Funky suits you."

I suspected funky didn't suit me at all, but I was stuck with it for now. "What's the significance of the dragon?" I asked, turning back to the shield.

"It's our symbol, I guess you'd call it. There aren't as many dragons in Elfheim as there used to be, but those that still live in the hills answer to the Tân."

I turned to stare at him. "You mean there are dragons? Real dragons?" Why didn't I know there were dragons?

"Of course." He said it as if I were an idiot for asking.

I pointed to the suspended copper structure. "What about the dream catcher? The fire in the stone looks alive."

"It is." He touched a finger to one of the jeweled feathers, and the fire inside the center stone leapt outside the confines of its metal setting. "It strengthens my dreamwalking skills as I sleep. It was my mother's. The dream catcher and the shield are the only things of my parents I brought here."

There was so much about the elves I didn't know or understand. Before he'd become besotted by Terri the vampire and let himself be manipulated into getting fangs, courtesy of his own father, Adrian Hoffman had been giving me lessons in elven history. I wished I'd taken them more seriously.

Speaking of which. "Have you heard anything about Adrian?" As annoying as I found the man, I couldn't help but feel sorry for him. He'd betrayed me, but he'd been played big-time by his father and Garrett Melnick. And now he was forced to hide out with them or be arrested by the Elders for whom he once worked.

"No, and I can't believe you'd care." Rand gave a dismissive wave. "Good riddance. Hope he enjoys life as a vampire."

Now there was the Rand I knew and despised.

"Do you have a transport that goes somewhere besides Elfheim, or do I need to make one?"

He leaned against the bedroom door. "Could you redo the transport in the greenhouse so it can go anywhere? It still goes only to Elfheim."

"I think so. Is that the one you call Rivendell?"

He smiled. "It is."

"Okay, let's check it out." If he'd transported into it from Eugenie's, he should be able to transport out with a quick reset.

We went down the narrow stairwell that opened into the front part of the Plantasy Island retail area. The cash register sat on a wooden counter, and every inch of wall space sported some type of outdoor doodad: garden gnomes in colorful outfits, flags, faux-classical statuary, ceramic birdbaths. "Don't you get tired of all this cuteness?"

"Yeah, but humans love it." Rand straightened a couple of oversize verdigris-painted metal frogs. "And when people come in to buy this junk, it gives me a chance to talk to them about plants and how to take care of them."

We walked through the wide door behind the counter, and the chill of the greenhouse went straight through my hippie dress. I'd been carrying my lambskin jacket, but pulled it on. Who the hell cared if it matched? It still beat the orange and purple nightmare I'd been wearing.

Rand fingered the soft leather. "You should've gone with imitation. It's more environmentally responsible and nothing had to die to make it."

Nice way to make me feel like a selfish lamb-murderess. "You do remember your promise to be considerate and sensitive to people's feelings today, right?"

"Of course."

Good grief. Things could go south so very easily.

"Is the transport still in the gazebo?" I eyed the confection of white-painted gingerbread trim with wariness. Rand had kidnapped me in this freaking transport, after which his Synod—including his mother—had inflicted mental torture on me I could only liken to rape. It had been physical and visceral and painful. Rand hadn't known that was going to happen, but I still blamed him for taking me against my will. And I'd never, ever forgive Mace Banyan, who engineered it.

"I'm sorry." Rand touched the delicate bloom of an orchid. "About the part I played in what happened to you."

"It's done." I knelt and touched a hand to the transport etched lightly into the floor of the gazebo. The magic still tingled but had weakened. "Could you bring my bag from the front counter?"

Once Rand retrieved the bag, I took out my portable potions kit and blended a bit of anise and clove in a solution of holy water, injecting just enough of my native physical magic to activate it. I spread it over the existing transport, waited a few moments, then touched my hand to the transport again. All traces of its magic had disappeared. Convenient thing, that deactivation potion.

Next, I recoated the transport symbols with iron shavings, touched the corners with dots of mercury, and used Charlie to inject a bigger dose of magic into the redrawn transport.

"This one should last awhile and take you to any other transport, as long as it's open." I looked up at him. "I deactivated the one at Eugenie's house so don't get any bright ideas."

He quirked up the edge of his mouth in an approximation of a smile, but didn't say anything. I'd have felt better with an *Of course I won't try to see the woman who's carrying my child, Dru,* but I probably wouldn't have believed him anyway.

I checked my cell phone. "Council meeting starts in half an hour. You ready to give the greatest elven performance of the ages?"

"I will dazzle them all with my earnest and heartfelt words," he said. "Although I still think it would be easier and faster to just kill Zrakovi."

It was going to be a long, long day.

CHAPTER 22

Within seconds, Rand and I arrived at the third floor attic space of F. Edward Hebert Hall, located near the front side of the Tulane University campus. Home to the history department, the late nineteenth-century yellow-brick building smelled of books, polished wood, and rarefied academic types.

I hadn't been here since my undergraduate days, when I'd dragged myself across the quad with my fellow chemistry majors, all unsuspecting humans, to do our prerequisite time in humanities hell. I'd developed an interest in history I hadn't expected, especially Louisiana history.

The transport had been drawn in a heavy chalk line outside an elevator that looked odd. I had to study it a moment to realize it had no up or down buttons. The handiwork of the Blue Congress team, I was sure. No prowling PhDs would be wandering up to the third floor of Hebert Hall today.

"Well, isn't this interesting?" The soft Mississippi drawl of Jake Warin came from behind me as soon as we arrived in the attic hallway, where he leaned against the wall in a discreet alcove just made for a security lookout. "You're keeping strange company these days, sunshine."

I glanced at Rand, who shrugged and walked down the hall without a word.

"It's a long story," I told Jake.

"Anything I need to be concerned about? Or should I say, is it anything my boss should be concerned about? And that's a pretty cool outfit, by the way. It suits you."

"Right." He didn't sound sarcastic, so maybe my inner goth girl had some appeal. What I found more interesting was that he didn't ask if my appearance with Rand was anything his cousin Alex should be concerned about. He did jobs for Alex on behalf of the Elders, but his real boss was Jean Lafitte.

"Nope. Jean only needs to be concerned with Truman Capote today." Because I had no doubt Alex had gotten the undead author subpoenaed last night before I'd been gone five minutes. My role here today was to testify about Jean's role in the fire, which meant I had to admit to publicly hibernating and then finding him in the bar. Nothing said "competent sentinel" like admitting you'd hibernated through a preternatural crime. "Is the star witness here yet?"

He shook his head. "No, and that is going to be one interesting testimony. If it goes bad, you better duck. I'll be helping our friend shoot his way out." His voice was soft.

Jake had no problem with clarity. His loyalty went to Jean, and never mind that Alex was his cousin or that the Elders had paid for his rehab and training after the loup-garou attack. In a lot of ways, Jean had saved Jake and given his life back to him.

"I met Collette," I said. "I really like her, and she's, like, seriously gorgeous."

He grinned, and those dimples made me smile in return. "That she is." He paused. "No hard feelings with us?"

"Nada." Finally, Jake and I could be friends, roles for which we were better suited.

After wishing him luck with the boss and hoping no shots would be fired this morning, I wandered around the hallway that formed a U shape before opening onto a large meeting space. It couldn't be more different than the courthouse room patterned after the Supreme Court. This one appeared to have been patterned after early industrial warehouse.

The overhead ductwork was exposed and wrapped in foil-covered insulation, which matched the room dividers of corrugated aluminum. Long tables were arranged in a square, and the name placards looked as if they'd been hastily scratched out on cardstock using a black Sharpie on the verge of running out of ink.

Every seat had a placard and a microphone, so I wandered around looking for my name. I'd been placed between "Florian, Faery Prince of Summer" and "Special Guest Truman Capote."

Awesome. Talk about an odd couple.

I spotted Alex directly across the room, talking to Zrakovi. Make that listening to Zrakovi. Even they were less formal than before. Alex wore a simple black sweater and pants, and Zrakovi a dark gray suit and striped tie. No robes or fake glasses today.

Jean arrived with Jake trailing a few steps behind. Ostensibly, he was working security for the Elders, but Jake took a place along the wall behind Jean's seat. The pirate scanned the room, paused long enough to give me a small nod, and turned his gaze to Christof, who'd taken the seat on the other side of the one reserved for Florian. They exchanged a long look.

What were those two hatching? I knew Jean well enough that shooting his way out of the meeting would be a last resort; it would close off too many of his options. He'd scheme his way out first, and I'd wager the cost of my blue sacrificial-lamb coat that he and Christof had their own plans A, B, and C.

"Oh good, I asked to sit by the prettiest wizard in the room."

I was glad I'd learned about the whole faery appearance-changing skill, or I wouldn't have recognized the black-leather-clad, rooster-haired punk rocker who slid into the seat next to me. "Thank you, Prince Florian, but I am the only female wizard in the room and the only wizard of any gender in the room under sixty."

He laughed, a grating, tinkling timbre that reminded me of his husky-voiced aunt Sabine. It made my skin crawl. I met the gaze of his brother, who was back in the short dark hair of the first council meeting. He nodded a greeting, and I wondered if this were his real face and hair. How would one ever know?

Faeries were creepy.

Alex left the room abruptly, and I tracked his progress down the hall until my attention was diverted by a pair of blue-gray eyes boring holes in me from the seat next to the one marked for Zrakovi. I squinted to read the print on his name placard, and my heart sped up. Holy crap. With all the drama, I'd forgotten Lennox St. Simon would be here.

We rose from our seats at the same time and kept our eyes on each other as we walked toward the center of the room, inside the square of tables.

He had Gerry's eyes. In fact, he looked a lot like Gerry, except his hair was shorter and still dark whereas Gerry's had turned silver by the time he died.

We stopped and fidgeted through an awkward few seconds before he finally spoke. "My God, you look just like your mother." His voice was deeper than Gerry's, but the accent was the same. Gerry had lived in New Orleans since about the time I was born, but he'd never lost his British accent.

I smiled. "I didn't realize you knew her. You and Gerry look a lot alike as well."

"Now." He laughed a little. "Not so much when we were younger. I suppose you know that your father and I . . ." He looked away. "This is bloody awkward, isn't it?"

Very. "It's okay. I know you didn't get along. Gerry had that effect on a lot of people. And I didn't know about you either." I laughed. "I didn't even know Gerry was my father until he died." Just before, but there was no point in going into that sad tale if he hadn't already heard it.

"I'd like us to get acquainted. My daughter, Audrey, is about your age. Perhaps you could be a good influence on her."

I coughed to choke off the guffaw that threatened to escape. No one in my life—ever—had expressed hopes that I might be a good influence on anyone or anything. Audrey must be pathetic. "I can't wait to meet her. I was excited to learn I had a cousin."

He smiled, and he looked so much like Gerry it made my heart ache and tears build up behind my eyes.

Until Lennox looked over my shoulder and mumbled, "What the bloody hell is that?"

I turned and saw Alex coming back down the hallway from the transport. At his side, moving with a bouncing gait, strode a short, slight man wearing orange-tinted glasses and a dark suit. Without his fedora of last night, Truman Capote's blond hair hung lank and thin, but his face still had the impish look he'd had even in his older years. A fluorescent purple scarf was draped around his neck. I suspected Truman might have enjoyed my ugly coat that was now probably resting inside a Dumpster behind the Monteleone.

Once they got in the room and Alex retreated to his corner to stand guard, Truman gave him an exaggerated wink, which brought a smile to my face. Alex blushed and looked uncomfortable. Teasing him about the flirtations of an openly gay man who was a member of the historical undead would be a great way to annoy Alex. After today, however, I wasn't sure how we'd ever get back to the teasing stage.

"I believe he's been asked to testify today," I told Lennox, who'd continued to track Truman's progress through the room. "He's a member of the historical undead, Truman Capote, the author. He wrote *Breakfast at Tiffany's* and *In Cold Blood*."

"Ah, right. I believe I saw them on the telly." Perhaps Lennox didn't share Gerry's love of books and arcane bits of knowledge. Gerry hadn't even owned a telly until I badgered him for one as a teenager.

We made hasty promises to stay in touch, and I returned to my seat.

"Hi, Truman, you're sitting next to me," I said, pulling out his chair. I figured after he'd asked me to suck on his cherry, we should be on a first-name basis. "Sorry you got dragged into this."

"Pish-tosh." His pupils were the size of pennies behind those glasses, and he smelled of gin. Not a good state for a star witness. "I have often been skewered by Johnny Carson on national television," he said. "So what the hell're the wizards going to do, kill me?"

He gave a broad smile to Christof before leaning over me to focus his attention on Florian. "Are you one of the Rolling Stones? I did so enjoy your early music. Even kept up with it after my human death, at least until the disco era. *Emotional Rescue* was such a mistake."

He turned to me and spoke in a stage whisper. "Why did one of the Rolling Stones make it onto your council and I wasn't even asked?"

I'd witnessed the entire exchange with openmouthed amazement, and it occurred to me that I had no business attending these council meetings, sentinel or not. I wasn't weird enough.

Florian leaned over. "What is the significance of a rolling stone? Does it have something to do with gathering moss?"

Thankfully, I was spared from answering by Zrakovi calling the meeting to order, then having to pause for the arrival of a red-haired bombshell poured into a low-cut leopard-skin dress. Only once she got closer, I saw it was a very ancient bombshell whose caked makeup looked more Bette Davis horror movie than glamour queen. Baby Jane had made her entrance. Florian sniggered; Christof looked annoyed.

"Yes, well, thanks to all of you for attending on such short notice," Zrakovi said. He introduced himself as the acting First Elder, explained that a warrant had been issued for the arrests of Geoffrey Hoffman, Adrian Hoffman, Etienne Boulard, and Garrett Melnick—and therefore there was currently no vampire representation on the council.

My eyes almost crossed out of boredom as a motion was solicited and approved and voted on to banish the Realm of Vampyre from representation on the Interspecies Council until matters could be resolved.

During all the ayes and seconds and motions, I slouched down in my seat and tried to keep my eyes open. Holy crap, but I was tired, and Zrakovi spoke in a droning monotone that did nothing to wake me up.

"Now, to new business." Mr. Monotone speared me with a decidedly unfriendly look. "Although I mentioned a warrant for the arrest of Etienne Boulard, we still must discuss the matter of the burning of his Wild Love club."

Guess it took too much effort to get the name of L'Amour Sauvage right, much like the name of my friend Eugenie. Or he considered neither of them important enough to care about.

"As it is well known that one of our council representatives, Captain Jean Lafitte, had recently threatened Mr. Boulard, we feel it is necessary for the continued integrity of this council to ask Mr. Lafitte to testify as to his whereabouts when the incident occurred."

Jean gave Zrakovi a small smile. "Pardon, Monsieur Zrakovi, but I know not of the incident to which you refer. Do you mean there was a fire? I hope my former colleague Etienne was not injured."

Zrakovi blinked at him, and I leaned back. This part of the meeting could prove entertaining. Zrakovi was a smart man; he couldn't have reached his level in the wizarding hierarchy without a certain degree of savvy. But he was no intellectual match for the scheming mind of Jean Lafitte.

"No, he wasn't injured," Zrakovi said slowly. He was already losing ground, and he knew it. "Could you tell us where you were during the hours of two and seven last evening?"

Jean nodded. "There is a lovely drinking establishment within the Hotel Monteleone on Royal Street, where I reside in the rooms of Eudora Welty when I am in *Nouvelle-Orléans*. I have found *Le Bar du Carrousel* quite an enjoyable means of passing the time of an evening."

I bit my lip hard enough to draw a bead of salty blood on my tongue. Jean could turn on the flowery bullshit better than anyone I'd ever met, and from the stunned expression on Zrakovi's face, this was the first time he'd experienced the brunt of it.

"Yes, but Captain Lafitte, were you—"

"When I learned that my dear friend Truman Capote had come to the city of his birth to witness its beauty in this rare snowfall, I was quite pleased to introduce him to the pleasures to be found at the *Carrousel*."

Zrakovi blinked again, and Jean settled back in his chair with a smirk much like the one my former cat Sebastian got when he'd cadged part of my dinner from under my very nose.

The acting First Elder cleared his throat. "Yes, well. Mr. Capote, can you confirm that you were with Captain Lafitte during this entire period?"

"Why, of course I can." Capote leaned forward, his high-pitched voice singsonging into his microphone. "I was telling him about how I used to boast that I was born in the Hotel Monteleone but, really, I was born in Charity Hospital . . ."

And on and on he went. Zrakovi's eyebrows got lower and lower until they were in danger of meeting his mouth, bypassing his nose altogether. "Thank you, Mr. Capote," he finally interrupted during a diatribe about the treachery of Gore Vidal that, as near as I could follow, was apropos to nothing. "You're free to leave."

"Not quite yet."

Everyone sought the source of the interruption, but I'd recognize that silky, suave, evil voice anywhere. Mace Banyan, seated on the other side of Sabine and across the room from Rand, leaned forward. The leader of the Elven Synod hated Jean, and the feeling was mutual. I'd been so sidetracked with the Eugenie situation that Mace's interference with Jean hadn't occurred to me.

"I believe we know that, in his human life, Mr. Capote was far from stable, and that he was notorious for telling untruths. Do you deny that, sir?"

Capote reddened. "A bit of embellishment is an author's privilege. You are a friend of that damnable Gore Vidal—"

"And from your nonsensical ramblings today, it is clear that you're either still quite unstable or else have been coached in the art of obfuscation by the most eloquent Captain Lafitte."

Mace was performing the classic exercise of destroying witness credibility. Unfortunately, he had plenty of fodder where Truman was concerned.

"This wizard was there," the author sputtered, jabbing me in the side with his elbow. "She wore a salacious sweatshirt and sucked the stem off my cherry."

I closed my eyes and tried to will myself to disappear. It didn't work. When I opened my eyes, everyone in the room was staring at me except Sabine, who was examining her zebra-patterned nails.

"Really." Mace turned beady brown eyes on me. "Then perhaps we should hear from our sentinel, who is duty-bound to tell the truth to her own Elders."

Freaking elf.

CHAPTER 23

The familiar sweep of déjà vu hit me, except at least this time I didn't have to sit alone at a table in front of an interspecies firing squad. Zrakovi sitting directly across the room from me was bad enough, and I had to drag my gaze away from Alex, standing directly behind him like a big old statue.

I took a second to collect my thoughts. "Of course, I'd be happy to answer your questions," I told Zrakovi, and mentally prepared myself to spend the next four or five minutes lying through my teeth. I would stick with the story I'd fed Alex. It was safe because it had enough of the truth in it to keep me from tripping up.

As per my assignment, I said, I had followed Jean Lafitte on his stroll through the French Quarter. I had trailed him all the way to Jackson Square, where he looked around a few minutes and then threw a snowball at Andrew Jackson's head before walking back up Royal Street. As I followed him along his return route toward the hotel, I became overwhelmed with what I later learned was ESS, elven survival syndrome.

Zrakovi interrupted. "And ESS is what, exactly?"

I'd hoped he either already knew, or wouldn't ask, although I could understand why elves didn't advertise the fact that cold weather virtually incapacitated them.

"If I get too cold, I go into spontaneous hibernation," I said through gritted teeth, daring him to comment. I didn't look at Rand, but I could hear him inside my head, laughing at my embarrassment like it wasn't his fault. Until I bonded with him, I'd gone twenty-eight years without hibernating. "It's an elf thing," I added, just to clarify.

I took Zrakovi's blank stare as permission to continue, but addressed the rest of my testimony to Mace Banyan.

I'd awakened a short time later to hear sirens, had gone downstairs, and had found Jean Lafitte in the Carousel Bar with Truman Capote. The men appeared to have been drinking for some time.

I saw on the TV behind the bar that the fire was at L'Amour Sauvage, so I walked over to Chartres Street to see if I could tell whether or not the blaze had a preternatural cause. There, I spoke to Etienne Boulard, who escaped before I could arrest him, and the Sauvage host, Marcus, who opined that the heating system had shorted out.

I saw no evidence that Jean Lafitte had been there and no proof of foul play, so I returned to the hotel, where he and Mr. Capote were still drinking. I joined them, although the cherry from Mr. Capote's cocktail went nowhere near my mouth.

I had to nip that notion right in the cherry pit.

Zrakovi didn't look happy with my testimony, but everything I'd said was true. I simply changed the order of events and left out a few details. I saw no reason to get Rene involved in this mess, nor to mention being duped by an Etienne look-alike.

"Obviously, she's covering for her *good friend* Jean Lafitte,"

Mace said. "She has been known to frequent his pirate den in Old Barataria. I myself have seen her there, wearing a scanty costume and consuming alcohol early in the morning."

Actually, I'd been wearing a fine early-nineteenth-century gown, and hadn't really been drinking. He was angry that I'd thrown a heavy cut-glass brandy decanter at his head—and hit the bull's-eye. "I only threw the brandy at you because you'd kidnapped and tortured me, you elven snake."

"Please." Zrakovi held up a hand. "Does anyone else have new information we should consider before concluding this matter?"

The sound of a chair scraping across the tiled floor sounded preternaturally loud. "Yes, Elder Zrakovi, I would like to add to the testimony."

God, what a zoo. I looked around for the source of this interruption just as Christof stood. "I too was with Captain Lafitte." He turned and gave me a stiff, formal bow. "Sentinel Jaco, I appreciate your honoring my request to keep my presence quiet, but this farce has gone on long enough. It's clearly a witch hunt."

Holy crap. Christof was pissed. I knew this not by his chilly words but because the temperature in the room had dropped at least ten degrees in a matter of seconds. I sure hoped nobody figured out it was caused by the anger of the Faery Prince of Winter and made the leap to New Orleans' suddenly arctic weather, from which a leap to Jean and then to me was an easy journey.

Zrakovi recovered with some difficulty if his sudden coughing fit was any indication. "Your highness, you were with Captain Lafitte at the time of the fire?"

Christof nodded. "Quite by accident, of course. I had decided to visit the city to see if I could be of help in my official capacity as the Winter Prince." He shook his head. "Such suffering in a place unaccustomed to these types of weather patterns. I'm happy to report that I should be able to relieve the problem and move this weather system away shortly."

"That's . . . wonderful news, I'm sure." Confusion wafted off Zrakovi's aura like toxic smoke. I fingered the amulet containing my little traveling mojo bag to control the antlike tickle as it washed across my skin from clear across the room. He was desperate to seize control of the meeting again. "And you ran into Captain Lafitte?"

Christof laughed, and it transformed his face into something playful and handsome instead of its usual hard planes. Of course, who knew if it was real or illusion?

"As you know, the fae are quite fond of carnivals and circuses and carousels, and I had heard of the famed Carousel Bar." He ducked his head and raised his shoulders to accompany his winsome little oh-aren't-I-a-silly-faery smile. "When I arrived to see it, there sat Captain Lafitte and Mr. Capote. They graciously invited me to join them. Ms. Jaco arrived some time later, and I asked that she keep my presence quiet."

Mace Banyan made a rude, scoffing noise. "Why would you care?"

Another friendly gosh-darn shrug from Christof. "Ah, our monarch, Her Highness Queen Sabine, does not approve of her people, especially the princes and princesses of Faery, consorting in the human world." He bowed his head and turned toward the woman in question, who looked like an ancient, slutty version of Ginger from the *Gilligan's Island* reruns. "Your highness, I beg your forgiveness, but I felt it unfair to see an innocent man wrongly accused."

Sabine held out her hand, and he kissed her oversize ring. I thought I might barf. "We shall speak of this later, Christof," she said in her husky, dry, cornsilk-rustling, creepy voice.

Jean stood up. "I believe this assembly owes Jean Lafitte an apology for pursuing what is clearly a personal vendetta on the part of Monsieur Banyan. I am most disappointed, Monsieur Zrakovi, that you should have been forced to behave thusly."

Oh, brother. Only Jean could pull a monstrous scam on the entire Interspecies Council and then demand an apology because they'd suspected him.

Of course, he got it. Zrakovi had no recourse but to apologize even though frown lines rutted his face. The shifter standing behind him looked as if he didn't know whether to laugh or weep. I was with Alex on that one.

They might yet catch Jean Lafitte doing something worthy of tossing him off the council or into a prison cell, but it would not be today.

I was a happy camper, at least for a few seconds.

Zrakovi flipped one folder closed in front of him, slid it aside, and opened another. I shot a sidelong glance at Rand. Time for act two.

"Now, I fear, we must address a rather sensitive issue—"

"Elder Zrakovi, might I say something? I promise to keep it brief, but it's important." Rand stood up, my annoying Russian snow prince with his gleaming blond hair and pale blue sweater and winter-white trousers, his eyes an impossibly rich shade of blue, his arrogance and petulance often heavy enough to sink a ship. I hoped he could keep it afloat, at least long enough to save Eugenie a lot of misery.

From across the room, I sensed Zrakovi's blood pressure rising. The man was going to have a stroke if this meeting didn't end soon. "Can't it wait, Mr. Randolph?"

"Please, I promise to keep it short—it's just a quick thank-you, really, and you're the one I wish to thank."

Elder Z's blood pressure ticked up another few notches, and he developed a slight twitch in his left eye. "Oh, very well."

Behind him, Alex wasn't looking at Rand. He was still looking at me, eyes narrowed. I gave him what I hoped was an innocent shrug.

"I am so honored to be a part of this group that I wanted to share some happy news," Rand said, oozing sincerity so thick I was glad I had on boots with a decent heel. "In about six months, I will become a father for the first time. It's a cause for celebration, although I regret to say my son's mother is only a human and was certainly not the person I'd hoped would bear my first child, which would be my mate, Dru, the New Orleans sentinel."

I glared at Rand. That long, run-on speech was *so* not part of the script, and so help me if he as much as thought my name again I would create a potion to encase him in ice until hell froze over.

"However," he continued, ignoring me, "I want to publicly thank Elder Zrakovi—I have no doubt the permanent First Elder position will be yours very soon—for your unwavering support and personal assurance that no harm will befall my son because of any political differences."

The silence swelled to fill the room. Rand's performance was Oscar-worthy. "Anyway, I just wanted to say thank you for that personal promise to protect my child. It only strengthens our alliance between wizards and elves, and proves what a man of character you are."

Rand sat down. What could Zrakovi do? We'd backed him into a very tight, very public corner. "You're welcome, of course," he mumbled, then cleared his throat. "A child's impending arrival is always a joyous thing."

Not a note of joy sat on his face or rang in his voice. I'd encountered cheerier demeanors at funerals.

I didn't dare look at Alex. Instead, I watched my uncle. Lennox St. Simon had sat quietly throughout the proceedings.

Several times, he'd cocked his head and settled a very sharp, Gerry-like gaze on whoever happened to be talking, including me. Now he watched Zrakovi with a slight smile curving his mouth at the edges and a glint in his eyes. He didn't know to shield his feelings when his part-elven niece was lurking about, apparently, so I knew he was gleeful and greedy and enjoyed his superior's discomfort. He wanted Zrakovi to fail. Uncle Lennox wore the hunger of an ambitious man who sensed a weakness in his rival.

Fingering my amulet again, I sought to lessen the emotional drag of both wizards. While Zrakovi physically wrapped up the meeting, his mind was rapidly morphing from frantic annoyance to outright fury. He ended with an announcement that the council would reconvene in January unless the wizarding body elected a permanent First Elder before then or one of the outstanding warrants was filled.

His fury wrapped around me despite my shielding. He'd been blindsided. He'd been outplayed.

And he didn't like it.

My part of Plan Eugenie was about to begin; I could only hope Rand backed me up, or Eugenie and I would both be taking flight.

My first option, however, was leaving without any close encounters of the Elder kind. I looped my arm through Truman Capote's and talked about utter nonsense as we edged our way toward the door laden with our bags and notebooks and coats. We'd made it almost as far as the entrance to the hallway when I felt a tug on my arm and looked up to see Alex.

Granite statues had more animation in their faces. "Willem wants to talk to you."

I gave him a sunny smile. "Sure. A lot of surprises today, weren't there?"

"Surprises. That's one way to put it." He looked down at me, his gaze roving over my face. I thought a tiny doubt flickered, as if he wasn't sure what I did and didn't know. That was purely a guess, however. Alex knew how to shut me out, and he was shielding his emotions like they were gold nuggets within Fort Knox.

I waved good-bye to Truman and turned to Alex. My first impulse was to begin making excuses, to assure him I'd gone to Eugenie's last night but hadn't been able to go through with it. But it was heading down a deep well of lies that might eventually drown me.

"DJ, I don't want to know what happened." Alex at least had the decency to drop his voice. "I'm not going to ask and you're not going to tell me."

I caught the edge of anger in his voice; we both knew I'd gone around him, but I'd done it for his sake as well as Eugenie's. "That's best. I don't want you stuck in the middle."

"And yet here I am, in the middle."

I wanted to come clean, to try to explain, to say whatever it would take to smooth things over between us. But those words would be lies, too, because I'd done what I thought was right. Still, his anger and hurt leaked through those formidable mental barriers of his, and they broke my heart.

What did you do that was so wrong? A little, nagging inner voice—my own, not Rand's—posed that timid question. *Why should you have to lie to make him love you, or pretend to be what you're not, or sneak around to do what you think is right so that he won't be mad at you? Why can't he just love who you are?*

Why can't you love who you are?

I usually ignored my own still, small voice, but the inner DJ had hit me hard with those last two questions. I'd done the right thing. I shouldn't have to beg or lie or sneak around in the hope

I could make Alex love me more and, maybe, eventually accept me or respect me.

You shall not pass. Another figurative line in the sand across the chasm at Khazad-dûm or, in this case, Uptown New Orleans. I wouldn't apologize for what I'd done, but I wasn't ready for an ultimatum either. "I'm sorry I hurt you," I whispered.

His eyes softened and he pulled me into a hug. I held on to him with both arms, as if by holding on, I could prevent the chasm between us from growing any wider. "It can't be easy, can it?" His voice was soft enough that the others still milling around couldn't hear him. "Where do we go from here?"

Where we went from here was that I wouldn't put him in the position of having to lie for me. I pulled back and swiped a couple of stray tears off my cheeks. "I'm going to talk to Zrakovi, tell him the truth, and see what happens."

Alex dropped his voice lower still. "Don't push him too hard. He's stressed out over your uncle as well as all the other shit going on. Lennox is ambitious. You want me to stay with you?"

I shook my head. "I need to do this alone. I'll call you as soon as I can."

He took a reluctant step back and gave me a smile before turning and disappearing down the hallway. Everyone else had gone except Rand and Zrakovi, and Rand was on his way toward the door. I didn't plan to rat out Jean Lafitte, but I was going to tell Zrakovi that I'd gone to the elf last night. I needed to warn my coconspirator, so I dropped my mental shields.

Rand!

His shoulders gave a quick jolt. *For God's sake, Dru, I'm standing six feet away. Stop yelling.*

I'm going to tell Zrakovi the truth. Nobody was hurt, your baby is safe, and I'm tired of lying.

Long pause. Really long pause. *Are you sure? I can keep you out of it.*

No, I disagreed with his orders and I need to stand up for what I believe.

Does this mean I can go ahead and kill him?

I closed my eyes. In my head, I heard Rand laughing. *Just kidding.*

Jerk.

"Elder Zrakovi, can I talk to you for a few minutes?" God, I hoped he was still the wizard I'd always thought him to be—calm, rational, and fair.

And, today, angry. "I think that's a good idea. Would you wait outside, Mr. Randolph?" Zrakovi frowned at Rand, who hadn't moved any closer to the door.

"I think I should stay, Mr. Zrakovi, at least for a minute. I would like to explain something."

Zrakovi's temper began simmering. Again.

Rand, let me handle this.

He ignored me. Again. "I'm sorry I blindsided you. But when Dru came to me late last night, she said you were concerned that my child could be used to manipulate me and asked if I could think of a way to keep that from happening. I thought—we both thought—that if the fae, in particular, saw wizards and elves united, it would make them less likely to take any kind of action against Eugenie or my child."

Zrakovi's anger didn't drain away but it leveled off. And damn if the elf hadn't given me a partial loophole to slide through; he never said I'd revealed Zrakovi's desire to destroy the baby, but only his concern that it would be used as a pawn. Maybe it was enough of a loophole to save my job.

"Thank you, Mr. Randolph. I don't think we'll need to speak further. Again, congratulations on your pending fatherhood."

Rand nodded and squeezed my shoulder on his way out the door. *I'll wait for you, Dru.*

No, go home, I need to talk to Alex after this. I had no idea what we'd say, but Alex and I had worked too hard to let politics pull us apart.

Zrakovi closed the door and returned to his seat. I pulled a chair to the other side of the table, facing him.

"Is what Quince Randolph said the whole truth, DJ?" Zrakovi leaned back in his seat and rolled his neck around, popping stiff tendons.

I took a deep breath. I'd keep Rand's loophole, at least for now. But I had to try and explain the rest of it. "Not exactly, but I'd like the chance to tell you why I disobeyed a direct order. It wasn't something I did lightly."

"Very well." Zrakovi loosened his tie and unbuttoned the top button of his dress shirt. Trying to relax, but not successfully. "I realize Eugella is your friend."

"*Eugenie* is a very good friend," I said. "But I doubt I would have done anything differently had she been only a casual acquaintance."

He frowned. "You have that little respect for me, for your position, for your own people?"

"This isn't about respect, or power, or politics, but about right and wrong."

"So it was a moral issue, or a religious issue?"

I leaned forward, propping my elbows on the table. "Look, it's not about whether I think ending a pregnancy is right or wrong. I'll admit I'm all over the map on that topic. If it were me, if I were carrying a child with this much preternatural baggage? I don't know. I might choose not to have the baby. I don't know without actually being in that position." Which would, hopefully, be never.

I took a deep breath and chose my words carefully. "The point is, it needs to be Eugenie's choice. I will absolutely tell her your feelings about it, and why you strongly believe that ending the pregnancy is the best solution. I'll tell her you believe this baby has the potential to cause a lot of strife in the prete world and that it might endanger both her and the baby. But I can't use my magic to take the decision away from her. I won't. It's wrong."

Zrakovi didn't respond, just leaned back in his chair, crossed his arms, and frowned.

Plus, it wasn't just Eugenie involved. "I have my issues with Quince Randolph," I said, my voice softer. "You know our bond was a business deal and not a marriage. But this is his child; he can already tell it's a boy. Preemptive strikes are all well and good, but not when it's a strike against a threat that might not even exist. Sure, this baby might cause chaos. But he also could help broker peace."

Zrakovi steepled his fingers in front of his face and stared at the floor a long time. When he looked back up at me, I realized he'd been shielding a lot better than I'd thought. He was still furious.

Well, screw him. I was right, damn it.

"Let me clarify." His voice was cold. Two days as interim First Elder and his political animal had taken over. "Did you understand my direct orders to go to Eugenie and talk to her, and to perform the procedure yourself if she would not agree?"

"Yes, you made that perfectly clear."

"Was Alex Warin under the impression that you were going to follow my orders?"

He was going to try to implicate Alex in this, but that wasn't happening. "I lied to him. I told him what he wanted to hear and then I went to find a solution I thought was fair. When I left his house, he thought I was going to Eugenie's."

"Did you talk to her at all?"

"No I did not." I paused, taking a second to tamp down my own rising anger. "I was on my way to Eugenie's house when it occurred to me that Rand knew the political landscape better than I. I thought he might have a way to neutralize any threat his child might pose." I didn't admit to selling Zrakovi straight down the Mississippi.

"I see. And do you still stand by your testimony regarding Jean Lafitte's involvement in the burning of Etienne Boulard's club—or his lack of involvement?"

On that matter, I'd developed clarity. Selling Jean out would hurt a lot of people and accomplish nothing. No one had been hurt, and telling Zrakovi that Christof was hanging out with Jean and manipulating the weather to torture the elves? That would just make the future First Elder more paranoid.

"Yes, I stand by my testimony completely. I apologize for not revealing Christof's presence but didn't feel it had any bearing on the matter."

Zrakovi speared me with a hard look. "You're a talented wizard, DJ, and your elven magic makes you an extremely valuable asset to our people in these troubled times." He leaned forward and smacked his hand on the table, his flat palm cracking against the wood like a gunshot and making me jump. "But don't *ever* think you're untouchable. Don't ever make me think you'd turn your skills against me or the wizarding council. Don't disobey me again. I'd hate to see you follow the path of your father."

I looked down at my hands. Hands that mixed potions, wielded a staff of fire, and held on to things too tightly out of a deep-seated fear that I'd lose yet another person I cared about.

It always came back to Gerry, didn't it? Gerry had followed his beliefs, betrayed his kind, and paid with his life.

Yet the path Gerry followed had been a selfish one, carved out of a desire for power. I'd sworn when he died that I'd never go down the road he'd trodden.

I'd been naïve.

In the end, I had to do what I believed was right, even if it meant letting go of old promises. Maybe even letting go of people I loved. But it would not be out of selfishness, and it would not be for power.

I looked back up at Zrakovi and said the only thing I could. "Do what you think is best, sir. But I am not my father."

I was, however, my father's daughter.

"Go home, Drusilla Jaco. But watch your step."

I pushed my chair back and stood. God, I was so tired. The floor even felt shaky, and I staggered a little as I edged my way around the table toward the exit.

"What was that?" Zrakovi stood up, looking around the room.

A muffled boom sounded from the hallway, and I ran toward the door.

I'd just grasped the knob when the ceiling came down and blackness descended.

CHAPTER 24

I came to consciousness in a pitch-black world of choking, chalky dust. The taste and smell of old, dislodged plaster was one I'd come to associate with those horrible months after Hurricane Katrina, when New Orleans had become one massive, sweltering site of both destruction and construction.

Coughing, I rolled to my knees and cracked my head against something solid. Damn it, where was Charlie? I'd pulled the cross-body strap of my messenger bag over my head before the ceiling came down, so it had to be nearby. I felt along my chest for the strap and followed it to the bag, but no elven staff stuck out the top.

I focused on the staff, calling it to me using an elven phrase Rand had taught me: *Dewch i mi, Mahout.* Instantly, a spark of red fire shot out near my left foot. I reached back and felt along the debris where the light had been, and when my fingers brushed against the polished wood, it heated to a soft glow.

Now I could see that I was in a cave with walls formed of plaster and broken lathing and wire.

"Elder Zrakovi? Can you hear me?"

It took a few seconds, but finally he answered with a muffled "I'm a few feet to your left, I think. I'm all right. Are you hurt?"

I did a mental body check. "I don't think so." At least not beyond the throbbing shoulder and ribs that seemed a constant these days. And maybe a new lump on my head.

"I'll try to make my way to you," I said, holding Charlie up to see how to best dig my way out. I needed another source of light, preferably one that wouldn't set the room on fire.

Wedging Charlie between two boards with the glowing end closest to me, I felt inside my bag for the smooth wooden surface of my portable magic kit. Pulling it out, I held it closer to Charlie's glow and picked out a small packet of crushed bioluminescent mushrooms. I tapped a small amount into a plastic container, added an ounce or two of holy water, and used my finger to stir it and also shoot a bit of my native magic into it. The phosphorescent green glow sprang up instantly, so bright that I had to blink a few times so my pupils would adjust.

"What the hell is that?" Zrakovi sounded closer than before, and debris fell and shifted somewhere to my left.

"I made a light so we could find our way out." I stuffed Charlie back in my bag and held the container of light above my head. There was a beam just above me—that's what I'd cracked my head on—but open space on either side of it.

I began pushing debris out of the way in front of the beam, careful to stay clear so it wouldn't hit me if it shifted again. By the time I'd cleared out a space big enough to crawl through, Zrakovi had made his way to me and peered in the opening. "How did you make the light—is it elven?"

"No, just good old potion magic." If not for his voice, I might not have recognized him. He was covered head to toe in white dust that glowed a little in my phosphorescent light. He held out a milky hand to help me crawl clear of my rubble cave. "I keep a portable magic kit with me most of the time."

Crap like this happened often enough that I needed it, sadly.

"Enterprising." Zrakovi stared at the light a moment, then around the room. "Let's see if we can get the door open to the hallway and find our way out of here."

I did a quick rundown of who might be left in the building.

"Alex?" I stilled, straining my ears for a response, but crackling wires and shifting rubble was all I heard. He'd probably been gone long enough to transport out before the explosions, or whatever they were. But my elf probably hadn't.

Rand! I felt a mental stirring through the pain that stabbed through my temples, but no answer. *Rand—are you okay? Are you still in the building?*

His answer was faint and sluggish. *I'm stuck near the transport. I need help getting free.*

We're on our way. Have you seen Alex?

He left before the explosion.

I hoped he was right. "Rand is stuck between here and the transport; he needs help getting clear." I held the light nearer the door, from which Zrakovi was methodically clearing rubble. "That's too slow. Stand back."

He gave me a sharp look, probably not liking my pushy attitude, but moved to the side. I pulled Charlie from my bag and pointed the staff at the door. I couldn't shoot it full force or I'd start a fire, so I fed the tiniest trickle of magic into it I could, and willed it to singe rather than flame.

The end glowed like the tip of a lit cigarette, and I touched it to the door, moving it in widening circles until there was a big, round scorched hole in the middle. Then I punched my fist through it. It wasn't pretty, but it was big enough to climb through.

Or it would have been for anyone not wearing a freaking elven hippie dress.

"Damn it." I used the staff to burn a hole in the dress about mid-thigh and ripped off the bottom. Once my legs were freed, I stepped through the hole in the door and was glad to see the hallway beyond wasn't nearly as wrecked as the meeting room.

I looked back to find Zrakovi examining the hole in the door and stepping cautiously through it. "Enterprising," he said again.

Yeah, well, some of us were working wizards whose skills hadn't rusted from too much political nonsense. Zrakovi was Green Congress, and had to be a strong wizard to have made Elder. Or maybe not. Maybe one only had to be ambitious and politically savvy.

The ceiling hadn't collapsed in the part of the U-shaped hallway leading to the elevator, but the walls had lost their plaster and part of their lathing. The footing was tricky, and we moved slowly over land mines of nails poking out of wooden strips and enough white dust that it was hard to tell the floor from an uneven invitation to a sprained ankle or pierced foot.

Rand, where are you?

About six feet ahead of you to the left, I think. I'm trapped.

With Zrakovi crunching behind me, I held the light up and began searching for my elf. I finally spotted him against the wall with some kind of support beam over his legs. It had to be heavy. Elves had a brutish, preternatural physical strength. I'd seen Rand pick up a sofa without straining.

"You can't kick it off?"

"Sure I can. I just wanted to see you try to lift it."

"No point in being a smartass." I settled the light onto a pile of rubble and studied the beam. Wooden, solid, thick. "Did you see what happened?"

"I'm not sure. Bombs, maybe. The first blast was back where you were; the second was between here and the transport. I saw Jake Warin just before the second blast."

A chill stole across my shoulder blades. Why was Jake still here?

I turned to my silent accomplice. "Elder Zrakovi, could you dig through some of that blockage while I try to free Rand? Jake Warin might be over there."

He didn't respond, but walked toward the cave-in a few yards in front of us. I didn't think Zrakovi appreciated me barking orders at him, but he'd proven himself fairly useless so far. Not that I'd be sharing that opinion.

I saw somebody else, Dru.

Who? Obviously somebody Rand didn't want to identify in front of Zrakovi.

Garrett Melnick. He was fighting with your loup-garou friend.

Another chill stole across my scalp. The thought of Jake with that bloodsucking freak made me ill, but if Jean had taught me anything, it was that Jake could take care of himself.

I think Melnick was trying to take out Zrakovi, and maybe you and probably me. There's not much he can do to Lafitte.

Wait. That didn't make sense. *How could Melnick be here? It's daylight.*

"What in thunder's name are you two doing?" Zrakovi abandoned his excavation job and stepped up beside me. "Are you so besotted that you can't take your eyes off each other? We need to get out of here."

Zrakovi didn't know Rand and I could communicate telepathically, and that was for the best, even if it meant he thought there was besottitude at work. "I'm trying to figure out the best way to move that beam," I said.

Zrakovi leaned over and grasped the beam, but couldn't budge it. "We will have to go for help."

"No, no. I can find something." I squatted down and pulled my portable kit out again. "Rand, is there some elven thing that can mimic telekinesis?"

He frowned, his facial movement cracking off a marble-size chunk of plaster from his forehead and sending it tumbling down his cheek. "The air and earth elves can do it, but not fire elves."

I studied the neatly labeled vials in my kit, then the pocket containing three recycled mint tins filled with different gemstone chips. *Aha.*

Pulling out the tin marked BLUE, I scanned the blue and blue-violet stones. Maybe a sapphire, but . . . I picked up the small blue-green mineral chip called spinel. Its element was fire. I dropped it into an empty vial and poured holy water over it, then touched the edge of Charlie to the liquid. Might as well infuse it with the magic of the fire elves rather than that of a wizard.

Because no way would it strengthen me enough to lift that beam, or even Zrakovi. Rand was already super-strong, however. With him, it might work.

Once the mixture had boiled, then cooled off a little, I crawled over the rubble and held it out. "Drink this. Don't swallow the stone, but just hold it in your mouth. Wait a few seconds and then try your hardest to push off that beam. I don't have much of the mixture because the stone chip is so small, so it won't last long."

Rand sniffed the vial, and for a moment I thought he was going to put on his petulant I-Am-Elf face. But he nodded, upended the vial, and waited a few seconds. Gritting his teeth, he jerked his left leg up toward his body. As soon as the beam lifted from that leg, he slid his right leg free and pushed on the beam with his foot. It tumbled away from him with a crash.

He spat out the stone and grinned at me. "It worked."

I smiled but it was halfhearted. Jake might be over there somewhere, and instead of digging, Zrakovi stood there with his thumb up his ass, giving me a weird, assessing look. Useless.

"Can you walk?" I turned back to Rand, but he was already on his feet.

"Yeah, that stuff even cleared up my headache."

Great. It hadn't done a thing for mine. "Then help me dig."

The potion wore off quickly, but Rand still had his prete-strength, so with his help we made quick work of moving rubble from the blocked-off area. Zrakovi finally got with the program and helped pull away pieces of lathing and chunks of plaster.

The closer we got to whatever was on the other side, the tighter my throat grew and the more labored my breathing, not from plaster dust but from fear. Jake had to be okay; he had to. He'd been through too much, and was finally finding happiness.

At last, Rand lifted off the last big barricade, and I heard the sounds of a struggle to our right. I ran ahead, stopped at the corner, and peered around, with Rand and Zrakovi right behind me.

Traces of two images disappeared so quickly I wasn't sure I'd seen them—at least not until Rand said, "Melnick. And a big red wolf."

"Jake," I said. "Let's go."

I started toward the transport, but Zrakovi grabbed my arm and pulled me back. "You aren't going anywhere."

Excuse me? "Melnick just bombed Tulane University's history building and tried to kill us. Jake Warin's gone after him and we're not going to follow?"

"We don't have a warrant to arrest Melnick in Vampyre, only

in New Orleans. We don't have jurisdiction. And we don't know there were bombs. It could be a coincidence. Besides, it couldn't have been Melnick. It's daylight."

Voices wafted up from the stairwell. "And there's another coincidence: the arrival of the fire department and a boatload of cops to an Interspecies Council meeting," I said. "Do you want to stand here and explain things to them?"

"We'll transport to Mr. Randolph's house and continue our discussion there."

Rand and I looked at each other.

Help me.

He nodded and walked to stand next to Zrakovi, placing a friendly hand on his shoulder. "Don't you think it would be wise for you to go to Edinburgh to report to the Elders, and send DJ to Vampyre to make sure Jake Warin is safe? He's one of your enforcers, after all."

Halfway through that speech, Zrakovi's eyes had glazed and lost focus. "Yes," he said, "I should go to Edinburgh. DJ should go to Vampyre."

"Is that a direct order, sir?"

"It . . ."

It might have been, if Jake hadn't rematerialized in the transport right in front of us. He was still in his wolf form, and sat with golden eyes blazing and blood dripping from his teeth.

Judging by the mangled, crimson-covered body of Geoffrey Hoffman lying at his feet, it wasn't Jake's blood.

CHAPTER 25

As soon as Rand released his arm, Zrakovi looked around in confusion, heard the approaching humans, and snapped back into Elder mode.

"You fools, get in the transport." We all crowded around the wolf and the former First Elder. I grabbed the bristly ruff of Jake's wolf to keep him from bolting, which he seemed inclined to do, judging by his wide eyes. Now that I'd bonded with Rand, I couldn't be turned loup-garou, but the humans rushing up the stairwell toward us certainly could. The first firefighter crashed through the emergency exit, ax first, just as we dematerialized.

I'd suggested the safest place I thought of to go—Alex's house.

Poor guy. When we all materialized in the middle of his living room, Alex was sacked out on his sofa a few feet away from the transport, wearing a pair of baggy camo shorts and a black T-shirt, barefooted, his head buried in a copy of *Sports Illustrated*. He pretended to be cool about our arrival, barely raising an eyebrow, but his shifter vibes went from mellow to startled to confused in a matter of seconds, finally settling into annoyed.

I really, really needed to get back to Gerry's frozen house in Lakeview and replenish my mojo bag. My own emotions were exhausting enough; adding so many others made me want to hibernate, and not from the cold.

"Mr. Randolph, if you don't mind, we need to discuss matters of concern to the wizard community." Zrakovi was all brisk business now, back in charge and ready to herd Rand toward the front door. "I'm sure we'll set up another council meeting right away to complete our business."

I wondered what building we'd destroy next time? And what business was left?

Rand, would you call Jean Lafitte at the Monteleone and tell him Jake might be in trouble?

The elf looked out the front window, where the snow fell heavily again, the flakes coming down at a wind-driven forty-five-degree angle. *Sure. Think Alex would let me use the transport to my house?*

I glanced at Alex, who'd returned from ushering a bloody Jake to the bathroom and now stood with evil eyes fixed on Rand. Zrakovi had knelt next to the body of Geoffrey Hoffman, whom I assumed was dead. *No transport,* I told Rand. *Just run fast.*

At least he had his coat, dirty though it might be. My four-grand lambskin would be found amid the rubble of F. Edward Hebert Hall. Coatless again.

As soon as he left, I collapsed into one of Alex's wooden dining chairs. I was too filthy to sit on his sofa.

"What happened?" he asked.

"I'm not hurt—just a bump on the head, thanks for asking." I rubbed my aching shoulder, which hurt worse than my head. I'd undone all the benefits of my healing potion.

"Sorry." He didn't sound it. "What happened to Hoffman? Why are you guys covered in . . . dirt?"

"I'm not sure about Hoffman, the building exploded, and it's ashes and plaster dust." I went through my version of things, omitting the details of my dressing-down by Zrakovi and the mental conversation with Rand. "It looks like Garrett Melnick set off the explosives, but who he was after—Rand or me or Zrakovi or all of the above—I don't know. When we got clear of the rubble, Jake and Melnick were dematerializing in the transport. Then Jake reappeared in wolf form with Hoffman and no Melnick."

I left out the part about Rand using elven mind control on the Elder, too.

"How'd Jake get in the middle of it?"

"By doing my job, asshole." Jake emerged from the bathroom, his face covered in cuts and bruises but clean, which was more than I could say for me or Zrakovi. I'd kill for a shower.

Jake sat at the table. "I didn't kill Hoffman, no matter now it looks. I caught Melnick triggering the last explosive and tried to stop him. The bomb had a short trigger; we were fighting when it went off. We eventually fought our way into the transport and off we went. He threw the body in the transport in Vampyre and sent us back."

Nobody had answered my burning question. "How could Melnick be there during the day?" I knew vamps could move around in light-tight areas and the Hebert Hall attic had no windows, but how had he known to transport directly into the attic?

"Melnick must have an open transport in Vampyre and knew where the meeting was being held," Alex said.

Great. Future meetings should be held outdoors, where there

would be no buildings to destroy and thus no surprise visits from bomb-happy vampires. The NOFD would appreciate it, no doubt.

Zrakovi joined us at the table. "Hoffman's dead, and doesn't appear to have been drained. He appears to have been chewed on. What would you know about that, Mr. Warin?"

Jake went through his story again, and I could sense Zrakovi's doubt just as I could tell Alex wasn't sure what to believe. He loved Jake; they were more like brothers than cousins. Jake was two years older, but Alex had always been the golden boy. Star athlete, star student at Ole Miss, star FBI agent, star enforcer. Jake was divorced, had been badly injured in his first tour of duty as a Marine, drank too much, and struggled with his identity as loup-garou—a rogue, non-pack werewolf with control issues. It would be easy to set him up for killing Geoffrey Hoffman, but why? Jake was a non-player in the grand scheme of prete politics.

"DJ," Zrakovi said, breaking my reverie. "As difficult as it is to believe, this trouble doesn't seem to involve you, so feel free to leave."

He'd get no arguments from me. I got up and stopped next to the chair Alex had claimed. "We need to talk," I said softly.

His voice was equally soft. "I'll call you as soon as I can get free." He reached out and caught my hand. "I really am glad you're safe. Are we okay, the two of us?"

I stopped and thought about it for a second, then leaned down and kissed him, leaving a smudge of ash above his upper lip that looked like a milk mustache. I smiled. Yeah, we were okay. Somehow. So far. "We're good."

I walked to the transport, stopping when I realized Hoffman's bloody body still lay in it, and Zrakovi looked annoyed that I was still there. I'd go to Eugenie's instead.

Until the wind blew the shreds of my dress up and treated

my nether regions to a subfreezing assault of icy wind, I'd forgotten I was not only coatless but half dressed.

I hurried as fast as the heavy snow would allow, calling Eugenie on the way, thankful my phone had survived the blast. "Let me in before I freeze," I shouted before she'd even gotten out a hello.

By the time I skated across her frozen front porch, she had the door open. "Lord, girl, what are you wearing?"

"Not much."

She laughed. "Yeah, I see that. You have more chalk on you than clothes. I guess that's chalk. Is that chalk?"

I shook my head. "Plaster dust. It's a long, ugly story. Can I get a shower and borrow something warm?"

Here, at least, I felt at peace. No politics, no relationship worries, no judgment, no marauding vampires or elves. At least for the moment, no imminent baby crisis.

The shower helped rinse away the last of the post-meeting aches. I towel-dried my hair and smiled at the clothes Eugenie had brought me. The teal sweater, my favorite color, was cashmere, which she could afford even less than I. She'd given me her best, which was so very typical.

"DJ?" She knocked softly on the door. "Rand's on the phone and wants to come over. Should I let him?"

"Only if you're comfortable with it." As much as I hated to admit it, Rand had behaved better than my boss today. Zrakovi had been contemptible.

She smiled when I walked out of the bathroom. "I always liked that sweater better on you than on me. It's a good color for you."

Since Jean and Alex thought so, too, it must be true. I followed her into the living room. "Is Rand coming?"

"Yeah, I thought about it a lot last night, and I figure I'm gonna need him. I mean, I don't know anything about his people, and this little guy"—she rubbed her belly—"is going to be a part of that world. I'm just gonna have to stop looking at what he's done in the past and keep looking forward, you know?"

Yeah, too well. I curled myself into one of the armchairs near the fireplace and rested my head on the chair back. "I'm so tired."

"You want to stay here tonight? You can, anytime. Or are you staying at Alex's? When's he gonna put some heat in your house?"

That would be never, the way things were going. Then again, it wasn't his job to install a heating unit in my house; it was my responsibility. If I wanted to be treated like a strong, independent woman, I needed to act like it. When I could find enough time between crises.

"I'll probably go back to the Monteleone tonight, but thanks for the offer. Or maybe I'll go to Alex's if he finishes up with Zrakovi in time." Alex wasn't angry, which was a relief, but I still felt a widening gulf between us, partly because of our different personalities but mostly because we couldn't find time to be together. We badly needed some alone time.

"I think Alex has changed," Eugenie said out of the blue. "Or maybe he hasn't changed, but the world around him has. He doesn't seem to be handling all this political mess very well, at least from what I've seen. He always seems, I don't know, restless." She chuckled. "Of course, what do I know? I didn't have a clue your world even existed a few weeks ago."

Eugenie might be sensitive about not having a college degree, but she was plenty smart and had good intuitions about people—well, except for the whole hooking-up-with-Rand business. "Tell me what you mean."

She tucked her feet under her on the sofa. "I just mean with the pretes all living here now, coming and going when they want to . . . Alex is a guy who has it fixed in his mind that the world's a certain way and he's comfortable there. Then the world changes, and he doesn't like it. And it keeps changing. Seems like something new comes up every other day."

Or a few times a day. I'd thought Alex's problem was only with me and the chaos that always seemed to surround me. But maybe I was just a symbol of the chaos he saw infecting everything. It was easier to blame my nature for his discontent than to fight windmills and shadows, or elves and vampires who demanded equal access to the modern world.

"I think you might be right." I rubbed my eyes, which felt like a bucket of sand had been poured into each one. "Unfortunately, I think he sees me as part of the problem."

Eugenie laughed. "It's because he doesn't understand you, DJ. He wants you to be like him but you're not. You're okay with change. You roll with it where he fights it and gets thrown off-balance by it."

"But I—" A knock sounded from the front door. "That's probably Rand." I didn't know what else to say anyway. Even if Eugenie was right and Alex was having trouble adjusting to our crazy new world with its lack of absolutes, I wasn't sure how to help him if he saw me as part of his problem.

Rand had showered and transformed himself back into his usual snow prince look, albeit a very cold snow prince with lips that had turned an alarming shade of icy blue.

"You want something hot? I'll get you some cocoa." Eugenie hustled toward the kitchen. Rand stood in front of the fire, holding his hands toward the flames, flexing his fingers.

"Lafitte wants you to call him." Rand smiled at Eugenie when she brought in the mug of hot chocolate; she smiled back.

Good. At least these two were behaving themselves. For now. I wasn't deluded; the bad old Rand we all knew and hated would return eventually.

"I'll talk to Jean when I get back to the hotel." I wasn't sure I could hold up to the pirate's complex verbal sparring tonight. I just wanted everybody to leave me alone for a while.

"He says he knows what really happened to Hoffman, but he needs to talk to you before he can say any more."

I groaned and slumped down in the chair. "Oh, holy crap. I can't handle one more disaster today."

Still, I dug my phone out of my bag and speed-dialed Jean.

"You did not call me with proper haste," Jean said by way of greeting. I really needed to teach him proper phone etiquette. "Or did your elf not relay my request? He is quite impertinent and self-important."

"Quite." Because if anyone should recognize a self-important man, it would be my pirate. He saw one in the mirror every day. "What's up?"

A long pause while he translated "up"; I was too tired to do it for him. "Some information has come to my attention of which you should be aware, Drusilla."

Great. "What?"

"I do not wish to impart such information on the telephone. You must return to the hotel *tout de suite*."

I'd toot his sweet, all right. "Jean, can it wait? I'm exhausted."

"Do you wish to help your friend Jacob?" he asked. "Do you wish to prevent a war?"

Well, when he put it that way.

"I'm on my way."

CHAPTER 26

I had two surprises awaiting me on my return to the Monteleone, neither of them good.

First, when I arrived at my room after a harrowing forty-minute cab ride through snow-strangled streets, my key card didn't work. I trudged back to the lobby to get it rekeyed.

"I'm sorry, Ms. Jaco, but your card was declined," the oh-so-polite desk clerk said, looking embarrassed on my behalf since I was too tired to do it myself. "Would you like to provide us with another form of payment?"

Zrakovi had cut me off, the jerk. Then again, I guess my job of tailing Jean Lafitte was over and he saw no reason to continue paying several hundred bucks a night for a hotel room.

I dug out my own credit card. It was eight p.m. and I was a zombie. I'd worry later about how to pay the bill. As soon as Christof followed through with his promise to send this weather system somewhere else, I'd check out and call somebody to install a heating unit in Gerry's house. I still couldn't quite think of it as mine.

I trudged back to the eighth floor, dragged myself down the hallway, and dumped everything in my room except the staff. Then I knocked on the door of Jean's suite.

There are many people I could have found inside who would not have surprised me. Truman Capote wouldn't have surprised me. Christof wouldn't have surprised me. I'd even have been unsurprised to see Jean's brother Pierre, half-brother Dominique You, or one of his pirate cronies. I half expected Rene.

But not in my wildest dreams would I have expected to see Adrian Hoffman, fangs and all.

He looked even worse than when I'd summoned him to my hotel bathroom to ask about elven pregnancies. Vampires always seemed to look elegant and refined and the prettiest version of whatever their human countenance had been. Adrian had always been very handsome, like a tall Montel Williams who enjoyed some ear bling.

He was still handsome, but had been completely stripped of his cocky attitude. In fact, he looked scared.

"Adrian." I nodded at him and gave Jean a narrow-eyed what-the-hell look.

"Would you care for a drink, *Jolie*?" Jean had his usual brandy; I didn't see a cup of blood for Adrian.

"No thanks. What's this about?" One drink, and I'd be under the table, snoring and drooling.

"Monsieur Hoffman came to me for asylum. Before I granted such a favor, I wished for your counsel."

After being dissed much of the day, I wasn't sure whether to be flattered or suspicious that anyone would seek my counsel. Or fearful, because Adrian Hoffman spelled trouble, and I had enough already.

However, I sat down on the sofa opposite Adrian and reminded myself of how sorry I'd felt for him when he learned his father had conspired with Garrett Melnick to have him turned vampire. He'd sold me out, but he'd been sold out worse. A lot worse.

"Better start at the beginning," I said. "And tell me why I shouldn't call Zrakovi and turn you in. He's pissed off at me right now. I'd earn some Brownie points by turning in a wanted man."

Adrian swallowed hard, his Adam's apple bobbing above the collar of his gray band-collared shirt. Silk, with charcoal trousers. Now that I thought about it, he'd always dressed like an urban vamp, even before he became one.

He looked at the floor. "I don't blame you for being angry, DJ. For whatever it's worth, I am sorry for my part in what happened to you last month."

I sighed. "Look, we were never buddies. We probably never will be. You got caught up in something you never intended, though, and you paid dearly for it. So let's forget what happened and start over."

"This is as I told you, Monsieur Hoffman," Jean said, settling in on the sofa next to me. "You did not believe she would help you, but our Drusilla has a generous heart."

Yeah, yeah. Save the flowery speeches for someone who'd slept in the last three days. "So do you, uh . . . do you know about your father?" I know he had to be angry at his father, but still, the man was dead.

"I saw it happen." His voice trembled, and he kept his gaze fixed on the carpet. "Maybe I could even have stopped it but, God help me, I didn't." He closed his eyes. "I didn't. I let someone kill him, then tear into him like a dog."

Or a wolf. "How'd Jake Warin get mixed up in it?"

Adrian looked at Jean and made like a clam.

"Drusilla, if Monsieur Hoffman tells us what he knows, he says that his life will be in grave danger," Jean said. "Therefore, he will not reveal the killer's name without assurance of his safety." He leaned back and sipped his brandy. "I wish to know how the other members of the council would view such a thing?"

That was a good question. "Well, it depends on who's involved. All the alliances are shaky right now. Could you provide asylum to Adrian without anyone knowing?" Yeah, there I went, advocating lies and secrecy again. I was hopeless.

"Perhaps, if Monsieur Hoffman is willing to live in Old Barataria," Jean said. "No one who is not trusted by me or loyal to me is allowed to come there now. I have destroyed all but one transport, and have armed men watching it at all times."

I stared at him. It sounded as if Jean Lafitte were preparing for war. "And who are among those trusted and loyal people?"

He gave me a small smile. "Other than my men? Jacob and his future wife, certainly. Rene and his father Toussaint. Christof. You, *Jolie,* and your friend Eugenie. And Adrian, should I determine he is deserving of my protection. No others at this time."

Interesting. Jean already had trusted allies among the fae, the water species, his own historical undead, the loup-garou, and me, a wizard. Eugenie, a human. Plus the vampires, if he took Adrian in. He'd collected quite a ragtag army.

"Okay, then, let's assume you can supply Adrian with protection and that the wizards don't have to know where he is. How can he help Jake without going before the Interspecies Council?"

Adrian cleared his throat. "I'd hoped you would intercede on my behalf."

Oh hell no. "Define intercede."

"I thought perhaps I could give my testimony on a video and you could present it at the hearing."

I closed my eyes. "And then they'll demand I give up your

location and I'll have to lie to Zrakovi." Again. "Won't you be safe in Vampyre?"

"No, and neither will Terri. She will have to come with me," he snapped, sounding very much like the old Adrian. I hadn't missed him.

That meant he was going to sell out the Vice-Regent. "Melnick will track you down, even in Barataria."

Adrian looked away too quickly; I'd nailed it. Holy crap, Melnick was up to his fangs in all of this. "Look, I can't make a decision without hearing the facts. All I can promise is that if I decide not to help you, I also won't turn you in. That's the best I can do without knowing more."

He didn't speak right away. I went to pour myself a glass of water, and returned. I more than halfway hoped he wouldn't tell me. If I had a lick of sense, I'd walk across the hall and go to bed, leaving Jean and Adrian to scheme and plot on their own.

"It was Melnick, as you guessed," Adrian said. "He killed my father because he'd decided to turn himself in and throw himself on the mercy of the Elders. His magic doesn't work in the Beyond, he didn't like being a feeder for the vampires, and he couldn't see a role for himself. He, of course, wouldn't consider letting them turn him even after paying Melnick to turn me."

I couldn't blame him for being bitter, except he had almost gotten me killed. "How did Jake get involved? And what was the point of Melnick setting the bombs?"

Adrian clammed up again, so I waited, and he finally spoke. "Jake happened to be at the wrong place at the wrong time. He saw Melnick setting the bombs, so Melnick lured him to Vampyre, had one of his men tear up my father's body while he and Jake fought, then he trapped Jake in the transport and sent it back. Perfect timing."

Perfect indeed. And there was Zrakovi standing at the transport when Jake arrived. Talk about rotten luck.

"Here's something that's bothered me all along." I set my glass on the coffee table. "Who was Melnick's target?"

"Quince Randolph." Adrian got up and began pacing. "It was all to get rid of Randolph, and if you got killed in the process, all the better."

I was missing something big here. "Why would Melnick want to kill Rand?"

Adrian stopped and looked down at me. "You're missing an important question."

That much, I knew. "Which is?"

"Ask yourself this: How did Melnick know when to strike, and where? How did he know Quince Randolph was still in the building, as were you, but that the rest of the potential vampire allies had left?"

A chill stole across me, goose-pimpling my arms. "He was working with someone on the inside." Who wanted Rand dead? Crap on a stick. "Melnick was working with Mace Banyan?"

"Give the girl a prize," Adrian said, sitting again. "After the bollocks of the first council meeting, Melnick was desperate for allies. He'd blown it with the wizards, and everyone knows the fae are crazy. So he and Banyan made a deal. He'd kill Rand, and the elves would align themselves with the vampires against the wizards."

God, my head hurt. With Rand gone, there would be nobody to oppose Mace, and unless the wizards secured an alliance with the fae, which would be difficult, they'd be outnumbered by a landslide.

Forget Adrian. Maybe *I'd* move to the Beyond and ask for asylum.

"So you see why I can't go before the council," Adrian said.

"Sure." I rested my head against the sofa back. "I need to think about this." I needed to talk it out with someone, but there was no one I trusted. Maybe Jean, but he was too close to it.

Wait. That wasn't true. There was one person. I stood up. "I need to go back to my room and think a while."

"Very well, *Jolie,* but I request that you do not think too long," Jean said. "I received a message shortly before your arrival that the council is to meet tomorrow to discuss Jacob's fate."

Well, wasn't Zrakovi efficient these days? Trying to prove himself decisive First Elder material, no doubt.

"Where's it going to be?" The cabbie who'd brought me to the hotel from Eugenie's house had talked of nothing but the explosion on the Tulane campus.

Jean retrieved a sheet of paper from the end table, shrugged, and handed it to me.

I scanned it. "The New Orleans Museum of Art, at ten p.m.?"

It made some sense, I guess. NOMA would be closed by then, and the Celebration in the Oaks holiday light show, which spread behind the museum through City Park, would be closed as well. They'd been shutting down early each night because of the weather.

Still, the museum had quite a good collection, and the council meetings had proven destructive. I hated to see priceless art in jeopardy.

"Okay, I'll let you know something in the morning," I said. "For now, I'd recommend you at least go into Old Orleans for the night, Adrian. I think you're pretty low on Zrakovi's to-do list right now, but you can be tracked eventually if you're in New Orleans."

Adrian stood. "Yes, I just wanted to talk to you first. I hope you'll do the right thing, DJ."

That made two of us.

I said good night and returned to my room, pulled a diet soda and a candy bar from the mini-fridge, and took out my cell phone.

I needed some advice.

CHAPTER 27

An hour later, I sat on the bed in my hotel room, watching Rene Delachaise take me at my word when I said, "Order whatever you want from room service."

After he'd placed an order for turtle soup, grilled grouper, pecan-crusted trout, and cheesecake, I stopped trying to tally up the financial damage in my head. Good thing my credit line had recently been increased.

He held his hand over the phone and spoke in an exaggerated whisper. "What you want, babe?"

"A plate of andouille and a bottle of bourbon." I stretched out on the bed, pulling a pillow over my face and wondering if I could suffocate myself without chickening out. It would solve so many problems.

Rene jumped on the bed with a bounce and sat cross-legged; I could see him from underneath the edges of the pillow.

"Okay, you said you needed to talk, and lucky for you I was already in town 'cause the roads to Plaquemines done been closed again and I can't get home. It's too damned cold to swim." He grabbed my pillow and tossed it aside. "We could cuddle up in bed again, but you look like hell, babe."

"Thanks." Glad to know my looks matched my mood. "I needed to talk preternatural politics with someone neutral."

Rene scratched his chin. "I ain't exactly neutral, DJ. My papa's the head of the water clans and Jean, he's my friend and business partner."

I sat up and scooted until my back rested against the upholstered headboard. "I know, but you're familiar with the players yet not involved in this particular problem."

Rene stretched out and bunched up my face-covering pillow beneath his head. "Okay, shoot."

I went through the story as Adrian had told it to me.

As usually, Rene's sharp mind distilled it into its simplest issue. "So you're wondering who can get this information to Zrakovi and cause the least amount of shit to fly."

"Right. Let's go through the possibilities, assuming we have a taped version of Adrian's testimony against Garrett Melnick and Mace Banyan. Melnick won't be at the hearing tomorrow night, but Mace will. Adrian doesn't dare show up in person."

Rene pursed his lips. "You think they'll believe him, even on tape?"

Good question. "I don't know. Maybe. I think even Zrakovi would admit that Adrian's real crime was getting in over his head and succumbing to blackmail. As far as I know he doesn't have any personal grudge against Adrian."

Rene nodded. "Why can't Jean take the tape in?"

"The biggest problem with Jean is that Zrakovi already distrusts him." Never mind Alex. "And Jake works for him, so they'd expect Jean to come up with something to get Jake off the hook. Mostly, though, Jean only understands a recording in a very theoretical sense. If he shows up at the council meeting with a DVD, they'll know Adrian's hiding out with him or else someone is acting as go-between." Someone like yours truly.

"Yeah, you right," Rene said. "Mark the pirate off the list."

I was pretty sure Jean had come to the same conclusion, or he wouldn't have called me in the first place. "Mark me off the list, too. If I show up with Adrian's testimony, not only am I already in hot water with Zrakovi for disobeying a direct order, but I have a history with Jake and . . ."

Holy crap. Double holy crap. Mace Banyan knew that Jake had lost control and infected me with the loup-garou virus a couple of months ago. He couldn't prove it, but he knew damned well that I'd bonded with Rand to keep from turning loup-garou. He had witnesses to plundering my memories and learning about Jake.

A loup-garou losing control meant a death sentence in our world. And now he could claim Jake had lost control twice, with me and now with Hoffman.

All of which I shared with Rene as soon as he forged my name for room service and wheeled over the huge tray of food. "I hate those fucking elves," he said amiably, inspecting his dinner options. "What direct order did you disobey?"

I filled him in on Eugenie's pregnancy and Zrakovi's orders, delivered via Alex. "I lied to him, Rene. I couldn't do what Zrakovi had ordered."

"It was a stupid order. Bet Alex didn't like it either, but the shifter, he'll always try to follow orders 'cause that's how he's wired." Rene chewed for a moment. "Gotta tell you, my papa don't like Zrakovi much. Says he's too ambitious now that he's seen an opening in the power structure. He don't much like your new uncle, either."

Rene opened the bottle of bourbon, poured a generous few

inches into glasses for each of us, and shoved one toward me. "This is a big mess, babe."

Tell me about it. "I thought about having Adrian send the tape to Alex, but he's got a credibility problem, too. Jake is his cousin." Plus, there was no way in hell I'd put Alex in the middle of this, making him choose between saving Jake and lying to his boss.

"Zrakovi'd believe Alex, though." Rene slurped up a spoonful of rich, reddish-brown turtle soup that had a fine sheen of sherry floating on top. I munched a hunk of smoked sausage. Freakin' elves.

"Probably." As far as I knew, Zrakovi still trusted Alex.

"Definitely," Rene said. "Alex is in Z's back pocket, or at least Z thinks so. Papa thinks he's angling for head of the shifter/were group. Notice they didn't have a representative at the last meeting? Alex was filling in."

I frowned. No, I hadn't noticed. I'd assumed Alex was strictly security. But I thought Rene was wrong. Alex might be named head of the shifter/were group, but it would be because he earned it, not because he'd played politics. "Alex would never sell himself out for a seat on the council. He's a good enforcer, and Zrakovi knows he's loyal."

I worried that he'd confused loyalty with blind loyalty somewhere along the way. To me, there was a big difference.

"What about your elf?" Rene asked. "Seems if anybody would be able to take on Mace Banyan, it would be Randolph."

I'd thought about that as well. "It would be a stronger case if Rand were genuinely surprised by it during the council hearing," I said. "Part of that's selfishness on my part. Zrakovi's already furious at me for running to Rand with his plans to get rid of the baby. He'd suspect that anything coming from Rand also involved me. The elf needs to be clueless." Which is why

I'd had my mental loins heavily girded throughout this conversation.

We ate and drank in silence for a while. In the background, the local weather forecaster broke in the middle of a sitcom to issue another freeze warning and blither on about another foot or two of snow expected overnight. New Orleans' weather had become the focus of nationwide pontificating about global warming. The Weather Channel was broadcasting live from the Quarter daily now, with meteorologist Jim Cantore bundled up like an elf in a deep freeze.

"What about Christof?" Rene said. "He and Jake hang out some in Old Orleans and they've gotten to be buddies. Nobody on the council knows that except Jean and us."

I chewed on my andouille and thought about it. Using Christof was an interesting idea. "Plus, he has no stake in this," I said. "That's perfect, if he'll do it. We just need to make sure Jean has a way to get Jake out and back to Barataria in case everything blows up."

Rene nodded. "You can set up—"

A knock on the door silenced him, and I crawled off the bed and went to answer it, returning with a folded sheet of paper. I stared at it a moment in horror. "Holy shit."

Rene sat up. "What?"

I read: "Your presence is required at tonight's Interspecies Council meeting. Please be prepared to testify regarding an incident in November involving Jacob Warin that allegedly left you exposed to the loup-garou virus. Also be prepared to explain how you were able to avoid contracting the virus and why the Elders were not notified. The meeting time has been changed to eight p.m."

It was signed *Willem V. Zrakovi, First Elder.* No *Acting* in front of his name.

Mace had already struck. "This is an automatic death sentence for Jake. Why the hell does Mace want to destroy him? He doesn't even know him."

Rene sat, drank his bourbon, and thought a few seconds. "Jake's just a means to an end, babe. Banyan wants it all."

I crawled back on the bed. "How does getting Jake executed get him anything?" Other than ripping my heart out again and destroying a good man who'd worked hard to put together a life for himself. And destroying Alex. Surely Z wouldn't order Alex to take out his own cousin.

"It changes everything," Rene said. "Alex loses someone he loves. He loses ground with Zrakovi because he kept your and Jake's secret. You'll lose your job, at the very least; maybe you and Randolph even get accused of conspiracy since your bond was the main reason he got on the council. If you're on the outs with the wizards and Randolph's connection to them is gone, it leaves Mace Banyan stronger, the wizards' dependence on him greater, and the vampires with nice, clean hands."

Damn it, it was a brilliant plan. But we might be able to stop it.

"Christof's the one to take it to the council, as long as Jean trusts him." I rubbed my temples. "But we need a backup plan to get Jake out. Even if he's cleared of killing Hoffman, they'll know about what happened with me. I think Alex will be okay."

Alex knew Jake had infected me, and he'd kept that secret. But he didn't know about the bond with Rand until after it happened, and he went to Zrakovi immediately. His hands were mostly clean.

Mine were not. I'd probably lose my job, maybe even be stripped of my Green Congress license. I could be mixing illegal potions to sell on the black market.

Rene belched and pushed the tray away. I swear, for a wiry

guy not an inch over five-nine, he could put away prodigious amounts of food. "I got an idea about getting Jake free if it all goes to hell, but we need Christof for that, too."

After another hour, we'd moved our planning base back to Jean's suite. I'd called the concierge, and they'd been oh so happy to run through the blinding snowstorm to Canal Street and pick up a video camera and DVD equipment.

By the time Adrian had recorded a halting, but effective, testimony, complete with the dates, times, and locations he'd seen Mace Banyan and Garrett Melnick together, Christof had arrived.

I thought Adrian was going to have heart failure when he realized who his delivery boy was going to be.

"You can't trust the fae," he whispered, pulling me aside. "We don't know where their loyalties lie."

I stepped back and gave him a hard look. "You need a reality check, Adrian. If there's anything I've learned in the last couple of months, it's that every group's loyalty lies only to itself. That includes the wizards. Nobody's looking out for the greater good. Nobody's looking long-term."

He glanced down, and when he lifted his gaze toward me again, his face was vulnerable and naked. "Unfortunately, you're right. I . . ." He took a deep breath. "I'm sorry for having been so weak. I feel like I set all this in motion. I love Terri, but it shouldn't have come to this."

Christof had entered the suite carrying a half-gallon of generic store-brand ice cream and now was in search of a spoon. "There's one on the tray in my room," I said, and Rene went to retrieve it. "If you like ice cream, you should buy Blue Bell."

Christof paused with an ice cream–covered finger stuck in his mouth. "It is good?"

"I would almost kill for it."

"Bring it to me."

I studied his face to see if he was joking—and to see what face he'd worn. Mr. Imperious today was about eighteen, with a Justin Bieber haircut and dimples. It was downright freaky.

"Fine." I called my friend the concierge and asked if there was anyone who'd trudge through growing heaps of snow to buy two or three gallons of Blue Bell Ice Cream. "Make sure one is the homemade vanilla flavor," I said. "Surprise us with the other two."

If I had any money left on my credit card when I checked out, the concierge was getting a big tip.

Fortunately, ice cream seemed to put Christof in a jovial mood, especially when the Blue Bell arrived in fairly short order and he dipped a big spoonful of vanilla directly from carton to mouth.

A wide smile crossed his face. I'd looked in the bag. Wait till he tried the pralines and cream.

"What can I do for you, my friends?" he asked around a pint-size mouthful of ice cream. A literal pint-size.

Jean explained the problem, and posed the idea of Christof being the one to present the magical testimony at the council meeting. In hindsight, Jean was probably the last one who should be explaining video.

"Of course," said the gluttonous Prince of Winter. He'd eaten a third of the vanilla while Jean talked, and now peeled off the top of the Tin Roof.

"Chocolate?" he asked, brows raised.

I nodded, being unfortunately well acquainted with the company's entire roster of flavors. "Fudge and peanuts."

He handed it to me. "Cocoa is harmful to the fae; even small amounts make us ill."

What a sad, sad thing. No chocolate and no dogs. I said a

prayer of thanks that I had no fae blood. I'd rather risk spontaneous hibernation than be forced to give up chocolate.

"You're safe with the pralines and cream," I assured him,
watching in fascination as he peeled off the lid and dug out a
mound of ice cream the size of a softball. It balanced delicately
on the bowl of the Monteleone silver spoon while he licked his
way around it with the tongue from his Justin Bieber mouth.

"We also wanted to see if you could help get Jake to safety
if things go badly," I said. "I'll let Rene explain."

"I will already say yes." Christof finally set the carton of ice
cream down, although he looked at it with regret. "Jake is a loyal
friend. How could I do otherwise?"

I sort of liked this guy, in some freaky, otherworldly, totally
surreal kind of way.

"Here's my idea," Rene said. "DJ and I can go to the park
early to see the lights; I'll run interference while she sets up a
new transport behind the museum somewhere on the grounds."

So far, so good. Although I was finding a polar fleece outfit to wear beforehand. "How do we get Jake to the transport
if he's wearing chains?" They'd shackled the prisoners the first
time.

"Make up one of your little potions that could take care of
it. You create a diversion while I use the potion to free Jake. I'll
get him out of the building."

"What do you wish from me?" Christof, showing signs of
sugar shock, had slumped on one of the sofas with his eyes at
half-mast.

"You create a diversion outside," Rene said. "Some of this
thick snow—maybe even thicker. Enough to give us a camou-
flage. Then somebody'll have to break the transport."

"I'd say whoever gets there first." I figured it might be me.

Unless I was testifying or they had me in chains myself, I'd probably be pretty low on everyone's radar if pandemonium broke loose. I could create a diversion in the room without being near the source. A nice smoke bomb or something. "And Jean, you should go to Barataria with Jake. If anyone tries to follow, you need to make sure your ducks are in a row."

He frowned at me. "*Les canards*? I do not trade in poultry, Drusilla. I shall be prepared nonetheless."

I wanted to sleep so badly my bones ached, but there was no time. I had to warn Alex that Mace was going to rat out Jake, in case he didn't already know. I had to warn Rand that we might be in deep-shit trouble. I had to go to my freezing house in Lakeview and cook up some potions. And I had to check on Eugenie.

All in time to meet Rene in City Park at seven p.m. to set up an illegal transport in the midst of a blizzard.

Running away from home had never sounded so good.

CHAPTER 28

I checked my cell phone on the way back to my room and found two missed calls from Rand, and two from Alex.

Any conversation with Alex would be an emotional wringer, and Rand had probably been pounding on my mental stronghold, so I dropped my shields. *Rand!*

Where the hell have you been? Transport here now. And stop yelling.

I took a quick shower and put on four sweaters. After a moment of thought, I tugged on the bottoms of my flannel Harry Potter pajamas and managed to get my jeans over them. Housekeeping kept vacuuming up my transport, so I dug out my vial of salt and laid a new one, grabbed Charlie and my messenger bag, and transported to Rivendell.

Rand was sitting in the gazebo, looking like the world's most petulant elf. I'd known the real Quince Randolph would show up eventually, but I wished he could've behaved until I'd gotten some sleep.

"I know, I know. There's trouble."

He already had a slight glow. "Where is she?"

Huh? "Where's who?"

We sat in confusion a second. Clearly, we had two different crises. "You start first. Where's who?"

"Eugenie, of course. She's gone. Car's gone. House is locked up tight. Sign on the salon door says it's closed until further notice."

Holy crap. "What did you do?" I should never have left her alone with him. Dumb dumb dumb. He'd lured me in by being reasonable. I'd known it was out of character.

"I did nothing but try to protect her. She's too stupid to understand."

I reached out and gave him a good zap of magic with my right hand. I'd pull out Charlie if Rand didn't get rid of the attitude.

"Ow!" He moved farther away on the gazebo bench.

"Eugenie is not stupid, you oaf. She's afraid, especially when you start being your overbearing self. She has a good, pure heart, and you wouldn't recognize a pure heart if it bit you on your elven ass."

Okay, maybe I'd gone too far. His glow increased.

"Stop doing your glow-worm impression and tell me exactly what happened." I had too many other things to worry about for this crap, and so did Rand.

"I told her to get packed up so I could move her to Elfheim for the rest of her pregnancy. I have people there who can keep her and the baby safe."

Yeah, I bet that went over really well. "Rand, she needs to stay near her friends. She's scared. You need to keep her calm, both for her sake and your son's. Scaring the bejeezus out of her isn't going to help.

"Besides, we have bigger problems."

"What's more important than my child?"

Oh, I don't know . . . your miserable elven life? "Mace is making his move against you."

He grew still, his restless baby-daddy energy bleeding away. "How?"

I showed him the letter from Zrakovi. "It was delivered to my hotel room. Mace has obviously told Zrakovi that Jake infected me, and that our bond was a deal so I wouldn't turn garou and you'd get on the council. I'll lose my job. I might be arrested, and so might you—all Mace has to do is convince Zrakovi that we conspired to impact the makeup of the Interspecies Council."

Which is exactly what we'd done, although I'd made the deal before figuring out Rand's agenda.

"It's our word against his." Rand's voice was tinged with uncertainty.

"Nope. Other people knew. Lily's dead, of course, and your mom, but Betony was there at the regression." Which was a nice word for the mental rape and torture they'd put me through, stealing my memories—including that one. "And Alex knew."

Rand growled in a very Alex-like way. "Will he talk?"

I looked at the wide-planked floor of the gazebo, painted a pristine white. "I don't want Alex to be forced to lie to Zrakovi."

"Even to save Jake or to save you?"

"He'll do what he thinks is right." And I wasn't sure what that would be. I didn't envy Alex the decision, but I couldn't see a way to keep him out of it.

Rand got up. "You need to leave."

"What? We need to plan a strategy. At least make sure we're saying the same things."

"Don't worry about it. I have things to take care of. I'll see you tonight at the council meeting."

He got up, walked out of the gazebo, and a few seconds later

I heard the sound of his boot heels as he climbed the stairs to the second floor.

I had no idea what just happened, but at least he was focused on Mace instead of Eugenie.

Fortunately, I still had a key to Eugenie's house, so I pulled a thick garden flag from Rand's inventory, wrapped it over my head babushka-style, and slogged my way across the thick snow that had settled onto Magazine Street. Technically, the street wasn't closed, but it might as well be. The few vehicles inching along were of the high-riding military type.

When I got to her porch, I looked back to make sure Rand wasn't watching. Otherwise, he might follow me, and I needed to snoop and see if I could figure out where she went.

I tried the obvious first, calling her cell phone, but it went straight to voice mail. I left a message for her to call me and promised I had nothing to do with Rand's attempt to move her to Elfheim.

After a half hour of poking around the house and finding nothing of help, I sat and tried to clear my mind. Eugenie had a sister in Shreveport; she always went there when we had to evacuate for hurricanes.

I didn't think she'd go to family, though. There was no way to explain the real details of this pregnancy to anyone, or why she was hiding. Eugenie was a really bad liar; she made me look like a pro. Normally, the person she'd go to was me. If she went to the hotel and I wasn't there . . . Well, of course I knew where she was.

I punched speed dial: P-for-pirate.

"Hello, Drusilla. Why did you not share your lovely friend's delicate condition?"

Well, that answered my question. "Is she okay?"

"*Oui.* Christof heard her at your hotel door and fetched her. She is quite frightened of your elf."

God, even I had been calling him my elf, albeit in the way one would say *my dog* or *my car.* "Yeah, well, my elf has bigger problems right now, and so does Jake." I filled Jean in on my summons to the hearing. "You're probably going to have to bust Jake out of there and get him to Barataria," I told him. "I can't see any way they're going to let him go." Adrian's tape would prove his innocence in killing Hoffman, but not in losing control with me.

"This will be done, but my concern is for you, *Jolie.* Your Elders will know that you lied to them about Jacob and your elf."

"So did Alex."

Jean made a rude noise into the phone. "*Monsieur Chien* is much like a *Monsieur Chat.* He has many lives and lands on his paws."

"I'm on my way to talk to him now. Will you keep Eugenie there and make sure no one finds her?"

"But of course, Drusilla. I have already offered her the protection of Jean Lafitte and his men."

I ended the call and sat for a few minutes, staring into the cold fireplace. It struck me once again that Jean was assembling quite an army of misfits and the disenfranchised—which was exactly what he'd done in his human life. His legion of a thousand pirates, all of whom swore loyalty to him, weren't formed of whole cloth. He'd collected them, offering them safe haven and potential wealth in exchange for their loyalty and service.

And so it was again.

Time to get busy. I didn't see any way I'd get a sane cab driver willing to take me out to Lakeview to put together potions, wait for me in the thickening snowfall, and then drive me back here, so I plundered Eugenie's kitchen and bathroom for ingredients that might be helpful for simple potions.

Sitting at her kitchen table, I put together some basic charms—confusion, smoke, fire, laughing potion, hive inducers. Two ice charms made especially for Mace Banyan. Those I'd enjoy using. I powered them up using the elven staff.

Finally, I loaded everything up and checked the time on my cell phone. I was supposed to meet Rene at City Park at seven, and it was four. That left just enough time to talk to Alex.

CHAPTER 29

I punched in Alex's speed dial and he picked up on the first ring with a very piratelike lack of greeting. "We have to talk. Where are you?"

Hello to you, too, Alex. "At Eugenie's."

"Come here. You can use the transport."

I paused. "Is Zrakovi there?"

"No. God, no. We need to talk without him here."

Wasn't that the truth, and it did my heart good to hear Alex admit it. "On my way."

I took my bag and the staff, powered up the transport in Eugenie's living room, and a few seconds later, stood facing the man I loved. How could we survive this mess?

He looked the same as the day I met him, just after Hurricane Katrina. He had the same beautiful eyes, the perfectly shaped, strong mouth, the wonky shapeshifter energy. He had the same dutiful sense of right and wrong, except life no longer matched up to his black-and-white sensibilities. The world had moved on, but Alex hadn't figured out how to move with it. Eugenie had been right. He was miserable, and even his enforcer shielding powers couldn't hide it from me.

"I've missed you," I said.

His gaze softened, and he smiled. "Me too."

I finally stepped out of the transport and hugged him, breathing in his scent as if it might be the last time. His arms slid around me and squeezed for a few seconds, then he kissed me, hard and deep. I slid my hands beneath his sweater, desperately needing to be with him. He stepped back. "We can't. I want you so bad I ache, but we can't. We have to talk."

I was so damned tired of talking. "Yeah, we do."

We sat at the dining room table, which is where we tended to have uncomfortable conversations. When we talked on the sofa, we ended up not talking. "Did you get your subpoena?" he asked.

I reached in my bag and pulled out the sheet of paper. "If you mean the letter sent to my hotel room, yes. I gather Mace Banyan has decided it's time for Jake to be sacrificed in the name of power and greed and the elven way."

Alex winced, and nodded. "It's worse than you know. Mace visited Zrakovi this morning, and Willem came here just afterward, breathing fire."

That didn't surprise me. "Mace wants to take down Rand, and this is the first step." I paused. "I hope you told him the truth about not finding out about my bond with Rand until after the fact. You only knew about Jake infecting me, and for most of the time you didn't even know where Jake was. I don't think Jake would want you lying for him either; he has a life in Old Barataria now, and a fiancée. The council can't get at him there."

Alex stared at me as if I had andouille growing out my ears, which was possible. "Jake has a fiancée?" Then he shook his head. "No. Don't tell me. I can't deal with anything else. And, yeah,

I told Willem the truth. With Hoffman dead, I don't see any way to help Jake other than to sneak him out of New Orleans, but they've already arrested him despite his insistence that he's innocent. Even if we spring him, I'm worried about the rest of Zrakovi's agenda."

That I probably didn't want to hear, and a deep pang of dread knifed through me at hearing Jake had been arrested. Arrested wasn't dead, though. They wouldn't do anything until after the council meeting.

I took a deep breath and hoped Alex could handle one more surprise. "Would it change anything with Zrakovi to know there's proof Jake didn't kill Geoffrey Hoffman?"

Again, Alex stared at me, eyes wide. "Proof? What proof?"

I'd been trying to figure out how much to tell him. I didn't want Alex stuck in the middle of this huge cluster, but he was already there. I didn't want him having to lie to Zrakovi any more, but I also didn't want him telling Zrakovi anything that would keep us from getting Jake out safely.

"Adrian Hoffman saw the vampire Vice-Regent, Garrett Melnick, killing his father, and he heard Mace Banyan give the order. Mace and Melnick set Jake up."

Alex sat back with a frown. "How do you know this? And why would they want to set up Jake?"

My laugh was bitter. "Adrian wants out of Vampyre, and he went to Jean Lafitte seeking asylum." Alex blinked but didn't comment. "And setting up Jake accomplishes a lot. It weakens Zrakovi, since he clearly doesn't have control of the people working for him—me or you or Jake. Rand is discredited because of his bond with me and the way it came about. Mace wants Rand dead, so he'll probably charge him with treason against the elves. Zrakovi will have to rely on Mace to hold the wizard-elf truce together, so it gives Mace a lot of power."

Alex closed his eyes. "And all the while, Mace is secretly working with the vampires to stab Willem in the back."

"Stab *all* the wizards in the back," I corrected. "Elves plus vampires outnumber us, even if the were-shifters are on our side. That leaves the fae as the wizards' only hope, and they're busy with their own power struggle."

Alex pushed his chair back and paced around the table. "You're wrong about one thing. Mace isn't trying to kill Rand; he's trying to control him."

That didn't make sense. "Why would he want to control him if he's getting him thrown off the council?"

Alex took a deep breath. "Mace doesn't want Rand off the council either. Zrakovi came to me with a deal. And you aren't gonna like it any better than I do."

This sounded bad. Really bad. "What kind of a deal?"

"I keep my job. You keep your job, with basically a slap on the wrist for not revealing the true nature of your bond with Rand. Rand keeps his seat on the council."

It was my turn to slump back in my seat. That all sounded good. Too good. "Drop the other shoe. In return for all this, what is it that Zrakovi wants?"

"It isn't what Zrakovi wants, but what Mace has demanded in exchange for not tearing the whole goddamned Interspecies Council apart."

I raised an eyebrow in an unspoken *what*.

"Mace wants Eugenie."

The other shoe dropped right on my best friend's head. If Mace had control of Eugenie, and by extension Rand's unborn son, he controlled Rand. No doubt about it. He'd found the only thing that would bring Rand to heel. Then, once the baby arrived, he'd kill Eugenie. She'd have no further use to him and her potential to bring charges against him would pose a threat.

My rage level had been tamped down for a while, but it took only seconds for it to boil again. "And if we refuse to turn Eugenie over to Mace?"

Alex closed his eyes. "I'm to take you into custody and deliver you to the hearing tonight, pending charges of conspiracy to manipulate the Interspecies Council. If I don't go along with it, we'll both be charged."

Damn it. A week ago, I might have begged for forgiveness and tried to figure out how I could make things right with Zrakovi. A week ago, I'd have sworn I was loyal to the wizards, to my own people.

But this was now, and I felt pure, ice-cold fury.

"So, how do we do this? Do you put me in handcuffs?"

Alex took his seat again and twisted the plastic water bottle between his fingers. "I haven't agreed to anything. DJ, I don't know what to do."

His misery and conflict and indecision wafted over to me and settled on my shoulders like a mountain of lead. "Will Adrian's testimony make any difference at all? I mean, it proves Mace is manipulating Zrakovi."

"Maybe. It's our only hope. Who's going to deliver it, though? Who would the council believe wasn't biased in some way? Or wouldn't face more charges of harboring a fugitive?"

Oh boy. Here was the part I didn't want to tell him. "The Faery Prince of Winter, Christof, has agreed to present the testimony and verify its authenticity."

If we weren't all on the way to hell in one big handbasket, I'd have laughed at Alex's expression.

"Well, that's . . ." He paused as if searching for the right word. "Interesting."

I laughed. "Yeah, but kind of brilliant. Who's going to argue with him and risk pissing off the potential future fae monarch?"

There was one more loose cannon we needed to talk about. "What about Rand?"

Alex shrugged. "There's a subpoena out for him, too, but we haven't found him yet. Zrakovi is working with Mace Banyan to see if he's in Elfheim."

Mace Banyan might not like what he found. I had a feeling everyone sold Quince Randolph short. I had once, when we bonded. Now I knew better.

"Would you get in more trouble if you weren't able to find me before the council meeting?" The real question is whether he would lie and say he hadn't been able to reach me.

Alex had been staring out the window, but slowly turned to look at me. "Come to think of it, I don't think I have been able to find you. You never answered your phone, and I've left messages, you careless woman." He paused. "Go to Old Orleans so you can't be tracked, just for now. If you don't show up at the meeting and Mace gets exposed, everything might settle down. Give me time to do some damage control."

My heart almost broke at that; it felt swollen and heavy in my chest. Alex was going to lie for me. He was going to protect me from the people who should be my allies, but weren't. Neither of us said it, but it could very well make things bad for him.

"I love you." I'd never thought the first time I said those words to him I'd be crying.

"Me too." He smiled to make up for those words guys had such trouble saying, for some reason. "Do you know where Eugenie is?"

I nodded. "Hiding out at the Monteleone, for now. I might have Jean take her to Old Barataria."

"Good move." We stood looking at each other, unwilling to take that next step. "You probably shouldn't use the transport in the living room." His voice cracked.

"I'll make a new one." I kissed him like it was the last time, my own tears tasting of salt and bitterness, my arms trying to memorize the feel of him.

"It's just for a few hours, until the meeting is over," he said. "Once Mace is exposed, Zrakovi will listen to reason. We might even be able to get your uncle to side with us."

I hoped he was right.

"Destroy the new transport as soon as I'm gone," I told him, pulling a vial of salt out of my bag and forming a slapdash interlocking circle and triangle on his dining room floor.

I stepped inside and powered it with the staff. "Rivendell," I whispered, trying to smile at Alex as I felt myself sucked into the transport. Rand wasn't home, so it was my perfect base of operations.

First, I called Rene. "Change of plans," I told him, explaining what had happened.

He whistled. "Babe, you are in some shit. You wanna come out to Plaquemines and stay with me till the meeting is over?"

I'd been thinking about it on the way to Rand's and decided I wasn't letting Alex throw himself on Zrakovi's mercy by showing up without me as his prisoner. "No, I'm going to that meeting. It's almost five. Can you pick me up a block behind Rand's and we can go on to the park to set up the transport?"

"Sure thing. Give me fifteen minutes. I'm still at the pirate's suite. Need me to bring anything?"

I thought a second. "Get Eugenie out of there—see if Jean will take her to Barataria to keep her safe. Is Adrian still there? If so, see if he'll come with you to the museum. He can stay hidden, but if something happens to me, he can make the transport and get Jake out."

Rene's voice grew muffled as he talked to whoever was still in the Monteleone suite. "He'll do it. And, DJ. Ain't just gonna be Jake we're gettin' out." He spoke a few more muffled words, then, "We're not leaving you there if things go bad."

I let the tears fall as I ended the call and stuffed the phone back in my pocket. But only for a minute. It had never occurred to me that I might actually be forced to leave for real. When I'd been faced with the loup-garou crisis, Jean had offered me a home in Barataria, where I'd be safe from the wizards and not endanger those around me.

The thought of leaving my house, my job, and, most of all, Alex—those had been the things that made me most desperate. That, and protecting Jake, had been what drove me to agree to Rand's bonding proposal in the first place.

Rand had done the bonding out of greed and the desire for power. I'd done it out of love—not for him, but for my life and the people in it.

I laughed a little as I picked out another garden-flag babushka scarf for my walk to meet Rene. My house across the street was gone. Within a few hours, my job might be gone. Maybe even my freedom. Alex would do what he could, but I wouldn't let him throw everything away to save me if it came down to it.

Then my wallow in self-pity took a hard veer to the left. I wasn't a run-of-the-mill wizard and I needed to stop thinking of myself that way. The Elders could strip away my wizard's certification. They might even be able to strip away my limited physical magic. But I doubted anyone in Edinburgh's hallowed wizarding halls had a clue how to get rid of my elven magic. I had skills they didn't know about, as well as one righteous elven staff.

It made me stronger, and it made me a bigger target.

I rambled around Rand's greenhouse and pinched off a few herbs, just in case I needed to make a potion on the fly. Then I slipped out the back door and walked as fast as I could back toward Tchoupitoulas Street and the river. I saw Rene's black pickup waiting and wasted no time climbing inside.

"You okay, babe?" He reached across the front seat and pulled me into a hug.

"Rene, if you don't stop being nice to me I'm going to cry."

"Damn, don't want that." He pulled carefully onto the road, skidding into an icy U-turn, and drove toward the Quarter. "So shut up and fasten your seat belt, witch."

I laughed and watched the white world glide slowly by as the snow crunched under the tires of his heavy truck.

"So what's the next step?" Rene asked. "The pirate took Eugenie to his house, then he's gonna meet us at the council meeting. What are you gonna do?"

"Get Jake's escape hatch set up," I said. "And then get myself arrested by one surprised enforcer."

CHAPTER 30

The entrance to City Park was barricaded, with a sign announcing that Celebration in the Oaks was canceled this evening due to weather. About half of the sign was already covered in snow. The closure made our job both easier and harder. Easier because there were no humans around; harder because there were no humans around. Rene and I were the only things moving.

It was already growing dark, so Rene killed his headlights and eased the truck past the barricade. Not that there was anyone to see us.

We drove into a darkened Disneyscape. Wires stretched above the narrow drive and through the mature live oaks on either side of us. With the flip of a switch, all those lights would become twinkling animals and holiday scenes and fairy trees—or at least as humans might imagine light-filled fairy trees. I had no idea if the Monarchy of Faery had trees, but since some of their royalty had nature magic, I assumed so.

At the end of the long front drive, we reached the wide, neoclassical marble building that housed NOMA. Rene circled behind it. "How far you wanna go?"

"Not far. You need to be able to get Jake there fast."

Rene stopped beneath a grove of trees with a small clearing tucked behind it. "This'll work, but first we need to talk."

"Rene, I'm talked out."

"Good, then you can shut up and listen. I wasn't kidding earlier. You need to get the hell out of here, DJ, at least until things settle down. Zrakovi is setting you up; I talked to my papa this afternoon. Don't worry—I didn't tell him nothing. But he said I should warn you. Zrakovi thinks . . . let me see, how did Papa say it . . ."

Rene broke into a heavy South Louisiana accent that would've made me giggle if the words hadn't scared me so badly. "You tell dat wizard friend'a yours dat Zrakovi's gunnin for her, him. He thinks if he makes an example of dat Gerry St. Simon's girl, it'll show he's a hardass."

I looked out at the snow, or at least what I could see of it in the near darkness. "So if he gets rid of me, he thinks nobody will have the guts to challenge his authority?"

"Somethin' like that. The way I figure it, you scare the shit out of him because of that elf stuff you can do. Plus he thinks he'll get Eugenie in the process, sounds like."

"Right." Because both Eugenie and I were just so scary.

"I'm serious, DJ. You can do some shit, you think on your feet, and you're smart. And me and Jean and Christof, we talked about it this afternoon. We ain't leaving you there tonight. So my question to you is: Are you gonna come with us, or are we gonna have to force you?"

I laughed at the notion of Alex arresting me on one side and my posse of misfits rescuing me on the other. "Jean just wants to add a wizard to his collection of followers."

He grinned, his teeth shining white in the dark truck cab. "Nope. He's got Adrian. And I think your old wizard buddy is finally growing a pair."

I tried to imagine what my life outside New Orleans, outside the only world I knew, might look like. A world where I spent quality time with Adrian Hoffman, vampire at large. I couldn't quite do it.

"Let's just see what happens in the council meeting. We have a wild card unaccounted for. Rand is missing; my guess is that he's gone after Mace Banyan. Calling Rand a wild card is like calling . . . well, something." I couldn't think of a suitably outrageous analogy.

Rene pulled up the hood of his jacket and opened the truck door. "Fill me in while we work. Is this transport gonna get buried by the snow?"

"Yeah, but it won't matter. We just need to use landmarks as corners, like this bush." I walked off an irregular interlocking circle and triangle, spreading the salt. It melted the snow beneath it, but quickly filled back in. I should've asked Rene to bring charcoal.

When I completed the figure, I placed the beads of mercury at the corner landmarks and touched Charlie to the clearest edge. A ripple of fire in the shape of the transport raced around the clearing, leaving a clearly marked edge.

"Did you know it would do that?" Rene asked.

"Just a guess. Snow transports are a newly acquired skill."

"As long as we remember this tree is at the head of the triangle, we're golden." Rene pulled the white scarf from around his neck and tied it around the tree, high enough to allow for another foot of snow.

Okay, what's next? "Let's transport inside and take a look at the layout before the council arrives. You gonna leave your truck back here?"

"Yeah, I'll move it farther under the trees, but we might need it. You never know."

That was the God's honest truth.

"I need to warm up first." My limbs had gotten that bad old feeling that signaled impending hibernation.

"Come on." Rene opened the door for me, then hopped in the driver's seat and turned on the heater full blast.

"How long is Christof going to keep this cold business going? I thought he was about to get rid of it."

Rene laughed. "He was gonna stop it tonight after the meeting until he met Eugenie. Now, he's so pissed off at the elves he says he might let it snow until the Fourth of July. Got a soft spot for babies, him."

I pulled my babushka flag aside far enough to see if Rene was joking. I didn't think he was. "Christof is . . . interesting." That word kept popping up in relation to the faery.

"Ain't that right." Rene cracked his window; shifters and elves did not share the same opinion of cold, even aquatic shifters like the mers. "He asked questions about her when you guys came to Barataria couple of days ago. He was glad to see her again, even if she is knocked up with an elf."

I winced. Rene wasn't the most sensitive guy, but I adored him anyway. The idea of Eugenie getting mixed up with the Faery Prince of Winter made me physically ill, however, so I changed the subject. "How'd your date go the other night?"

He shrugged. "It was okay. I need to find a good mer woman, but I'm related to most of 'em around here. Might have to go on an ex-plo-ra-tory trip over by Lafayette this summer. Need to widen the gene pool . . . get it? Gene pool?"

"Don't tell me—an old merman joke."

"Yeah, you right." Rene leaned over to get a better look at me. "You don't look like a corpse anymore. Wanna go?"

"Sure." Some days, not looking like a corpse was the best one could do, I guess.

Snow blew straight into our faces as we hunkered down and made our way to the NOMA loading dock. "Can you unlock one of these doors?" Rene had to shout to be heard over the howling wind. Christof had outdone himself tonight.

"Yeah." I half walked and half skidded my way down the dock, and touched the edge of the staff against the lock. Might as well save my native magic in case the staff got taken away from me, although I had a feeling Charlie would always find me eventually. I felt rather than heard the dead bolt sliding open, and pulled the heavy door toward me.

Once we got inside, it took another twenty minutes of wandering the bowels of the building to find our way to a stairwell. When we found the meeting room on the second floor north gallery, the clock on my cell phone read seven p.m. One hour until showtime.

The gallery had been transformed into an art-filled conference room, which we observed from an alcove across the hallway. A couple of Blue Congress wizards were experimenting with different coverings for the conference table: a burled wood, a dark cherry, an oak. They finally settled on mahogany. Lives were at stake tonight, and these twits were debating proper veneer etiquette.

"Sometimes I hate wizards," I muttered.

Rene grunted. "Me too, babe. I been trying to tell you."

"There aren't any rooms off to the back, so reckon where they've got Jake?"

"No idea." He looked up and down the hallway. "This place is bigger than it looks from outside. He could be anywhere."

"That means you're gonna have to stage his rescue from the council room, most likely."

Rene nodded. "I agree. I'm gonna leave you to it and find the shortest route out. Two things first."

He grabbed my arms and turned me to face him. "We ain't leaving you, so don't make one of us get killed trying to find you."

I nodded; we'd see what happened. "What's the other thing?"

"Can you take that thing off your head? It has smiling frogs on it, babe. Ain't nobody gonna take a woman serious when she's got frogs smiling on her head."

I snatched off the babushka garden flag. "It's all I had."

He grinned and, with another look up and down to make sure things were clear, slipped away.

Next, I had to decide how I'd make my entrance. I was pretty sure Zrakovi expected me either to not show up or come in wearing Alex's handcuffs. If I walked in with Rand, it would show a certain defiance—or stupidity. I could walk in last, wielding the staff and making a grand entrance.

Or I could walk in and zap Mace Banyan, although the satisfaction would last only as long as my death sentence.

The big question was what Rand had up his sleeve. I was pretty sure he'd gone to Elfheim, probably to make some kind of deal with Mace. I figured he'd protect me if he could, simply because it was in his best interest.

I hoped Rene was right about me thinking on my feet because all I could do tonight was react.

My heart took a nosedive into my ankles when Zrakovi strode by with Lennox St. Simon. I bet he no longer considered me a good role model for my cousin Audrey. No doubt Zrakovi had filled his head with stories about how much like Gerry I'd turned out to be.

Funny thing, that. I'd started sometime in the last twenty-four hours to consider it an asset.

I finally spotted Alex, dressed in black and leaning against the wall near the second-floor landing. A swell of love filled my chest, making it hard to breathe. When pushed to the wall, he'd chosen me. That's all I needed. It would give me the courage to do what I needed to in order to protect him from whatever happened.

I knew how I needed to make my entrance. I stepped out of the alcove and waved to get his attention, then motioned him toward me. My pulse thumped so hard I could feel it throughout my body.

Then he was there, fear and love and hurt and anger, all wrapped up in one snarly shapeshifter ball.

"Does Zrakovi know I got away?"

"Not yet. What the hell are you doing here, DJ? We had it worked out."

I held out my wrists. "Bind them, and take me in, or whatever you were supposed to do with me."

"What?" Alex blinked. "Why, DJ? Why not let them think you outsmarted all of us? Why did you even come here tonight?"

Maybe he didn't know me that well after all. "Because I want to have my say. I owe that to Jake, and to you, and to myself." I gritted my teeth and closed my eyes, willing away the urge to cry. I didn't regret a thing I'd done. I was finished apologizing for putting people before politics.

He blinked once, twice, and looked away. "DJ, I don't want this."

I stood on tiptoe and kissed him. "I know."

"Are you sure?"

I nodded. "Absolutely. Just remember that Rand is an unknown factor, and Mace will be desperate once he's exposed. Be prepared for anything."

He pulled out handcuffs and snapped them around my wrists. "Where's your bag? You didn't bring your staff?"

"I have it. It's hidden." Charlie was currently tucked inside the leg of my Harry Potter pajama bottoms, which were beneath my jeans, but that fell under the category of TMI.

"Did I ever tell you how smart you are?"

If I was that smart, I wouldn't be marching into the Interspecies Council meeting in handcuffs.

CHAPTER 31

I was pretty sure protocol called for Alex to grasp my upper arm and steer me to a bench that stretched along an inner wall—the prisoner area. I also was pretty sure protocol did not call for him to walk me in with his arm around my shoulders, almost protectively. Well, except for the whole part about me being handcuffed.

Zrakovi and Lennox had been talking, but Lennox stopped mid-sentence when he saw me. I thought a small smile crossed his lips before he squelched it. Zrakovi turned and his aura virtually leapt with joy to see me this way. "Good work, Alex. I can't tell you how disappointed you've made me, DJ."

How did he really expect me to respond to that? Apologetically? I wanted to say "Blow me," but instead I smiled and kept my mouth shut. Lennox reached out and grasped my wrist as I walked past, which he really shouldn't have done. I could read him like a first grade *See Spot Run* primer. He was excited, which I didn't understand.

He stepped closer to me. "Hang in there, love. You've done

the right thing, and we'll get this overblown toad out of office before long."

I smiled at him, too, mostly to keep from letting my mouth hang open in shock. Lennox was a player; that much I knew. What I didn't know was his game. Right now, it appeared to be *Get Rid of Zrakovi the Toad*.

"Will you be okay sitting here?" Alex stopped in front of the bench.

"Sure. Is this where they'll bring Jake and Rand?"

My ploy to find out Rand's status worked. "Jake'll be here in a minute. We never found Rand to even deliver the warrant."

I'd spotted a familiar halo of wavy blond hair near the doorway. "There's your chance."

Alex whirled. "Shit. I guess he didn't know we were on to him."

Oh yeah, he knew, thanks to his non-wife. But what he'd done about Mace—that was the question. Rand scanned the room until he found me, and treated me to a wide smile.

Whatever I say, just go along with it, Dru. When you get the chance, make a run for it. Stay gone for a while, until I give you the go-ahead to come back. It's gonna be fine.

Oh, I so didn't like the sound of that. Alex approached Rand, who turned a sunny smile in his direction and said a few words that caused Alex to shoot a bug-eyed look toward Zrakovi.

Alex shrugged, though, and walked back to me.

"He doesn't get handcuffs?"

"Not yet," Alex said. "He says we don't have jurisdiction to arrest him here since he wasn't served with the summons, but that if we want to get one trotted over here, he'll be happy to comply." He looked back at Rand. "He's up to something."

Yes, he certainly was. This was going to be interesting. I felt relatively sure that Rene and Jean would be able to get Jake out safely. I had no idea what I'd do, and I hated that my fate lay in the hands of an overly ambitious wizard, a temperamental faery, and a freakin' elf.

Christof was the first of the contingent from Faery to arrive, and I was glad to see he'd abandoned his Justin Bieber face for a Viggo-Mortensen-as-Aragorn look, complete with the dark shirt, black, distressed-leather hooded cape clasped at the neck, and two-day stubble. Nice. Except for the little chocolate problem, being a faery could be fun.

Except oh-em-gee Eugenie could get into such trouble with him.

Florian was pink-haired and wearing a floral suit tonight, and Sabine had gone conservative with a severe black pant-suit and white blouse. The effect was ruined only by the rhine-stone peacock pin and green glittery heels.

Jean arrived with a flourish, wearing the suit he'd donned on our only official dinner date. Buttery fawn trousers with a cobalt-blue waistcoat that matched his eyes. He was smiling and greeting the fae contingent until his gaze fell on me and imme-diately dropped to my hands, cuffed in my lap. His face lost its animation and his eyes sparked with the blue fire of fury. That man could shift emotions faster than anyone I'd ever seen.

I made a face at him, bobbing my head to try and get him to come close enough for me to tell him it was okay. He leaned over and spoke to Rand, who apparently appeased him enough that he took a seat. He did not look happy, however.

"Hey, sunshine. We have matching jewelry."

I looked up and my heart broke a little at the sight of Jake. His blond hair had been brushed back, and his face had already healed of its cuts and bruises. "Sit down, we have to talk fast," I said through my grin.

He slumped on the seat and waved a cuffed hand at his guard, a grim-faced shifter I'd never seen before. Speaking of which . . . I looked around the room and saw that, once again, there was no shifter representative. Toussaint Delachaise had arrived. In fact, the only missing council member was Mace Banyan.

What in God's name had Rand done?

"What's up?" Jake leaned his head against the wall with his eyes closed and whispered out the side of his mouth.

"We have proof that you didn't kill Hoffman." I tried to talk without moving my mouth, but I'd never make a decent ventriloquist. "Mace told everyone about the loup-garou incident so there's no getting around that, though. Stay on alert. Rene and Jean will bust you out. There's a transport right behind the museum so you can go to Barataria."

"What about you? DJ, you can't stay here."

I sighed. I didn't want to run away because I didn't think I'd done anything wrong. Surely once Mace was exposed, the new First Elder would see that.

Zrakovi called the meeting to order. "If the council doesn't mind, I'd like to wait a few more minutes to allow time for the head of the Elven Synod to arrive. He has obviously encountered a delay."

"No, he hasn't." Rand stood up. "Mr. Banyan will not be attending tonight's meeting. If I might address the council?"

From at least twelve feet away, I could feel Zrakovi's blood pressure starting to spike again. If the council had many more meetings, he was going to stroke out and Lennox would get his shot at First Elder without having to work for it.

"Mr. Randolph, I don't feel it's appropriate for you to address the council, given your involvement in tonight's agenda. So if you don't mind . . ." Zrakovi lifted a brow.

Rand gave him the sunny elf grin. "No problem. I can wait."

Christof stood and cleared his throat, and I swore Zrakovi dropped an f-bomb under his breath. "Elder Zrakovi, I have something that was delivered to me anonymously this afternoon which might explain Mr. Banyan's absence."

Zrakovi's brows lowered in confusion, and, I was pleased to note, so did Rand's. He knew about Mace's plot, but not the proof. Jean maintained a pleasantly blank expression, and I bit my lip to avoid giggling. One should never giggle in handcuffs unless one were naked. I was sure I'd read that rule somewhere.

Of course, naked reminded me of Alex, which made me look at him, and the tense look on his face wiped out my amusement.

"You know what this is about?" Jake whispered, leaning slightly toward me.

"Just watch. It's good."

Christof walked to the front of the room with a laptop, which he set next to Zrakovi's chair. He held out a disk in a plain white envelope. "Shall I?"

Zrakovi nodded, a sour look frozen on his face, and watched while Christof slid the disk into the computer and adjusted the sound.

A jittery picture fuzzed in and out until it finally focused on Adrian Hoffman. There was mumbling in the room until Adrian began talking. Alex moved to the side to see better.

"Most of you know me," Adrian said in his oh-so-proper British accent. "My name is Adrian Hoffman, and for many years I was employed by the Congress of Elders." He went on to explain briefly what happened to him, and his father's role in having him turned vampire. He also took responsibility for his part in what happened to me.

"I was weak, and Sentinel Jaco paid for that weakness, as did Captain Lafitte, and Enforcer Warin."

There were a few others he owed apologies to, but that was a good start.

"I apologize for delivering this testimony by video rather than in person, but I believe you'll understand why I now fear for my life. I recently overheard conversations between two individuals who were planning the death of my father, Geoffrey Hoffman, as well as the bombing of the Interspecies Council proceedings."

Now the mutterings grew so loud that Zrakovi paused the video until it quieted down.

"I can tell you without a doubt that Garrett Melnick killed my father," Adrian continued once the video started again. "I witnessed it myself. And he made it look as if an animal had done it in order to implicate Jacob Warin."

"That doesn't make sense," Zrakovi muttered.

"Garrett Melnick also set two explosives in the building where the council met yesterday. The target of the bombing was the clan chief of the fire elves, Quince Randolph, and his bondmate, Sentinel Drusilla Jaco. Melnick was acting on information supplied by Mace Banyan in exchange for a political alliance between the elves and vampires, against the wizards. He wanted Randolph under control to secure his spot on the council and with the Synod."

Adrian went on a while longer, but the point had been made. Rand leaned back in his chair with a thoughtful expression, no doubt figuring out how to spin whatever it was he had to announce.

Finally, with the video done, Zrakovi turned to Christof. "Your majesty, could you share with us how you got this recording?"

Christof nodded, and I reconsidered whether I'd made the right choice in daydreaming of Sean-Bean-as-Boromir instead of Viggo-as-Aragorn. He made a fine-looking fake *Lord of the*

Rings character. "Of course, Mr. Zrakovi. I was working in my office in Faery about two o'clock local time, rewriting weather coordinates to help the dire situation of New Orleans. A courier left the disk in a plain white envelope in my inbox, and my secretary delivered it with my afternoon mail. I questioned her, and would have brought her along if I thought it would help, but she had no recollection of who left it."

Faery princes had offices and secretaries, and plotted weather coordinates on computers? Since I was probably soon to be unemployed, I'd have plenty of time to catch up on my faery research.

"Very well. It's clearly Adrian in the video—many of us know him quite well. And he didn't appear to make the statement under duress. Mr. Randolph, would you like to add something about this particular matter?"

"Yes." Rand stood up. "I'm so sorry to announce that my colleague Mace Banyan met with an unfortunate accident in Elfheim this evening. I was called about it by Betony Stoneman, chief of our earth clan, and by the time I arrived in Elfheim he was dead."

Zrakovi's mouth opened and closed several times before he could get himself under control. "How . . . how did Mr. Banyan die?"

"I believe he was crushed beneath an airplane," Rand said, as if that were the most normal death imaginable. "He was an amateur pilot and enjoyed working on his own planes." He paused, then added, "It's quite common among the air clan.

"But," Rand continued, "in light of that, I would like to inform the council that with the vacuum of leadership in Elfheim, we held an emergency meeting a short while ago and I humbly accepted the position as head of the Elven Synod. I would like to nominate my colleague Betony Stoneman as the second elven representative if it meets with council approval. He will be here shortly." Rand looked around the room. "Thank you."

Holy crap. He'd killed Mace. Not only killed Mace, but taken over the Synod. Too bad he was about to get his own set of handcuffs to match mine and Jake's.

CHAPTER 32

Zrakovi called a brief recess so those who wished to do so could stretch their legs. I suspected he needed to regroup.

"Did you know about that?" Jake asked.

"Not at all." Thank God. That's one secret I didn't want to carry around.

What do you think, Dru? Rand had turned his sunny smile toward me.

I think you better not ever tell me what really happened.

Rand smiled, but I caught a hint of attitude on his face that I didn't like. His surprises weren't done.

"If everyone could be seated, let's get started again." Zrakovi banged a gavel he'd come up with from somewhere. "I think it's clear that the charges against Jacob Warin for the death of Geoffrey Hoffman must be dismissed, and apologies to Mr. Warin for the false accusation."

Jake's expression didn't change. He'd been working on that blank-face thing.

"However, before Mr. Banyan . . . died, he passed along information that we've been able to verify independently."

"Alex is a rat," Jake breathed, and I elbowed him. Alex wasn't a rat, and Betony could very well have corroborated Mace's story before Rand bought him off, or however he got to the head of the earth clan.

Zrakovi continued. "It concerns an incident that occurred in November shortly before Thanksgiving, in which Mr. Warin infected Sentinel Drusilla Jaco with the loup-garou virus following an argument during which he lost control. This, of course, is a grave offense with the loup-garou, and it has been my experience that once a loup-garou shows an inability to maintain control, it will continue to happen."

Blah blah blah. I wondered who was writing Z's speeches now that Adrian wasn't the Elder office toady anymore.

". . . first like to question Sentinel Drusilla Jaco, if she would take a seat here in front, please."

Sure, trot me out in front of everybody. No problem. I was getting used to it.

I plopped into the seat next to Zrakovi and clanked my handcuffs on the ugly mahogany veneer that so many wizards had gone into creating. I swear that Elder Sato, who had arrived late, and my uncle were both fighting laughter.

"Ms. Jaco, I'd like to ask a series of questions and, if you would, please keep your answers precise, succinct, and to the point."

Who did he think I was, Truman Capote? Or Jean Lafitte?

"Are you aware of the incident referred to in this report?"

I'd show him succinct. "Yes."

"And did Mr. Jacob Warin lose control during an argument and infect you with the loup-garou virus?"

"No."

Silence. Zrakovi repeated his question. "Would you like to reconsider your answer? Lying to the council will only add to the repercussions."

"We were not arguing. We were having a discussion."

"Ms. Jaco . . ."

"You asked me to be precise."

Zrakovi was getting pissed. Maybe I could push him into a stroke myself.

"Very well. Did Mr. Jacob Warin lose control during a *discussion* and infect you with the loup-garou virus?"

"No."

Zrakovi took a deep breath. I think I heard another f-bomb.

"Ms. Jaco, tell us what did happen, in words of which you approve."

"Sure." Exactly what I wanted. "Jake and I were having breakfast after visiting the crime scene of one of the Axeman of New Orleans' first crimes last month. We got in a discussion about how he was adjusting to being turned loup-garou after Katrina. I was waving my hands around as I talked"—I waved my cuffed wrists in the air and banged them on the table again—"and my arm accidentally grazed against Jake's tooth hard enough to break skin. He was horrified."

Except for the part where Jake had been snarling and holding on to my arm and trying to fight off his wolf, that account was entirely true.

Zrakovi tapped his pen against the folder in front of him. "So you're telling me that Mr. Warin never lost control?"

"He never lost control." Which was true. He left to keep from losing control.

"But you were infected with the loup-garou virus."

"Yes."

"How did you find out the virus was active?"

I paused. How much detail had Mace gone into? "I gave myself a blood test and began having symptoms."

"Symptoms such as . . ."

"Healing faster than normal." No point in mentioning the low-grade fever or the short temper.

"And did you, indeed, turn loup-garou?"

"No." By God, I wasn't volunteering anything. I'd make him ask me.

"How did you avoid it?"

Rand?

Go ahead and tell him the truth—you know, about how much we love each other.

Oh, brother.

"I was told by the man I was dating that he was immune. He offered to exchange blood to share that immunity with me." Okay, maybe I'd volunteer a few things, just because I could sense Zrakovi getting pissed again. "I mean, Rand and I were headed toward being bonded anyway.

"We couldn't stay away from each other."

Because he was stalking me like a sociopath.

"We could finish each other's sentences."

Because he could read my mind.

"He'd know what I wanted for dinner without me saying so."

Ditto.

"If I had shifted, it would have ruined the life we had planned together."

Crap on a stick, but I was a good actress. Kiss me and hand me the Oscar.

Alex coughed, and I swore I heard him mutter "bullshit" right in the middle of it.

Zrakovi rubbed his eyes, and if I hadn't been so annoyed with him I'd have felt sorry for him. It must be frustrating to try and manipulate people who wouldn't roll over and cooperate.

"Ms. Jaco. DJ. When you bonded with Mr. Randolph, were you aware that he was in line to inherit a seat on the Synod?"

"Yes. His mother, Vervain, was on the Synod at the time."

"Was the intent of Mr. Randolph in bonding with you to strengthen his position within the Synod and, by forming an alliance with a wizard, assure himself of a seat on the Interspecies Council?"

I pretended to consider the question. "It's an interesting theory, sir, but I don't believe it's possible. I mean, at the time we were bonded, Rand's mother was quite healthy, and either she or one of the other Synod members would be on the council. There was no way Rand could know his mother was going to pass away so suddenly." I paused. "Bless her heart."

Bravo, Dru. I hadn't even thought of that angle.

Neither had Zrakovi, from the pained look on his face.

"That is all, Ms. Jaco. You may return to your seat."

"Bench," I said. One must be precise.

He ignored me.

Zrakovi sat in silence for a while, flipping through papers.

"Very well. I don't see the point in belaboring this further," Zrakovi finally said. "In light of today's testimony, I believe this to be a matter for the wizarding community and not the full council, so I'll ask your patience as we conclude this issue.

"Jacob Warin, will you stand, please?"

Jake winked at me as he stood, then gave Zrakovi a look of utter contempt.

"You were in the employ of the Congress of Elders and the enforcers at the time of this incident. I understand that rather than reporting it, you left New Orleans and began living in the Beyond. Is that true?"

"Sure is," Jake drawled.

"Given that the incident appears not to have been malicious, as First Elder I hereby terminate your employment by the Elders and shifter community, and sentence you to one year of imprisonment for failure to report this incident. Said imprisonment will begin immediately and will take place in the wizarding facility at Ittoqqortoormiit, Greenland. Do you understand?"

"Yep. Sure will be cold."

"Drusilla Jaco, will you stand?"

I stood, lecturing myself inwardly. I'll channel Jake and be insolent. I won't cry. I won't cry. I won't cry. It's just a job.

"It is the duty of a sentinel to not only uphold the laws of the wizarding community as established by the Elders, but to set an example to other wizards. By failing to report this incident and, indeed, by covering it up, you failed in this duty. I hereby terminate your status as sentinel of the Greater New Orleans Region, and am revoking your Green Congress license pending further investigation. During this investigatory period, however long it might take, you will be imprisoned in the wizarding facility in Ittoqqortoormiit.

"Until a new sentinel can be appointed, Elder Lennox St. Simon has agreed to fill the sentinel post on a temporary basis."

That snake. They were putting me on ice indefinitely. On *ice*. A non-weather-related chill washed over my skin. I was bonded to a full-blooded elf. I couldn't be on ice.

Dru, you can't go to Greenland. You'll die. Get away from them and hide until I get this cleared up. I'll create a distraction after I do one more thing.

"Ms. Jaco, do you understand your sentence?" Zrakovi asked.

"Oh yeah, I understand all right." I understood I was going to get back at that son of a bitch. It might not be tonight, but it would happen.

I looked at Alex, who stared at me with eyes widened one step short of panic.

Sitting down again, I reached over and grabbed Jake's hands as if to console him, and shot some of my native magic into his cuffs. I heard the tiny clink as they released, and he had the presence of mind to keep his hands still. No one would suspect he was free. Then I did the same thing to my own cuffs. Stupid wizards. Even a baby with no magical training could unsnap regular handcuffs.

Once again, Zrakovi had underestimated what I could do.

Now we had to wait on Rene or Rand to cause a distraction. Then Jake and I needed to get the hell out. I wasn't going to Greenland to either rot in prison while my case was "under review" or "accidentally" get locked outside and go into permanent hibernation if Rand couldn't fix this right away.

"Elder Zrakovi." Rand stood up, and I took a deep breath. Here came the rest of whatever he'd been plotting this afternoon. "I have one more item of business I need to put before the council."

"Can't it wait, Mr. Randolph?" Zrakovi sounded tired. Good. I hoped he was exhausted and miserable.

"No, it can't."

Rand walked around the corner of the table, past Zrakovi, and opened the door. He moved out of sight for a few seconds, and when he returned he wasn't alone. Betony Stoneman, head of the earth clan and new council member, was with him.

Between them, looking like she was a few loads shy of a full deck, was Eugenie.

CHAPTER 33

I sat up straight so fast it was a wonder I didn't drop my handcuffs and give myself away. I looked at Jean, whose jaw was clenched tightly enough that the scar running along his jawline stood out. The temperature in the room dropped at least thirty degrees, and, across the room, both Sabine and Florian looked suspiciously at Christof.

How had Rand found Eugenie? And how much elven mental crap had he and Betony done to her? Her hazel eyes were glazed, and her pupils were the size of marbles.

"What is the meaning of this, Mr. Randolph?" Zrakovi stood up and looked appropriately appalled. Like what he'd done hadn't been worse.

"Earlier today, I informed Ms. Dupre, who is carrying my son, that I'd made arrangements for her to spend the rest of her pregnancy living in Elfheim, under the best medical care and with a life much more luxurious than the conditions she lives in now, which are deplorable. She washes other people's *hair*." His snarling Elvis lip told what he thought of that occupation.

What a horrible thing. She made more money than I did. She had a house with working heat and a car, which was more than I could say.

When he began talking, Rand had let go of Eugenie, and now that he no longer touched her, awareness seeped back into her eyes. She turned her head wildly from side to side, finally spotted the door, and made a run for it.

Alex blocked her way, and she ran into him with an *oof.* He leaned down and put his arms around her, whispering furiously.

She looked at him, her brows drawn together in uncertainty. She trusted Alex, liked him, had been one of his biggest cheerleaders. Our world might be getting pulled apart, but bottom line? He was a good guy. If push came to shove, he'd protect her. I was sorry I had ever doubted that.

Alex led her to a seat, pulled it out, and pressed on her shoulders until she sat. Finally, she spotted me. *Help me.* She mouthed the words.

I nodded and gave her what I hoped was a reassuring smile.

"I repeat, Mr. Randolph, please explain yourself." Zrakovi was pissed. "This is a closed meeting of approved Interspecies Council members. We do not allow uninvited guests, especially humans. It is part of our bylaws, adapted at the meeting on Nove—"

"I realize that," Rand said, wincing when I screamed at him: *Rand! What the hell are you doing?*

I felt his mental wards go up, which was strange. I shut him out all the time; he'd never done the same to me.

"Ms. Dupre not only refused my overture to improve her life and ensure the safety of my child, but she ran away. My fellow Synod member and new council member, Mr. Stoneman, found her hiding in the Hotel Monteleone, where I believe she awaited a chance to reach asylum in the Beyond. I know for a fact that there are those who have encouraged her to abort the child, including some in this room tonight." He looked pointedly at Zrakovi.

"Should anything happen to my son before he is born or after—anything—I will hold the wizards personally responsible, and will advise those on the Synod and among our people that our long-standing truce is at an end."

Holy crap. Rand was threatening Zrakovi with war, and he was doing it in a way that threw me under the Ittoqqortoormiit-bound bus. He'd made it clear he knew Zrakovi had threatened the baby, and the only way he could possibly know that was from me. I'd be in Greenland until I hibernated permanently.

As if he heard my thoughts, Zrakovi turned to me with a look that would've curdled Christof's gallon of Blue Bell pralines and cream. I didn't need my empathy to read the promise in that expression. It promised I would live badly and die worse.

"Mr. Randolph, those are harsh words. I'm sure when you've had a chance to calm down and realize someone has given you false information, you'll—"

"My words aren't idle, Zrakovi. My information wasn't false and you know it." Rand reached toward Eugenie, and she edged away from him so fast she'd have toppled off her chair if Alex hadn't caught her.

"There's only one way this situation can be rectified." Rand's voice dropped into a smooth, reasonable timbre. "Only one, and I request that you make it tonight, right now, or else I will consider the elves no longer a participant in any interspecies negotiations. I have already obtained the support of my fellow Synod member Betony Stoneman for this move, and as the air clan is currently without a leader and the water clan leader is not yet an adult, that is all the approval I need."

Shit. Rand had Zrakovi over the proverbial barrel and he

knew it. Z was fidgeting so badly he was practically dancing in his chair. "Well, there's no need for such measures, of course, Mr. Randolph. What is it that we can do for you?"

Zrakovi might never recover from this humiliation, and when my gaze met that of good old Uncle Lennox, his delight couldn't be more obvious.

"I demand that Eugenie Dupre be turned over to me for the duration of her pregnancy. She'll be placed in protective custody in Elfheim until the child is born, at which time she will be free to return to her little life of washing hair and painting fingernails."

I'd hated Rand before. I hated him when he treated Eugenie so badly before we bonded. I hated him when he'd taunted her with it afterward. But never like I hated him now. All this scene needed to be perfect was him to trot out the nonsense about me helping him raise Eugenie's child.

"Well, of course, that seems perfectly reasonable."

"No! You can't do that. DJ, help me." Eugenie jumped to her feet and Alex again tried to soothe her, whispering, rubbing her back.

Rand, this is wrong. Please let me talk to her. We'll find a compromise.

He ignored me.

The temperature dropped again, and I glanced at Christof. His face had grown the color of a snowball, and his green eyes shone silver. He was the scariest damn thing I'd seen since the Axeman came after me, Aragorn or no Aragorn.

Sabine leaned over and whispered something to him, and the temperature seemed to level off. Not warm—I could still see my breath condensing—but at least not growing colder.

We were going to have to take Eugenie out of here with us. That's all there was to it. Jean had already offered her sanctuary.

In fact, I hoped Jean had plenty of room, because his house was going to be crowded. The Elders had no reach and no authority in Old Barataria, and whatever question I had about leaving had been answered by my elf. He wasn't going near Eugenie without her permission, and I was going to make sure of it.

My future landlord seemed to be engrossed in a series of nods and gestures with his infuriated faery friend.

Christof lowered his head and, beneath the table, I could see him raise his hands, palms up.

A loud *pop* sounded in the room, and everyone looked around. Another, this one lasting longer, made us all look up. A wide crack zigzagged across the ceiling, and I experienced a horrifying few moments of déjà vu.

Oh, God, please tell me Christof wasn't going to bring down the ceiling.

CHAPTER 34

Christof was going to bring down the ceiling.

This time, instead of a crash of plaster dust and lathing, Sheetrock and roofing materials and snow rained down. Lots and lots of snow. And pandemonium. Sabine screamed and tried to levitate, but the stuff on top of her was too heavy. Florian pushed himself free and tried to dig her out. Zrakovi was completely buried, and I saw Alex wrapping his arms around Eugenie and pulling her free.

Jake had grabbed me before the first part of the ceiling fell and had shoved me to the ground, our handcuffs lost in the scramble. Now, we both climbed to our feet, looking around. Somehow, everyone in the room floundered under Sheetrock and snow, subroofing and nails—everyone except Christof, Jean, Eugenie, Alex, Jake, and me.

How had he done that?

Jean rushed to Jake and me, herding us toward a ladder that had dropped down from one of the holes in the roof. "*Courir! Dépêchez-vous!* We must fly."

"Where's Eugenie?"

"Alex got her to Christof," Jake said. "They're already at the ladder."

The ladder. Were they nuts? I ran to the back corner and looked up into a black sky dropping snow on my head so fast it already felt frozen. Eugenie's feet disappeared out of sight and, satisfied, Christof nodded at Jean and ran back to excavate his queen.

"You must climb, *Jolie. Tout de suite.*"

We were going to have a talk about that *tout de suite* business, and soon, but for now I grasped the metal rungs of the ladder, wincing at the cold. Couldn't they have used a wooden ladder, for crying out loud?

My feet kept slipping, but there was no danger of falling because Jean was right behind me with his hand on my ass, pushing me upward. We'd be talking about that, too.

Finally, I reached the top where Rene waited, hand outstretched. "C'mon, babe, move it."

With Jean's help, which gave a whole new meaning to *assistance,* I managed to climb onto the roof. A gust of wind would have knocked me off but for Rene's grasp on the back of my sweater.

Jean climbed out, followed by Jake.

Then the five of us stood and stared at each other. We'd gotten to the roof. I sure hoped they had a plan to get us down. And where was Alex?

I turned and grabbed Rene by the lapels because I figured he'd be the least likely to take offense at being manhandled. "How the hell do we get down? Did you think that far ahead?"

"Hold on, babe. It's coming. You're gonna love it."

"What's coming?"

As if on cue, City Park sprang to life around us. The lights blinded me at first, but eventually I could make out shapes. Alligators the size of single-engine planes, built out of bright green lights with yellow teeth and eyes, rose over the snow, suspended in midair, their lights casting colorful shadows on the white mounds beneath them. Beyond them, in the snow-covered, frozen pond, rose the green humps of a sea serpent. Purple and silver fairy lights strung along the twisted limbs of the massive live oaks created surreal vistas everywhere I looked.

A red and green Tyrannosaurus rex ran back and forth across the main road through the park, a neat trick I remembered from the last Celebration in the Oaks light show. Now, the dinosaur ran over snowbanks. Music from the nearby carousel tinkled. Christmas music from the Cajun Christmas Village wafted through the snow, carried by the gusts of wind.

This was beautiful and I'm sure if I survived I'd appreciate it, but in the meantime, my feet had gone completely numb, as had my ears. I was in dire need of my lost babushka flag scarf.

And I was hallucinating, because I could swear the nearest light-covered live oak had changed position.

"The tree is moving!" I screamed at Jean, who'd fixed a broad smile on Papa Noel, the Cajun Santa, who rode his red-lit sleigh across the frozen lake, pulled by eight grinning green-lit gators.

"Yes, *Jolie*. We must climb down when the tree grows near," he said, as if, duh, I should've known the escape route lay down the trunk of a moving three-centuries-old tree.

I was almost jerked off my frozen feet by Rene, who shoved me toward the edge of the roof. Holy crap; the tree had arrived. I reached out and grabbed hold of a branch the girth of a half-dozen baseball bats, grown warm from its covering of lights.

Whoever had come up with this bright idea for an escape needed to be horsewhipped, and I knew just the wizard to do it.

I crawled across the widest limb and stopped when I reached the trunk, which was wider than my SUV I blew up last month. I needed a strategy.

"C'mon, sunshine, follow me." Jake skirted past me, and quickly figured out a way to dangle his legs off one branch and slide onto the one below it. Luckily, live oaks had a dense array of limbs so the method even worked for my short legs. The lights kept the snow off so it wasn't as miserable as it might have been.

Also, live oak branches grow all the way to the ground, so we were able to slide off the last one straight into a fluffy snowbank.

When I struggled out of the snow, I almost tripped over a sweating Adrian Hoffman, deep in concentration as he twirled his fingers in intricate movements and chanted words that were incomprehensible to me. He was doing all of this—running the whole freaking City Park light show using his pretty Blue Congress magic. Which he shouldn't be able to do anymore since he'd been turned vampire.

"Pretty cool, ain't it, babe?" Rene wrapped his arms around me from behind, sharing some shifter body heat.

"I thought wizards lost their magic when they were turned vampire," I whispered, not wanting to break Adrian's concentration. At least that's what Etienne Boulard had told me.

"He says he'll lose it eventually but it takes a few decades," Rene said. "Come on, let's get to the transport with the others before he runs out of juice."

I turned to follow Rene, but before I'd taken two or three steps through the deep snow, there was a loud crack and everything went black and silent.

"Rene?" I whispered. "Adrian?"

Nothing. Just wind that screamed like a woman in pain, and heavy snow, and bitter cold.

Something shuffled to my right, where Rene had been, and I stumbled blindly toward the sound, holding my hands in front of me to feel for what I hoped would be a nice merman.

Instead, another loud crack sounded, from my left again, and a sharp pain lanced through my left calf. My leg buckled under me, and I hit the snow as another shot rang out. Because it was definitely a shot. In the pitch blackness, that last blast had been accompanied by a flash of red fire.

I dug inside my jeans and pulled Charlie from his makeshift holster inside my Harry Potter pajamas. *Don't glow,* I told him. *We have to stay hidden. But if you can help keep me warm, I'd appreciate it.*

Later, I'd worry about how Charlie knew what I meant and what I needed. For the moment, he was not only failing to glow, but had heated up with a delicious warmth that spread through my arm and into my body. My feet were still frozen, but by holding the staff two-handed, I thought I could avoid hibernation.

I couldn't see, though, damn it. I crouched in the snow and listened, sorting out wind and snowfall from cracking branches and distant traffic.

I reached out with my other senses, sifting through the input. Fresh, clean snow, wet wood from the trees, gunpowder. I noted those and pushed them aside, looking for energy signatures. Rene's wonky shifter aura, or the buzz of Adrian's wizard signature.

I felt both, although they were faint. The strongest aura I read was wizard, off to my left, where Adrian had been. I moved slowly, trying to make myself a small target in case the shooter had night-vision equipment, and praying the wizard I was moving toward was Adrian and not Zrakovi.

The aura was strong now, and I stopped again, trying to pinpoint it. Ahead and just to the right. I crawled now, not wanting to make myself a big target by standing up. Charlie touched the ground with each movement of my hand, melting the snow with a faint sizzle.

Here. I laid the staff beside my knee and felt around me in a wide sweep of my arms, touching something warm to my right— something that grabbed my hand and twisted my wrist violently. I couldn't avoid a sharp intake of breath.

"DJ?"

Oh thank God. "Adrian? What happened?"

"Somebody shot at me, so I dropped the lights. He's moved back toward the transport."

Damn it, who was the shooter? "I'm hit, too—left calf. You okay?"

"I'm a bloody vampire. Bullets don't do much."

Right. I'd forgotten.

Rand!

Silence, but not an I'm-injured-and-unconscious kind of silence. He was still shutting me out. He wouldn't be out here with a gun, either. For one thing, it wasn't his style. Plus, he wouldn't risk hitting Eugenie.

Zrakovi wasn't the shooting type. He'd send someone else to do it. Like Alex. Alex wouldn't be out here shooting blindly, though.

Lennox crossed my mind, but why? Letting us all escape would make Zrakovi look bad, opening the door for my uncle to ride in on his white Bentley and save the day.

No point in worrying about the shooter's identity, only his location. "Let's try to go toward the transport," I whispered. "Rene's out here somewhere, too. I lost him when the lights went out."

Which worried me. He hadn't been that far away, so what

if the shooter got him? Of course, like vampires, shifters healed from most things. "D'you know if the bullet was silver?" I asked Adrian.

"I don't think so." He shuffled alongside me, also crawling. "You think the transport is this way?"

Hell, I wasn't sure anymore. I could have crawled around in circles. "Let's try it. We can't do anything except freeze sitting here."

He stood up, and I tried, but my left leg kept giving way on me. "Here, try this." Adrian bent down and pulled my left arm around his shoulder. "I'll help you."

We moved slowly toward the direction I thought the transport lay, each with one hand on the staff for warmth.

"I think we've walked too far." Adrian stopped. "We've got to have some light."

"Don't start up the whole park again. I'll use the staff." I held Charlie up and asked for light. Again, he understood, flooding the area around us with a golden light.

"Oh, bloody hell." Adrian let go of me, my leg gave way, and I crumpled back into the snow.

The distinctive sound of a gun chambering a round sounded, and I sat up, holding Charlie out in front of me, ready to confront our shooter.

CHAPTER 35

Betony Stoneman, the newest council member, stood there with his gun pointed toward us, and gestured for us to stand.

"What are you doing?" I struggled to my feet and held on to Adrian for a second to make sure my leg was going to hold me up.

"Part of my deal with Rand is I help him get the mother of his child. You'll lead me to her."

Betony was a short, stout, swarthy man who'd had little to say during the great elf kidnapping and torture session, although he had participated in it. Rand had told me once that he was a weak leader of the earth elves, and had always been easily swayed to follow in Mace's wake. Guess now he followed in Rand's wake.

"I can't believe you shot me," I said. "Just wait until Rand hears about this. I'm his bond-mate, you know."

"He won't care—it's just a leg wound. Now walk to the transport," Betony said, gesturing with the gun.

With Charlie lit up like Obi-Wan's lightsaber, I got my

bearings and stumbled toward the transport. We'd gone really far afield, and between the heavy snow and yet another gunshot wound, I couldn't move fast.

"Damn it, Betony. You know Rand won't like you having a drawn gun around the mother of his child. Eugenie could be hurt with you out here firing into the dark."

"Would you shut the hell up?" Adrian hissed. "You're just pissing him off more."

"Keep walking, you stupid wizards."

I glanced back at the gun-toting elf, who raised the weapon and pantomimed taking a shot. He poked me in the back with the barrel to hurry me along.

"You touch me with that thing one more time, buddy, and we are going to have a talk." But I kept walking and, even with Charlie's warmth, I felt the makings of a hibernation threatening.

Finally, I saw the tree with Rene's scarf flapping from it. "Just past that tree," I said, and was relieved to see a small group of people gathered there. Jean and Eugenie and Jake. "Where's Rene? Damn it. Was he hit?"

I saw a figure on the ground—Rene—when I stumbled closer, and another, taller figure in the shadows behind. A figure with a gun.

He stepped out of the shadows. "Stop there."

I fell again, only partially because of my injury. The rest was confusion. "Alex?" Where'd he come from? And was he trying to help us or stop us?

"DJ, are you hurt?"

He walked toward me as I stumbled to my feet again.

"Another council meeting, another building destroyed, another gunshot wound." I wanted to hug him, but more than that, I wanted his gun focused on Betony.

"Betony's here on Rand's behalf, to take Eugenie," I said. "I am not letting that happen."

"I think you're wrong, DJ. You should let her go."

I stared at Alex. He couldn't mean that, not after all we'd gone through to make this happen. He gestured with his gun. "All of you get over there together, and you"—he jerked his head toward Betony—"throw your gun down or join me, whichever you want. I think we're on the same side."

"Very well." Betony lowered his gun and went to stand next to Alex.

This particular elf was an idiot, as was proven when Alex raised his gun and whacked Betony in the head. He dropped like a rock.

"You guys need to get out of here." Alex unhooked a big flashlight from his belt and propped it on a tree branch, throwing a yellow-white glow around the clearing. "Lafitte, you're not hurt—make sure everyone's in the transport."

"Go with us." I clutched Alex's arm. "We can keep tabs on things and come back when it all settles down."

Alex looked at the transport, at me, and back at the museum, where, so far, no alarms had sounded. "I can't, DJ. I have to stay here and try to fix this so it's safe for all of us. You and Jake and Eugenie have to go. Zrakovi still trusts me, mostly. I'm the only one who can do this, and you . . ." He paused and closed his eyes. "I won't lose you. I'm going to stay here and fight for us. For what's right. Even if it means fighting Zrakovi."

I understood what that cost him. But we all had to draw the line somewhere. We all had to stand on our own Bridge at Khazad-dûm and raise our staff and say "You shall not pass" to the monsters of indifference and pride and ambition.

"You shall not pass," I whispered.

Alex frowned. "What?" He turned as voices sounded in the distance. "DJ, you have to go."

"Everybody get in the transport, and go now," I said. "I'll follow in a minute."

I heard shuffling behind me, and Alex's flashlight put out enough light for me to see in my peripheral vision that they'd transported out.

Then it was just Alex and me, him with a gun, me with the staff, face-to-face.

I dropped the staff to my side and he reholstered his gun, pulling me to him for a kiss that was teasingly sweet and achingly sad.

"Be careful," he said, stepping back and nudging me toward the transport. "I'll stay in touch and let you know when it's safe to come home."

I had a bad feeling about this. Alex was strong, but all of his potential allies had just hightailed it to the Beyond. There was only me.

I took a couple of steps, then stopped. "You won't be able to fix this, Alex. Zrakovi knows I told Rand about his orders for me to kill the baby and now Rand will be after us, too."

He looked at me and in his eyes I saw he knew the truth of what I'd said, but it was in his DNA to fight, to try and make things right, to work within the system.

I was Gerry St. Simon's daughter and it was in my DNA to fight, too. But I had to fight the system from the outside. I prayed that when the fighting was done, Alex and I would meet in the middle somehow, and be together again in a world that wasn't so broken.

You shall not pass.

"I love you, Alex," I said, and took a step backward into the transport.

He stood there, a beautiful, genuinely good man who'd placed his loyalty in a system I no longer believed in. I whispered the words, "Old Barataria," and as space and time compressed around my crushed heart, he dropped his arm to his side, and the light of the clearing shone on his tears.

The last words I heard were, "I love you too."